ROGUE DEFENDER

Lethal Nannies, Book 1

Kat Lewis

CHAPTER 1

M usic is one of the most powerful and triggering stimulants to the human brain.

Normal people used it to soothe battered emotions and restore a sense of balance; be it drug addicts, insomniac children, or the average Jane dealing with stress from work.

But when *I* heard the music, it was time to go to war. To waltz through a sonata of civic duty, horror, and blood until I rose in victory with a gore splattered face and my target in hand. If Homeland Security had told me that joining their ranks would forever taint one of the great joys of my life and twist it into some hideous, violent thing, I might have chosen to become a psychiatrist instead.

You'd think they'd warn you—those no-name, whisper-in-the-dark government agencies that spend millions of dollars transforming you into an efficient, lethal machine. Warn you of the volatile emotion and irreparable trauma of the job. Remind you that signing the dotted line means risking your sanity. Your humanity even.

They spend taxpayer dollars turning you into government assassins...and then have the audacity to blame you when you snap like old cello strings.

The military trained you to repair yourself on the go—to never stop taking ground just because you had a hole in your chest or your ankle was twisted in an unnatural direction. Win at all costs. No matter how bad your wounds or how deep your fear. And that's exactly what I'd do...even if I lied to them, and myself, to do it.

I peered at the mansion in the woods through night vision googles, searching for signs of movement at the balconies and entrances. Intel suggested that the kidnappers intended to transport our VIP to another location shortly after sunrise yet the activity level of the house had remained minimal. I would not be fooled though. This was my redemption mission and anything other than flawless execution of the plan was not an option.

The route, time, and tactic were all up to me, down to a limited cache of weapons and transportation. Everything except the most critical element—my team. Randomly assigned, they said, so they could ascertain if my incident a few months ago who wholly circumstantial and not a result of inadequate leadership or my inability to create a cohesive team dynamic. Or was it because I was a woman, a black woman at that, and perhaps my sex made me uncapable to lead in this capacity? Homeland Security's director team was exhausting every option to make sure that I hadn't, one way or another, intentionally sabotaged the mission in Syria.

I flexed stiff fingers around the butt of my gun and breathed in a lungful of frosty air to hold back a surge of anger. Control— this mission's success hinged on whether I could keep my shit tight and locked up. I checked my watch, careful not to rustle the tall grass that hid me and the large man beside me. His codename was Bach and last I heard, he'd fumbled a weapons exchange with a highly wanted terrorist and those weapons ended up in the hands of local radicals...who of course used them to bomb the village of contact. There were four us on this mission and all of us had something to prove.

Determination was a steel plate around my chest. This time, I would not fail.

As if in tune with my thoughts, the first rays of sun peaked over the horizon. The south Carolinian sun rose hot even though it was the end of October and that heat caused the heavy dew on the ground to sizzle and evaporate, creating a thick mist that rose off the ground like a cirrus cloud. That little bit of light illuminated the field of the grass razed down to the dirt that intentionally provided no protection whatsoever from searching eyes.

A comm crackled in my ear and man's baritone came over the line. "Guard change has started and there are no hostile near the west entrance." That was Strauss, a communications expert currently on parole due to questionable satellite usage on mission. "You have two minutes to clear the field."

"Copy that." I muttered. I flicked a hand to signal Bach and we rose with that mist. Silent and synchronized. Waifs of death ready to neutralize anything that stood in the way of completing our directive. We simultaneously broke out into a fast, low sprint across the open field. Knees slightly bent to absorb shock and sound. Guns high and tucked close to our bodies, ready for anything. The field was close to half a mile of thick grass, large rocks, and pitted ground but if we cleared it without being seen, phase two of the mission stood a chance.

"Ninety seconds," Strauss muttered in our earpiece.

A gentle slope creased the landscape and Bach and I barely slowed. As we crested the hump, we saw that the ground was littered with large boulder and made minor adjustments to skid past or leap over them. But when I went to leap over one rock, the boulder moved with me. Crap—it was a man in camouflage. He slammed into me with the brunt of his body causing both of us to fly through the air and hit the ground with a teeth clattering thud. I rolled with the impact, brought up my gun, and shot him two times in the chest as he flung himself at me. A boulder near my leg shifted and I swung my leg in a vicious kick before letting loose two rounds.

"Sixty seconds."

I popped to my feet just as Bach flipped a man decked out in drapey green camo to his back and shot him in the head with a pistol.

"Rocks are bogies." I said as I launched into a run once again. "Tag 'em if you can, Strauss."

"Roger that."

We ran in a full out sprint, trying to beat the clock. Bach hit the west wall before me and immediately started search for the window-like depression we'd found on the map. I stuttered to a stop and kept my eye on the field, ready to silence a passing guard or a bush that turned out to be a hostile.

"Thirty seconds."

Behind me, Bach shuffled across the base of the house, searching for our way in. "The entrance should be three feet from base of the wall at the south corner," I reminded him.

"It's not here." He shot back.

Unacceptable. "Switch me." I ordered.

He grumbled but took the sentinel position and I frantically searched for entrance. The map made it seem obvious, a dumbwaiter entrance used to drop food for picnics or heavy loads for wash day.

"Ten seconds." Strauss crackled.

I ran my hands along the wall. My fingers caught on a ledge like projection and I tugged. The wall gave way with a small groan and revealed an opening barely four feet across. Bingo.

"We're in." I said.

Bach was already pulling on the state of the art gloves with gecko pad fingers that was strong enough to hold up the weight of an average person. Thankfully, Bach and I were both built like Olympic track sprinters and were slender enough to slide into the small opening but strong enough to free climb the musty shaft.

We'd just crawled our way past the second story when a loud rumble made us both freeze. My military watch glowed green as I checked the time but my earpiece crackled before I did more than glance,

"We've got a problem. Motorcade is fifteen minutes too early."

Shit in a bucket. "How many vehicles?"

"Four SUVS and two motorcycles."

Significantly more men than we'd planned on.

Bach shuffled beside me. "Do we keep going?"

The odds blitzed in my head. Even if we could get the target, the chances of our own transport slipping through unnoticed was slim. Unless we switched our extraction location.

"No stopping." I told them both. "Notify Bernstein to switch to plan B but we stay the course."

"Roger that."

Exactly three minutes later, my watch flickered as I hoisted myself level with the dumbwaiter entrance on the fourth floor. We'd made it. Bach lifted himself beside me and used a thin sliver of light to locate the depression that would be our exit. He counted down from three before shoving open the panel which groaned loudly. I stuck my gun through the entrance and sprayed the room with bullets but yanked back quickly to allow Bach to hoist himself through the opening and roll into the room.

We took out the four men stationed in the room before turning our attention to the limp white body dummy was duct taped to the chair at the wrist, ankles, and chest. Our tactical knives sliced through that and Bach hefted the form over his shoulder with a grunt that told me it was heavier than it looked and I led the way out the door.

It suddenly swung open and the man who pointed a gun at us from the other side made me jerk to a halt and my blood ran cold. Deep olive skin...black beard draping thickly from a rounded chin...shifty eyes the color of the blackest dirt. No turban framed his face but his features were more familiar to me than a few distant relatives.

My nightmares and I knew that face.

In the far recesses of my mind, I knew that the possibility of this man being caught and captured by the American government was slim. He'd been the leader of a small insurgent group in Syria, one of dozens flagged by Interpol every week, and had not been seen since my escape. But Beastie roared and loud crescendo of music overrode everything else as flashes of that cave prison flicked like a horror reel inside my head.

An enraged scream tore from my lips and I charged across the room. Bach yelled my name but it was a haze amidst the tormented memory ruling my thoughts. Nothing mattered. Not the mission. Not my reinstatement. Nothing computed.

The man raised a handgun and fired but I was too fast. I tackled him in the midsection and carried us both back into the hallway, slamming into the far wall. He tried to wrap an arm around my shoulders even as I smashed an elbow into my back but I broke his hold and straightened enough to punch him in the face. I grabbed his shoulders and drove my knee into his solar plexus two times; when he sagged, I shifted just a bit a pummeled my knee directly into his face. Something crunched and blood gushed as he groaned and stumbled to the side. But he wouldn't get away that easily. I swept his lung out from under him and was on top of him, battering him, before he hit the ground.

I vaguely registered the sound of men rushing into the hall. Beastie and I were only focused on annihilation. Someone shouted my name and rough hands grabbed my upper arms just as I pulled a dagger from my tactical belt and tried to slash him. I screamed, infuriated, as men in military camo dragged me off him, and I fought against their hold.

"Kill him," I snarled wrenching against the hands, trying to get free. "Kill him now!"

But they did the opposite. Several men knelt beside the gasping terrorist, face a bloody mess, and immediately began basic first aid. Beastie roared and the sound came out of my mouth. Why were they helping him? They should help me cut him into little pieces and toss him into the nearest body of water. One of the men reached forward and gently pried at the skin around the terrorist's neck, peeling it away like thick tape. It took only a few seconds for him to gently peel back the thick layer of facial covering to reveal a face I'd never seen before. Not the terrorist of my nightmares. But a stranger with blonde hair and brown eyes rolling back into his skull.

Dread slammed into me like a fist to the temple.

I'd just beat the shit out of someone and had no idea who he was. Because he wasn't my tormentor at all—but a plant. And just realized how horrifically I'd failed this practice mission.

* * * * * * * * * * * * * * * * * *

Remember what I said about the inevitability of shattering? Yeah, this was case and point.

Part of me already knew that Homeland would lay this entirely at my feet. Because when you break—and it's a time game because destruction was unavoidable—they blame it on you. Your lack of cunning, speed, skill, courage, intel, prework, etc… The ultimate CYA program. Cowards.

Which is why I sat inside of the main office waiting to get my discharge.

This was a different kind of prison, white walled and air conditioned, yet I couldn't say I preferred this to the moldy cave that kept flashing just behind my retinas. The blinds were up, a hint that this wasn't confinement or isolation, revealing a hallway busy with a stream of men and women in the customary bland colors of the intelligence office world. Look at the people, was the subtle message, don't you want to be good and normal and functional like them? But that was no longer an option for me. I was the best agent in my department reduced to a fracturing bundle of violent emotions. And now, all of Homeland knew it.

The door finally opened and I was only mildly surprised at

the man who took two steps inside before shutting the door. Figured they'd send him to give me the boot. Wesley Brandon Lawrence was everything you'd expect the director of Homeland Security to be—an innocuous, brown haired, 5'11 man dressed in an expensive dark suit but was unassuming enough to fit in anywhere, be it a baseball game or board room. He gave off Kevin-Costner-meets-CIA vibes and I dared anyone of debate that.

And he was one of the few people I could truly call friend in this entire organization. Here to deliver the death blow to my career and ego. His eyes were blank like the bottom of an empty coffee cup. Unreadable.

I looked away and refocused on the smear on the wall. "You planted him on purpose." My voice was hot with accusation.

"We had to make sure your test results were accurate." His voice was carefully bland, so bland that I knew he was holding back.

Too bad I couldn't do the same. "So you set me up to snap and some poor rookie to get his face beat in so badly he'll probably need a plastic surgeon? And if you feed me some line like, "He knew the risks", I'll literally lose it."

So he said nothing at all.

A frustrated breath flew past my lips. Government people are so irritating.

"It's only been 6 months, Serena." He started. "Most agents take twice that long just to finish PT recovery from something like what you experienced yet you blasted through PT and your psyche evals. It set off our alarm bells."

"I was ready. I am ready." I insisted.

"It's time for you to rest, truly rest. Take a load off for a few weeks and don't worry about work."

"With all due respect, sir, I don't need rest. I need work." I need to atone for my mistake. I looked at him. "What about the Hirzel case?" His quirked eyebrow said all it needed to. That was highly classified, something I should know nothing about. Oh well, we all have our sources. Still, I pressed on. "It's only a two week gig with light security at most. A perfect reintroduction mission."

"I'm going to be pretend like I didn't just hear you mention the details of Dutch diplomat's personal security mission that is still buried in someone's budget pile right now." He replied.

"Unfortunately, the board and I are not confident that you are ready to be back in the field. You're on 12 weeks of mandatory rest starting now. Think of it as a vacation. Either way, your sole focus is to get better and get functional so I can get you back into the field." He pulled a white envelope and tossed it on the dresser. "Most agents would thank me for giving them a paid holiday."

I shot him a cool glance that did nothing to hide my fury. "I've got other things I'd like to say to you, sir." But I was a good little soldier, trained to obey the most minute command even if everything in me revolted.

But even that statement was pushing it. This *was* my boss after all and one of the most powerful men in the nation. That's the trouble with becoming friends with higher ups—the line was crossed at some point.

A smile ghosted on his thin lips. "Your plane leaves in an hour. There's a card with my number on it. Where you're going, I doubt there will be any drama but if you have any trouble at all or need anything at all, don't think twice, call me."

Emotion choked the words in my throat. So I let my silence speak for me.

Again, that smile. "Enjoy your vacation, Serena." He said before stepping back into the hall and shutting the door.

Which is how I ended up standing in the middle of Reagan National Airport with a tactical backpack filled with my most basic belongings and that stupid envelope crumped in my hand. I hadn't bothered to check its contents until I arrived at the terminal—it didn't matter where Lawrence sent me, I'd hate every minute—but I didn't realize how stupid a mistake it was until the clerk pulled up the details of the location.

There was a handwritten prescription from the doctor on base and a single plane ticket. To Oklahoma City.

What are the chances that my magnanimous, compassionate, understanding boss would freeze my personal bank account to keep from buying a new ticket, a ticket that would take me anywhere but the city listed on the landmine he gave me?

Pretty effin' high.

It wasn't that there was anything wrong with Oklahoma City. Nestled between Dallas and Kansas City, it was the heart of eclectic tastes; everything from southern hospitality, midwestern cuisine, and postmodern art. It was funky—uniquely western and distinctly conservative and all Oklahoma. But I wanted to be there like I wanted to facilitate another tri-nation hostage swap in the middle of the desert with a single wave walkie-talkie and a foil antenna.

Read: not at all.

What was the source of my deep rooted aversion? Simply put: my family. A fact Lawrence was all too aware of.

Beastie growled and I silently hummed a few bars of my favorite concerto until she retreated, soothed by the music. If my goal was to convince him that I was fully functional, going berserk in an airport was the last thing that needed to happen.

I took a breath and weighed my options. But really there weren't any. That's the thing about working for the government—they won't blink an eye to use those resources to manipulate those around them into playing their twisted chess game. For the good of the public, of course. I gritted my teeth. I really didn't want to do this. But vacation was a direct order and, like any good experiment rat, I'd been trained to obey those commands at all costs. I'd been given the order, the location, the transportation...the message couldn't be any clearer.

So, I trudged toward my departure gate with a growing sense of dismay and ready to strangle something. A black security orb caught my eye and I waited until I was directly under it before lifting my middle finger and waving it around in a circle. There was a slim chance that Randall's was watching me but, just in case...

Half an hour later, the small airliner jettisoned down the runway and I struggled to suppress memories of the last time I'd been on an aircraft. Things were different without the frantic beeping of medical equipment and the whirring of helicopter blades but that drop in my stomach took me back to the moment of landing on an airstrip at some heavily restricted government military base eight weeks earlier. Fuzzy images flashed in my head—struggling against hands trying to strap me into a stretcher, the jolt of pain when the copter finally landed, and a wave of unfamiliar faces speaking in garbled tones over me.

The dark growl rumbled inside my head only spiked my anxiety. Losing my chili on this plane wouldn't help my case that I was better, more balanced, and ready to return to the field. The thought of another six weeks of forced rest and PTSD therapy made me want to vomit. I so needed to get my crap together. I spent the next several hours deploying a handful of techniques I'd learned over the years to calm myself down; counting backwards from one hundred in Farsi, dynamic breathing exercises, and mentally visualizing the orchestral chords to Bach symphonies.

By the time I landed at Will Rogers World Airport, the cold in my stomach and the unstable feline in my head had receded yet again. Before my...incident...in Syria, I didn't have the black sleek cat roaming my mind, triggering spasmodic PTSD events. But I was learning to deal...I didn't have any other choice.

One botched mission and everyone treats you like a basket case.

CHAPTER 2

I landed in Oklahoma City with all the fanfare appropriate for a prodigal daughter slinking back home in the shadows. Meaning, nothing at all. There were no tearful embraces, heartfelt statements of forgiveness and unconditional love, no long overdue reunions that permanently healed a cracked part of my spirit. My family didn't even know I was here. Nope, I slipped through the Will Rogers International Airport like the shadow I was trained to be and flung myself into the process of getting settled for the next eleven weeks and six days of my life. Within forty-eight hours I'd secured a line of credit, found an adorable apartment in the Art's District downtown, and haggled the price with the apartment manager I came away with the rent lowered by fifteen percent and he agreed to leave all of the stage furniture for my use. It made no sense for me to scour the city for a new love seat or bistro table when I was only here temporarily—that and interior design was at the bottom of the list of my resume quality skills.

Oh, and I bought a car. A sleek Chevy Camaro ZL1 that was the deep gray color of the residue a gunpowder left on your skin and packed with all the latest features that made it racetrack ready and sexy beyond belief. The engine's growl vibrated through the seat and into my thighs in a way that felt indecent and I'm pretty sure the sales associate that I was having a personal moment with the V8 engine.

Was it a complete waste of the government issued, bland-as-sin sedan that Lawrence had secured for my use while on "vacation"? Yes. Did I care one single hair on a rat's behind about that? Absolutely not.

But trying to reacclimate to civilian life as a highly trained assassin was...inconvenient....and I found myself slugging through difficult moments that I wasn't mentally prepared to handle.

Moments no one tells you about when they release you back into normal society.

Like when you're at the grocery store and a little old lady creeps up behind you, innocently reaching for the oatmeal. But you respond like she's a terrorist, barring and pinning her arm to the cereal shelves in three seconds flat.

Or when you're driving down the highway at night and swerve to avoid a landmine...which is really a Walmart sack floating in the wind.

Two days in and I was one hundred percent certain that I was a walking danger to the normal people of the world. Yet staying locked away in my apartment wasn't an option. Solitude I could handle. I was an introvert and the thought of being by myself is often what propelled me through a hard mission filled with uneasy children and aggressive parents. It was the silence that got to me. The silence that stirred unstable things in the dark corridors of my mind. Things like the fact that my family had no idea I was in town and I wasn't sure I wanted them to know. Like the countdown clock of how much time my dad had before his cancer won the battle. Like how much of a coward I was for avoiding all of the things. And, of course, the extraction mission I'd failed that had landed me here in the first place.

By Thursday afternoon, it was mission critical that I get out and do something, anything, to keep myself occupied and, let's be honest, distracted from all of the things that I should be handling. Which is what led me to the Krav Maga gym in a run-down part of the city.

I was no stranger to this place. In fact, in all six hundred square miles of the city, this goldmine nestled within a shoddy shopping center was the one place I felt most comfortable. Home even. It had been a haven during the turbulent days of high school and when my dad remarried. The trend these days was to rent out garage space in a ritzy part of the city and charge top dollar for a "gritty" martial arts experience. Not here. The Forge was nestled into an old strip mall and, on its best day, someone might look at it and think "dingy". But those really looking to gain insight wouldn't mind.

A warning voice groused in the back of my head. The shrink assigned to me at the military base warned against "trigger" environments, essentially anything linked to violence or a spike in my adrenaline that could trigger a PTSD episode. I wouldn't be able to heal that way, he'd told me. But I'd been dealing with this for longer than I wanted to admit and I knew the things that set Beastie off. This place wasn't a danger. Just the idea of going made me feel more grounded and peace that I had for a long time.

This I could control.

A cool late October breeze ushered me through frosted glass doors into a space that was lit only by sunlight pouring in from ceiling height windows and a few white lightbulbs that considerably brightened the space that used to be a supermarket back in the day. Now, the shelves were cleared and the entirety of the floor was covered in thick black mats except for a ten inch or so gap between the wall so people could walk the perimeter. The regulars immediately kicked off their shoes and placed them on the metal rack just left of the door. I kept mine on and slid off to the side, watching.

The atmosphere quivered with an undercurrent of controlled violence and I let the hum of activity sink into my skin—grunts, swearing, the sound of bodies hitting the mat, the rhythmic *thawp* of strikes to a punching bag. All of it struck a familiar chord, and something foundational within me notched into place. I inhaled the acrid scent of sweat, blood, and pain. Yes, pain had a smell. It was the aroma of discipline and correction and determination—of pungent sweat and iron-tinged blood and rubbery exercise mats. Excellence vocalized through cries of defeat and victorious roars. This, more than any other place, felt like home.

The standard black outfit was intentionally innocuous and put everyone on the same level. But don't let the five foot woman with turquoise painted toes or the scrappy looking man with a tattoo on his neck fool you. Most people who came here wanted a no holds barred, hands-on experience that mimicked the unexpectedness of real life. It's the reason the gym appealed to law enforcement on every level. Private investigators, cops, current Marines, ex-Army rangers...those who knew that a quick, rough, and dirty fight was the only way to ensure going home at the end of the day.

Even with the AC going full tilt it was still hot enough for sweat to bead on my skin at the back of my neck where my braids lay hot and heavy. The door opened and the cool air was momentarily sucked toward the new entry as two men stepped inside before rushing back through the room as it closed heavily behind them. A harsh vacuum of air in and out. Like the very room itself was breathing.

Anxiety fluttered through my clenched stomach. It wasn't unpleasant. It was the jitters you got after being away for a while. I was excited, mildly nervous, and ready. All good things.

There was a small door in the further corner of the room and it opened, revealing a tall man built like a bulldog who strode inside. Travis Blalock was no ordinary Krav Maga master, and it was obvious in the calculating, watchful way his eyes roved over every person in the room. You could almost feel his gaze, like a breath on the back of your neck. A former marine and self-defense instructor for the US military, he carried the art of tactical defense in his blood. Though he stood on the far side of the room, I was sure that everyone was aware of him.

My stomach twisted as his dark gaze landed on me. He probably didn't recognize me. I was taller and had put on thirty pounds of muscle that showed in the ripples in my biceps and thighs. I looked like the military security professional that I was, not the scrawny girl who'd graced his door a decade before.

When he strode across the mats toward me, I forced myself to remain where I was and not slip out the door. I hated that small part of me that cared about his opinion and craved his acceptance. I knew from experience that giving people too much access invited them to destroy, and most did. If there was a single ounce of hesitation in his demeanor, I'd bounce and not return.

He stepped off the mat, and I moved forward to meet him and offered the traditional greeting. A deep bow at the waist, chest high, with my fists firmly anchored on my hips. I bowed low and stayed there. In my peripheral, I saw him return the gesture.

"Serena." The warmth of his voice made me glance up into espresso-black eyes. I wasn't at all prepared for him to step close and wrap me in a tight, muscly hug. "Welcome, home." He breathed in my ear, patted me firmly on the back, and released me before my brain fully processed what was happening.

I smiled at him. "Thank you, sir."

"Have you been in town long? I talked to Julien the other day, and he didn't say anything about an upcoming visit."

My younger brother's name sent a sharp sensation through me. Our relationship had been tense before I left for the Airforce and ten years of silence had withered it down to a single thread of hostility. Still, I kept my voice emotionless and even as I said, "A couple of days ago."

"Janet will be upset that the one night she chose to stay late at the hospital, our prodigal daughter decides to surprise us." His eyes crinkled talking about his wife, a woman who'd been one of my greatest influencers. "You planning to join the class?"

I glanced at the mats filled with the midweek crowd scattered across the mats and chatting comfortably, waiting for him to start the session. "If it's not too late."

"I think I have a good reason to wait." His wry smile was a rare gift. "There's an extra uniform on my desk. It probably won't fit perfectly, but it'll suffice for now."

"Beggars can't be choosers." I headed for the small office at the very back of the building. It took less than five minutes for me to snag the uniform, at least a size too big, strip and fold my own clothes, and pull on the surprisingly soft black pants and short sleeve T-shirt. The moment I stepped from the office, Master Blalock called the class to attention and moved us through a rigorous warm up that left sweat dripping down my face.

Blood pumped through my veins as I moved through the standing defense and gun disbarment techniques. I was having a blast.

Homeland was wrong to be worried about me.

Dad was wrong too.

I was fine and totally in control.

When the group switched to choke holds, I didn't think twice about it. I loved practicing breaking standing chokes because they were so practical and applicable in real combat situations. Standing chokes were glamorized by Hollywood which made it the first attack for the everyday, Joe-the-jerk fighter. Something unpleasant and persistent stirred at the back of my mind when we added a takedown element, but I tamped it down. This was a safe space. I was fine.

Until I wasn't.

Until, in an attempt to avoid the flurry of elbow strikes I furiously rained down on him, my partner flipped me over his hip and pinned me to the floor. Ugly memories broke free of the vault and swallowed me in a dark wave before I fully comprehended what was happening. Beastie roared as flashes of thought, of memories, barraged my mind.

The hands gripping me turned into chains shackling me to the floor, pinning me in place for an endless onslaught of blows that came from every direction. A face rose out of the sea of pain. A face that drew a hiss from my lips even as I scrambled to get away. That face was the architect of my torment, and I would not be his plaything again.

I screamed and struck out, music suffusing my mind as I careened straight into combat mode. My fist buried itself in the large muscle of his thigh, a nerve strike, and the man on top of me faltered. I punched him again brutal strike to the kidneys, and he gurgled. Good, I wouldn't waste the opening. I canted my hip and tried to roll us, but he was too heavy. I landed several vicious blows to his ribs until he shifted his weight trying to get away. Voices frothed around me and multiple pairs of hands grabbed at me.

I screamed in fury. They'd captured me once and I wouldn't

go back easily. I flailed and kicked and scratched but still they dragged me away. Strong arms wrapped around my torso and pinned my arms to my sides, limiting my range of motion.

"It's me, Serena." A man's voice muttered, lips brushing the shell of my ear. "You're safe. Stop fighting me."

My legs turned to lead but my heart pounded. I knew that voice...more intimately familiar than I wanted to. That voice helped push back the fog so I could think.

"Talon?" My throat was scratchy, as if I'd been screaming, and I tried to force myself to think past the tide of adrenaline coursing in my veins. Beastie snarled in my brain, telling me to keep fighting. Fear rose, sharp and caustic—if he was there, I must be back in that hell hole. Danger all around. I had to get us both out of here. They'd kill him too.

I wrenched to the side but the arms only cinched tighter. Talon spoke again, yet all I registered was the deep rumbling in his chest that vibrated against me as we moved.

It was his gentle crooning that brought me back. There was nothing gentle in this world, nothing that exuded warmth or welcome and if it did exist it was a façade. But music, my fractured brain understood. The song slowly drew me from the dark shores of trauma and back into the present with a quivering gasp as if coming up for air after being held underwater.

I forced myself to relax against him and focused on taking a series of deep breath, each inhalation washing away the horrible memory. He kept singing but switched his grip from a restraining arm bar to simply his arms around me, holding me upright.

For a moment, I let myself enjoy the feel of those arms and let peace wash over me.

Until I opened my eyes.

The scene before me was a triage nightmare from medical documentary. Blood was everywhere—splattered against people's skin and pooling on the black mats like dark, lethal wine. And in the middle of that pool was Frank. He wheezed for breath, hoarse whistling gasps moving his chest. Half a dozen classmates clustered around him, one holding a t-shirt to his nose, another palpating his upper leg. He looked like he'd taken on three guys and lost, horribly.

Nausea overwhelmed me. "Oh my god, Frank!" I lurched in Talon's arms trying to get to him but Talon tightened his grip. Something wet and tacky covered my hands and I glanced down to see blood caking my fingers. What the hell had I done?

My voice made several people look at me, some with carefully blank faces but not everyone could hide the judgement in their eyes.

I tried taking a step. "Did you stabilize his—"

A woman with spiky blue hair couldn't quite keep the hostility off her face. "You've done enough," she spat.

And looking around the room, the quiet judgment in their eyes, it was too much. My stomach rolled and I gagged. Talon's arms loosened and I ran for the back door. I barely made it outside to empty my stomach on the cracked concrete. Every time I thought of Frank's broken body another wave rolled over me and I ended up on my hands and knees gagging bile as penance for my stupidity with hot tears trailing down my face. Someone swept my braids free of my mouth and I immediately knew it was Talon. He rubbed my back until the last wave subsided.

My stomach was empty but my soul felt chained by guilt.

"Don't." I choked out, wiping my mouth with the back of my hand. "Don't coddle me. Frank needs your support, not me."

"We both know that's not true."

I spit one more time, wishing for some water to swish and get rid of the bile tainted funk, but there was no help for it. I stood and turned to face him.

There were a dozen things that stood out about Talon. Tawny bronze skin and chiseled cheekbones which hinted at Native American heritage. Six-four frame roped with thick muscle. The thick braid that fell to his waist and was interwoven with a thin piece of leather. But it was his eyes that were my favorite—gunmetal gray starbusted with silver. giving him a rugged handsomeness. Unusual and enthralling. Eyes that I had labeled lightning eyes when were younger.

Now, I met his eyes and flinched.

"Serena," he took a step toward me. "I know you're better

than you were but what made you think sparing was a good idea?"

The words hit me in the face and burned all the way to the bone. "I needed to do something and this was the first place I thought to come. Someplace I could be comfortable and myself."

"So you came to Krav Maga gym?" His tone was bland but there was a wealth of accusation in all the things he didn't say. "I'm not well versed in the psychological needs of someone who survived what you have but I think rule number one is probably stay out of triggering environments."

"Don't lecture me, Talon. I've had plenty of those the last two days."

"Clearly not anything that penetrated."

I stared sightlessly over the parking lot as Beastie growled in my head, evident that some demons are too entrenched in who we are to easily let go of.

"How long has this been going on?"

He would start with that question. A question I didn't have a good answer for. I shrugged

"I'm not judging you, Serena. Anyone who's ever seen a minute of combat knows that it changes you, fundamentally. But some...events are more damaging than others. Are harder to fully recover from."

"I don't know what you want me to say."

"Anything. I want you to tell me why you haven't gotten help. Why you walk around with this trauma so close to the surface?"

My lips twitched with a soundless scoff. He had no idea of the dozens of hours of therapy. Countless meetings with psychiatrists and therapists specifically trained to help soldiers deal with the trauma of the job. None of it had helped.

A gentle hand pressed against my chin and I didn't fight him as he raised my face to meet his eye. "You had no control over what happened in Syria. It wasn't your fault."

The words hit me in the face like acid and it burned all the way to the bone. I smacked his hand away. "You know nothing." I snarled, anger a cold flush that made my voice shake.

"Maybe," his eyes gleamed, not backing down. "You know what I do know? That nerve strike you dealt Frank will make his leg numb for hours. He'll limp for days."

"That wasn't supposed to happen."

"I'd bet my right kidney that you have more "wasn't supposed to happen" moments that you'll admit." He sighed, still an angry sound. "Serena, just tell me. How often?"

I couldn't hold his gaze and looked back towards the parking lot. I sucked in a breath. "Often."

"How. Often?"

"I don't keep track, Talon."

"Bullshit," he snapped. "You thrive on data analytics. It's how your brain works. You probably can tell me how frequently, what time of day they're happening, and any established patterns."

I gave in. If I answered his question, maybe he'd get off my back and leave me alone. "At least once a day...on good days."

Silence.

That was worse than his yelling.

"You can't thrive like this. No one can."

His voice was a familiar rumble that I wanted to relax into, know that I could trust. But deep down, Beastie and I knew we couldn't.

"I know a good psychiatrist who can help. He helped me when I just got back and struggled to reacclimate to...life. He offices out of Tulsa but that's not too bad a drive—"

"I'll pass," I cut him off. "Been there, done that and it was waste of time. The last thing I need is for new people stirring things up so they figure out what to prescribe to help my "instability"."

"So you'd rather be dangerous?" His voice was matter-of-fact, almost bland but it didn't lessen the cutting of his words. "Continue to hurt the people around you for what? Because you're afraid of what they think? That sounds more of you being a coward than them being judgmental."

"Everyone's judgmental when they don't understand. You show them part of yourself and they pretend to understand what you're showing them and all they end up doing is stabbing you in the back with it."

"If that's what you project, then maybe you're creating your own future. People don't walk around trying to figure out how to screw you over. Not me, not your family..."

A derisive snort popped out before I could hold it back.

He shoved my shoulder, both playful and a bit chastising. "People change, Serena. You wouldn't want them to hold you to the person you were when you left town would you? Try and give them the same courtesy. Who knows," he shrugged. "You might just be surprised."

"Doubtful," I muttered.

"You know the family barbeque is Saturday, right?" he asked. "Your dad insisted we hold it as usual, the full works and everything, and Yvonne couldn't say no... especially now."

Especially now. Two words that caused a sharp pang to explode in the center of my chest. My stepmother was a diva in every way and reticent to change plans or be forced to give priority to something other than her expensive charity fundraisers or days at the spa. Unless there was an overarching reason...like a terminal illness that was getting so bad she didn't want to waste time on petty arguments.

"Might be a good time to reconnect." He stood and held out his hand to me. "If you don't get a handle of this, there'll be many more Joe's in your life."

Talk about it. Easy to say...far harder to do. I took his hand and let him pull me to my feet. His words resonated, though. Every passing day brought a new and unwelcome side effect of PTSD. Together, they were getting harder to hide. He was right, but how was I supposed to open myself up for healing when I didn't trust the people around me? What if I couldn't open up? The damage was more severe than Talon could ever know. If he knew, if any of them knew, they'd look at me like some pitiful, broken thing that needed to be coddled. Weakness makes people lie to you, tell you pretty lies about everything being okay. I'd had enough lies.

He didn't press me further but let me stare with unfocused eyes at the traffic lazing down the street. Talon had never been afraid to let words linger. I'd always taken that as a sign of character, his inner strength and lack of dependence on what others thought of him, and I liked that.

The whine of a siren interrupted the peaceful scene.

"Think on it," he said. "I know some good people who can help when you're ready." The siren was getting louder, nearly drowning out his words. I looked over my shoulder to the street just as an ambulance pulled into the tight parking lot and rounded to the front of the building.

Fear pulsed in my chest. I started to walk around the building, but Talon grabbed my bicep, stopping me. "It would be best if you didn't."

Didn't what? See how much damage I'd caused that an ambulance was needed? Maybe someone else had gotten hurt. But the kindness lingering in his eyes that made my stomach clench with nausea.

I jerked my arm, but he held firm. "An ambulance? You pulled me off him!"

"Serena, don't beat yourself up—"

"Tell. Me." Again, I noticed the blood caking my hand and the words gurgled in my throat.

He was silent a moment. "We knowing nothing until the EMTs confirm but, the way he was wheezing, there might be a punctured lung."

"He's trained for crying out loud."

"He was trying not to hurt you."

Emotion overwhelmed me, and I swayed with it. Frank was my friend, a good friend back in the day. But PTSD didn't care who was friend or foe. "I need to go." I straightened but didn't meet his eye.

"Serena."

His warm voice made Beastie snarl. I couldn't...didn't deserve his understanding and patience. I turned on my heel, bare feet catching on the concrete, and walked away. I rounded the corner of the building just as the paramedics slammed the back doors shut and hopped inside. Wet misted my eyes, and I watched through blurry vision as the two men hopped inside the van and drove away, siren blaring.

I felt a presence at my back and knew it was Talon. For a

brief second, I wanted to crumple against him. But this mess had nothing to do with him, and I wouldn't share the burden.

Master Blalock stood at the doorway. When the ambulance was out of sight, he walked toward me.

I wanted to shrivel away and hide. I didn't want to see the innumerable reactions on his face or in his eyes—disappointment, horror, condescension. Beastie growled that it wasn't my fault, that I'd had no choice. With the siren echoing in my ears, I knew she was lying. I was tempted to dart around Talon and pretend that I wasn't there. Weakling move.

Instead, I stepped away from him and stood tall, chest out, shoulders straight while I waited for Master Blalock to stop in front of me. As he neared, I couldn't hold eye contact and stared at the concrete.

The weight of his gaze made my knees buckle but I forced myself to a parade rest. I'd made a bad judgement call and should be woman enough to face the consequences.

"Would you be available to look at Justin? He wouldn't let the paramedics see his injuries, but he was limping pretty badly when he went to the bathroom."

My gaze snapped up, and I realized he was addressing Talon.

"Of course," Talon rumbled.

The tension was stretched tight, but I was the one to snap. "Master Blalock, I am so sorry."

"I know you are." The compassion in his voice made Beastie snarl in my head and I shushed her. "Sometimes, we don't realize how close our demons are to the surface until something triggers them and we find ourselves swimming in a murky sea of memory. I suspect you knew something wasn't right. I wish you'd shown better discernment in coming tonight, making sure you were fully ready."

I nodded but couldn't meet his eye.

"Good. What I'm going to say next is going to sound like a punishment, and I want to tell you, eye to eye, that it isn't. I will support you in whatever way you need to help you find healing."

I wouldn't balk at punishment. I curled my hands into fists and Frank's blood tightened against my skin.

"But, until you've sought professional help to address your PTSD, you will not be allowed back into class." His tone was remorseful yet firm. "I must think of the safety of my other students. We all know what it is to carry demons. Not one of us here would lecture or condemn you. We've all been there in our own way, traversed that very river ourselves and, at moments, wanted to drown ourselves in it. But healing is always on the opposite shore and the length and duration of the journey is up to us." He held out my key fob and phone to me. One of the other students, a tall, broad woman who I knew was a local firefighter, stepped forward with my clothes folded in her arms.

Humiliation burned and I dipped my head so he wouldn't see the tears that blurred my vision. The best thing in my life… my second home…and I'd let my weakness ruin it. I cleared my throat. "I understand. I'm sorry." Humiliation burned deep in my chest. I had to get out of here, away from the sympathetic looks and accusing whispers that floated around me.

I spun on my bare heel, gravel digging into my skin, and walked to my car.

"Serena!" Talon yelled as I pulled open the door. "You're in no shape to drive. Let me take you home."

I dumped my stuff in the passenger seat and started the engine. My sympathy meter was in the red and any more coddling from them and I'd snap. Without another word or glance their way, I backed out of the parking lot and sped toward the highway.

Thoughts ping-ponged through my skull, rapid firing accusations and judgment faster than I could keep up. How could I have been so stupid? Putting myself at risk was one thing. Blindsiding a friend and forcing him to choose between his safety and mine? My stomach churned.

Being broken sucked.

CHAPTER 3

*B*ang-bang-bang.

The quick raps tore me from sleep as Beastie roared in my mind, awake and immediately alert. Danger!

My fingers wrapped around the Smith & Wesson handgun strapped beneath the coffee table, and it was cocked and pointed at the door before I fully opened my eyes. Thoughts tried to filter in—the bright sunlight streaming through the open curtain, the fact that I was curled up on the couch wearing only a pair of track shorts and a sports bra, and the lack of attackers in the immediate area—but Beastie drowned out everything else.

It took three slow breaths for me to realize the sound wasn't gunshots or the sound of sniper fire. Someone was knocking on my front door.

Bang-bang-bang.

"Serena? This is Elana Orsoto."

Talon's aunt? How in the world…?

Air whooshed from my lungs. Adrenaline vaporized from my system as quickly as it came and left me shaking. Bone-deep weariness crashed over me in a wave, and my arm dropped to cover my face in the crook of my elbow. Beastie yowled in protest that we were still in danger and raked her claws against the bars of her cage. I winced as pain radiated down the back of my neck. It physically hurt to ignore her.

"Talon told me you moved back to the city, and I was so surprised when he told me you'd moved to my apartment complex. I live in the next building. He said you were taking a break from working with Homeland Security." The voice that came through the door was both cheerfully familiar and jarring. The last thing I needed was a reminder of last night...and Talon. "What's with our children and wanting to save the world? Anyway, I made a casserole for you. I'll leave it on your welcome mat and you can snag it when you're ready. It's good to know that you're back home. I feel safer already."

Mrs. O was practically a mom to me, and I couldn't leave her standing on my doorstep like a beggar. I slid the gun between the cushion and couch arm and stood upright and swore aloud. Every muscle in my body was tense and on fire. How had I ended up on the couch? I then remembered the late-night kickboxing session that lasted until 2am that I used to exhaust myself enough to sleep. This morning, I was definitely paying for it. I quickly snatched my shirt from last night from the floor and pulled it on as I walked to the door. Quick glance through the peephole confirmed it was just her and I pulled the door open as she started to gush about her grandchildren.

Her face lit when she saw me. "Serena!" She balanced a blue and white floral baking dish in one hand and stretched out her free arm toward me.

I bent down and let her arm wrap around my neck as she went on her tiptoes to hug me. The smell of buttery pastry combined with her herbal scent had me relaxing into her grip as familiarity washed over me. "Hi Mrs. O." I greeted, voice gritty with sleep.

She stroked her hand down my braids, comforting and motherly, as she pulled me in tighter. "I've missed you, sweet girl."

My arms convulsed around her before I dropped them to my sides and stepped back.

Barely five feet tall with silver streaked black hair cascading down to her waist, Elana Orsoto was the very definition of dowager Native American queen. There was strength in her jaw, a regal air around her, and kindness in her dark, deep eyes.

I didn't mean to wake you," she apologized, scanning my

face with concern. "I thought I'd waited long enough in the day. Talon says that the military turns everyone into morning people, but he's been more a night owl than I've ever seen him since he's been back."

Just cause the military forces you to function in the morning, doesn't mean you necessarily enjoy it. "Don't worry about it. I needed to get up anyway." I stepped back and held open the door for her, despite the prickles that traveled down my fingers at having another person in my space. My apartment in the one place I could deal with my crazy in solitude, with no judgement. Even though I'd missed Miss Soto, having her in my place of regeneration made me...antsy.

"I'm just dropping this off. I know you probably have a mile-long list of things that need to get done." She walked to the marble bar, trailing tantalizing smells of sauteed onion and grilled meat, and set the baking dish down. "When Talon moved back last year, his first week or so was hectic as he tried to sort things out, and he refused to let me help. Do you even have plates?"

I shrugged. "Paper ones." But I wasn't sure where I'd put those.

"Guess that's better than eating off your palm like a gorilla," she muttered. "I'm going to consider this a don't ask, don't tell situation, so if you end up eating straight out of the dish, I don't want to know."

She seemed so put out by that idea that I couldn't help the slight smile that tugged my lips up. This from the same woman who used to help Talon, my brother Julien and I make mudpies and pretend not to notice when we shoved handfuls into our mouths.

"All good things come from the earth," she used to say. "Why should eating it be bad for you?" Very philosophical. But now that I'm older, I suspect she was just desperate to keep us hooligans out of trouble and out of her house.

"I will immediately add plates to my list of things to buy just to put your mind at ease," I teased.

"Good." She said. "Do your parents know you're back?"

The smile disappeared. I appreciated that she didn't just assume that I'd communicate my plans with my parents. Our family had been intertwined through fate early on. My dad had practically adopted her into the family after his partner of twelve years suddenly committed suicide and Elana had stepped up to raise Talon and his two sisters. She'd witnessed the budding tension between me and my stepmom that exploded when I was in high school and knew on what strained terms I'd left.

To answer her question, I shook my head. "I'm giving myself a few days to settle, and then I'll reach out."

She nodded in understanding, though a quick look of chastisement flashed across her face. "Don't wait too long. More time will only deepen the canyon of distance between you and your family and will make it harder to cross when it's time." She glanced around the nearly empty space. "You might think about asking Yvonne to help you decorate."

I almost laughed aloud—she and I could barely go to a grocery store without starting World War Three. Debating over furniture and decorating knickknacks would be a nightmare. I gave her a look that told her what I thought of the idea.

She shot me one back. "Yvonne has great style, and it might be one of those necessary tasks that can be a natural ice breaker. I'm just saying."

"The only thing that comes naturally to my mother is forcing people to agree with her opinion that, usually, no one asked for." My tone was mild, almost placid to my own ears. But the tightening in my throat and flash of emotion made Beastie stir in the corners of my mind.

"What your relationship looked like when you left is not how it has to be now," she said gently. "Whatever your reasons for coming home, maybe reconciling with your family is part of God's plan for your unexpected return."

Pretty words. Too bad me, God, and my stepmom rarely saw eye-to-eye. I wasn't surprised Mrs. O pulled the God-and-

His-masterful-plan card. Elana was one of the most devout Christians I knew, but it wasn't pretense or haughtiness that drove her. She'd experienced a lot of hideous things in her life —burying a husband and brother—yet still turned to God as her source of strength and perseverance. I admired that about her. Even though I'd been raised in church, I'd seen too much ugly, done too much ugly, to really believe God circulated in my life.

At best, I was just one of the headaches that He occasionally had to deal with.

At worst? Well, my time in a Syrian cave prison pretty much told me where I listed on His priority list when it came to emergencies.

The white bulb over the door that was connected to the pressurized mat outside blinked twice just before a knock sounded. Who in the world? As I walked to the door, the irony wasn't lost on me that I could spend thousands of dollars on state-of-the-art security but balked at spending a few hundred for a couch of my own.

I peered through the peephole. The tall man on the other side was already familiar, but the trademark leather vest and swinging braid would've given him away even if I couldn't see his face. Talon. A deep sigh left my lips. What did he want? If he came to follow up on last night's quality conversation, I was all talked out. The temptation to ignore him and wait for him to leave was strong—I had enough to deal with without him in the mix. But that was the cowardly way out, and *coward* was not a label I'd wear in any lifetime. I pulled open the door before I could overthink it.

A wide chest covered in a tight black T-shirt filled my vision, and I followed that line of sight up until I met his striking eyes. He'd leaned an arm against the door jamb which caused him to lean forward and dip his head to stare at me. I inhaled the scent of leather and musk. Didn't he know that it was against the law for her brother's best friend to be so freakin' hot? I forced myself to ignore all that and hold his gaze, which swirled with a hazy emotion that made my gut clench.

I swallowed. "You're just in time for casserole." That was a safe enough topic.

"Oh yeah?" His eyes sparked with humor. Damn those eyes.

"Your aunt brought it over. I had no idea she lived here when I chose this apartment."

"It slipped when I was talking to her last night. I told her to give you a couple of days to get yourself sorted, but you know how she is."

"I don't need to settle. I'm fine, and I appreciate the gift."

He stared at me, eyes speaking volumes.

I cleared my throat. "Did you need something?"

"I wanted to see how you were doing."

Flashes of memory. Flesh striking flesh. The slick feel of blood on my knuckles. Nausea washed over me in such a powerful wave that I swayed with it. If I hadn't been clutching the door frame, I'd have fallen. "If you're concerned about someone, you should be checking on Frank, not me," I snapped. "He needs your sympathy, I don't."

"Talon? Is that you?" Elena's voice made us both jump.

"Hey, Auntie." Talon's voice rumbled so close that it seemed to vibrate the air, tickle my suddenly sensitive skin. "I was just dropping by. I can't stay."

"You're always too busy to relax," she admonished. "You need to rest more, *kipenzi*," a Cherokee term I'd heard countless times over the years, "Or stress will age you before you're due."

The affection and love between them was clear and hit a sore spot. Affection that I never seemed to be able to foster in my own family. Beastie stirred in her cage.

"I hate to rush you," I said, "but I have a few errands I need to run, and I'd like to knock them out before it gets too late in the day."

"Of course," Mrs. O agreed. "You're probably swamped with a dozen things to do." She closed the cabinet she was rummaging in. "Just rinse out the pan when you're finished.

31

You can drop it outside my door or wait for me to swing by to grab it. No rush at all." She looked up at her handsome nephew. "Walk me home? I made some of your favorite clove cookies."

Talon's eyes brightened. "Won't say no to that." He offered the small woman his arm. He was so much taller than she that she had to reach up to loop arms with him.

He shot one last concerned look over his shoulder at me as she led them toward the stairs. It pissed me off. Who put him in charge of the check-on-Serena-and-make-sure-she's-not-losing-her-crap committee?   No one. He could take his concern and burn it in some redneck's trash pile for all I cared.

After I closed the door, I pulled back the foil on Elana's dish to let the aroma infuse my senses. Philly cheese steak hash brown casserole. My favorite. I made myself search through the kitchen drawers until I found a plastic wrapped cutlery set I saved from takeout a few nights before, ripped it open, and shoved a huge bite into my mouth. I groaned in delight. Who cares if this was technically a brunch dish—breakfast hit the spot any time of day.

A gust of wind fluttered through the room—those freaking windows were still open—and something fluttered in the breeze. Stretching over to pull the curtain open further, I stared at the prescription note I'd contemplated shredding the night before. I must have shoved it in a random spot hoping it would disappear. I grabbed it and set it on the counter. When the military psychologist gave it to me a week before, I'd resented it, swearing I'd never use it. After last night, I was re-thinking things.

What I really needed was to get out of the house. Go explore and enjoy the bright Friday afternoon that shone through the windows. Autumn was my favorite season in Oklahoma, and I was missing it.

I dressed in my standard outfit but pulled out the clothes that were easiest to reach—skinny jeans, a flowy halter top, belt, and boots. It didn't matter that the jeans were black and textured to resemble leather or that the top had a cross wrap neckline and the material was soft as silk. The only thing I'd thank my mother for was my love of high quality clothes—just because my style was simple didn't mean it had to be cheap. I pulled on open toed booties that were too sassy to pass up but had a thick stiletto heel that would me balance if I ended up doing anything more strenuous than walking.

I swiped my key fob and prescription from the counter, grabbed my favorite leather jacket from the coat closet, punched in the alarm code, and was through the door and down the steps before the high pitched beeping that signaled the alarm had activated stopped. Happy yellow sunshine warmed my skin as I made my way down the steps and across the sidewalk to where I'd parked Blade. He started up with an energetic growl. We roared out of the parking lot, tiles squealing, and I grinned the entire time. Why have a hot sports car if you aren't going to drive it wild?

I spent the first few hours just driving around. When I visited a new city for a job, I usually spent at least two days becoming familiar with street patterns and traffic flow and familiarizing myself with popular places. Even though this was home, the city had grown so much since I'd last been there that it felt like a completely foreign place. Over six hundred square miles, Oklahoma City consistently ranked as one of the largest cities in the U.S. In layman's terms, that meant it could take at least twenty minutes to drive from one side of the city to the next, on the interstate and with no traffic.

I was shocked at all the new construction. From swanky neighborhoods and shopping areas in the northwest to freshly black-topped road in the south. Downtown was the major highlight of the retro area, and I drove straight toward the tall, metallic building that added so much personality to the city skyline—the Devon Tower. With its sharp, geometric lines and distinctive blue color, it dominated the view at every angle, even looming in my rearview mirror when I finally diverted from downtown and drove into other parts of the city.

The sun had dipped below the horizon by the time I punched the address to the pharmacy into my GPS. I decided to get it filled, but I'd use it only when necessary. What could it hurt? I was halfway there, weaving through Friday night traffic, when my cell phone rang, Sam Smith's ringtone crooning loudly on the car's stereo system.

"This is Black."

"If you're planning on bailing on us for the barbeque tomorrow night, I will never forgive you." My stepmother's voice —one I hadn't heard in years—whipped across the line like an arctic tundra wind and left frost seeping into my bones. Some people remember their mom's perfume or tone of voice or favorite recipe. Me? Her disappointment-laced accusation was a tangible taste on my tongue, sweet for its familiarity but pungently bitter for the ever sharpness she never could seem to hide.

A sigh welled up in my chest but I stuffed it down. "It's taken longer to get things settled than I—"

"Don't give me excuses," she snapped. "I just got off the phone with Elena Orsoto, and she said that Talon told her that you've been in town for days. Days! As if we haven't waited for years for you to remember that you have a home and a family who would love to hear from you occasionally. I shouldn't have to beg you for a little common courtesy, Serena."

Such warmth…such invitation. Was it really so surprising that I wasn't foaming at the mouth to reconnect with them? Or maybe I was. Foaming, that was. Even as I thought it, guilt churned in my head but Beastie was having none of it. She yowled at my mom's tone.

"Yvonne, I—"

"Your father doesn't have much time left. I shouldn't have to remind you of that."

Pain slammed into my stomach and I sucked in air through my teeth as sharp emotion crawled up my chest. Low blow.

Beastie snarled.

"Look, I plan to be at the house for the barbeque. Me and my banana pudding." The GPS flashed for me to turn, and I guided the car into an old strip mall that had recently undergone an upgrade and parked. "I have to go now. I'm in the middle of something."

"You always are." She muttered the words so quietly that I knew she hadn't meant for me to hear, and the line went dead before I could respond. She always knew how to get to me. I was pissed that I made myself such an easy target for her. I should know better by now.

With an angry huff, I shoved open the car door but took a moment to calm myself before walking into the building. I knew that my annoyance and tension pulsing through split my awareness and was a risk. I shoved the chaotic emotion to the back of my mind, Beastie' playground, and focused on the environment around me. The drugstore was tucked into the far corner of the NorthPark Mall shopping center on the north-west side of the city. My friends and I used to convince our parents to take us to the dollar movie theatre there—a dingy, grungy, and at times halfway-to-being-condemned place that was often used as a cheap birthday party venue for elementary and middle school kids. If you didn't mind the risk of lice, that was.

From the outside, the theatre looked the same, give or take a new sign and repainted parking lot. What's the saying about slapping lipstick on a pig...? Even down to the gaggle of pre-teen girls clustered beneath the awning and loudly debating what movie they wanted to spend their precious allowances seeing. Reminded me of how my brother and I used to spend our Friday nights. The rest of the shopping center, however, looked fresh and updated, with a few new storefronts showcased on the southeastern edge and that's where the pharmacy was nestled. I pulled the curved metal handle and stepped into the cool interior.

"Welcome to Medical Supply."

A man in a white shirt restocking a shelf behind the long white counter covered with a transparent plexiglass shield that cascaded from the ceiling. A cluster of small pumpkins were arranged on a bed of fake greenery; a man's attempt to add Autumn cheer to the space.

I slapped the prescription order on the counter. "Are you able to fill this for me?"

"Could be," the wiry man pulled down a pair of thin glasses from his head but still squinted at the paper like they didn't help much. After a moment, he said, "I should have some in the back. Can you wait?"

I nodded and bounced on my toes as he disappeared around a row of shelves. Less than ten minutes later, he returned carrying two white bags.

"Okay, this one," he pointed to the bag on top. "Is an antidepressant. You need to take one pill in the morning with food."

"I'm not depressed." It came out more defensive that I intended.

"Doesn't matter. That medication improves the functionality of this one." He pointed at the second bag. "This one is Olanzapine and will help voices in your head, bouts of unconsciousness, the whole works."

Beastie eyed both packages with contempt.

"How much?"

He swiped the handheld scanner from the side of the computer. "War does that to you, marks the soul in ways you'll never fully get rid of."

His words made me watch him instead of his scanning hands. "I never saw active combat," I told him, which was only half true. My years with the Air Force had been shortened due to my accelerated track to join the Secret Service. I'd only spent a year and a half at Tinker Air Force Base, just long enough to complete the basic courses necessary to move on. Combat came years later.

The clerk nodded. "You've got war veteran written all over you."

The scar above my eye twitched at that. I looked away from his probing gaze and stared through the tinted glass door as he finished scanning and bagging my items. Seeing the parking lot through the molasses tint forced my eyes to adjust. What was that?

A man in a red leather jacket half dragged, half carried a limp girl across the parking lot. I knew it was one of the girls that had been loitering outside the movie theatre by the thick curtain of tight golden curls that now hung limply around her face. It wasn't as if he couldn't have lifted the girl, but it seemed he was trying to keep it from looking like he was taking her against her will.

The clerk gave me a price, my brain scrambled the words as if hearing them through water.

I was reaching for my wallet, never taking my eyes off Red Leather Jacket, but froze when he popped the trunk of his navy blue Charger and flung the girl inside.

Cold emotion swirled in my gut. Part of me screamed to ignore it. To call the police and let it be.

Beastie agreed, turning her back. This wasn't Syria and getting involved wouldn't change the past.

Perhaps. But the argument seemed hollow as the Charger started backing out its parking spot.

I looked at the clerk. "You know what, can you put a hold on these for me?"

Confusion flashed on his face, but I turned away, tore open the pharmacy door, and ran to my car. The Charger pulled onto 122nd Street just as I yanked open my car door and punched the start button.

Blade growled to life.

Weekend traffic clogged the streets and I had to work to keep the kidnapper's car in sight. But I kept my movements smooth and calm—jerking from lane to lane was bound to get draw attention. Tipping him off that he had a tail wouldn't help me or the girl, and nervous criminals tended to make dangerous mistakes. My gut clenched as I thought of the exhaust fumes swirling through the trunk of a car like that. Drugged or unconscious, the girl's breathing would be slower than normal, and the trunks of small cars sat closer to the exhaust, increasing the level of carbon monoxide in the air. It was only a matter of time before the levels became deadly, and she'd drift into eternal sleep.

That wouldn't happen on my watch.

I activated the car's dialing system, but as soon as the dial tone buzzed through the car, I paused. Calling the police should have been a no brainer...and perhaps, if Julien didn't work for the local PD, I wouldn't have hesitated. His face streaked across my mind. The jaw and nose strongly showed the family resemblance, but that was where the similarities ended. His skin was golden beige, and mine was the color of sun kissed umber.

But it was his lips, curled into his trademark sneer, that made my fingers hover over the screen uncertainly. Disdain and condescension seemed to be the only emotions he was capable of when it came to me. It had been that way since we were in high school, and I still didn't know what I'd done to make my younger brother despise me. And he'd always been so talented at making people anything that slid out of his mouth. The last thing I wanted was to have to explain why I was tailing a kidnapping suspect instead of visiting dad like everyone else. "Flake" was a sin I didn't need added to the list of crimes against my family.

No police. No judgmental, condescending younger brother. Just me, myself, and my badass new car.

That suited me just fine.

CHAPTER 4

W hen the blue Charger merged onto Broadway Extension, I followed but kept several car lengths between us
and dimmed my headlights. The reckless way he sped through
a construction zone and aggressively bobbed among what little traffic was on the roads told me he wasn't interested in
subtlety. I dropped back until half a dozen cars filled the
road between us to make sure that he hadn't spotted me. Ten
minutes later, he exited onto Fourth Street, and I followed him
into the heart of downtown OKC.

The nightlife district had boardwalks, restaurants, and
nightclubs lining the Oklahoma River. I slowed to let a group
of laughing men and women cross the road and idled at the
light on Sheridan Avenue to watch his next move. The Charger
stopped in front of a black brick building with a line of people
trailing down the metal staircase and along the sidewalk. A
beefy man in a tight black T-shirt detached from the group of
bouncers working the door and caught the keys that Red Leather Jacket tossed in the air and slid into the driver's seat. The
Charger eased from the curb and pulled an immediate right,
going down an alley alongside the building. Meanwhile, Red
Leather Jacket bounded up the steps past the people waiting in
line and slipped through the main entrance.

I drove slowly past the alley just in time to see the rear
lights disappear behind a silver garage door. Private parking. I
glanced at the clock. Without the car running and providing
a flow of fresh air, the girl had roughly twelve minutes or so
before the CO_2 concentration in the car spiked to a dangerous

level.

I whipped my car around and pulled into one of those private entry parking lots that had a massive fee attached with it. I ignored it. One of the perks of being a cop's daughter? In the right circumstance, one didn't have to worry about parking tickets. You drop the right name, and people were more than happy to look the other way.

As I stared at the club's entrance, every training instinct honed by blood and pain rebelled at the thought of strutting into a nightclub blind. Especially knowing who owned most of the clubs in this part of town. I eyed the two burly men checking people and doing general crowd control but didn't see any telltale bulges of concealed weapons. Didn't mean they didn't have any. For a moment, I thought about taking my gun. But trying to waltz into one OKC's hottest nightclub with a Glock 47 strapped to my hip was a bad idea, and I didn't want to waste time trying to bypass pushy bouncers. *Though we could*, Beastie whispered in my mind. Another reason she wasn't allowed to run the show.

Damn it. There were too many unknowns that could turn this into a shit show fast. I was usually confident of my ability to handle unstable situations, but last night had proved I was not nearly as in control as I'd been telling myself I was. I didn't mind beating the snot out of kidnapping creeps and imprinting a lesson they'd never forget. I did mind being so strung out on a flashback that I couldn't tell reality from fiction.

I punched the buttons on the car's dash before Beastie convinced me to chicken out.

A crisp male voice answered. "9-1-1, what's your emergency?"

"Uh…yeah…I think I just saw a man shove a girl into the trunk of his car." I kept my voice shaky, slightly uncertain, to make a more convincing case, and watched the call time clicking on the dash.

"You think you saw a man shove a girl into his car trunk? Are you sure about that?"

"I think so. She looked underage, like a teenager or something."

"Where are you?"

"I'm at"—I looked through the windshield at the perpendicular glowing sign on the outside of the building—"Club 115 in downtown Oklahoma City."

"And what's your name?"

I grabbed an old receipt and crumpled it in my fist. "Sorry... you're cutting out there."

"Ma'am can you tell me— "

I hit "End" right at twenty-five seconds. Anything under thirty seconds and they'd have a hell of a time tracing the call back to me. Good. Less ammunition for Julien to crucify me with, were he to find out.

I popped open the glove compartment and pulled a wad of bills from an envelope that I always kept stashed there. It seemed archaic to people in America—where the convenience of credit cards trumped everything else—but, in the rest of the world, cash still held top spot for most immediate swaying power. Credit and debit cards were useless if there wasn't anything to put in the bank. And cash made even the grimiest of eyes sparkle. Start waving cash around, and you had instant swaying power.

But if cash didn't work, force usually did. I snatched out a pair of six inch black cylinders from the glove box and twisted myself into an awkward contortion to shove them into the holster at my back. Just in case things got crazy. As I walked, I lifted my arms to make sure the two small holsters strapped to my back didn't peak through beneath my shirt's hem. They did, a little. To most, they would look like the straps of my panties or some intricate lingerie.

I shoved the bills into my bra, ripped off my jacket, grabbed my phone, and stepped out of the car. With the sun completely gone, chilly autumn air swirled around me, making me miss the jacket, but the fitted black shirt and leather skinny jeans would work as "nightclub casual". I watched traffic for a moment, getting a sense of its rhythm, before jogging across the street to the crowded sidewalk.

I followed the sidewalk but into the alley where he'd pulled in and immediately saw the large garage doors on the opposite of the building. A black staircase led back into the nightclub and on the other side of the alley, a gleaming metal garage door gleamed in the streetlight. A large man--another rental from Big Dumb Bros Anonymous--lurked at the entrance back into the club, ensuring no unpaid guests could gain access. I followed the sidewalk just beneath that staircase trying to keep out of sight as long as possible but also getting a better view of the garage.

A keypad glowed against the bricks but it wasn't your normal number entry system. No, it looked like something you placed a hand on and it was scanned. Who need custom, print protective access in the middle of the fun district in Oklahoma City? Again, one name ran through my head.

Slade.

The most notorious drug dealer and kingpin in the Midwest and the man who owned half of the nightlife entertainment in this district. He's the only person that would feel the need to install high level security like this.

My stomach twisted. If he was involved in anyway, the girl's fate was certainly sealed to that of a coked out prostitute or drug dealer's bookie. Either option was unacceptable. Looks like I needed to find another way to get to that car ASAP.

I jogged toward the stairs and the guard at the door straightened in alert.

"Just joining my friends inside," I told him as I climbed the rail toward him.

"Where's your stamp?" He asked. "If you don't have stamp, that means you weren't checked in at the front, and it means I'm not letting you inside."

"This stamp?" I held a hand at chest level and it was obvious I didn't have a glow in the dark stamp but I use the angle to pull several bills from my bra and hold it in front of him.

His lip curled. "Can't do that."

"Look, I dropped a friend off but left my keys with her. By this time, she's too drunk off her rocker to answer her phone so I all I need is my keys and I'll be out of your hair." I waved the three bills again. "Fifteen minutes and I'm out of here."

A pause. He snatched the bills from my hand and stuffed them into his jean pocket. "Ten minutes and then I'm pulling your ass outta here." He said as he yanked open the door and music immediately assaulted us.

I nodded and slid past him into the dark fray. Immediately the sounds of the club suffused my senses. Punchy music. The muted roar of hundreds of voices talking, laughing, singing over the high pitched clink of glasses sliding across the bar. The sharp scent of liquor and sweat and perfume mixing into a noxious aroma in the air. People flowed around me, and I was on high alert instantly. Sounds muted in my ears, as if I were underwater, and my vision blurred with the ocean of faces and noise.

Beastie roared with confusion and worry.

Nightclubs and PTSD...a bad combination. What the hell was I thinking?

A group of men shoved their way through the narrow passageway and one of them, a man in a fluorescent orange button down with a streak of white in his cropped hair, roughly jostled me as he moved to keep up.

Beastie snarled at him, ready to do damage.

Effing nightclubs.

I hummed the first few bars of Bach's cello suite number one under my breath, letting rhythm wash through my mind like a cleansing tide. Calm, I told myself, civilians are nice...civilians are good. My feet found the rhythm on the upswinging of the vivace music in my head and I used that pace to shuffle, slink, and maneuver around bodies as I moved calmly, lithely through the narrow entryway.

At the landing, I immediately moved left into a shadowed corner and gained my bearings. I stood in an oversize balcony that ran the perimeter of the second floor and looked over the entirety of the club. Patterned glass sloped from the ceiling and connected with a gray-and-black swirled marbled half wall that was just transparent enough that I watched him disappear into a crowd of the beautiful, glamorous, and exclusive. Obviously an area for VIPs. It was full, not uncomfortably so— I no longer felt like chopped salmon in a can—but there were easily close to one hundred or so people scattered throughout the area. All of them gorgeous, perfectly groomed. Beautiful women flicked long sleek hair over their shoulders as they eyed men or crossed smooth legs perched on charcoal grey leather couches. The men were decked out in expensive, custom clothes, everything from casual shirts tucked into slacks to full on three piece suits, the majority paired with cowboy boots in all textures and colors. They slouched and prowled the area with confident ease across the white tiled floor. The "elite" class, whether self-titled or assigned by a person of lower attractive or financial status.

My eyes flicked over huddled groups of women or men throwing back beers and laughing loudly, hyper focused. Seeing them without seeing. Taking in intent, motive, direction, and energy all with a glance. Body language alone often gave away a person's true intent—the difference between reaching back to adjust your panties and reaching for a gun was the angle and intent and forward momentum of your muscles.

Swirling smoke refracted the dim blue lights, giving the entire club a sleepy yet energetic glow. Still, the red jacket stood out and I found my target leaning against the bar on the other side the lounge. I walked the length of the balcony, eyes riveted on my quarry. Red Leather Jacket turned to grab the fresh drink the bartender handed to him, but his eyes cut across the loft, only a brief glance, before he went back to casually flirting with the woman next to him. I followed his gaze.

The only thing that didn't fit the loft area was a door parallel to a smaller staircase with a red exit sign glowing above it that led back down to the main floor.

The man was biding his time. Whoever would walk out of that door would likely give him payment or his next instructions about what to do with that girl locked in his trunk. Every possible option was unacceptable. I quickened my steps but kept my gait long and seemingly unhurried. As long as I intercepted him before whatever sleazy rat exited those doors, I should be able to save her.

For some reason—a suicidal sense of curiosity perhaps—my gaze drifted back downstairs, to the dark corner on the far side of the dance floor. To the cluster of tables where another man sat, also waiting. I spotted him immediately...mainly because he was staring straight at me.

My eyes locked with vibrant, shockingly deep Prussian blue eyes. My stomach dipped at the full effect of those eyes inside his ridiculously handsome face.

His lips curled up in a smirk, and the look on his face... Heat. Warmth. Undeniable awareness of my feminine presence, and enjoyment of what he saw. My muscles locked, and air whooshed from my lungs. Oh...that look was trouble. That smirk teased, taunted me to traipse back down those steps and meet him face to face. I glared at him instead. Filled the look with all the disdain I could muster and hoped that it hid the real way his gaze affected me.

He wasn't fazed. The smirk widened to a full out smile, and it felt like I'd been punched in the gut and dazzled by the sun at the same time. He leaned back, our eyes still locked, but the energy shifted. His head tipped left, just slightly, but I was watching so closely that I didn't miss it.

He was intent. Listening.

Suspicion roared back to life. He was trained enough not to give it away so obviously, but I knew the look of someone listening into an earpiece. My eyes darted across the room, searching.

I saw it then. Untrained eyes would miss it, but I saw clearly the man on the other side of the crowded first floor bar casually leaning against it but with bright, alert eyes. There was another one, same dark suit staring out over the dance floor, lethal readiness tensing his muscles. It was the earpiece lazily dangling from the ear of a fourth man, this one the size of a brick wall, that gave him away.

By the time I rounded the corner, I'd counted a total of six of them.

I didn't know if they were government agents, private contractors, or the effing mafia. None of that mattered. Shit was going down, and I wanted the girl and myself gone before the drama started. Time to move.

I hugged the wall and slunk toward the bar, watching Red Leather Jacket's increasingly agitated movements as he spoke to a brunette woman in a gold dress that was a size too small. I walked up in time to hear him say, "How many ways can I spell it out for you, Katie? It's over. We're done. I'd commit a dozen crimes right now just to make sure I never had to see your washed out face again."

Judging from her stringy tawny hair and watery hazel eyes, she was at least two drinks past her limit and looked every inch as drunk as she was.

"Just give me another chance." She grabbed his arm, desperation etched on her face, but he was having none of it. He ripped out her grasp, making her wobble unsteadily, placed a hand in the center of her chest, and shoved. She flew backward, and I lunged left so that she'd stumble into me and the momentum caused us to stutter step back several feet.

"Hey man, you need to cool it or take it outside," the bartender barked.

The woman in my arms trembled. "Danny." She whispered his name under her breath, the soft, surprised hurt in her voice more than I could handle. I hoisted her upright until she was halfway steady in her platform spike pumps.

"Go rejoin your friends." I told her. "You're better off without the scum bucket, and you've got good people waiting on you."

"But..." She swayed on her feet, and I reached out steadying hands in case she tried to play chicken with the floor. "I love him. He just needs to understand that, and we'll be happy."

I glanced at the man who leaned casually against the bar and chatted with the woman next to him, his violent display already forgotten. I looked back at her. "Something tells me you'll be better off without him."

Tears shone in her eyes.

I turned her and walked a few steps with her, mainly to make sure she stayed on her feet. When it looked like she wouldn't collapse, I let her go and turned back to the man at the bar just as Beastie let out a menacing growl. She paced back and forth, eager to unleash a world of hurt on the woman-hitting creep. Yeah, me too.

I sidled directly to him, leaning casually against the bar with so little distance between us it immediately caught his attention. He angled his body to mimic my position and gave me a once over, slow and creepy, and it ratcheted my anger from a simmering five to an explosive eight.

"You're just what the doctor ordered, *mamita*." he said. "You look like a woman who's confident that she's about to get what you set out for."

I smiled, cold and dry. He had no idea. "And *you* look like an abusive jerk." I stood close enough to count the red lines streaking his eyes and gag on his bourbon-laced breath.

"She had it coming, *chiquita*." He flashed me a charming smile. "But, you know, I'm really a nice guy."

"Hmmm.. I bet you are. You're nice to everyone in your life, right?"

"Exactly."

"Children...animals..." I leaned forward, "Pretty underage girls with curly hair."

He gave me a sharp look before turning back to the bar. Too late. The shock on his face gave him away. He let out a slow breath and took a sip from his tumbler, but his shoulders bunched beneath the jacket. Suddenly, his left hand struck out in a closed fist as he tried to smash my face with his bare knuckles. I rocked back a half step back, just enough to let his hand sail past my nose. I grabbed his arm at the wrist and just above the elbow and used torque and pure force to slam him into the gold swirled gray marble of the bar.

Glass tinkled and broke as he hit face-first.

I grabbed the back of his neck and dragged him across the surface, sliding him across the glossy finish like slick rain.

"Hey!" someone barked.

Danny kicked out, aiming for my knee. Music filled my mind, and I let the passionate rhythm guide me as I twisted my leg out of range. A large hand wrapped itself around my braids at the base of my neck and jerked. Pain shot down my spine, but it acted as an electric shock, the music in my head clanged viciously as adrenaline sparked in my blood. Beastie hissed, and the sound echoed out of my mouth. I craned my neck to see the bartender reaching for something underneath the counter with his beefy hand buried in my scalp. I let go of Danny's arm and kicked him in the ribs at the same time that I snatched a stray tankard off the bar. I turned and smashed it across the bartender's temple. The man's grip loosened, and I angled away and punched the bartender in the throat.

Danny stumbled away, clutching the bar as he tried to gain his feet.

Beastie snarled.

I picked up one of the bar chairs and hurled it at him. The chair smashed into his back and both loser and chair clattered to the floor just as thick arms wrapped around my chest and hauled me off my feet. He'd trapped my arms by my sides, trying to trap me in an immobilizing bear hug. I braced my feet on the bar and shoved. We stumbled backwards across the balcony until the man slammed into the half-wall with a grunt.

Another man flung himself at us, raising a small handheld weapon that crackled with white light. A taser. Not good. My leg caught his outstretched arm and swung it away enough for me to follow up with a vicious kick to his chin which made his head snap to the side. I twisted my left wrist up and pulled one of the retractable batons from the sheath at my waist. Even at the strange angle, when I buried it into my attacker's inner leg, the sharp studs that ran the baton's length buried into the large nerve that ran up into the groin. Read: instant, fiery pain. He screamed and dropped me.

A third man pulled a gun, and I lunged forward, swiping at his wrist as bullets punctured the glass wall behind me. Piercing screams filled the club as people ran for the only exit, the stairs. I smashed my left baton into the meaty area between his shoulder and neck and then slammed the right baton across his temple, the sharp studs slicing his skin. Blood spurted as he fell unconscious.

Another man launched himself at me from a nearby bistro table, a wild attempt at tackling me. I rolled to my back, catching his weight and momentum with my feet and guiding him over my head before pushing off powerfully with my legs. He sailed over my head and crashed through the cracked partition.

Glass glittered like diamond rain as he fell and people below screamed.

The music screeched to a halt, and chaos broke out on both floors.

I jumped to my feet and glanced at the doorway across the balcony where men poured out of it like rats scurrying to leave a discovered nest.

A hard body slammed into my side and took me to the floor. The man rolled us and rose above me, fist raised to strike. It was Danny. I swung the baton up and caught his wrist, twisting sharply to one side so that the punch sailed past my face. I canted my hips and rolled us until I was on top of him and proceeded to smash the baton over his arms, face, and chest over and over.

Men in suits flooded the floor yelling, "Police."

Strong hands grabbed my arms and dragged me off Danny. "That's enough," a man growled in my ear, dragging me across the lounge.

I didn't fight him, though his hands on my skin made Beastie fling herself against the bars of her cage, demanding that we teach him a lesson about invading our space. I was breathing hard, and adrenaline still pumped through my veins in harsh pulsing beats as the music in my head shifted from intense and energetic to something to soothe Beastie back into a lull. I was so checked in to keeping her from breaking loose, I didn't realize they'd cuffed me until the sharp metal dug into my wrists.

I forced myself to focus on the men who stood in front of me. Both wore black suits and looked every inch the cop with buzzed hair and hard eyes. Must be some kind of special unit. Something hostile must have shown on my face because both of their faces changed: the younger one looked slightly uncertain, but the older one frowned and put his hands on his hips, closer to his gun.

The action made Beastie smirk. *Weaklings,* she taunted.

"I saw you beating that man." He jerked his head at Danny, who was currently being cuffed by another pair of suits. "You'll be questioned just like everyone else before we make any determinations about whether or not you go free."

My blood cooled as irritation set in. "It was self-defense," I snapped.

"Maybe it was, maybe it wasn't. We'll get the whole story out of you once things calm down," the older suit said. He spotted my batons rolled up and picked one up with the corner of his blazer. "Officer James Dunningham with OKCPD." He held it out to the other man. "Micah, take this and set it aside as a suspicious item."

"Be careful—" I warned but I was too late.

When the younger officer grabbed the butt end, he depressed the hidden button that caused the baton to lengthen with the razor studs on full display. Micah was standing so close that he almost stabbed the other officer accidentally.

Both men swore, and Micah dropped the weapon. It clattered to the marble floor.

"What the…?" Dunningham gave me a look at was pure suspicion.

Hadn't the man seen a retractable baton before? The military had been using them for years as easy-to-conceal weapons that wouldn't trip most sensors. He was either out of the loop or liked to do things old school, with a gun and grit as his only defense.

"You'll be detained for questioning," Dunningham said. "You'll be lucky to escape an overnight stay in county."

"I'd bet my favorite body part that she's one of the more interesting people in the room." The words came from a deep, smooth voice.

Both officers turned, and I looked over my shoulder at the new player.

Prussian blue eyes met mine, twinkling with hidden mirth.

The man from the corner table.

He wore dark slacks and a midnight blue shirt that turned his eyes into liquid pools, dressy club wear but obviously quite different from the suits the other two men wore. Deep cover. Even slouching against an intact portion of the glass wall, he had a solid four inches on me. The shirt he wore was tight, straining against his chest and thick biceps. He was built like a muscled swimmer and dressed like a French GQ model, but the sharpness in his eyes gave him away for what he really was—a cop. A smile tilted the corners of his lips, refracted in his eyes, and my irritation spiked. That damn smile.

My stomach dipped as I met his bold, amused gaze, and I scowled at him.

The smirk widened to a full grin. "I'll take it from here, boys. I'll question her and determine what to do with her."

Micah stepped forward. "That's outside your jurisdiction."

"Normally, you'd be right," he said. "But since it was my tip that led us here and my case to begin with, I think the captain would find you debating that a waste of everyone's time."

"You'll get no argument from me." Dunningham pointed at the baton on the floor. "That was found on her person. You may want to check to make sure she's not hiding any other dangerous items."

"Oh, I will." His tone was bland, but the look in his eyes was anything but.

Officers Dunningham and Micah moved to the front of the lounge where a group of officers were getting orders from a man in charge.

Prussian eyes glanced at the weapon the men pointed to, and his blond eyebrows disappeared into his hairline. He crouched beside it and studied it a moment before glancing back up at me.

"A bit bigger than your average nail file, eh?"

Depended on what you were trying to shrink down. Some nails came off with a bit of extra flesh, or limbs, attached. I shrugged and gave him a blank face, trying to ignore the irritation bubbling in me. Judging from the arrogant still smile hovering over his mouth, I didn't entirely succeed.

"Not much of a talker? That could have its benefits." He stood and studied me. "But I have plenty to say. I know that you walked in armed, though I couldn't tell exactly what you were packing. I know that you incapacitated eight men before my team could clear the stairs. So, you're either highly trained and used to lethal situations, or you're She-Hulk with an abnormal talent for mixed martial arts. How am I doing?"

I wasn't impressed.

It must have showed because laughter twinkled in his eyes. "And I know that this" he toed the weapon—" once standard police baton has been modified, which means you either are a cop, were a cop, or have someone in your life who is."

"Any half decent cop would be able to tell all that." The words fell out of my mouth before I could shove them back. Perceptiveness was the difference between a successful bust or a bullet in the head.

"So you do talk." The smug smile he shot me told me a reaction had been his goal all along. He'd played me. I mentally slapped myself.

"Apparently only to fools." I looked at Danny, sitting pathetically with his back against the bar and bleeding down one side of his face—did I do that?—and back to the man in front of me.

"You know how to shoot down a man's ego."

"Perhaps you should tuck it back in and not leave it out where it can be damaged."

He guffawed loudly, the sound echoing down the lounge. "You're brutal." His expression told me he didn't find that a bad thing. "Detective Lucas Thorne, DEA. You can call me Luke."

His smile made his handsomeness ratchet up several degrees, and my stomach fluttered. I tried and failed to squelch the sensation. So I did the one thing I was best at—I got mad.

"Save your flirting for someone who cares," I snapped. "While you're being Casanova, there's a teenage girl stuck in a car somewhere hoping that we find her instead of some rat bastard kidnapper."

"What?" The humor dimmed from his face. "What girl?"

"I followed that scumbag," I jerked my chin at Danny. "After I saw him shove a girl into the trunk of his car outside of a movie theatre. Now, with Oklahoma being the largest human trafficking motorway in the nation, you and I both know that there're only two reasons someone would stop at such a public place instead of carrying on to a secluded location. Either he's an amateur or—"

"This was a drop off point." Luke finished. "Where did he park?"

"Uncuff me and I'll show you."

He gave me a look. "No disrespect, but for all I know you might be an accomplice and, if nothing else, a disrupter of public peace."

Beastie growled low and, for once, I agreed. When someone finally educated him about who I was, I hoped I was in the room. If he was going to make an ass out of himself, I desperately wanted to see it. But as much as I yearned to swipe the look of his face, there was a drugged and terrified girl who needed to know that the world around her wasn't collapsing.

"There's a private garage directly behind the building. Blue Charger with New Mexico plates."

"How long's it been since you tailed him in here?"

"Hopefully not long enough for whoever was supposed to grab the girl to do so. Especially in the middle of all this chaos."

Harsh swear words left Luke's mouth. "Don't pull any more contrabands out while I'm gone." He turned and jogged through the lounge. He didn't, I noticed, tell anyone where he was going or signal for backup. The entire club could be wired with cameras and traps or men lurking in dark corners despite the heavy police presence. Reckless.

I tuned into the action around me. Men in black suits still pulled club vermin from secret party rooms, gathering everyone into the main space. A separate group of suits actively went through the clubgoers asking for ID and giving some the green light to scurry on home while others were forced to remain behind. Part of the confusion was the fact that the local police force stormed in just as the DEA made their move. You wanna see more confusion than a bunch of huge elephants trying to unicycle at a circus? Get multiple law enforcement agencies going after the same prize with no prior communication. It made for a great show.

A cop with graying hair and a pouchy gut looked down at Danny, who squinted his good eye up at him

"'Ole Danny Verengaz," the officer began. "It's been a hot minute since we've seen your ugly mug. Thought you'd moved to another state or something. But drug possession and traffic tickets always manage to catch up to you. Wonder how many bags of cocaine would I find under the seat of your car right now?"

Danny spat a hunk of blood at the officer's feet.

I mentally added "stupid" to his list of crimes.

The officer reached out and hauled Danny to his feet, ignoring the man's cry of pain when he jostled his obviously bleeding shoulder. "Doubt you'll be so mouthy in the back of my squad car." He turned, forcing Danny to turn with him, and our eyes locked. Recognition lit up his eyes.

"Hayes," he barked, and a young officer with wheat-colored hair and still twenty pounds too small detached from interviewing witnesses and approached.

"Yes, sir."

"Escort this scum bucket to my car and lock him in." Dunningham pushed Danny toward the other man, and the young officer took firm hold of him and led him across the balcony toward the stairs.

"I'm gonna remember you, *mamita*." Danny spat as he was dragged away. "I'm gonna find you."

Hayes shook him hard. "Anything you say can and will be used against you, buddy, so I suggest you keep your mouth shut."

I met Danny's burning eyes with a cool stare of my own. I'd looked terrorists in the eye after they licked their victim's blood from their scimitar swords. I wasn't at all intimidated by a thug wannabe. When his stench finally cleared the area, I looked at the older officer in front of me.

"I'd recognize that scowl anywhere," Captain Dawson of the OKC Police Department said, a broad smile on his face. "Even if you've grown two feet taller than I remember."

"It's good to see you're still terrifying the roaches," I smirked.

He huffed a laugh. "Gotta do something with my time. Besides, it's an old game with even older tricks. If these idiots haven't realized that now, then they deserve what they get. Speaking of—" he gestured at my cuffed hands "—how'd you end up in this little situation?"

"Wrong place, wrong time." The details weren't important. My mind kept flickering through a half dozen possibilities of what would happen if Luke didn't find the girl.

"We all have those moments." he reached over and unlocked my cuffs.

"Thanks." I muttered the word as I stared over his shoulder at the now fully lit club. A tall man strode through into the heart of the club. Everything in me tensed, and warning bells rattled in my brain. Familiar skin tone, familiar stride...yeah, it was my younger brother in the flesh, and I was shit out of luck. Julien. All-star on the OKC police force. Yvonne's darling child that she'd dragged into our family. The son dad always wanted. And the one person I could have waited another thousand years to see in person.

Beastie snarled at him.

He moved through the now fully lit downstairs area, circumventing crowds of guests that were still being escorted out and greeting other cops in uniform. His gaze swept over the area, taking it all in, and as if he could feel me looking at him, his eyes snapped up to the second floor. When he saw me, he stopped walking so abruptly he almost tripped. A myriad of expressions flared across his face, from surprise to confusion to disgust, but settled on his favorite emotion: rage.

Dunningham chatted about how his wife's Pitbull had finally had a litter of puppies, but it was white noise as I watched Julien storm his way to the staircase.

"You might want to keep those on until you figure out what she's been up to this time." Julien's voice was as familiar as the tide of acid that accompanied his words. Hostile eyes the color of frosted dirt glared at me.

Dunningham took one look at Julien's expression and frowned. When he glanced my way and saw that my face was not any more pleasant, he cleared his throat.

"I'm going to check on how my partner's doing with ID'ing the guests." He beat a hasty retreat, hoping he'd done it quickly enough to avoid frostbite from the chilly atmosphere.

I didn't want to fight with my brother, but it seemed that no matter what I did, he couldn't wait to spew the hate.

Even after a decade apart, tonight was no different.

"Is this how you spend your time now, Serena? Starting bar fights in ritzy nightclubs? Oh, how the mighty have fallen."

"Don't complain just because this is a world better than the sleazy hell holes you find yourself stuck in," I shot back.

"Those sleazy hell holes are part of my job, a job that makes a difference for my community and my family. Oh, wait, you wouldn't know anything about family loyalty and duty, would you?"

"My duty looks different than yours."

"It always has, hasn't it?"

There was no use trying to talk to Julien. I said nothing.

"Why'd you come back? I didn't expect to see you until funeral."

His words were a straight punch to my heart.

I must have failed to hide the hurt because his face twisted into a scowl. "Dad's been sick a long time, Serena. Of course, you wouldn't know that because we had no way to get ahold of you, and we weren't entirely sure that you'd care."

"You have no idea—"

A commotion downstairs drew my attention, and I looked in time to see Luke striding into the club with a gangly bundle spilling out of his arms. Relief flooded through me so strongly it almost made me dizzy. He'd found her. I started to move around Julien so I could go to them, but Julien moved with me, not touching me but fully blocking my path.

I swung my gaze to meet his angry one. "Move, Julien."

"You always look for an excuse to avoid the hard conversations. Trouble seems to trail you like an evil shadow," he spat. "You might as well not come to the barbeque on Saturday. Dad will get his hopes up, but Mom and I know you'll find some excuse to not come, something we won't be able to criticize because Dad won't let us."

"Hate to break it to you, baby brother, but I'll be there." He hated it when I called him that.

"I'll believe it when I see it."

Whatever. I stepped around him and hurried downstairs to where Luke had set the girl in one of the corner booths. She'd curled her knees into her chest, leaned to one side of the cushioned booth. Curly golden hair partially covered her face.

I knelt in front of her but kept enough distance so she

wouldn't feel like I was crowding her space. "Has an EMT looked her over?" I could see her pulse beating against the skin of her neck. Poor girl was still on high alert, and I didn't blame her.

"All of them were busy patching up clubbers who were injured trying to exit when things got crazy," Luke explained above me. "I asked one of them to check in when they were done."

"The car?"

"Was where you said it would be. She helped out, though. She was already banging on the hood by the time I got there. It took a little coaxing to convince her to come with me, but I worked my magic." He gave her a smile and a reassuring wink. "I impounded the car, and we're tracing the plates now. I doubt it'll trace back to the guy who snatched her, but hopefully we'll get a lead on a bigger fish."

I nodded to let him know I heard, but my focus was fully on the girl. The erratic pulse and clammy skin were probably an after effect of whatever Danny had used to drug her.

I spoke softly, keeping my voice low and even and soothing. "My name is Serena, and I'm a friend. I work with Detective Thorne." I nodded to Luke. "He works with the police department. We need to know if you have any cuts or bruises that we need to take a look at. I won't touch without your permission, but I need to know if you're okay."

Her eyes opened to slits, and she stared at me from beneath her eyelashes. Still, she remained quiet.

I smiled at her reassuringly. "It's been a rough night. Can I call your parents for you? We can get them down here to take you home lickety-split."

"Dad?" Her voice was muffled by the blazer she partially spoke into, but I understood well enough.

"Your dad will grow wings and fly over here once he knows where you are."

She bit her lip. Her eyes flicked between me and Luke as she pondered the offer. After a moment of indecision, she held out her hand. "Can I call?

I smiled at her. You sure freaking can. I handed her my cell phone, careful not to accidentally touch her as it passed to her. She dialed the number with shaky hands.

"Daddy?" Even though the phone was turned down, I heard his shout of emotion. "I'm okay. I didn't run off from my friends. A strange man took me from the bathrooms and shoved me into his car." Her voice warbled as fear crept in. "Can you come get me? Yeah. I'm at..." She trailed off and looked at me. I mouthed the name of the club to her. "Club 115 down-town. No, I'm not alone. A police officer found me and brought me inside." She paused to listen, then said, "He said I had to stay with him until my parents arrived. Yeah. See you soon." She held the phone out toward Luke.

I snagged it from her instead. "Sir? My name is Serena Black, and I wanted to reassure you that your daughter is under my personal protection until you get here."

There was a three second pause, but when the man spoke, he didn't waste time with basic questions. "Are you the cop who found her?"

I glanced over my shoulder at Luke, who raised an eyebrow but didn't try to take the phone. Smart man. "One of them."

"Thank you." His voice was gruff when he spoke. "I'm less than ten minutes away."

"I'll be here."

I looked at the girl as I slipped the phone into my back pocket. "He's on his way, hon."

She nodded. "Yeah. Probably with the whole security team."

I quirked an eyebrow and glanced over at Luke who tilted his head and frowned. So he didn't know any more than I did. Either her parents were overprotective, bordering on paranoid, or we'd stumbled upon the child of a VIP.

Luke crouched down on the other side of me and shot a bright smile the girl's way. "What's your name, honey?"

It took her a moment to answer—seeming dazzled by the handsome smiling man in front of her. I couldn't blame her.

I'm sure he'd get that reaction from a ninety-five-year-old woman.

"My name's Alyssa Jackson."

It was a pretty name, a bit on the tame side. In Oklahoma, you could have a white-bread name like Susan Smith or redneck something more redneck chic like Susie Picadillio. The name meant nothing to me, but Luke suddenly seemed so tense I thought his muscles would hulk out of his shirt. He stood and I did the same.

"What's wrong?" I asked, reading the tension in his face.

"Nothing," he replied, smile no longer dazzling but tight at the corners. "I need to go give my captain a report, let him know that we have a state senate candidate's daughter in our protection for the time being."

I looked back at the girl, who had huddled into herself once again.

"I can handle it from here," Luke said. "You're free to go."

Beastie growled at him. I didn't know him from Adam, and my history with choosing people to trust was shoddy enough that I wasn't about to leave the girl unprotected.

"Thanks, I'll wait."

We didn't have to wait long.

A few minutes later, a man dressed to the nines stormed into the nightclub like a Viking invader—face thunderous with concern-laced anger and a glint in his eye that made it obvious he was ready to slay everyone in sight if necessary. Encased in an expertly steel gray suit made from some slick, shiny cloth that made it gleam like real armor added to the illusion he marched his way past a cluster of cops and club goers into the heart of the club. Several men rushed in after him, including a six foot plus muscled ogre of a man with a bald head who was the poster child for "bruiser security" and skinny man with hair a color I could only describe as mangy tabby cat chic. Julien and Captain Dawson brought up the rear.

"If you'll just wait outside, I'm more than happy to make inquiries on your behalf," Captain Dawson said.

"I'm done talking, Captain. I don't want to hear another word until—"

The girl jerked like she'd been zapped the moment she heard the man's voice. "Daddy!" She flung off Luke's blazer, scrambled out of the booth, and ran to the man at the head of the group. He barely had time to crouch before his arms were filled with a sobbing tween girl.

He clutched her tight. "It's all right, Princess. I've got you. Are you alright?" His face was partially concealed by her wild curls, but his voice trembled. He looked around the group but his eyes landed on me. He struggled to find words. "Is she...was there...?"

I knew what his eyes were silently asking. "We got to her in time," I told him gently, addressing that desperate fragileness in his eyes. "Only a few scrapes and bruises that an EMT has already checked out."

He clutched her tighter but the lines around his mouth and eyes softened, the fear of father receding enough to allow him to take in a full breath.

Some might call me deluded but I liked him more because of it. I'd been on security details for countless foreign dignitaries that were concerned if someone had gotten handsy with the daughters. A father who genuinely cared whether or not his barely teenage daughter had been raped was a check in my book.

"How could something like this have happened?" The mangy haired man asked, tone snippy.

"From the information we've gathered, it looks like Alyssa was kidnapped from the theatre when she left the group to go to the bathroom or concession stand," Luke said. "Normal circumstances might make us look at this as a crime of opportunity but, knowing the Jackson's...reputation, I'd suggest we look at every angle before we label this as a crime of opportunity."

"And you are?" mange man snapped. He reminded me of the yapping dog that often barked from the shadow of the wolf.

Luke extended his hand. "Detective Luke Thorne, recently

transferred from Scottsdale."

The other man didn't take it. "Scottsdale? What do they have there? Angry skiers?"

"More like rampant serial killers." Luke shot him a half grin but his shoulders were tense. Nothing like a snub from a peon to get a macho man's back up.

"Hmmmp." and that high pitched snort that managed to be equally derisive and ridiculous sealed it in my head. I knew him. Brendan Michaels, notorious nerd, seriously lacking in the social skills department...and the boy I stood up for senior year prom. Looking at him now—hair stylishly cut but still that horrendous orange color that was his family trademark and wearing a designer suit that was a size too big like he'd gotten it off the sale rack...and put it on without ironing it—it embarrassed me to even think I'd agreed to go in the first place. Add mouthing off to cops and it was the cherry on the cake. He was still as much of a social ditz as ever.

The uniforms in the group glanced at one another, the cop version of a straight faced eye roll.

Captain Dawson smiled but couldn't quite hide his irritation "I didn't realize we had the politician's daughter in custody. How did you know that she was on the premise?" He looked at Luke.

"I got a tip that the girl might be in a precarious situation in the parking garage and I checked it out."

The Captain lifted an eyebrow. "A tip?"

Luke looked at me.

All eyes swung to me, half of them confused and the other half carefully curious. Except Julien, his eyes blazed and he muttered something under his breath I couldn't quite catch.

Crap. As much I'd give anything to slink off into the shadows and pretend that my hands were still shaking from adrenaline and not from my waning control of Beastie's death mantra in my head, that wasn't going to happen. "I saw her get snatched from the theatre," I told

"Are you willing to give a statement?" Dawson asked.

I nodded. "Of course. I tailed him here and saw almost everything except for when he parked in the garage."

Brendan's voice was a bit smug when said, "Seems we'll need someone on your end to fill in the rest of the details, detective."

"Enough," Jackson's voice was soft and he nailed Brendan with a look that made the other man's mouth snap closed. "We wouldn't even be having this conversation if the security team *you* hired did their job to begin with."

"I-I-I have reached out to Cheryl but she's not responding to any of my calls." Brendan sputtered. "I had no idea she'd renege on the job. I'll find a replace—"

"Not a chance," Jackson snapped.

The ogre-man took half a step to the left and it put him directly in the Jackson's line of sight. "I know some people. I can have a few recommendations in the next day or so." His voice was deep and thick, like a boat horn in deep fog.

"I appreciate that, Dane, but no. The next person my daughter has will be a professional, vetted bodyguard, not some nanny who knows Karate."

Captain Dawson cleared his throat, "I have half a dozen top notch officers who would gladly do the job. Just give me a few hours to make some calls, and I'll have a new bodyguard for you by sunup."

Julien stepped forward. "I'd be happy to volunteer for the job, sir. I have an extensive background in—"

"I appreciate that, son," Jackson said but his eyes traveled the group and landed on me. "Are you the woman I spoke to on the phone?"

All eyes swung to me, most curious and one hostile. I ignored them and stepped forward, extending my hand. "Yes, sir. I'm Serena Black, Homeland Security."

That got several raised eyebrows and Dawson swore loudly.

"I'm on leave," I explained before the local PD flew into a tizzy and started spouting piss off jargon of "not your jurisdiction" nonsense. "I don't represent Homeland in any official capacity."

"What made you risk your neck for a stranger?"

I shrugged trying to keep it casual but Beastie rumbled in my head. "Call it instinct...habit...tactical security was what I did for HS and it's an old habit to break I guess."

"Don't try and break it just yet." He nailed me with a piercing look. "You interested in a job?"

CHAPTER 5

I accepted the offer.

Why shouldn't I? I specialized in child protection and excelled at it, regardless of the fresh past that implied otherwise. Besides, how was I ever going to convince Master Blalock that I was mentally and emotionally healthy by sitting on my butt? This could be a way to show everyone that I was fine, functional, and didn't need or want their coddling or interference.

Julien protested, loudly and vehemently, until Captain Dawson pulled him aside and tell him to get his act together.

I avoided Julien's hostile gaze as I exchanged numbers with the ogre—who turned out to be Jackson's head of security—and we set a time for me to start. I suggested immediately. I wouldn't make strides in convincing Master Blalock that I was no longer a threat to be around by sitting on my butt at home. A job would give me a way to kill time…and hopefully distract the feline mass of psychological instability prowling my mind. Expending energy was a good thing, right? Both men seemed surprised but quickly got on board with the idea.

But the lazy tigress simply looked on with hyper focused energy. The moment there was a slight moment of weakness, she'd pounce. Which meant I couldn't slip up and give away how close to the surface she really was.

The sooner I got to work, the quicker I could placate her patient, waiting, killing energy. Somehow, I didn't think the family barbeque was going to contribute to the Zen that I needed, but I couldn't avoid it. Dad was waiting.

Yay for internal stress.

CHAPTER 6

The Jackson family lived in a ritzy, gated community in Moore, Oklahoma. The city had once only been known as a small suburb outside Sooner Town (Norman), but it had experienced a renovation and boom in the last fifteen years. What was once endless cow fields speckled with the rare neighborhood was now a metropolis with strip malls, swanky new home editions, the premier luxury Warren Theatre, and traffic to rival any big city in the state. During non-peak hours, it was a solid forty minute drive. I made it in twenty five.

What fun was having a sports car if you weren't going to open up the engine every once in a while? I rolled down the windows, cranked Yanni radio on Spotify, and let Blade steadily accelerate until we cruised at a spry ninety-five miles an hour. With the sun steadily lowering in the horizon, the wind that whipped against my skin made my face feel like a popsicle by the time I exited the highway.

I followed the directions Dane had texted me, which I'd already memorized, to a gated community on the east side of the city. Spectacular homes loomed—this was definitely one of those neighborhoods with high curb appeal. I punched in the access code at the entrance gate and turned down my music as it slowly slid open. Already, kids in a colorful array of costumes skipped and ran past the gate—fairies, aliens, and superheroes all gleefully laughing over their hard earned rewards. I eased along the streets, crawling at less than ten miles per hour just in case a ninja turtle tried to dash after an errant trinket without checking the road. I turned down the second street on my left, bypassing a gaggle of Disney princesses in glittery tiaras and singing a popular song, before turning into the Jacksons' driveway.

On the left of an intricate black iron gate sat a small building that I guessed was the security room. It was pretty intense, the kind of thing you see reserved for political officials or high members of state. Instead of pressing the red button on the silver panel, I waited. It was more than mere curiosity—I wanted to see how alert this team was, and there was no better way to measure that than the strange-car-at-the-door test. I expected their immediate response, especially considering the recent kidnapping. When everyone stayed sharp, alert, and aware, it created less stress and a more balanced team, but even one slacker meant the rest of the team could be strung out trying to compensate for the hole. I needed to see what I'd signed up for. The response now could hint at the work it'd take in the following three weeks to bring this operation up to my standards.

After four minutes of idling, no one came to check on me. I had my answer.

Freaking perfect.

Four minutes doesn't seem like a huge amount of time. Most people can scroll on their phones for a full fifteen before they become aware of the passing of time. But in that time, I'd spotted both security cameras situated on the far sides of the porch pointed at close to sixty-five degrees, the yard gnome hidden in the bush with a winking left eye that was likely a motion sensor, and the onyx jewel in the center of the gate's emblem, which was likely a decoy for a minute camera.

I assumed there were two smaller sensors somewhere on the periphery of the fence or security booth. In the security world, the flashier something was, the less likely it was actually the thing to be concerned about. I rolled down my window so they—assuming anybody was watching—could catch my face on camera.

Nothing. At nine minutes, I pressed the tomato red button in the panel.

Another minute passed before a buzzing sounded on the other side.

"I see you." Dane's voice came over the line. "I'm opening the gate now. Park on the left of the Denali, and I'll meet you at the back kitchen door." A high pitched buzz sounded before the gates parted down the middle and slid open

"Will do." I maneuvered Blade along the wide circle drive and spotted the black Yukon Denali backed up to the front door, facing away from the house and ready to drive at a moment's notice. I parked just as the back door swung open and Dane's massive frame filled the doorway.

"You're early," he said.

"In this business, being late makes people nervous."

I grabbed my Smith & Wesson M&P Shield out of the glove compartment. It was a small gun that was easy to conceal but still packed the punch of a 9mm.

Dane stood on the single step porch with the side door wide open. "Seems you found your way easily enough."

I shoved the gun into the holster that would hold it against the small of my back, which I'd strapped on before I went to my parents' house, and adjusted it to make sure it felt secure. The snakeskin leather jacket I wore hit at my waist and would cover any ridges or bulges that might peek out. I climbed from the convertible and walked over to him. "Thought I'd misread my GPS or something. When the gate didn't immediately open, I thought I'd turned down the wrong street."

"Things have been more hectic than normal. The camera connects to my phone but the last two days it's been short circuiting and there's a delay."

"You plannin' on having someone come out to repair it?"

"I need to make a few calls but I'll make it happen."

Read: he hadn't made those calls and the camera would remain a liability until then.

I frowned at his blasé attitude. "I'd encourage you to make time. I wouldn't want to see one or both kids in a compromising situation because we couldn't fix something as simple as a camera." Normally, I was a bit more tactful. Close protection officers were muscled bodyguards with an analytic eye and an instinct that could sniff out trouble and we tended to wear their ego close to the skin. Having a new team member single out a weakness in the process was the quickest way to piss people off.

But Alyssa had been kidnapped less than twenty-four hours ago and that meant this entire operation needed to tight. No mistakes. I wouldn't put another client in danger because I didn't go with my gut.

The look in his swamp brown eyes told me he didn't appreciate me stomping on his male-in-charge toes and, for a moment, emotion swirled that was downright hostile. I thought he'd call me out. But he rolled his neck a few times then shot me a brief nod.

"Might have time after the kids get settled." He hedged.

Beastie grumbled. She wanted him to take a swing at us so we could pound our studded batons into his skull. "What are we on tonight?" I asked, scrubbing the urge from my mind.

His face never moved, but I swear I caught a hint of desperation in his eyes. "Halloween duty. The neighborhood hosts an annual Halloween Festival on one of the empty lots at the back of the addition. It's a big deal apparently."

A loud clatter from inside the house made my gaze snap past the door and scan the luxurious kitchen.

"It's fair to warn you," Dane warned without turning to check the source of the noise. "The kids are jazzed today. Don't know if their mom tweaked their food just to mess with us or what, but they're both on one tonight."

Toward the front of the kitchen, a wide staircase with golden oak paneling shot straight to the second floor. A small figure sprung from the top of those stairs, jumping down every other stair and making fighting noises under his breath. He leapt down the final three stairs to land on the kitchen floor with an explosion noise.

I recognized him from the internet search I'd run on the

Jackson family. Logan, nine-year-old budding genius. Soared through his sixth grade classes because the work was not challenging enough. He won a local highly competitive science fair competition when he was seven with a working model of a supernova explosion. Definitely preferred studying over team sports or physical extracurriculars. Attended the same middle school as his sister. Was generally well liked by his classmates, and his teachers adored him. Floppy golden brown curls that were his and Alyssa's trademark, the hair a gift from their interracial parents. All dry, clear cut facts.

But the boy who ran up to Dane was all energy and enthusiasm and not one bit intimidated by the hulking man. "She's here, can we go now?".

"Is your sister ready?" Dane asked.

The little boy turned back to the house, cupped his hands at his mouth, and yelled. "Alyssa!"

Because, you know, yelling in a house that size always worked. I rolled my eyes but bit back the small smile pulling at my mouth.

"I like your costume," I told him. "What are you supposed to be?"

"Falcon from the Avengers," he replied, stretching out his arms to show off the fabric intricately etched like wings that flapped between his arms. "He's the best because he's an army veteran, and Dad says that if anyone could turn into a superhero in real life, it would be them."

I smiled at that. Hard to argue with that logic.

Logan's were a gentler version of his father's blue eyes, more like the bluebonnet flowers that grew up the slopes of highways in the city. "Are you Alyssa's new bodyguard?"

I nodded.

He stared at me, calculating. "You don't dress like the other one. She looked more like Dane."

"Most bodyguards dress like him," I told him. "Even the women. But my approach is different: I don't *want* people to know that I'm a bodyguard."

His face scrunched in confusion. "Why not?"

I noticed he lacked the twitchy energy that most kids his age had, the pure inability to stand still. "Because people tend to be more relaxed and reveal their true motives when they don't think their every move is being watched. I prefer to come across more like a babysitter or nanny, hence"—I gestured at my outfit—"my clothes."

"But you're trained like Dane, right? You can take someone down if they tried to hurt me or Alyssa? That's why Dad hired you?"

"Right."

"So you're not a *normal* nanny." He said it like a revelation, a juicy secret that only he knew. "You're more like…a *lethal* nanny."

The smile I'd been fighting broke through. "Yeah, something like that." This was part of why I did what I did: that quivering wonder and revelation that kids naturally possessed was something to be protected. It was one of the reasons I preferred working with children. There just weren't enough people dedicated to making sure that the unjaded minds of children went untainted. Childhood was a beautiful thing but often ended too soon, and I wanted to help kids remain in that season as long as possible before the world tainted their view.

Something flickered in my peripheral and I looked to see the girl from the nightclub storming down the steps. The fury that contorted her face was completely at odds with the crisp white ballerina outfit she wore—complete with a tutu covered in intricate white embroidery, crisp white panty hose, and a white multi-petaled flower adorning a pristine bun at the top of her head.

"I hate you!" she screamed. "You slinky, little, know-it-all loser!" She hurled something that made Logan dodge to one side with his arms protecting his head.

"What did I do?" He yelled.

"You know exactly what you did you stupid loser!" Another projectile flew through the air and hit Dane's chest with a thump before clattering to the tile.

I glanced down to see that the thing she'd thrown seemed to be a chunky doll leg.

"Not again," Dane muttered.

Alyssa stormed up to her brother and I read trouble in the lines of her body. When she was only a few feet from him, she flung herself at him, something raised in both hands ready to clobber him.

Dane and I sprang into action. I caught the girl mid lunge and held her back by her shoulders while Dane stepped in front of Logan who stared at his sister in confusion and a hint of anger.

"I didn't do it, 'Lyssa."

"Dad told you to leave my stuff alone and stop breaking my dolls. We even hid them so you couldn't get to them." She clutched the torso of a doll dressed in a similar ballerina outfit —sans the legs—with anger glittering in her eyes. "I hope he grounds you for a year."

"It wasn't me!"

"Liar!"

The doll clutched in her arms was pretty pathetic. It was considerably larger than a Barbie and reminded me of that line of dolls based on a historical book series…American Lady? American Child? Whatever it was, it now was legless.

At his words, she jerked against my hold and swung the doll, trying to hit him around my body.

I let go of her shoulders and caught the doll mid-air. "That's not going to help anything." I told her. "Dane, why don you boys start heading to the festival and we'll catch up with you."

"Roger that. Take this." Dane grunted behind me. He held out a black walkie talkie no larger than the palm of my hand, and I took it. "We're bound to get separated, and I don't want to worry about trying to hear my phone above the noise. Festival's on the northwest end of the neighborhood, and we'll be on foot the whole night."

Alyssa jerked against me as Dane turned Logan by the

shoulders and marched him out the front door. When she did it again, I let her go. She took several large steps back and stared at me furiously. "It's not fair. He's always getting what he wants and getting out of trouble.

"If it makes you feel any better, I have a brother who makes me feel the exact same way." I knelt and picked up the detached doll leg. It was heavier than I would have guessed, the glass thick and smooth except for the jagged hip joint when Logan smashed it. Or ripped it off with his bare hands. I frowned. Determined kid.

"Did he break your dolls?" Alyssa asked.

"I never really played with dolls. He'd do things like deflate my favorite basketball or tear my posters."

"So, what did you do?"

Suffered through until I was old enough to escape. I shook off the thought and looked up into her blue eyes. "I learned to ignore him."

"Yeah right."

"Take it or leave it but that's what I did." I walked through the kitchen until I came to a utilitarian looking cabinet with a bunch of random tool stuff inside. I pulled it open and shuffled inside. Batteries, tape, and a variety of knickknacks filled bins of every height and size to the brim with the junk. I found the glue sticks and my eyes zeroed in on what I wanted.

I held out my hand. "May I see her?"

"She can't get wet," Alyssa clutched the doll more tightly.

I nodded and wiggled my fingers. After a tense minute, she placed the doll in my palm. I carefully ran the super strength glue around the outside of the leg and, just as carefully, before holding the leg up to the hip joint and pressing hard. A few seconds later the leg was reattached.

Alyssa's eyes were huge!

It wasn't my first go round with emergency surgery on a doll. Hazards of the job, I guess. She pulled it from my hands and gave it a big hug and then looked up at me, embarrassed.

"It's, uh, a limited edition collectible," she explained. "If this one breaks, there's no telling if I'll be able to get a new one."

I nodded. But by the way she cradled the doll in her arms belied her words. I wouldn't be surprised if it was a special gift that she cherished more than she let on.

"How about we join the boys, eh?"

She nodded. "Let me run this upstairs and put her in the cabinet." She turned on the ball of her foot, making the movement far more graceful than it should have been and peppered up the stairs. A few seconds later, she ran back down and immediately headed for the door.

I stepped out and punched in the security code Dane had showed me before jogging up to catch her.

"Just so you know, I don't need a babysitter...or governess or..." she sniped as she flounced down the sidewalk. "In short, I don't have any use for you so be sure to stay away from me."

I studied her face. Back to being an impulsive brat? Whatever I could handle it.

The sidewalk was a crowded, noisy mess. Young children dressed as animals toddled and skipped down the sidewalk herded by parents in matching costumes. Gaggles of teenagers in video game characters or superhero outfits strolled slow, taking Instagram videos and stopping every few feet to snap the obligatory "selfie". It was like Noah's Ark being manned by X-box and Marvel characters. And all of them followed the thick scent of corndogs and the sound of carnival music.

Alyssa tried to jet in front of me, but her legs were only so long and I easily kept pace with her, staying behind and to the right. By the time we turned at the corner farther along their street, we were suddenly swallowed whole by the revelry of a street festival. Food trucks, colorful banners, face painting, and an endless array of colorful, flashing booths were packed into a tight four-block radius. There were even a few happy clowns on stilts passing out candy bars the size of a preschooler's arm.

It was the happy chaos and energy of hundreds of kids. Normal people might revel in the joy soaked atmosphere. It only served to make Beastie pace with anxiety and I could feel

Beastie's hackles rise. I sucked in rhythmic breaths as we entered the crowd. At least two hundred kids and adults in a parade costumes mingled, and the night was still early. If it were up to me, I would have avoided this stimulus-heavy atmosphere that was a potential minefield. Clearly, the kids didn't feel the same. I spotted a tall, shiny bald head in the flashing lights and guided us toward the face painting booth that Logan and Dane idled behind.

Logan tugged at Dane's hand, pulling on a single thick finger. "Come on! I want to try the Ferris wheel."

Dane muttered a swear word under his breath and looked at me. "You good?"

I nodded. I was hoping Alyssa was one of those kids with FOMO who really only wanted to be in the atmosphere, not trying to play every single game. As Logan dragged them both away, something told me Dane had his hands full.

"Alyssa!" A group of girls waved and my charge ran over to them. The next thirty seconds were filled the exclamations and approval of twelve year old girls over each other's outfits. Some twirled to some of the effects of their glittery skirts and hair and others flexed imaginary muscles.

Alyssa squealed. "Y'all look great too. Where's the photo booth? We definitely need to get a picture."

The alien and Wonder Woman giggled, and the three started away in a group. I followed, no further than three steps behind the last girl, Alyssa was sandwiched in the middle. I tried to make myself as invisible as possible but didn't intend to allow too much space in an atmosphere like this. People got snatched at things like this all the time. Judging from the foul look she shot over her shoulder, Alyssa failed to recognize the appeal of having a bodyguard working hardcore RBF.

"Can you give us some space?" she hissed.

I didn't bother replying.

"You deaf or something? You can watch me from, like, over there." She waved in some general direction, and I didn't bother looking.

"What's her problem?" one of the other girls said, skin painted green and black antenna jutting from the top of her head. A friendly alien?

Alyssa rolled her eyes with a dramatic sigh. "No clue. Dad just hired her, and now she's supposed to stalk me all over the place."

"No!" the taller girl said, adjusting her wonder woman shield.

A few minutes later, Alyssa tried a different tactic. "Hey, Serena," she called, her voice high and sweet and genuine as cobra laced honey. "Would you mind getting us some corn-dogs? Daddy gave me money." She held up a twenty-dollar bill and waved it in the air as if to tempt me.

I almost laughed. I'd been offered more than that to shirk my duties—houses, cars, even diamonds for a five minute window of negligence. And here she was waving her paltry twenty bucks as if it was a really tempting offer.

But the gleam in her eye was anything but funny. The little scene back in the driveway gave me a hint that she wouldn't make this process easy; paired with the open gate only a dozen yards away and the mischievous shift in energy from her friends, it didn't take a Harvard scholar to recognize that her intent was to distract me so she could sneak away. Beastie snarled at her, testy. It looked like I'd have to find a memorable way to prove to her that I wasn't a punk and wouldn't be evaded.

I stepped forward and grabbed the twenty from her hands. "Sure thing. A corndog for each of you?"

"Yeah!" Wonder Woman chimed in eagerly.

I turned and walked that way. After a few steps, I turned back around. "Wait for me right there."

Alyssa rolled her eyes. "Duh. I've done this before."

I'll just bet you have. I headed for the collection of food trucks but angled my path so I could keep the girls in sight out of the corner of my eye. I knew once they lost sight of me, they'd beeline it straight for that open gate. The crowd thickened closer to the concession area, and I used that cover to duck behind the food area and take off in a full sprint through the crowd to the far edge of the carnival and then cut back behind a few houses. It took less than two minutes to loop back around and approach the back gate from the far end of the street.

I arrived just as Alyssa and her friends slipped through the gate and skittered down the sidewalk. I switched to the same side, stayed in the shadows, and waited. Alyssa was squealing in delight, apparently thrilled I'd been so easy to lose, when I made eye contact with the girl in the alien costume.

Her black tinted mouth fell open and she stuttered to a halt.

"What?" Wonder Woman asked.

I stepped out of the shadow, and, as a unit, they came to a dead halt.

I locked eyes with Alyssa, whose open mouth twisted into nasty scowl.

I walked straight to her, not stopping until I towered above her and crowded her space. I rarely relished my height, but when I did, it was because I was punking idiot clients. I used every inch to my full advantage now. Frost swirled in my gut. Such recklessness, putting herself and potentially her friends in danger. And for what? Just to spite her lame *babysitter*? Freaking Unacceptable.

"I'll say this once." I got into her face, so close I'm sure she could pick up the scent of clove gum on my breath. "I don't play pissing games with twelve-year-old girls. From now until the time that your parents determine that I am no longer necessary, you exist in Serena's Rules of Order. My rules are simple: when I tell you to do something, you do it immediately. No questions. No flack. No back talk."

"You don't control me," she spat.

"I'm not your enemy, Alyssa. But make no doubt, if you insist on being difficult, reckless, and immature, I will shut down everything in your life until the election is over or the sick man who tried to snatch you out of a theatre is caught. Starting now." I shifted to face her friends. "This is what happens when y'all decide to be reckless and irresponsible. Party's over. Alyssa's going home, and we'll walk alone.'

"What?" said Wonder Woman.

"Not cool!" The alien pouted.

"That's not fair." Alyssa actually stomped her feet, a temper-tantrum move if I'd ever seen one.

I wasn't about to debate my decision with a bunch of tweens. I grabbed her upper arm and started walking.

Alyssa stumbled a step but caught my rhythm and tried to yank away.

"Get off me! I'll tell my dad you yanked me away from my friends. He'll fire you quicker than he fired Tiffany for leaving me at the theatre."

I kept my face neutral but snorted in my head. If the Jackson fired me over an accusation his manipulative little princess shot my way, he was a fool. And people who worked for fools tended to end up dead.

Alyssa yanked at my grip one more time and then stopped so suddenly that she stumbled. It was only my grip that kept her standing. The stark fear that shadowed her face put me on instant alert. I pulled her slightly behind me. What on earth?

"It's him." Her voice shook so badly that I almost missed the words. "Don't let him get me."

I scanned the crowd, searching. The array of colorful costumes made everything strange and obscure, except for one thing. My eyes riveted on a red leather jacket weaving its way through the crowd. Male, tawny skin, about five-three from what I could gather from the distance. Surely they hadn't let Danny Verengaz out of custody so soon?

The moment I clocked him, I turned us both around and started walking us back through the neighborhood at a rapid pace. It may or may not have been Danny Verangaz—I seriously doubted they would have let him out of custody so soon, since the kidnapping had taken place less than forty-eight hours before. Unless he had serious clout with people in high places, he was definitely cooling his heels in county jail, and, probably, an attorney. Right now, none of that mattered. Logic wouldn't soothe the girl who was so stiff with terror that she stumbled every few feet.

I pressed the button at the side of the walkie talkie. "Dane. We're headed back to the house."

A pause before static gritted across the line. "What's up?"

"Possible kidnapping suspect from Thursday spotted in the crowd. Doubtful that it's him, but Alyssa's spooked." In front of us, a group of people in no hurry slowed us down, and I led us both into the street to move around them, speaking into the handheld device. "I suggest you and Logan head back as well."

"On it. Over and out."

"Over and out."

Alyssa was limp as dead fish, and I needed her to loosen up. I shook her just enough to get her attention. "Move with me, Alyssa. Relax your muscles and do what I do. I'll get you home faster that way, okay?"

She sucked in a deep breath and let it out, and I felt her muscles relax beneath my hand. We moved at a quick jaunt until we were almost jogging down the sidewalk, maneuvering around clusters of weary parents and candy high kids. Alyssa didn't stop shaking until the house loomed before us, and I all but ran us up to the kitchen door and punched in a code. We spilled inside.

In the kitchen, I studied her. She was breathing hard, but I thought that was more from fear than from the exertion of getting home. I walked over to the cabinet and pulled out a glass before moving to the fridge and using the filter to fill it with water. Footsteps made me look up just as Brendan walked into the kitchen, flipping through a manilla folder.

He paused mid-step when he saw Alyssa huddled against the fridge. "Everything okay?"

"All good here." I said, voice chipper and upbeat. "We just got a bit overwhelmed from the crowd and decided to call it a night." I tipped the glass to stop the water and held it out to

Alyssa. She took it, hands only shaking a little bit.

"From what the Jackson tells me, the carnival is a crush every year. I'll bet it's easy to get...overstimulated in a crowd that size." His eyes lingered on Alyssa whose body still trembled with fear and adrenaline that was slow to leave.

"Large crowds aren't for everyone," I agreed. Alyssa downed the glass in a few gulps and tried to stand but her legs wobbled and I reached out to steady her. "I think it's safe to say that we need to go to bed and start over again tomorrow, hmmm?"

"Yeah." Her voice cracked and she cleared it.

"My bed always makes me feel better," Brendan said. "It's one of the few places I look forward to going back to and it never fails to comfort me."

I wanted to roll my eyes but focused on shifting my arm across Alyssa's shoulders and holding her weight as she stepped forward.

As we passed, he reached out to awkwardly pat her shoulder. "You've had a rough few days but things will calm down... soon."

Beastie growled and wanted to swipe at him. Didn't he know that touching recently traumatized girls only made them feel more powerless, out of control? I shushed her but turned Alyssa's shoulders so his hand only touched her for a moment. "True that,' I said. "With me around and the election almost over, things will return to normal before we can even miss the chaos." Most people wouldn't know that, wouldn't consider a touch meant to comfort as a violation of personal space. But her stiff body and flushed face was a dead giveaway of her discomfort, signs Brendan missed entirely.

We traipsed up the steps to the second floor and turned right to the large room that dead ended the right side of the hall.

"Are you staying the night?" She tried to keep the question casual but I could see the fear shadowing her eyes.

I smiled gently at her. "Not tonight. There's a police car that's patrolling the area and will drive by every few minutes to make sure everything's okay. Nothing to worry about."

By the time she finished getting ready for bed, Dane made it back with a mutinous Logan in tow. He tromped past me on the stairs, struggling to carry his bulging candy bag and didn't say a word.

Cutting any kid's candy collection time short was apparently a sure way to get on their crap list.

"He wasn't a fan of leaving early," Dane said as I reached the bottom of the stairs.

A door slammed closed. "I can see that. I hated to cut off his fun but Alyssa really freaked and I didn't want to risk their being a minutia of truth to the threat."

"I get that," he twisted his neck to the left until it popped sickeningly. "I'm on shift until the parents get home. You're free to go."

"I don't mind staying." All I had was an empty and sleepless night ahead of me.

Dane popped the otherside. "You're good. I can handle this."

I didn't argue though I truly would have preferred staying. I flipped my keys in one hand and exited out the kitchen door. An idea struck me. It took almost thirty minutes for me to do a lap of the house, yanking on every window and door to make sure they were firmly closed. Nothing was out of place and I drove away feeling better about leaving the kids in that mansion with only one and half men—Dane, full man, Brendan, definitely half man—to protect them.

CHAPTER 7

Monday morning was one of those hazy autumn mornings with a canopy of rose-hued clouds backlit by the rising sun and the air thick with the smell of rain. It was another windows-down drive to the Jackson residence. This time when I pulled up the black security booth, I barely waited thirty seconds before the gate buzzed and slowly opened enough to let me ease through. Looked like someone decided to show up to work today. I eased past the security booth, but the blacked out windows made it impossible to see anything but the reflection of my car. Even in dim light, Blade gleamed like a lurking predator, and a frisson of delight coursed through me. My car was so badass.

I parked and punched in the keycode to access the house through the kitchen. Even before I pushed open the door, melodic piano music teased my ears and swirled through the air. It was a classical piece that was so intricate that I could almost envision the notes sparking and dancing through the air. Where was it coming from?

Both Brendan and Dane were putzing around the kitchen when I walked in. Brendan scraped the magenta remnants of a smoothie out of a blender and Dane pulled a bottled water out of the fridge, eyes riveted on his cell phone His head jerked up when the door closed behind me.

"Morning," I said, but my lips snapped shut when Brendan pressed a single digit to his lips and gave a quick, sharp shake of his head. Okay...

He pointed, and I followed him through the kitchen and

around the staircase to a sunroom. Beautifully paneled windows draped down the wall and let the gray morning light fill the space with a sleepy, wakeful glow. A grand piano was shoved into the farthest corner, where Jackson played the lovely notes. The rest of the room was empty of furniture, covered with a dark wood floor where Alyssa pirouetted and arabesqued her way around the room. She leapt at an uptilt of the song and landed like a graceful flower petal before twirling around the room in a flurry of flowing arms and spinning hair.

"It's a daily routine," Brendan murmured so close that his breath tickled the hairs on my neck and I could smell the egg he'd eaten for breakfast. "It's a sacred time, and neither of them miss. The rest of us know better than to interrupt."

I didn't realize I was humming a cello accompaniment until I was forced to stop to hear him. They met like this every day?

At one point, Alyssa missed a move, and the Jackson seamlessly replayed the music without a hitch. Not once did he look down at the keys, but his eyes stayed locked on his daughter as she leapt and spun.

His eyes were filled with love. He seemed captivated by his little girl's dancing. My dad's face flashed in my head, and my throat tightened.

A minute later, the Jackson played the final crescendo and Alyssa gave a theatrical bow, feet in perfect position as she bent low at the waist with a dramatic flair as if she'd given everything she had to the performance. Yet, the moment the final note vibrated from the air, she snapped upright and launched herself at her dad.

Piano keys clanked as he caught her, wrapping her in a tight hug. "You look good, princess."

"I keep messing up the last part." She grumbled. "It's like I understand the movements in my head, but I can't get my feet to cooperate."

"Then you'll just have to practice more." His reply was matter-of-fact yet calm and free of judgment.

She leaned against him in the way of a gangly, growing

teenager, and he easily took her weight. "I don't do as well when I'm listening to the CD. I do better when you play for me."

"The only way you'll master this routine is by practicing more. I work too much to play for you as much as you'll need in order to become perfect, and I don't want you waiting on me. Excellence—"

"Waits for no one," she finished for him.

He smiled up at her. "Right." His eyes cut over to me and Dane in the doorway. "Looks like it's time for school."

When her eyes took us in, she scowled. "Can't I spend the day with you? I can shadow you like I did last week." It was a sweet ask, the genuine longing of a child to be around their parent, and the look on his face showed he knew it.

"This isn't a good week, honey. The election's next week, and the office is a madhouse. I'd be no fun to be around because I'll be running around like the big bad wolf." His voice was gentle.

"I know." Her shoulders sagged.

"Besides, the church's Christmas recital's rehearsals begin today, so your schedule will be full anyway."

"If I got out of school early, I could—"

"Leaving school early is out of the question," he said, voice firm. "Speaking of"— he glanced at Brendan and me— "I think it's time to leave."

Her lower lip jutted out, but he only tweaked her nose, forcing a small smile from her. She pushed away from him.

Alyssa brushed past me and Brendan and stomped her way up to her room. Apparently, no wasn't a word the Jackson used with her often enough. Maybe a few more of them would do her some good.

"Do you have my shake, Brendan?" Jackson asked as he stood and massaged his temples.

Brendan snapped to attention. "It's coming right up, sir." He squeaked as he rushed to walk around me. I followed him into the kitchen and watched him dump frozen strawberries into a high powered blender.

"Did you intend to pull in a job with one of the most influential Jacksons in the state or did that happen on your time off?" He joked but there was something in his voice that me study him.

"It just landed in my lap I guess." Yeah, like an airplane with a blown engine. I watched his shoulders tense as he tossed a banana into the blender. I'm sure it sucked working your butt off when it seemed like other people had all the luck. Beastie rumbled in my mind. If only he knew what I hoped this job would help me fight...better not to think about it.

"Seems like you've made something of yourself," I switched subjects away from me. "You always told everyone you'd make it into high society—and here you are. How long have you been managing campaigns?"

"Six years, seven city council elections, four state representative races, and one congressional race that will end us all," he recited the numbers in a monotone voice as if he chanted this to himself every morning while brushing his teeth.

I shot him an impressed look.

"If we win this race, it'll skyrocket us both to the top. Interviews, power, etc... the stuff most people dream of but can't really fathom cause it's so far from what they've known."

"You've always been a dreamer," I said as much. "What about the family business? What was it again...trucking?"

"It's a fourteen wheeler appliance transport company," Brendan snapped and I blinked with surprise. Touchy much? He cleared his throat. "Sorry. People hear trucking and immediately think white trash homegrown business out of a filthy garage. My uncle has created the very opposite. It's a multi-million dollar empire with enough moving parts to make your head swim. The demand is higher than ever."

"Any plans to take over if your uncle decides to retire?" I handed him the lid to the blender bottle.

"Uncle Leo's built like a tractor," Brendan joked. "You can always repair it."

"Some people might feel pressure to continue the legacy."

He shrugged. "Who knows what the future holds for me. I'd like to actually start climbing that success ladder instead of only making lateral moves, you know? The "Yes, sir" life gets...tedious after a while."

I definitely understand that. Seven years serving the country in some militant capacity and it never made it easier for those words to roll off my tongue. There were moments when it seemed glued to my dang mouth and refused to actually come out.

"Speaking of luck, I found two tickets to the philharmonic's annual fall concert. Thought it might be fun if we went."

Oh no, not this again. "Brendan..."

"It's nothing serious or formal," he rushed on. "Just two friends reconnecting on a beautiful night. No pressure. Besides, you probably just got back in town and don't know anyone and no one would recognize you—I know I sure didn't. I could introduce you to some people, we could mingle. It'll be fun."

Schmoozing wasn't a strong skill of mine. Add to the mix an unstable tigress who didn't do well in crowds and that made mingling a very bad idea. For me at least. The more time I spent around people and the higher the risk someone would recognize how close to the surface Beastie was. I was pushing things with this job already.

Before I could respond to the puppy dog question in his eyes, Alyssa stomped across the kitchen to the back door, and threw a cross look over her shoulder at me.

"You coming?" She pulled open the door and marched out before I could reply.

Logan skipped in from the living room, backpack bouncing against his back. "She's always in a bad mood in the mornings." He swiped a banana from the counter and ran to the door.

"Here are the keys to the Escalade," Dane said and chucked me a black key fob. "That will be your "on duty" vehicle."

A car honked and I frowned at the door. I moved to the window to see Alyssa through the open passenger door, leaning over the driver's seat and pressing the horn.

"Don't miss that," Dane muttered as he swiped the second key fob from the counter before walking over to the kitchen back door and pulling it open for Logan "This is one morning drive that I'm not sorry to hand over to you."

I can see why. I shot Brendan an apologetic shrug, grabbed a bottled water from the fridge and headed after her. I'd dealt with some of the brattiest behavior imaginable from the kids of the wealthiest, most powerful men and women on the planet. It would take more than a car horn to rattle me. Even though Beastie didn't like it. We settled into the vehicle, and the clogged traffic on I-35 North meant that it took us right at forty three minutes to arrive at her school. I drove past the drop off line that was thirty cars deep and around the building to a mostly empty parking lot.

"What are you doing?" Alyssa asked.

I didn't respond, just pulled up to the curb and shoved open my door. I walked around to open hers and waited until she climbed out, shoving her arms through her backpack.

"Tiffany never went inside with me." The implication was clear: you're not nearly good enough, skilled enough, or competent enough for this gig.

I was tempted to remind her that it was Tiffany nearly got her kidnapped. But I wasn't about to start a game of, "One Up You" with a twelve-year-old brat. I shot her an, "Oh really?" look and followed her inside and met her homeroom and third hour teachers, completely ignoring the angry looks she shot my way. Today, I was just dropping her off and Lang, the third man on the team, would pick her up and take her to ballet. Still, it was good for her teachers and other students to become familiar with my face and presence in case I asked them to do something strange like board the windows with their desks or lock the kids in a classroom.

I was back on the road within twenty minute with a specific destination in mind. Normally, I learned more information about a client before jumping onto an assignment, but I'd been flying blind with the Jackson, and that needed to stop.

The downtown Oklahoma City police station was such a beautiful building, surrounded by music halls and fancy restaurants, that it would be easy to mistake for an office complex or a mall if not for the abundance of police cars parked outside. With sloping, darkly tinted windows that covered the majority of the exterior and sharp geometrical elements, it seemed more like an extension of the downtown music hall. It definitely blended in with this upscale corner of the city.

Walking inside felt like a time hop back into my childhood. Dad used to "hire" me out as a desk worker. Essentially, my job was to go from desk to desk and clear off old coffee mugs and general trash from around the office. Really, I was just free labor but it usually involved a trip to the donut shop and cool stories from the other officers. It was how I got to know so many of the seasoned cops—I'd been their wide-eyed road dog on their daily routes and eager sidekick that helped pull pranks on the other cops.

A police station created a tornado of emotions for most people. Anxiety and fear, indignation...rage. For me? It felt like that friend's house you always knew you'd be welcome.

I walked to the front desk and waited for the receptionist to click off the phone. She had an expensive pixie cut and a sharp chin.

"Can I help you?" Her voice was pleasant, although her piercing eyes studied me.

"Can you tell me if Julien Black is in the office or out on patrol?"

"And you are?"

"His sister." I held my hand over her desk. "Serena Black. Nice to meet you."

The woman took my hand with a firm grip of her own. "Good to meet you. I've heard so much about your family from the old dogs. I'm so sorry to hear about your dad."

I hated when people said that. I gave her a tight smile.

Her fingers flew across the keys. "Looks like Officer Black is on patrol until three this afternoon. I can page you through to his squad car though."

"Don't worry about it." A thought struck me. "Is Officer Paul Dunningham in?"

A few clicks later. "He sure is."

"What's his desk number?"

"Thirty-seven."

"Thanks." I pushed off the countertop and jogged to the second floor. I counted the desks and spotted the man I was looking for.

Paul was chatting in a cluster of other officers when I approached his desk. Once upon a time, I would have known those faces but now they were strangers to me. Laughter broke out and Paul looked up just as I entered his row.

He blinked several times before a wide smile split his face. "Well, now, isn't this a blast from the past," he said, ambling toward me. "It's been a hot minute since I've seen you in here."

He extended his hand and we shook. "I'm sure you have a new culprit who's responsible for the cold coffee," I joked.

"Could be." His eyes twinkled.

"Hope I'm not interrupting. Seems like you and your boy were celebrating."

"Sure are," He beamed. "We just submitted the final paperwork to haul away one Danny Vergangaz for good. It'll take a few minutes to process the paperwork downstairs and then that no good trouble maker is gone."

"He won't make it six weeks in county before he's dead or somebody's wife," a brown haired officer chortled.

"Not nearly long enough for his kind," Paul muttered. "Anyway, what can I do for you? I seriously doubt you came up here just to see this old officer."

I smiled. "Maybe I did."

He raised an eyebrow. "But you didn't."

I chuckled. "Not solely for you," I admitted. "Alyssa Jackson's kidnapping made me curious. Do we know if there's been a history of serious threats against the Jackson family, specifically since he started his Congressional campaign? I'm wondering if his security team should be on the lookout for any repeat attempts or other strange incidences."

"It's a good thought, but, unfortunately, I can't run such a search for civilians. Sorry, doll."

"I'm here in official capacity," I told him. "The Jackson family hired me as Alyssa's personal bodyguard the day of the kidnapping."

His eyebrows rose. "Well that's impressive. In that case, follow me on over and let's see what we can dig up."

His mess was a cluttered jungle of papers with brown stained disposable coffee cups perched here and there. Paul plopped into his seat and let his fingers fly over the board.

"Serena!"

I glanced up from reading the screen over Paul's shoulder just as Detective Luke Thorne hit the second story landing and sauntered my way. A slick forest green shirt strained at his biceps and perfectly complemented the sand colored, straight slacks he wore. He looked like a fashion model on the way to a casual photo shoot. But *cop* was etched into the confident set of his shoulders and rhythm in his walk.

He was high-dollar eye candy, and it suddenly felt like years since I'd been to the candy store.

Beastie grumbled and looked at him through slitted eyes.

He strode over and leaned a hip against the desk. "What brings you out this way?"

"Just doin' a bit of homework." I resisted the urge to take a half step back and to the left to give me a bit more space.

"Yeah? What subject?"

"Davis Jackson. Seems like he's gotten a lot of negative attention in the last few months and I want to see if there's been an uptick in unfriendly gestures toward him."

"You think the nightclub wasn't an isolated event?" The way his eyes twinkled told me he had intentionally invaded my space and found my ire amusing. Stupid man.

"Can't say. But I'm wondering if there's been an increase in actions against him that would lead up to such a bold move."

He nodded. "From what I've heard, Jackson definitely inspires...strong emotion. It would be interesting to see if there was a precursor to the kidnapping attempt."

"I think I've got your answer, doll," Paul cut in, still scrolling through the page. "It's nothing exciting. According to Davis Jackson's file, there have only been a handful of times where the police were called. Looks like two were stalker concerns after a big rally and the other was on the night of the kidnapping, around ten pm, which came directly from his cell phone after learning that Alyssa was at the nightclub."

I skimmed the information for myself. There was nothing conspicuous enough to scream clue or danger but my gut told me something was off about this situation.

"Would you mind printing me a copy of this report?" I asked.

"Anything for a fee."

I smiled. "I'm more than willing to swing by the donut shop and grab a half dozen just for you."

He looked affronted. "A half dozen? If you're gonna spend your money you better make it a dozen crullers and a vat of black coffee."

I laughed. "That crap will put you in the E.R."

"But I'll go a happy man," He chuckled. "No, my fee is that you give your dad a message from me."

Just like that my laughter drained like a recently cleared pipe and Beastie outright growled. I swallowed past the tightness in my throat. "Of course. Dad would love to hear from an old friend who's still working."

"You tell that man that when he's in fighting shape again that I want a rematch at arm wrestling to try and win back the two hundred he rickadooed me for that night." The memory made him chortle but I fought the cold that hardened by gut.

"Well that will be a long time, Paul." I said, voice icy to my own ears. "Dad won't ever be up to fighting strength" ever again."

The light cleared from Paul's eyes.

I should have been gentler, more understanding, taking his words for the encouragement. But I couldn't handle jokes right now. He was dying and I shouldn't be forced to put on a cheery facade to make people more comfortable.

"You still here?" I asked Luke.

He held both hands in a surrendered position. "I wanted to apologize for how my men treated you on Saturday."

"They were doing their job." My voice was sharper than I meant and I forced myself to take a breath. "Things always get a bit skewed in the heat of the moment. The handcuffs didn't leave a mark so I think I'll live."

"Shame," he murmured. "Still, I feel like I owe you a drink as a proper apology."

So that's what this was about. Pretend that your professionalism was affronted and the only way to make things right was buy me dinner or some such nonsense. If he thought he was the only man to try that crap with me, he'd have to get in line with all of the other failed attempts at suave apologies.

I opened my mouth to retort but a loud popping noise and the unmistakable sound of glass cracking resonated through the building. Someone was shooting...directly at the police station.

Luke dropped into a crouch by the desk, pulling me down with him. Beastie roared in panic and I cursed myself for leaving my gun in the car.

"What the hell?" Luke growled, pulling a handgun from a holster at his back.

More shots rang out. Half the officers crouched behind desks and chairs while the other half ran for the stairs, guns high and ready to take on anything.

Luke turned to me, his eyes gleaming. "Stay here. I'll be back." He stood and half crouched, half ran with the second wave of officers flowing down the stairs.

I cocked an eyebrow. Since when did I strike him as a stay out of the action kinda girl? Or the type of woman you could teach to "sit and stay" by the sheer force of your macho manliness? Puh-lease. I waited for him to disappear down the steps before I cautiously crept down the row of desks and stopped behind a desk with a familiar family picture facing outward. Desk twenty—Julien's desk. Pulling open the bottom drawer, I lifted a thick stack of yellow files folders to reveal a black pistol and holster tucked beneath. Bingo, baby. I snatched up the gun and stood, as the cops who stayed behind made phone calls or continued to hide beneath the desks.

I paused at the top of the stairs and listened but no further shots rang out. I jogged downstairs. The receptionist desk appeared empty but I caught a flash of red hair as the receptionist curled on the floor next to the desk despite her calm and clear voice as she spoke through her headset to request backup. A buzz of voices drew my focus and I followed the noise through the main police station entrance.

At first, it seemed to be pure chaos. My eyes riveted on the bullet holes puncturing the police cars lining the street. The bits of shattered glass from windows and windshields that glittered like water on the sidewalk. And the blood splattered on the steps and sides of vehicles. Beastie flung herself against the cage, screaming danger. Officers in various states of uniform were all over the place, taking pics on their cell phones, huddled together, some staring in confusion at what possibly could have happened.

Once I really looked, I could see that the majority of the damage was concentrated on a patrol car parked directly in front of the building. A crowd of people huddled around that I took a couple of steps down to get a better view. One cop was being helped to peel off the bullet proof vest that now looked like a cat had raked it's claws down the front and another was giving his statement to a group of friends. But the body, twisted and full of bullet holes, that was splayed out on the bottom two steps held my attention.

I knew that face. It was Danny Verangaz.

Who had done it and who was suicidal enough to do it in

front of the police station. As I stared at the red river burbling from his grey lips, I knew whatever answers this man had were long gone. The question was: what did Danny know or do that made him so much of a threat that someone would risk high exposure to kill him in such a public way?

I shook my head. Murder On The Steps Of The Police Station...how about that for a front page news story?

CHAPTER 8

I left as they were debating whether or not the FBI should get involved. Generally, the Internal Affairs Unit is responsible for conducting investigations within a PD but because Danny was linked to the most powerful drug lord in the Midwest, some thought it called for higher authority to make sure there was no foul play.

I didn't think you could get any fouler than a corpse rotting at the PD's front door but no one asked me. With Beastie in full freak out mode, I probably wasn't a reliable source anyway.

Luke was hot in the middle of the debate and I waved to him as I walked down the street to where Blade was parked. Never before had I been so glad to have been forced to park so far away. I did a quick walk around to make sure there wasn't any unseen damage, checked the tires for punctures or slits, before sliding inside and roaring away.

I swung by my favorite local smoothie shop on the way back to my apartment. I loved this place because they used real, fresh veggies and fruits to make their drinks, and everything always turned out in vibrant colors. As I waited in the drive thru, I scrolled through my texts to a name toward the bottom of the screen.

Hey you. Up for a little research project?

A few seconds later, my phone lit up. *That's how you're going to start? No, hello or hey buster or what's up, blockhead? Just hey you. Tsk, tsk, Tsk.*

Sorry. Gotta a lot on my mind. Let's start over. How art thou, oh most immaculate of friends?

Best friend. She corrected

Best friends

I'm neck deep in the most ridiculous shit storm imaginable. Thanks for asking.

I laughed as she'd meant me to. Leah Jones was as ornery and obtuse as they came. She'd dubbed herself my bestie almost the moment we'd laid eyes on each other three years ago. Apparently, she thought I was some sort of friendless, lost soul who needed a buddy to help guide me through life. She proceeded to attach herself to me like some type of algae and I'd stopped fighting her about it. If she wanted to hitch herself to my sinking boat, who was I to stop her? .

I didn't respond right away, just let my request linger. Her naturally persistent curiosity would do the work for me.

What do you need? she asked after a minute of silence.

Bingo. I shot her the first and last names of each member of the Jackson family and asked her to pull records and drum up dirt. In this day and age, *politician* was almost synonymous with *scandal,* and I wanted to know what skeletons dangled in his coat closet—be it inconsistent voting records or a male stripper job in high school.

Through the drive-thru window, a girl with bubblegum-pink hair handed me the avocado smoothie with chia seeds just as Sam's Smith's voice rang out through my car. I transferred the drink to the cup holder, wiped my hand of green smoothie goo, and pressed the button on the screen's dashboard.

"This is Black."

"Hi, there. Is this Serena?" A perky alto voice twinkled across the line.

"It is."

"My name is Brianna, and I'm calling from Apparently, I Do. I saw that you recently submitted a request to begin the interview process, and I wanted to confirm your information. Is now a good time to chat?"

Normally, I'd think this was a spam call. My phone was programmed to block all calls except recognized numbers for the express purpose of preventing junk calls from cluttering my inbox or making my phone constantly buzz like a possessed maraca. But something about the name struck me as familiar.

"Who are you with again?" I asked, reaching for my smoothie and taking a sip. I'd learned that if you go with the flow, oftentimes you'll find out more information than you would by peppering questions. "Who are you with again?"

"I'm a client coordinator for Apparently, I Do, a fresh, modern, and scientific take on dating. We're an arranged dating service that uses relationally integrated science to pick out matches for approved clientele." She laughed a bit self-consciously. "Of course you already know all that. I wanted to touch base with you regarding the form you submitted on August twelfth."

What was this woman talking about? Homeland hadn't forced me to pack my bags until September, and before then I was stationed in Mumbai. Even if I'd had access to the world wide web, which I didn't, I wouldn't have wasted my time filling out an application for a shoddy dating program that seemed to have the credibility of Frank Exotic's animal farm.

"You have the wrong person," I told her. "I would check the contact information and try again." I reached for the disconnect button, but she wasn't giving up that easily.

"The contact information I have on file is 405-555-7828 for the phone and the email listed is policechief97 at gmail.com. Would you like to update that to a more current email?"

Tendrils of cold swirled in my gut. There was only one police chief in my life who would have the audacity to sign me up for a dating program behind my back. The kicker was that he'd tried to tell me about it and I'd shut him down.

"Actually, Brianna, I'm caught in the middle of something right now. Would you be able to call back?"

"Certainly," she chirped. "Just so you know, this application is time-sensitive, and it would be best to get this done as soon as possible." She ran through a handful of times to call back, and I picked one at random. The moment she confirmed the reschedule, I disconnected the call—in the middle of her cheerful farewell. I hit the gas and sped toward my parents' house. When Brianna called again, I wanted to have my facts straight enough to shut her down.

But first, my dad had a lot of explaining to do.

It took me half the usual time to get to my parents' house. I spent most of the drive trying to calm the beast pacing the cage of my mind. Did Dad think he could pressure me into a program like this? When he'd mentioned it on Sunday, he'd made it sound like a suggestion, not something he would go behind my back to do.

Correction: Something he'd already gone behind my back and done.

He knew me well enough to know that pressure only made me simmer and turn the other direction. What had he been thinking?

Beastie paced in my head, and I forced my thoughts in a different direction. Negative emotions made her more restless, and speculating on Dad's absurd motivations wasn't helping. I tuned out the growling and focused on replaying a complicated cello solo from one of Yo-Yo Ma's recent performances. The music calmed the tigress but now the anger pulsing in my gut.

Ten minutes later, I pulled into the pristine circle drive and propelled myself from the car. I marched across the cobblestones to the front door and inserted my key.

The air smelled heavily of cocoa, warm vanilla, and browned flour when I stepped inside, the smell of baking cookies a scent that enveloped most people like a warm, welcoming hug. It turned my stomach. I knew Dad was on a strict, gut healing diet, and sugary baked goods weren't on the list. Which meant Yvonne was most likely crafting the most perfect, delectable treats for one of the many charities she volunteered for. Playing philanthropist to most yet taunting her dying husband with food he'd never again be able to enjoy.

I ignored the jolt of bitterness and shut the door harder than necessary.

"It's me." I shouted toward the kitchen but walked through the spacious living room, decorated in classy hues of off-white and brown, to the stairs. I heard the TV before I was halfway up to the second floor, and my mouth twitched in a smile as I recognized the commentator's voice. Dad and his old football reruns. It was so loud that I could tell which football teams were playing before I hit the landing.

"Yeah!" he roared. "Go, go, go!" He rattled the IV drip at the massive hundred-twenty inch TV. "Run for your life, you useless Kason!"

His energy and vigor stopped me dead on the last step. Most days his lively demeanor was an act, cracking jokes and harassing anyone within earshot, but with a raspy voice and very little volume. His constantly gray skin and watery eyes proved how tired he was. We all played along, knowing that he kept in high spirits more for our sakes than his.

Today, though, his cheeks were more pink than gray, and his voice was strong as he screamed at the television. My anger evaporated like smoke, and sadness flooded its place. Seeing him bright eyed and animated, remembering the man he used to be—and realizing he'd never really be that man again—left me with a flood of emotions that I didn't know what to do with.

That suited Beastie just fine as she encircled the swirling chaos and smothered it with her body.

"I can feel you staring at me," he said as the game switched to commercial. "If you're not bringing food with you, go back down and try again."

"Spoiled old man." I tried to sound chipper as I made my way through the den to his couch. I leaned in and kissed his cheek. "I could make something for you. Have you had your smoothie?"

Wrinkles creased his skin as he frowned, but his blue eyes sparkled. "I only drink that green death juice because Yvonne is convinced it helps my gut, and I was raised never to hurt a pretty lady's feelings."

"So if she were ugly, you'd tell her to get that crap out of your face?"

"You said it, I didn't."

I chuckled and gently sat on the couch next to him, careful not to jostle him. Sadness welled up inside me like a flood, but I viciously shoved it back down. Stupid. *He's alive today*, I hissed at myself. For the here and now, that was enough. It had to be.

We watched a few minutes of the game in silence. That was one of the best things about Dad and me—we'd always been so comfortable around each that we didn't need to fill the silence with frivolous words. Peaceful silence was just as much a testament to friendship as insightful words. He never forced me to talk or spill my deepest darkest feelings, unlike Yvonne. She was pushy by nature.

"Anything you needed to talk about?" His words no louder than a grumble yet still I heard them. "I heard the way you stomped up the stairs. Surely your stepmother couldn't have made you that angry between the front door and the staircase." His ears were still sharp as a hawk's. You could emaciate his body and leave him weak as a child, but you'd never take the cop out of the man.

I focused on the game as I tried to figure out how to answer him without giving into the cold pit in my stomach. "I got an interesting call this afternoon."

"Hmm." He grunted, body slightly weaving as if to encourage the man running on the screen.

"At first, I thought it was a wrong number, but the longer she talked, the more I knew she had to be legit."

"Telemarketers these days are sneaky bastards. Even with the most sophisticated technology, they can still waste your time."

The screen blurred. "Wasn't a telemarketer, Dad."

"Yeah?"

"It was a lady with an arranged dating service"

He stilled.

Uh-huh. Gotcha. "It happened to be the one you were telling me about the other night." I took the folded brochure out of my pocket and dumped it in his lap.

His eyes stayed glued to the TV, but his jaw flexed and his muscles vibrated tension.

I eased back into the cushions, fighting the anger that pulsed through me. The angrier I got, the more lax my muscles became. It was a trained response—never let them see how much they've affected you. The moment you allow your emotions to control the situation, you lose. Every time.

Dad cleared his throat. "It's probably a really great opportunity to meet quality men who have something to offer."

"Let me see if I understand you fully," I began. "You, without my permission or consent, signed me up for an untested, unvetted glorified arranged marriage social experiment?" My teeth clenched on the last word, and I felt the muscles around my scar twitch.

"Serena, I—"

"Do any of those words sound natural to you? Like they go together at all?"

"Serena—"

"Does any of that sound like something that I would remotely—and when I say 'remote,' I'm talking, undiscovered black holes in the far reaches of space harboring life to a translucent chanting alien species 'remote'—be interested in?"

Dad grabbed my hand, and I fought the urge not to rip it out of his weak grasp. Especially his next words. "You are not okay, baby girl. And you won't let anyone help you. When Brian explained this idea to me, it felt right in my gut, and I went with it."

"So all of the sudden, you have dictatorship over my life, and I'm just supposed to roll over and do whatever makes you happy? We both know what happened the last time Yvonne tried that particular—"

"I'm dying." His words were softly spoken, but not with sadness or fear.

Just pure, simple fact.

A fact that slayed me down to the fabric of my soul. My mouth snapped closed as the muscles in my chest constricted.

"The doctors know it. Your mother knows it. I know it. I've even come to peace with it. But my days are limited, and I don't have time to waste worrying about social niceties or even courtesy. Each day I wake up is precious, an extension of time and life that God's given me to cherish. I won't be here to hold my grandchildren. I won't be here to see Julien finally pop the question to Amber. Or see him make police chief, and I know he'll do it. I won't be here to walk you down the aisle with the man of your choice. Hell, I won't probably won't be here six months from now."

"Daddy…" Tears burned my eyes, and I didn't hold them back as they dripped down my face.

"I've known for a while that my days walking this earth are limited. So I've done what I can to set up those I love in a position to achieve the deep desires of their hearts. For you and for Julien. And I can't, I refuse, to leave my most precious gift without an anchor. All I ask is that you meet with Brian and let him ask a few questions. You may not even make it to the next interview, but at least try."

I looked into his once vibrant blue that were now dull with weariness and pain and knew I was going to cave. "So long as he doesn't try to get too deep into that emotional junk."

Dad smirked. "I'm sure a little bit of that is necessary, honey."

I grumbled and scooted closer to him on the couch and laid my head on his thin shoulder. The cotton of his shirt was soft, but his bones protruded beneath. "You know I'm not good with that kind of stuff."

He kissed the top of my head. "I also know that you're past the days of biting boys who get too close."

"Dad, that was a hundred years ago. And that buffoon knew better than to force himself on me."

"It was a hug, Serena. He was trying to give you a hug."

"A hug that I didn't want! It was unrequested and unre-quited. That kind of crap is how young boys get it into their heads that no doesn't mean no."

He chuckled. "Just promise that you'll keep your teeth sheathed until the guy's deemed worthy of that kind of power."

I rolled my eyes, but the corners of my mouth tilted. "What-ever."

We sat there in silence, content to stare out of the large bay windows. I was content to stay there forever. Just as the thought crossed my mind, my phone buzzed on the coffee table. I would have ignored it but the name that flashed across the screen caught my attention: Dane Matthews.

"I gotta get this," I murmured, and his beard chafed against my braids as he nodded. I snagged my phone from the table. "This is Black."

"Can you switch shifts with me tomorrow night? Alyssa has a dance recital, and I was supposed to drive the family there and back, but something personal came up."

"What are the deets?"

"Dinner reservations at the Melting Pot at five thirty, and from there you'll hit the Lyric Theatre. The performance should wrap up around eight o'clock, and then you take them to the house. Everyone's going to be at different places before then, but once they get the restaurant, they'll be all yours."

"I'm fine with that. As long as you don't mind an early shift the next morning."

"So you'll take it?"

"Yep."

"Great. I'll let Lang know. He's on duty before you, and he'll pass the family off to you."

CHAPTER 9

T he silver SUV had been following us for three miles. It was late Thursday night, and we'd just left Alyssa's performance as the lead dance in "Peter Pan." I'd stood at the back of the auditorium and watched as she charmed the audience with her soft, powerful movements and her cute smile. When the curtain fell, Jackson was the first to leap to his feet to applaud her. He spurred a standing ovation that made the young ballerina flush with awe and pleasure.

There'd been a small reception for the dancers and crew afterward, and the line of those wanting to congratulate and encourage Alyssa remained ten people deep for at least an hour. I'd placed her in a corner farthest from the entrance so I could keep an eye on the flow of people. Logan stayed glued to my side the entire night.

At nine, a few people still lingered, but I determined it was a good time to slip out. Now, we were on the road to Moore. Alyssa sat in the farthest backseat with her legs splayed across the leather, cold packs wrapped in towels on top of her aching shins while Logan watched a science documentary spread across the middle seat. Jackson had insisted on sitting in the front passenger seat. I'd argued. It was safer for him to be in the second row, but he wouldn't hear it. Probably some macho man thing.

The other car had been following us since we pulled out of the theatre parking lot. It'd closed the gap, so it loomed larger in the mirror. If he'd followed half a mile, that could be a coincidence, just another guy who happened to live in a neighborhood in this direction. Totally feasible. But I wasn't paid to cater to coincidences.

Just to make sure I wasn't overreacting, I slowed, hit the blinker, and made a left turn onto a side street.

"Where are we going," Jackson asked.

I ignored him, gaze flicking to the rearview.

As I'd feared, the SUV followed. I waited to see if the other car turned into one of the sprawling neighborhoods.

It did not.

I didn't want to alert the driver that they'd been made, which would be no easy task. I made a series of smooth turns that led us back out to 23rd Street, and the car followed through all of them.

A surge of adrenaline had my senses kicking into high gear.

The random turns caught Jackson's attention. He looked up from his phone and glanced around, taking stock of where we were. "Are you lost? "You missed a left about two miles ago." His voice was low, as if he didn't want to alert his family.

"Not lost." I countered, "Just taking a different route."

I could feel his eyes on me.

"Is something wr—"

The SUV behind us surged forward and rammed into our back bumper. The back of our car fishtailed slightly.

"What was that?" Alyssa asked in a voice thick with sleep.

"Did someone hit us?" The Jackson twisted in his seat, trying to get a look at the car behind us.

I straightened us out and stomped my foot on the gas so hard that the engine growled. The SUV shot forward. The speedometer hit sixty—a good thirty miles over the posted speed limit in this residential area.

The car behind us was keeping pace.

Something glinted in the corner of my eye and my brain registered it before I fully knew what it was. I slammed on the brakes, and a black SUV roared past us, the edge of its front clipping our car. If I hadn't seen him in time, he would have smashed into my side of the car.

Something rear-ended us, hard. The impact jolted us forward.

I threw up my forearm as my head smashed into the steering wheel, dampening the impact, but pain still splintered down my arm and through my head. I shot a quick look over my shoulder. The SUV back up, probably winding up to hit us again.

The impact had driven us into the back side of the SUV that'd tried to side-swipe us, and I wasn't expecting that extra momentum. Spots exploded in my vision. Beastie roared, outraged and afraid.

I pulled the gun from my holster. "Get down," I yelled.

The Jackson family ducked, crouching as low in the seat as possible, as I pointed the gun at the back window and fired off three rounds into the windshield of the ramming car.

Without waiting to see how they responded, I spun, shifted into reverse, and cranked the wheel to barrel around the other SUV, my gun still clutched in my hand. I had to get us out of there.

I maneuvered past the forward SUV, spotted an on-ramp to merge onto the highway, and took it. A car chase in the city was a multi-car pileup waiting to happen, even this late at night. Open highway was far easier to navigate. The ramp was a sharp spiral upward onto the highway and I took it.

The SUV followed.

Our cars scraped against the concrete wall lining the on-ramp, sparks flying as neither let up on speed as we took the sharp turn.

"He's gonna ram us off the road!" Jackson yelled.

No. He wasn't. I wrenched the wheel hard and swung our car into the side of the black SUV hard. Much farther past the need to turn the wheel and slammed the other car into the concrete wall. Metal squealed and sparked in protest.

A black gloved hand peaked out of the window, a pistol pointing directly at the Jackson. I wrenched the wheel hard and smashed the sides of the cars together. Just at that moment, the ramp did a final sharp curve, the concrete wall dipping slightly. The other SUV hit the curve at full force, the back end rose up in the air, and the car flipped and careened over the other side. A few seconds later a massive plume of black smoke and orange flame erupted high into the midnight sky.

We were all silent for a moment.

I cleared my throat. "Call the police and let them know what happened."

Jackson asked, "Are we going to stop and wait for them."

"Not a chance. If they have questions, they can ask them from your house." Where I would be hyper paranoid trying to monitor the sidewalk at night and keep the family safe.

Jackson dialed 9-1-1, and I listened to him recount the details of the chase to the operator. It took us ten minutes at top speed. I wasn't risking getting ambushed by another surprise attack.

By the time the police made it to the house, an hour had passed, and both Alyssa and Logan were tucked into bed. Once the adrenaline completely wore off, they both crashed. And Julien and his partner, Rhodes, happened to be in the happy party.

"Why didn't you call the police?" Julien's voice was tight, and he all but strangled the small notepad in his left hand.

He was kidding, right? Navigating a speeding car across a highway with another vehicle ramming into your side wasn't exactly an easy skill, no matter what videogames taught people to believe. I wasn't an urban car chase novice, either. In Syria, it seemed like all I did was race my clients away from would be kidnappers and assassins—and each time I needed both hands to keep us from flipping into a ditch or being rammed off a bridge.

I gave him a look that communicated what an idiotic question it was.

"Why didn't you have Jackson call?" Julien asked, eyes flashing accusation.

I snorted. "He was more focused on unloading his gun into

the other car than calling for back up. The kids were so terrified out of their minds they wouldn't have been able to tell you their phone number if you threatened the family pet."

"So you went maverick through the city? You could have killed a lot of people, Serena."

"Stop acting like I was blasting through rush-hour traffic with a nuclear weapon in the backseat. My clients were the ones in danger, and I tried to mitigate the threat to the public as much as I could. Why do you think I was trying to merge onto the highway? More open road to avoid the crazy who tried to kill us."

"There's always a risk. What if the SUV had fallen onto another car that happened to be driving past or stopped beneath the bridge. We'd be left with more bodies and you with your face hanging out saying you did the right thing."

"What would you have done?" I snapped. "In case you've forgotten, I don't work for you, the PD, the DEA, or any other agency. Yesterday, I asked if the tail was a viable threat to the family and several people at the police station told me no. Repeatedly. Your people missed the threat and now this jacked up situation is all your mess."

"Civilian profiles are not public access, and my people did the right thing by not letting a civilian rummage through them." He spat the word "civilian" like a curse word.

"You're withholding police cooperation for an elected official, soon to be Jackson. I think there's a word for that." He could stand there and try to shove crap down my throat, but I didn't have to eat it.

"Careful," he growled, taking several steps forward until he looked down at me, so close our noses almost touched.

"My job..." I stared into his eyes and forced my voice to be steady even as Beastie sent images of choking him in my head. "My only job is to ensure that my clients stay alive and as emotionally unscathed as possible. 'Calling the cops' isn't listed anywhere in my job description. To do so only makes sense only after I've contained the situation to ensure my clients come out intact."

"You and your do-or-die, hotshot mentality is going to get you killed."

"And your inability to see past your anger at me or anything to do with me is going to get you passed over for that promotion," I snapped. It was a low blow, like slam-your-balls-with-a-sledge-hammer blow that made your eyes water and your face contorted with pain. And Julien's face did contort...but with rage.

We glared at each other. "You need to be very careful." he muttered, voice thick with rage. "There are several people in the department who don't think you're fit for service and are jostling for any privileges you have to be revoked. You're on a hair trigger, Serena, and I'll happily be the one to pull the trigger and have you removed from this case."

Color me shocked down to my unpainted toes.

"Julien." His partner's voice made us both look his direction. "I've taken pictures of the vehicle and collected a bit of evidence. Only thing we're missing is a statement from Jackson himself, and we'll be ready to file a report."

I stepped back. "I'll let him know you're ready." I moved in the direction of the his office, which was situated at the back of the house.

Beastie yowled at leaving a fight. I sucked in a deep breath and relaxed my clenched fists. What had I done to make Julien hate me enough to try to sabotage my job? I knew he disliked me—had as long as I could remember—but this was out of hand.

I turned a corner and neared the sunroom where Alyssa danced. Voices—hushed and speaking quickly—made me slow. The double door was firmly closed when I approached. I heard Jackson's harried voice.

"You lied." His words were a vehement whisper.

I thought he'd gone into his office alone, but he was definitely talking to someone. Maybe Brendan was working overtime? I crept forward, careful not to signal my presence with a creaky floorboard.

He paused, and only silence answered. He must be on the phone. "You lied to me about where it was going. If I'd known, I never would have agreed to this. How could I? We had an agreement that I would back your man for very different reasons and you played me. You degenerate SOB, you played me."

Suspicion swirled in my gut. Keeping my ear pressed against the door in an open hallway where anyone could catch me was an amateur move, but I didn't want to miss a moment of the conversation. I shifted to a different angle so I could keep one eye on the hall and the opposite ear firmly pressed to the door.

"You reneged on our deal, and you don't get to call the shots anymore. Let's clear one thing up—I don't work for you, and I never have." He paused. "You think I'll be intimidated by a two-timing, middle man pauper who's too much of a coward to do the work himself? Think again."

A pause and then a loud smacking sound as if the Jackson had hit the table. "Listen, you sick bastard, you leave my family out of this mess." His voice rose a few notches. "Do you hear me?"

I shifted my weight, and the floor creaked underneath my feet. Crap. The doorbell rang. Who on earth was calling at this time of night? Several ideas popped in my head but I strained hard to listen to the Jackson's voice. Nothing came through. Either he was talking in near whispers, or he'd hung up the phone.

Brendan's voice was loud and unchecked. "The crash was all over the news and I knew it was along the same route that you guys would have taken to get home. I had to check for myself and make sure everyone was okay."

Crap. People headed this way. If I was caught lurking in the hallway, it would only confirm Julien's suspicion. I quickly rapped on the door and twisted the know. "Jackson? It's Serena." Something crashed on the other side of the door followed by the Jackson's harsh swearing. I knocked again, more urgently. "You alright, Jackson?"

"Come in."

I walked in and my eyes cut to the lamp that now lay in pieces on the floor, shards of glass sparkled on the top of the desk.

"I, uh, was moving the desk and bumped into it. Couldn't catch it in time." He sat at his desk, both hands cradled in his lap out of sight.

"I just wanted to let you know that Dane is on shift and I'm leaving for the night."

He nodded, but it was clear from the hazy expression on his face that his mind was elsewhere. "I think we'll take a trip, get out of town to let things simmer down. I don't know how things got so out of control. Alyssa's birthday's coming up, and there's a museum in California that she's been begging me to visit. Nerdy kid." I could tell he'd tried to put both amusement and love into his voice, but tension hummed beneath the words. "I'll have Brendan work out the details. We'll leave on Wednesday."

Wednesday?

The election was six days away, and he wanted to suddenly take a family trip? That was more suspicious than a tuna sandwich from a Korean restaurant. Still, all I did was nod and walk out.

What on earth had this man gotten himself into?

A loud rap hit the door a second before it pushed open. Julien and his partner stayed in the doorway. "Mr. Jackson? It's Julien Black with the Oklahoma City Police Department and we a few questions about the incident this evening."

"Sorry to interrupt your evening, sir," Julien's partner said, "But we ID'd the men driving both cars and just needed you to confirm whether or not you knew them." Julien's voice floated around the corner and my head dropped until my forehead touched the cool wood. Was he following me around or was I projecting? He was a shadow I just couldn't escape.

I stayed long enough to listen to the Jackson give reports to officers from both the OKC and Moore police. By the time they wrapped everything up, it was time to run Alyssa to an early morning Pointe class and then jet her over to school with barely enough time to avoid a tardy. The tawny gold sun was high and bright in the sky and helped keep the wafts of sleep on the edge of my vision at bay as I beeped the locks on Blade and navigated Tuesday morning light traffic as I headed back to my apartment. Dane was finally back on duty and he called in reinforcements, an old military buddy by the name of Lang, to help cart the family around. I didn't argue. Twelve hours strong wasn't abnormal in the personal protection community but it didn't make them any less sucky.

My mind filtered back over the events of the last twenty-four hours. This level of aggression wasn't generally seen in first world countries. Especially not in America. A child was more likely to be kidnapped and sold as a sex worker than for a major political candidate and his family to be nearly run off the road and shot at. That kind of move could only be fueled by a certain level of animosity and boldness that I wasn't sure most American politicians had the stomach to act on. Unless it was personal.

So, the question was: who hated Jackson enough to try to kill him and his family?

I'd just merged onto the highway when my phone buzzed. "This is Black."

"Yo!" Leah's voice came a bit garbled over the phone but no less welcome.

"Hey, you." I glanced at the clock. "What time is it in Bangladesh? You sound like you just woke up."

She scoffed. "Trouble never sleeps on this side of the world."

"At least not your kind of trouble."

"Damn straight." She yipped. "I got that dirt on the Jackson that you asked for."

"Oh yeah?"

"Yeah, but it's not dirt per say. More like election trouble that has the potential to spill over."

My mind conjured images of ramming the car off the highway and the plume of smoke that wafted from its burning remains. It may have nothing to do with the election...but if it did, we were well out of "maybe" territory.

"Hit me."

"It's conflicting information." She said. "According to a recent opinion poll based out of D.C., he's up in the voter polls nearly twenty five percent over the incumbent, Roland Hughes. But his rating among party leaders has tanked...like, big time. He's more popular in conservative circles right now than anywhere else."

I frowned. Numbers often shifted right before major elections—last minute power plays to swing the tide—but that seemed extreme. "Why the sudden shift?"

"Major policy changes." She replied. "Jackson's initial platform was built on one specific premise—decreasing traffic checks at state borders, specifically semi-truck regulations, in order to allow for freer movement and stimulate the economy. The Dems were all for that...until his focus shifted two weeks ago. Now, he's been quoted in several newspapers and radio shows saying that he plans to push for increased regulations on truck drivers and propose investing close to eight million dollars to send more staff to state border check-in ports. The liberals are losing their minds and the conservatives are conflicted—they're torn between voting him in or sticking with Hughes."

That wasn't normal at all. Altering his platform at such a critical time could seriously impact the donations that had carried his campaign up to this point.

"Has that affected his political donations?" I asked. "I can't imagine that PAC donors were thrilled to see him switch positions out of the blue."

"Let's just say, he hasn't made any new friends. One of the unions for truck drivers that had very enthusiastically backed him at the beginning of the race just published an article on their website basically calling Jackson a fraud and scoffing at how degenerative the political system is that candidates don't even wait until they're in office before they start lying." Something loud tinkled in the background, like glass shattering, and Leah swore. "They've been the most hostile about removing their support. Everyone else seems to be quietly withdrawing."

Which meant his financials took a massive hit. But from what I could tell, Jackson wasn't sparing any expense. Four-star hotels, private jets, front page newspaper ads...he'd even funded the restoration of a local school's mascot that had been damaged in a hail storm last month. All of this money going out...it made me wonder how on earth he could afford it if his relationship with his donors was so damaged.

It certainly was fuel for hostile feelings in the PAC community but was it enough to drive someone to do something drastic?

"Are they any other major donors who might be feeling... hostile about Jackson's sudden platform change?" I asked. "Maybe an individual or organization with a history of being hotheaded or extreme in their PR responses?"

"Why do you ask?"

I briefly gave her the rundown of last night's activities. When I finished, she whistled low under her breath.

"Damn. That escalated quickly. At the moment, the only party that would have that type of response is the trucker's union. Everyone is keeping it chill as far as I can tell."

I frowned. Not sure a union would make such a risky move —that didn't have the corporate communist Russia style that it would take to do something so ballsy.

"Keep an eye out for me," I told her. "Anything that seems extreme or unstable to you, let me know. I'm going to reach out to local authorities and see if they're have been any threats toward the Jackson family. Between the kidnapping and now the car chase last night, hopefully they'll be willing to share if there's been a history of malice that can give us an idea of who might be behind it."

"I'll tell you the other strange thing," she went on. "There was practically no news coverage about the kidnapping attempt of his daughter. I'm talking next to none. Local news stations only hinted at it and the major national channels did even touch it."

I frowned. How does the kidnapping attempt of a major US political candidate's child go unnoticed? "No way something like that fell through the cracks."

"Absolutely not," she snorted. "That type of story would skyrocket a anonymous paper pusher to the top for sure. I wouldn't have skipped out on it."

"Unless you were paid to keep it quiet." I mused aloud.

"Maybe. The question is: how much moolah would you have to dish out to convince CBS, ABC, and NBC to slide it to the mush pile? We'd be talking millions of dollars...per network."

Not many people would be flush with that type of buying power. That narrows the list but doesn't explain why someone would agree to that. If I were Jackson, I'd be milking the victim-but-stalwart-defender-of-American-ideals card so hard those udders would fall off.

Something clanged in the background and reverberated across the phone that it made my speakers pulse. Leah swore. "I gotta go. Later."

The line went dead just as my apartment complex loomed in the distance. Perfect. A dull throb pounded in the middle of my skull, and the thought of bed and a few hours of sleep made my eyes water. Beastie slammed against the bars of her cage with an irritated yowl. She was pissed she hadn't gotten to play last night, and keeping her in check was almost too much right now.

I pulled into a parking spot, shut off the car, and got out. I did a quick scan, searching for trouble, before I jogged over the sidewalk and up the stairs, more to keep myself awake than anything else. punched in the code, but the noise on the other side of the door made me pause. Beastie sat upright, body tense. I strained to hear it again. Silence. Was I tired? Sure.

Tired enough to be hearing things?

That thought made me slowly draw my gun from the holster at my back. I did a swift three count and shoved open the door and rushed in, weapon high.

What I saw made my jaw drop.

A squad of women moved throughout my apartment. One lady had her back to me as she steamed dove gray curtains that lined the floor-to-ceiling windows, hips bopping up and down to the Latin music that filled the air. Another woman crouched on the far side of the kitchen and peeled blue tape from the wall that had once been an ashen white but was now a sophisticated dark emerald. Half full roller trays and discarded paint brushes littered the drop cloth at the far edge of the kitchen and my punching bag was nowhere in sight.

Elana Orsoto and her daughter, Muriel, shifted a pale grey sectional across an intricately patterned white rug and dropped it into place.

Beastie snarled. This was our sanctuary. The one place, the only place, we could be ourselves and not have to pretend. Our space had been invaded...and I couldn't agree more.

The tenor in the room shifted, and one by one they realized I was there and turned to face me, all looking shocked and caught but pleased with themselves. Until they saw the gun, then it faltered to confusion. The last made cold satisfaction flush through my system. That's right. Be afraid.

I holstered my gun—I didn't plan on shooting anyone yet —and zeroed in on the ring leader. "What the hell is going on here?" I marched to Elana and stopped in front of her. This was exactly the kind of thing that she'd been she'd head up in the blink of an eye.

She wiped away a bead of sweat and smiled at me. "Just a bit of a welcome home gift. We were hoping to be done before you got here."

"How did you get in?"

"It wasn't easy." Her rueful smile set swing a paw at the cage bars. "I talked to the landlord and explained what we wanted to do. He wasn't thrilled about letting us in, but when I told him about your dad and your recent return home, he caved and let us in himself."

I shut my eyes and sucked in even, rhythmic breaths, trying to calm my pounding heart. The pain in my head spiked.

"I got the picture!" The chirpy voice came from behind, and I spun to see another woman maneuver her way through the door with a picture that was nearly as tall as she was. It was a framed image of a desert oasis, and my mind immediately thrust back to another desert, in another time, when I'd failed my client.

Beastie's roar echoed in my ears as if from far away. I snapped.

I walked to the woman, yanked the picture from her hands, and smashed it into the ground. "Get out! Get out! Get out!" With every word I slammed the frame into the floor again and again until it was a splintered mess of glass and wood.

"Serena! Stop it! What's wrong with you?" A hand touched my shoulder, and I gripped it and wrenched it away in an arm bar. Elana sucked in a breath, eyes wide.

"Get out." The pain on her face made me pull back. My voice shook as I said, "All of you, get out!"

They all but ran as I picked the candle off the new entryway table and flung it against the wall. It shattered in an explosion of glass and fragrance.

Elena cast one final glance back at me before she gently shut the door behind her. Silence swallowed the space and seemed to echo back at me, mocking me, judging me.

Beastie paced restlessly. I took deep, slow breaths, but jitters still raced down my spine. Everywhere I looked, evidence of their invasion filled my vision—the gleaming new refrigerator, the square vase of white lilies on the counter. Beastie roared in my mind, flinging herself against the cage in outrage. I crumpled to the floor and dropped my head into my hands. I had to get this under control, but nothing was working.

I looked up, and my gaze landed on the gorgeous cello that

sat elegantly in one corner of the room, gleaming as if some-one had taken time to buff away the dust that had collected since I'd moved in. My fingers twitched. I knew how to unwind. I stood and approached it, gently gripped the finger board, pulled the black padded bench away from the wall, and sat in a sunny pool of light streaming in from the patio doors. I pulled the bow across the strings.

Deep, vibrating sound filled the silence, and Beastie paused mid step. Beautiful...even if the instrument was heinously out of tune. I took a few moments plucking the strings and twisting the pegs to get a good sound, the correct sound, before pulling the bow across the bridge and launching into the first movement of Schubert's Sonata Arpeggione and letting the sonorous, lustrous music surround me. I played, song after song, and let the music whisk away the instability and shakiness. I played from memory—sometimes the same song two or three times—until the kinks and hiccups worked themselves out. It was a hodgepodge mosaic of music—one moment Bach, the next an instrumental version of Lady Gaga—but I kept the music flowing until the cold in my stomach ceased and I was lost to the music. Pain twinged in my stiff fingers and calluses caught on the strings as I let the music flow out of me—something smooth and sonorous and visceral as the beast was finally at rest in my head.

If not for the flashing white light above my doorway, I wouldn't have known to look up. When I did and finally looked around, I could hear it —incessant pounding on my door. I stood, pain zinging down my neck and shoulders from holding them stiffly at such a strange angle for so long. The pounding continued, and I walked over to the door and peered through the peephole.

Talon stood on the other side, fist raised and beating on my door hard enough to make it vibrate on this side.

I pulled open the door.

The moment there was enough space for him to make it through, he stormed forward, braid flying out behind him, and

I scrambled back to avoid being run over. He slammed the door shut and shot me with a look sparking with anger. I could almost see lightning flashing in his silver eyes.

"You can't just barge in here and..."

He was suddenly in my space, a six-foot vibrating mass of emotion that was so close, I could see each little hair on his chin. The leather musk of his cologne swirled through my senses.

"You've got a real talent for pushing away people who are trying to do good things for you."

"They invaded my space," I shot back.

"Muriel called and asked me what would make you go off like that. Seriously, Serena. What the hell?"

"I—" Anger choked the word in my throat, and I sucked in a deep breath to calm the frost swirling in my gut. "I didn't ask them to be here."

"You know why? Because you don't have to ask good people to do good things for people they love. Trying to decorate it because they know you've been working yourself to the bone for Jackson."

I shook my head. "They crossed a line. Not okay—"

"You put my aunt's wrist in a brace."

My mouth snapped close.

"Do you even remember that? Harming a woman who has done nothing but support you and love you and cheer you on when everyone in your *real* family had given up?"

Bile rose from my stomach. I raced to the kitchen sink and emptied what was left of last night's dinner.

"You should be sick," Talon said once I finished heaving. "You *are* sick, Serena. And everyone seems to know it but you."

I rinsed out my mouth with shaky hands and didn't respond...because I knew I didn't have any room to argue.

He stepped closer, filling my space with a movement meant to be intimidating, but all it did was flood my nose with the leather musk of him. "You can work yourself down to dust for Jackson—a man who cares nothing for you other than what you can do to protect his reputation—but it's not going to erase the past or make your problems magically disappear. Sort yourself out, Serena, but don't do it while shitting on those who give a damn about you."

He ripped open the door and stormed out...at least, he tried to. He stumbled, hard. He quickly righted himself when lesser men would have face-planted on the concrete stairs.

Laughter bubbled in my throat, but I swallowed it down —Native American warlords tended not to appreciate being laughed at.

"What the—?" He spun and looked down to see what tripped him just as I spotted a pair of boxes sitting on the edge of the door mat.

My humor dimmed.

One was a FedEx box and one was a plain brown box with my name elegantly written in some fancy scroll across the top of it. The unmarked box sat on the very edge of the door, far enough to not activate the sensors but close enough that I wouldn't have been able to walk past it without noticing it. Most delivery services would have planted the box directly on the mat in the middle of the walkway—but no, this one seemed intentionally placed.

Beastie stirred in my head. It was as if someone wanted me to know that they were aware of my security and weren't intimidated by it.

Talon's voice made me look up and stare into his eyes, which swirled with the same questions mine did. It was a message, but what exactly had the sender been trying to say?

CHAPTER 10

"If you're not going to let me open it out here," Talon said, "then you should call the police."

"Calling the police will only lead to a bomb squad and robotic disarmament, and for what? A FedEx package that skipped a label. I haven't been in town long enough for someone to want to mail a bomb to my doorstep—calling the cops is definitely overkill."

"After you destroyed half of a nightclub, not to mention foiled an attempted kidnapping?" he shot back. "You've always had a knack for pissing off the wrong people. If nothing else, you should call the police to protect your neighbors."

"I don't *have* to do anything except live, die, and kiss my momma good-bye." Though knowing the ongoing dysfunction with my mother, the last item had always been optional.

"Don't be childish."

Part of the function of the censored mat was to detect any explosive or unstable elements within any package or on the person of anyone who stepped up to my door. Call me paranoid, but I'd seen one too many designer shoe boxes and jewelry cases laced with enough C-4 to take out a city block in my life to trust the scanning systems of the postal services or delivery systems or the moral integrity of the drivers. Anyone could be bought. Anyone. So the fact that the mat wasn't lit up like a Christmas tree put me at ease about the contents of the box.

You wanna know what childish really looked like? How about a grown man trying to force his help on someone who didn't ask for it or want it belligerently arguing outside as if he could bulldog his way back in. Yeah, that checked the boxes. Too bad Talon didn't feel the same. We'd passed the point of this being ridiculous fifteen minutes ago.

Talon grabbed a knife off his belt and flicked it to life and moved to step around me. The leather braided handle and gleaming blade was gorgeous. His audacity, less so.

I blocked his path. "Touch that box, and I'll skin you with that knife, Orsoto."

Talon shot me an offended glare, but his eyes sparkled. "If you manage to disarm me with me fully conscious and expecting it, then I deserve whatever your twisted little mind has in store."

Oh the things that surged through my *twisted little mind.* I opened my mouth to paint a gory picture for him, but a man's voice from down the corridor cut me short.

"Excuse me? Would you mind taking your lover's spat somewhere else, please? Some of us are trying to watch "General Hospital" without interruption."

I looked past Talon and saw the elderly man who lived on the far side of the corridor from me, Earl Robitussin, peeking out from his doorway with a glare wrinkling his face so much that it almost seemed as if his eyes had disappeared beneath bushy white eyebrows. He usually kept to himself, barely returning a wave or "Good morning", so I knew that for him to feel the need to quiet us meant we'd really been loud...that or he really resented his soaps being interrupted.

"Sorry, sir." Talon said. "We'll take our conversation inside."

Mr. Robitussin shook his head. "I feel for you, son. Women today are so headstrong they make it hard to take care of them."

"The good ones are worth the headache."

I glared at each man in turn. "The good ones are the women who can take care of themselves and don't rely on a man to help them clip their fingernails."

"Let the man carry the package inside," a woman yelled.

I looked past the steps to see two women in their sixties,

one with walnut hair that had just started graying and the other a sunflower blonde, standing at the base of the steps with two small leashed dogs eagerly sniffing around them.

"If I had a man who looked like that, he wouldn't need to fight his way into my apartment," the blonde chimed. "I'd lock him in it."

Talon chuckled, low and deep, a sound that vibrated in the pit of my stomach.

When had this turned into group discussion? I glanced at the balcony rail. It looked to be about fifty or so feet to the ground. If I flung myself off just right, I could sprint to the car and escape this madness before anyone could stop me.

Talon must have seen the desperation in my eyes because he stepped around me, grabbed both boxes, and walked inside my apartment before I could protest. I shot a glare at the ladies and over my shoulder at Mr. Robitussin, who was turning back into his apartment muttering about difficult women, and followed Talon inside.

He placed the boxes on the countertop.

"I figure since neither exploded when I picked it up, that we're in the clear." He flicked out his knife and sliced into the FedEx box without invitation or permission.

I seriously considered grabbing the knife that was lodged between the coat rack and the wall and throwing it at him. Nothing fatal. Just nail his hand to the marble or something. I took a deep breath, counted backward from one hundred in Mandarin, and approached as he carefully shimmied the knife down the center of the box, cleanly cutting the tape away. He gently pried apart the cardboard lids and peered inside. I came up beside him and peered inside as well.

An intricately carved black mahogany box was nestled inside. A swirly white emblem was branded onto its top box, and I instantly recognized it as a bottle of vintage Macallan whiskey, a nearly seventy-five grand liquor.

I reached into the box to lift it out, but Talon placed a staying hand on wrist.

"I probably should check it to make sure it isn't armed."

He was right. I removed my hand so he could run the edge of his knife along the underside of the lid. When he was satisfied there weren't any triggers, he stepped away.

I lifted the wooden top. Inside, an etched-glass decanter filled with amber liquid nested inside an emerald velvet interior. I pulled it carefully out of the box and pulled the cork. The familiar, woodsy scent of whiskey siphoned up my nose.

A small white card lay nestled in the forest green paper and I pulled it out and read it.

Miss Black,

The behavior of my associates last weekend was abominable. Please accept this bottle from my private collection. May this atone for any mistreatment and prevent any ill will from festering.

Yours,

Slade

My blood froze.

Slade, otherwise known as Nicholas Stone. In most circles, the name probably wouldn't even resonate, but every cop's household between Santa Fe and Baton Rouge was intimately familiar with the most infamous drug lord in the region.

And he was sending me apology gifts.

Shit.

Half a dozen reasons for the gift blitzed through my mind. He could be trying to make amends with the daughter of one of the cops who'd dedicated his entire career to bringing him down. Avoid shaking the boat and risking dozens of local cops descending upon every known operation. Or it could be something else. The fact that he knew I loved whiskey told me he'd done his homework. And that was more unsettling than the gift itself.

"Been making friends, huh?" Talon read the note over my shoulder, his tone bland.

"Not on purpose." I replaced the stopper and nestled the

decanter back in the box. "Not when my current *friends* are so helpful."

He leaned a hip against the counter and crossed his arms, studying me. "You gonna send it back?"

"You gonna stop treating me as if I'm a green -eared novice and let me handle it?"

He quirked an eyebrow but lifted his hands in a gesture that could either mean I'm-sorry-you're-right or placate-the-crazy-lady. The smile ghosting his lips made me think it was the latter.

I had several options. I didn't have firsthand experience with Slade, so I couldn't speak to whether he was the sort of man to get offended. But I knew one thing for sure—keeping gifts from drug lords rarely did dazzling things for one's reputation. Especially in this town, where nearly a third of the force had dedicated their lives to taking down this guy, and he still roamed at large. It was a slap in the face to all the work and sleepless nights and dead leads Dad had suffered trying to bring the man to justice.

I couldn't accept a peace offering from the enemy. Plus, Julien would never let me live it down.

That thought sealed the deal. It could rot inside the bowels of the post office for all I cared. The sooner it was out of my house, the easier I'd be able to breathe. But the box was blank and left me no return address or way to track who it came from. I glanced at the fancy white brand and a thought struck me.

"Look up the company and see how big it is. If it's a smaller operation, we might be able to call and get reverse tracking information or something."

He smirked at me. "Would a please kill you?"

"It might." I reached for the second box. This one had a FedEx, label and when I saw the name messily scribbled into the address field, a smile tugged at my lips.

I tore into the box and pulled out an index card with messy handwriting scratched across it.

Saw these damned things and thought of you.

XO

Leah

Short, terse, to the point. Definitely Leah.

Excitement gurgled in my stomach as I reached into the box. My hand connected with something soft and plastic, and I wiggled my fingers around until I grabbed hold of it. I pulled out a mass of bubble wrap and quickly unwrapped it. In the palm of my hand lay an exquisite blue-and-white ceramic shot glass. I turned it upside down to look at the description and nearly screamed. It was him, Theodor Van Burren, my favorite antique designer.

I pulled out the rest of the tightly wrapped bundles, and each revealed the same thing—a tiny blue-and-white ceramic shot glass. Four in total. I titled up the box, and a small card with information about the pieces fell into my palm. These were Russian shot glasses, estimated to date back to the seventeenth century.

A smile played at the corner of my lips. Leah was crazier than a road lizard, but she knew me so well.

I gathered one in each hand and walked across the room to the large antique glass hutch in my kitchen. I had two nearly full shelves lined with antique shot glasses from across the ages. From tarnished silver to gleaming ceramic, the collection had started when I was stationed in Morocco. Later, get a place card holder but that would do for now. Now, I wished I had some good quality liquor to pound in honor of my new present. I already knew that my fridge and cabinets boasted no such thing.

Talon's serious expression vaporized any momentary happiness I experienced from the shot glasses.

"You need to get help," he said. "Seriously. See a counselor, a therapist, a homeless man with good listening skills. You're a danger to those you love until you do." With that, he turned on his heel and stomped out of the building.

Leaving me with the satisfied purr of Beastie in my mind and a heart at war. Was he right?

CHAPTER 11

I stared at the door in front of me and clenched my fists. Beastie clawed in my mind, unhappy with the urge that had me out of my apartment and subjecting myself to the elements of a chilly November evening. But the light tremors flowing through my core had nothing to do with the chilly wind and the crystalized breath that hovered in front of my nose.

I was such a coward.

It was deeper than that though. My vision blurred as pain pounded in my head. But I knew I had to do this.

My hand shook as I raised my fist and knocked on the door that reverberated through my knuckles, down my forearm, and straight into the pounding in my chest. "Miss Soto?"

Silence.

Her car was parked in its usual spot, but I wouldn't be surprised if she weren't home.

Talon's face flickered through my mind, but it wasn't the anger etched into his jaw that shook me, it was the disappointment lingering in his eyes. Those eyes that were so beautiful and expressive they should be illegal. I hated that his look gutted me, but it did, and I wasn't interested in figuring out why.

I knocked the second time. "It's me, Serena...I, uh...wanted to come check on your wrist." I licked my lips, and cool air wafted across them. "I don't...I-I didn't...I haven't been myself. I have a problem, and it's getting worse. I can't control it." I laid my hand and my forehead against the door, and the words poured from my lips. "Something happened on my last mission with Homeland, something I couldn't control or foresee.

I was betrayed, and people died. My team. Our guide. My client was a twelve-year-old girl. She loved soccer. She reminded me a lot of Julien. They shot her in front of me. And it broke some-thing...something I don't know how to fix. Something I don't think can be fixed. And it's why I hurt you today, and that's not something I would have ever done in my right mind." The words clogged in my throat on a sob.

The door opened, and, finally, Miss Soto stood on the other side, cascaded in a warm glow of light. She stared up at me with kind, welcoming eyes, and it crumbled something inside of me. My knees buckled under the emotion, and I fell to my knees in front of her, gently wrapping my arms around her waist and burying my face in her stomach. I trembled as I fought the tears spilling down my face.

She pressed her lips to the top of my head. "I don't know how to help you," she murmured against my braids. "All I can do is give you the only advice I have when I'm lost or confused. You need to pray."

I jerked against her but forced down the movement for fear of hurting her more. But she couldn't be serious, right?

"After my brother killed himself," she continued, "I was in a dark place. I'd just lost my husband, and I still hadn't re-covered when Michael couldn't handle the pressure of being back in civilian life. Later, my counselor would label it extreme emotional PTSD. At the time, I only knew it as living hell. The only thing that kept me afloat was taking care of Talon and his sisters and praying, sometimes hourly, that God would remove the dark thoughts from my brain."

I stiffened and started to pull away but she wrapped her arms tighter around my shoulders. I didn't want to hurt her so I stayed put.

"I know it sounds simple, too good to be true. But what do you have to lose? Pray for Him to still those thoughts that make your mind race and to calm any spirit of instability that prowls our minds like a beast in dark times."

Her description made my stomach drop. There was no way

she could know…how could she? My knees hurt, and I was already late to leave. I gave her waist another squeeze and stood.

"Thank you," I said as I reached down and picked up my duffel. "Sorry to bother you this late at night."

Her smile was warm. "I've always seen you as a bonus daughter, Serena, and that comes with all the privileges. Knock anytime." She looked at me with a mother's shrewd eyes. "And at least think about what I said."

Praying wasn't really my style. "I don't know how much I believe in God. At least, not in my own life."

"Don't focus on that too much. He believes in you."

Her words caused a small jolt through me. I forced a smile, bent, and laid a soft kiss on her cheek that made her skin crinkle with a smile.

With a final glance, I turned and jogged down the steps to my car.

CHAPTER 12

Herding a gaggle of chimpanzees would have been easier than trying to get Alyssa and Logan onto the plane without squabbling. They argued with each other all the way from the house to airport but Jackson seemed oblivious to the noise. I wasn't so immune. By the time we drove onto the tarmac of Wiley Post airport, I was ready to rip out my braids one at a time.

"Help me out little man," I said, pulling open the car truck and tossing him a bag light enough for his nine-year-old body to catch.

"How come 'Lyssa doesn't have to work?" He grumbled, struggling to get a hold of it. "Everyone always picks on me for everything."

"It's cause you're special."

"I'm not dumb. Special people aren't made to *this* work hard."

I smiled. "Maybe you have a point."

He grabbed a small backpack and trudged up the steps into the heart of the private jet and I followed him. Out of the corner of my eye, I saw Brendan pull his phone out of his pocket and raise it to his ear. Whatever was said on the other line made pale and turn on his heel to walk back toward the waiting room building.

Dane helped me unload the rest of the luggage and Lang, Dane's friend who was acting as our extra security, helped him load it into the plane per the pilot's instruction. Jackson went over some last minute details with the staff staying in the city off to one side. I took it as a good opportunity to run Alyssa and Logan through some basic, vigorous calisthenics to help them burn energy. One hundred jumping jacks and thirty pushups later, I hustled the sweaty kids up the walkway, hoping it was enough to temporarily wear them out.

As we found our seats, I noticed a certain redhead's absence from the group. "Did Brendan forget something?" I strained to see through the window and see if I could see him on the tarmac. Only he would be able to get left behind with such a small flying party.

I stopped straining to see him on the tarmac when the Jackson answered. "Brendan's uncle was put in the hospital last night and apparently things are bad. Apparently it was an anomalous stroke and he's in surgery right now. Since he's the only close relative, he's staying behind."

"I hope that won't put you off your game for the interview," I said.

"We'll be in contact, email and texts make it easy to keep the pace," Jackson replied. "Worse comes to worst, he can email me my talking points. There's plenty of time to go over everything."

The plane engine whirred to life and drowned out further conversation.

I was too much of a control freak to relax during a plane ride. Something about levitating thousands of feet in the air with the naive prayer that whoever was driving the metal container wasn't sleep deprived or doped up on some substance just to keep them awake never really set right with me. It certainly didn't help that the private jet had been offered by one of the Jackson's constituents, and I had no idea who was flying and what his credentials were, despite the fact that Lang stepped in as co-pilot.

Beastie yowled, jittery and jonesing for a fight. Definitely not helpful in a pressurized flying Coke can. Which was why I had my ear pods tucked into my ears and let the sonorous refrains of a haunting cello solo resonate in my mind. But even

Schubert couldn't block out the nasty bickering of two bored children. I bit back a sigh. Freefalling through the clouds would have been more pleasant than listening to Alyssa and Logan lob insults at each other for the past two hours.

"You're a loser." Alyssa whipped around in her seat to snarl at her brother.

"I'd rather be a loser than ugly," Logan muttered. His replies were always soft and under the breath, yet his sister never missed a syllable.

She shot back an acerbic reply.

Their fighting was ridiculous, beyond ridiculous. I could feel a sharp chastisement welling in my throat, especially when Alyssa's insult made Logan fall back into his seat in a huff. From where I sat, I could see the quiver in his lip. Sharp words welled in my throat, but I swallowed them down. Reproaching a client's children was the quickest way to end up on the wrong end of someone's crap list. People tended not to appreciate the rebuke of their kids from their own parents, much less someone they considered hired muscle. And that mentality was magnified a hundred times worse for the elite of society. I glanced at Jackson, who was in the back of the plane with a portable desk over his lap scattered with papers. A public relations assistant sat beside him giving him the rundown on the latest criticisms from the newest opinion poll.

Too bad I didn't feel the same. I shot Dane a glance. He smirked at the look on my face and shrugged massive shoulders as if to say, *What can you do?* My mind filtered through several ideas before landing on the best one that wouldn't upset the parent's apple cart. Over the years, I'd learned to be more subtle in my approach.

"You're a frog-faced little—"

"Hey, Logan." I interrupted Alyssa's barb and shot her a reprimanding glance. "You want to come and review the security details with me. I've got maps." I held up the black three-ring binder where I'd compiled my notes and dangled the carrot shamelessly.

"Really?" His eyes lit up, and he scrambled across the narrow aisle to plop down into the seat next to me. "Are you sure this isn't classified or something? Do I need to take an oath of secrecy?"

I didn't fight the smile that pulled at my lips. "Nope, no oaths necessary." I selected a random tab and flipped the binder open.

"Is this an actual blueprint?" he asked, eager eyes scanning the page.

"Unfortunately, no. Most blueprints are copyrighted and, if the original designer doesn't give written permission, then we can't use it. But most people are willing to give security a close copy. Unless we're planning to use hidden tunnels or passages, most blueprints have more information than we need."

"Like the White House?"

I looked at him, impressed. "Just like those. I had a client in Bali, India, and there were hidden passageways interconnected throughout her entire house just in case bad men tried to surprise them."

"That would be so cool," Logan's voice was dreamy. "So, what are these prints?" He pointed at the page.

"This is the layout of the museum." I ran my finger down the page, pointing. "This is the main entrance, and these spiral looking things are stairs."

"Can I hold it?"

"Only if you promise not to leave this seat with it." It was a small plane, and I had a backup copy stored on my tablet, but I didn't want to be worried about sensitive information floating out there. Seemed stuff like that always ended up in the wrong hands.

He nodded, golden brown curls flopping on his head.

I hid my smile and transferred the notebook to his lap. He pulled it upright like a book and buried his face in it, nose scrunched as he studied the pages.

Land couldn't come soon enough.

We landed at a private airstrip just south of LAX an hour

later. Unloading suitcases and lugging carry-on bags gave the kids plenty to do with their abundance of energy and gave the rest of us a respite from their energetic dialogue. Small mercies. As the family piled into one of two Cadillac SUVs with blacked out windows, the men and I deliberated for several minutes before we decided that I'd drive the family in the main car and they'd trail us in the second SUV, which would be used to transport the kids to and from the museum camp. It took another hour to drive to the hotel—a thirty-story, four-tar affair just outside of San Francisco that was only twenty minutes from the TV studio where the Jackson had an interview Thursday night.

Jackson insisted on a far smaller security team that I was comfortable with. Dane would guard Logan, I would guard Alyssa, and our third man, Lang, would act as chauffeur for the Jackson and his wife and our backup if we needed it. Otherwise the Jackson was relying on local personnel and police escorts to protect him during his rallies. It was foolish, and I was surprised Dane hadn't argued more forcefully for extra security.

Logan and I settled on the couch in the main living area and I skimmed a magazine as he flipped through the various channels.

"Do you like the Avengers?" he asked, fiddling with bulky remote in his small hands.

"Do fish breathe underwater?" I teased. "If you don't then we can't be friends."

He shot me toothy grin. "Falcon's my hero. I want to be just like him—a veteran and superhero."

Wasn't a bad choice if you asked me.

"What about you? Which avenger would you be?"

I thought about it for a moment. "Probably Hawkeye." The door to Alyssa's room swung open and she marched out with something dangling from her left hand. It was a doll...a doll missing its legs. Crap. Not again.

"I can see that. You're both people of few words but you get the job done." Logan nodded, oblivious to the tempest of anger marching toward him with eyes locked on him. "Did you know that in the comics Clint Barton was actually introduced as a villain but changed his tune when Captain America—"

"Alyssa, don't." I said sharply.

She ignored me and swung the doll like an underhanded softball pitch. I reached out and caught the doll by the dress but the head still had enough momentum to slam into the side of Logan's face.

"I told you stay away from my dolls." She screamed, wrenching the doll against my grip, trying to free it for no doubt another strike.

I jerked the doll, hard enough that she lost balance and fell forward. I grabbed her thin wrist and did a light nerve hold. Her hand spasmed and she let the doll go. She launched herself at him, pounding her fists to the top of his head as he curled into a ball on the couch with his arms over his head.

"I hate you!" she screamed.

Over it, Logan yelled. "I didn't do it. It wasn't me!"

I grabbed Alyssa around the waist and hauled her off him.

"What on earth?" Jackson rushed out of his room and stared at his children. He took one look at the blood on the jagged doll leg and grabbed Alyssa by the arm and marched her out of the room.

I got up and went to the first aid kit that we set on the counter for easy access. Pulling out a bandage, alcohol, and cotton swab, I went and sat on the couch next to him.

"This is going to sting, little man," I murmured as I dabbed the cotton ball over his cut. It was long or deep, just a shallow cut that ran the length of his cheek. "If you did touch her doll, even accidentally, now's a good time to let me know."

His eyes flashed hurt. "I didn't do it." He yelled.

"I believe you, bud." I soothed. "Maybe now's a good time to go to bed, yeah?"

He nodded and slid off the couch and headed to his room

It surprised me but I did actually—he just didn't seem like the type to arbitrarily break things. He was too gentle for that.

Maybe Alyssa played rougher with her dolls and they broke from wear and tear. Valid but unlikely. Her performance tonight spoke to genuine hurt and anger. She was a dancer, not an actor.

The muscles in my neck hadn't relaxed since we'd left Oklahoma, and Beastie restlessly paced in my head. Tension shimmered in the air. Perhaps I was reading into things, but I learned long ago not to ignore that sixth sense that made the hair on my arms stand up. The election was only four days away, and I knew better than to expect trouble to stay away that long. I couldn't put my finger on it, but trouble like that tended to make itself known before too long.

I'd be ready when it did.

CHAPTER 13

Alyssa and Logan were up early the next morning, ready to get on the road for the museum, which was an hour away. They insisted that they could eat breakfast bars in the SUV, but I herded them downstairs to the parking garage while Dane swung by the complimentary breakfast buffet to grab something quick. He came back with a bag full of fresh blueberry muffins for everyone, to-go pouches of orange juice for the kids, and cups of black coffee for him and myself. It was my turn to drive, and I pulled onto US-101 N highway toward San Jose.

The Youth Action Climate Summit was a massive global technology conference hosted by The Tech Interactive Museum specifically for middle and high school students. It was a chance for students to hear from the top scientist, climatists, and legislators on the issues of climate change and give the students an opportunity to craft a science-based response to the issue. Apparently, it was popular because tickets seemed to sell out within days of opening registration. It was a four day camp that ran Monday through Thursday with a massive presentation and award ceremony on Thursday night.

Beastie was over it by day three.

Twelve hours of constant standing, going from painfully bright lobbies to dungeon auditoriums, surrounded by high energy middle school students with a propensity for shouting, squealing, dashing all over the place. It wasn't my idea of fun by any means, and she agreed. Too much noise. Too many unguarded exits where a threat could easily slip in and be lost in the chaotic sea of children. Too many unknown faces. I'd memorized the face and name of each museum staff member and camp volunteer logged into the system but that didn't account for hovering parents or parties of dignitaries that were given private tours despite the camp going on. There were several moments during the week when I thought I'd actually lose it —swipe at a child who brushed too close or scream until the noise ratcheted down. A pounding headache developed in my left temple and blasts of light pulsed in my vision.

This morning, I'd tried several different ways to secure my braids away from my face without pissing off my skull. Each time I started to pull my hair back, the pain would flare. Damn it all. The kids had been in an extra hurry to leave this morning, so I'd ended up with all the weave secured in a loose ponytail at the base of my head. Yet, by the time we walked into the museum, the ponytail holder had slipped halfway down my braids, and I ended up yanking it out and letting the mass flow freely.

The headache I'd been nursing for three days finally seemed to subside. Perfect timing. The urge to grab the nearest squealing tween and squeeze until all the noise and tomfoolery drained away continued to grow with every throbbing pulse in my scalp. Strangling children wasn't good public relations but it'd be effective.

That wasn't a guarantee though. Kids were resilient little snots.

The group of two hundred and twenty-six kids—this I knew to be an accurate number because I'd hacked into the museum database and pulled pictures of the all the kids registered to attend and then cross checked them with the program's list of names the first day—settled into the main auditorium by midday. It was the final day, and the program directors were determined to cram as much as possible into the last few hours. By eleven, the group had already FaceTimed NASA scientists and ecologists working to restore the rainforests in Brazil. Now, they were listening to a panel of national climatists explain the effects of the changing lunar cycle on weather patterns.

Personally, I thought it was a snooze fest. But these kids leaned forward, eyes bright as they absorbed all the information pouring off the stage. Their energy and intelligence made me smile.

It was nice to have all the students sequestered in one place instead of constantly flowing all around me all the time (two hundred moving missiles of mayhem). The seating sloped down towards the stage, coliseum style, which made it easy to scan the back of their heads as they scribbled notes. I sat in the last row, the highest point in the room. A few of the adult staff and volunteers, as well as a handful of clingy parents, congregated at the back as well, some lingering towards the doors so they could quietly converse. Alyssa sat in the fourth row on an aisle seat—good girl—several rows off to the left.

I kept myself at an angle from her in an attempt to be able to see her face at all times. They'd brought down the lights for the presentation, but not so much that it was a problem. Kids were no good at controlling their facial expression and body language, so I'd know if she picked up on anything amiss.

Which was why, when she abruptly jerked to her feet and practically ran up the stairs, I noticed immediately. I rose and moved across the row to intercept her. My eyes flicked to Dane, who mirrored my position exactly except that he was on the far side of the room—where Logan perched on the front row with his new "best smart friends," as he called them. He leaned against one of the pillars, arms crossed in a way that managed to be neither threatening nor bored. Simply ready.

I paused in the shadows of the only entrance into the room. Alyssa reached the top of the stairs and powered forward. I waited until she was close before stepping into her path. I timed it to where she'd either have to ram into me or stop. She skidded to a halt, glaring.

"Move, Serena," she whispered.

"Going somewhere?"

She shuffled her feet. "The bathroom." Anxiety twisted her

features. She looked both furious and ready to cry. Both of those emotions had yet to make an appearance this trip, so I knew something wasn't right. "What's wrong?"

"None of your business."

We'd played this game before. She could either tell me or we'd stand in the middle of the doorway looking interesting until she told me whatever was causing her to shuffle her feet, doing the pee dance in place.

She caved. "I'm bleeding, okay?" It was said barely above a whisper, still full of anger.

I flipped to high alert instantly. What was she talking about? "Where?" I did a quick body scan, but there were no obvious injuries.

"Just let me go to the bathroom."

The pee dance, face tinged with desperation...more hormonal than usual... A thought dawned on me.

"Have you started your period?" I asked in a normal tone. Clearly not normal enough.

"Shhhh!" Wide blue eyes frantically looked around to make sure no one heard before piercing me with an angry stare. "Say it for the world to hear, why don't you?" She was angry, but tears welled in her eyes.

"I've got what you need. Let's go." I stepped aside. and she bolted past. As we moved towards the door, a brown-haired lady with a massive purse standing near the door waved at me.

"Do you need—?" Apparently she'd heard.

"Yes." I cut her off, not wanting to humiliate Alyssa any more.

The woman pulled a tampon from her bag and held it out to me.

I snatched it as we walked past and shoved it into my pocket. "Thanks," I called over my shoulder. I actually already had a couple of tampons stuffed into the inside pocket of my jacket but knew Alyssa would explode if I prolonged the conversation.

We burst through the double doors and stepped into the

sun-drenched lobby. Because the auditorium was on the third floor, the full effect of the clear kaleidoscope dome flooded the area with heat and light. I moved Alyssa towards the bathrooms on the north side of the auditorium, weaving among the museum visitors who meandered about. When we got there, both the ladies' and men's restrooms had lines at least ten people deep. We didn't have time to wait that long.

"Let's try the restrooms on the other side." I led her in the opposite direction. I don't know how long she'd been bleeding before she'd decided to get up, and I already knew we treaded dangerous, panty-staining ground. But when we reached the other restroom, it was closed for maintenance.

Tears glistened in Alyssa's eyes.

I glanced at the door to the men's restroom and seriously thought about clearing it out so we could take care of this. The neon green shirt of a staff member danced in the corner of my eye and I called out. "Excuse me, ma'am."

The lady turned, looking up from her phone with a pleasant smile. "Yes?"

"We've got a bit of an emergency, and we need an open bathroom, stat."

"What kind of emergency?" Instant concern.

I glanced at Alyssa, trying to find a delicate way to say it. "Lady problems."

"I see." She began walking. "There are staff bathrooms on the second floor on the far side of the hallway. If you use the employee stairs, you'll exit right in front of it." She unclipped the plastic badge from her belt and handed it to me. She used the large map to show me where we were and how to get to the staircase.

"Thank you so much." We took off at a jog. "See? God does send angels."

Alyssa only said, "Whatever."

We made it to the door, and I pressed the badge to the scan pad. It flashed green, I wrenched the door open, and we flew down the single flight of stairs. I shoved open the door and we burst into the hall. This hall was empty, it being on the back side of the museum, and dimmer than the rest. Alyssa spotted the bathroom and took off, me close behind. A cleaning lady exited as we neared.

"Hold the door!" I yelled.

The lady started violently and looked up, surprised. Still she held the door as we dashed past and poured into the restrooms like frantic runaways. The marble floor gleamed from the fresh kiss of a mop as Alyssa sprinted to the handicap stall and slammed the metal door with a bang.

"Here." I held the tampon over the top of the stall door.

She snatched it away.

"Do you need help with that?"

"No!" she called out, disgusted. "They showed us how to do it in school. I can figure it out."

School? What business a private school had teaching girls to put in tampons I couldn't imagine. What happened to moms teaching their daughters that sort of thing?

I smiled at the cleaning lady, whose cart still propped open the door. "Sorry about that. She started her period today."

"Serena!" Alyssa called, voice shrill with horror.

The twenty-something cleaning lady smiled warmly but shook her head. "No English." she said, Spanish accent thick.

"That's okay," I replied in Spanish. "We'll be a few moments, and then we'll get out of your hair."

The young woman smiled and nodded and she exited.

A few minutes passed.

"You good, Alyssa?"

"Yeah."

The door creaked open, and a blonde who resembled Cate Blanchet walked in, staff badge swinging around her neck. She paused, clearly surprised to see me standing there. I wasn't wearing one of the obnoxiously cheerful neon staff shirts. In fact, I was in the exact opposite, black on black. Still, she only eyed me through the mirror as she walked and entered the stall next to Alyssa's.

The restroom door opened once more, and the cleaning lady struggled to push her cart through the narrow opening. Hadn't she just been there?

The hair on my arms stood up. I looked her over for weapons. None that I could see. This was a different woman altogether, taller with hair dyed dark burgundy.

Something was off.

A door creaked open, and I flicked my gaze to the mirror to see the Cate-wanna-be approaching the counter. Something banged, shut and I flicked my gaze to see that the cleaning lady had pulled the cart fully into the bathroom and angled it against the door.

We were trapped.

The air shifted behind me, and I flung myself to the left. Something glinted in the mirror and stabbed the marble counter in front of me. A dagger.

I kicked out behind me, forcing her to step back to avoid it.

The cleaning lady drew a wicked looking needle from the belt on her skirt. She lifted the needle over her head and flung herself at me.

I braced to deflect Red's attack, and Cate took the chance to drive a fist into my stomach. Pain sizzled in my ribs. I caught both of Red's hands in mine just as Cate hit me again. I stumbled to the side, taking Red with me, and we crashed into the doorjamb of the one the stalls. It rattled like a maraca.

"Geez, I'm coming," Alyssa groused. "It's not easy putting one of these things in."

Cate launched herself at me. but I kicked her away.

Red was stronger than she looked, and I struggled to control her hands. I had no idea what the needle was laced with and had no intention of finding out. I jerked Red close and drove my knee into her stomach. Her grip weakened slightly.

I slammed her hands against the doorjamb, and the empty stall rattled. Once. Twice.

An arm wrapped around my throat and jerked me backwards. I barely kept hold of Red's hands, and we all three stumbled to the left, crashing inside a stall.

"What are you doing out there?" Alyssa called.

I aimed a kick at Red's knee, and she slipped to one side dodge it. I viciously bit into Cate's arm, hard enough to draw blood, and she screamed, grip around my throat loosening.

"Stay in the stall, Alyssa!"

Cate's arm cinched around my throat tighter, and gray spots dotted my vision.

Red drove her knee into my ribs, sending pain rippling through my torso. I had no idea who these women were or what they wanted. Assassins? Kidnappers? It didn't matter. Beastie roared with fury, but I knew if I let her reign free, corpses would follow. I struggled against the darkening spots in my vision.

Red noticed my waning strength and pressed harder. The needle slowly inched closer to my jugular.

A gasp tore my attention to the mirror. In the reflection, I saw Alyssa standing just inside the stall, face white with shock. She looked like a little girl, unsure as fear clouded her eyes.

When Red turned to stare at Alyssa, the mirror reflected the look on her face, grim satisfaction. I realized at that moment who the true target was—not me, Alyssa.

Time slowed and music surged in my mind, and with the crashing crescendo came Beastie. A ferocious snarl left my lips as energy surged through me.

I slammed my left foot into Cate's shins. She groaned, and the death cinch on my neck loosened enough for me to suck in a full breath. With Red's hands gripped firmly in my own, I slammed blow after blow into Cate's ribs. Red tried jerking away from me. Bad idea. My left leg slammed into the inside of her thigh and she screamed, clutching her leg.

The move put me off balance, and Cate and I crashed into the stall wall. I ignored her for a moment. My foot flashed out again, catching Red across the chin, and she flew to one side. With space freed up, I stepped as far left as the space allowed and bent sharply and suddenly at the waist, forcing Cate to bend with me. My head slipped through the cage of her arms. I stood upright and drove my foot into the back of her knee. She went down to one knee ,and I slammed her head into the marble commode. Twice.

Red gathered herself and lunged, syringe in hand. I kicked the knee of her front leg, forcing the bone to pop with an ominously thick noise. As she screamed, I punched her in the throat, cutting off the noise with a sickening gurgle. I kicked the syringe from her hand as she slid to one side.

A small squeak leapt from Alyssa's throat as the woman slid to the floor before her, unconscious. Breathing hard, my gaze darted between the two women for a moment before I sprang into action. There could be half a dozen more on the other side of that door—hell, throughout the building, and we wouldn't be able to identify any of them. Shit.

"Wh-who were they, and why did you just wipe the floor with them the way regular people wipe peanut butter off a knife?"

My gaze darted to Alyssa, and whatever she saw in my face caused her twelve-year-old preservation instincts to chime. She clamped her mouth closed. Wise choice. I silently moved the cleaning cart far out of the way of the door.

"What are you doing?"

I sighed. Apparently those instincts didn't last very long.

I pushed on the door until it gave way slightly. I glanced into the corridor. Nothing. I debated whether we should stay here and ask Dane to come and get us or risk a mad dash through the lobby to the car. I scanned for another thirty seconds, watching the empty hall.

I turned back to Alyssa. "Wash and dry your hands and then give me a fresh paper towel." I squatted beside Red's unconscious form. The needle was lying on the floor beside her hand I rustled through her clothes, looking for any sign of identity. Of course, there was none.

"What are you doing?" Alyssa held out the paper towel. I snatched it and gently, careful not to touch it, picked up the needle. I rolled it fully in the paper towel and stuffed it in one of the inside pockets of my jacket.

"Can you run?"

"What did those people want?"

Great question. Questions were for later. "Are you good to run?"

She nodded.

I pressed the small button on the mic in my ear to activate it. "Ground hog." Our code word for "emergency" to get his attention.

"What's wrong?"

"Alyssa and I were attacked in the ladies' restroom across from the staff lounge. Two women. Both professionals. Alyssa was the target. We're on our way out of the building to the car."

He swore, and I heard a commotion over the phone. "Logan and I are on the move. We'll meet you there."

"Stay sharp."

"Got it." The line went dead.

"What about Logan?" Alyssa asked.

"Logan is with Dane, who will protect him with his life. He is completely safe. You and I, on the other hand, are not. I grabbed her arm and pulled her to the door. With my gun drawn and held against my leg, I said, "On the count of three. You run in front of me to my right. If I yell "duck," you hit the floor. Got it?"

She gave a jerky nod.

"One. Two. Three." I flung open the door and waited for her to dash through before I ran after her, scanning several yards ahead of us. Running with my gun out probably wasn't the most P.R.-friendly move, but once we were safely out of the building, most people wouldn't even notice, and by the time they did we would be gone.

As Alyssa and I sprinted through the building, I yelled into my phone, "Lang, we need car support at the south entrance now!"

"I'll be there."

Two people full out sprinting through a museum were bound to get some attention. A security guard and two staff members were gathered near one of the main check-in booths. We were two hundred feet from the main entrance when one of the guards noticed us. He stepped into our path, and I could tell by his body language that he didn't intend for us to get by him. Alyssa faltered and slowed.

"Don't stop." I dashed in front of her.

"Ma'am, why are running?"

Beastie snarled at him. I used my momentum as force and his forward step as motion. I grabbed the hand he extended and pivoted, rolling him over my back. Someone cried out, but we kept moving. We were through the glass doors before he hit the tile.

I'd send him apology flowers later.

Alyssa and I poured through the back entrance into San Jose's sweltering midday heat just as one of the blacked-out SUV's skidded to a halt in front of us. Excellent timing. I wrenched the door open for Alyssa, and she scrambled inside. I flung myself in after her.

I dove over the console into the passenger seat. "What were you doing, Lang, getting coffee for the building?" I asked, irritated. But the words died in my throat. That tends to happen when you're staring down the barrel of a handgun with a silencer on it.

"Not another word," Lang said calmly.

I looked past the gun to stare at him. His eyes were ice cold and determined. Dread slammed into my stomach. We'd been sold out.

"Serena?" Alyssa was sucking breath after our sprint.

"Shut up, kid," Lang snapped. "Sit down and you won't get hurt." Lang snarled but his eyes never left mine. "Gun?"

"Whatever is happening here, Lang, know that there's no coming back from this."

"Gun." Voice hard.

I slowly reached back and pulled the gun from my waist and

held it dangling in front of me.

"Drop it out the window."

The window behind me slid down as he pressed the button on his door. I tossed my gun outside.

"Where's Dane?" he asked, rolling the window back up.

I was tempted not to answer him. But I could see Alyssa out of the corner of my eye and didn't want her to get hurt if he decided to get violent. "He told me he was right behind me. Two minutes."

"With the kid?"

I nodded. "Lang, whatever is going on here, whoever's making you do this, we can figure this out."

He scoffed. "No one's *making* me do this. No one except a very large check and early retirement. Sounds good, don't it?"

"Traitors tend not to enjoy retirement for very long."

"They'll have to find me first." Something moved through the building doors and I could see Dane running our way with Logan tucked under his arm. Whatever was happening here, I absolutely knew that Dane and I would end up dead if Lang got ahold of both kids.

I lunged forward and used my elbow to block and drive his gun hand into the side of the seat. I slammed my palm into his neck. I grabbed the back of his neck and smashed his face into the steering wheel. The gun clattered to the floor.

"Alyssa down."

Lang's hand came up and slammed my head into the front console. I raised a hand to block it, but stars still exploded in my vision. I snatched the tactical blade from the holster on my hip and swiped at his wrist. He screamed in pain.

The split second was all I needed. I drove the blade into the small notch in his throat.

He gurgled. A hand came up as he twitched. The breath left his body, and he was still.

"Stay down," I told Alyssa, not wanting her to look. I was breathing hard as I shoved open my door and ran around the other side of the car.

The doors to the building glinted as Dane charged through carrying Logan under one arm.

"I'm driving." I told him as I pulled open the driver's door. Lang's body tumbled out.

Logan gasped.

"What the hell?" Dane ripped open the passenger door and all but threw the boy inside.

"He pulled a gun, and I had to act." I grunted as I pulled the body away so it cleared the car.

Dane took it in stride. "We can't just leave a body."

I sat in the driver's seat and grabbed the door handle. "His isn't the only one. You coming?"

Dane shot me a look that I couldn't quite decipher, but there wasn't time to evaluate. He could judge me all he wanted. We had strangers in play and no idea what the stakes were. I shut the door. Dane jogged around the front of the car and got in.

"Any issues getting out?" I asked him as I pulled into traffic.

"None. But that still leaves us needing to know who wants these kids so badly their willing to snatch them from a public place under armed security."

Right. Someone had just upped the stakes, and when bodies started piling up, it turned it into an entirely different game. The question was: who so disliked Jackson that they'd risk exposure to snatch his kids in public? It seemed an oddly intimate thing—the kind of risk you take when you had a personal beef with someone.

So many questions and not enough answers.

CHAPTER 14

"You really need to consider canceling the interview," I told the Jackson and Brendan close to an hour later back at the hotel.

"Out of the question," Jackson replied.

"We've already rescheduled once, and I'm not sure we could get Travis Gore to agree to host us if we tried to reschedule again," Brendan said, voice a bit warbly as he spoke over FaceTime.

"Is it worth the Jackson's life?" My voice was even, but I was trying not to scream.

"These threats aren't new. Besides, I'm sure we can request more building security."

"And if there are protestors?"

Brendan spoke slowly, as if in an attempt to calm the crazy person, raising the beast's ire. "You have to acquire a permit from the city for large gatherings, and, from what I understand, they're incredibly hard to get. The likelihood of there being a group protesting are slim to none."

I gave him a hard stare. Could he really be so dense? "Someone just tried to snatch your daughter out of a public place. That's bold. Maybe even desperate. Do you really want to give desperate people a chance to get to you or your kids? With all due respect, we have no idea what we're dealing with, and Alyssa and Logan are the most likely to get hurt."

"That's why they have you," Brendan quipped.

I shot him a dirty glare.

"This interview must happen," Jackson said.

"What on earth for?" Jackson's admin assistant asked. "The polls are showing that you're in the lead, especially since the policy change. You have this in the bag. Why do you feel like you must go?'

"Not many people get invited onto the show. It's a great opportunity to solidify the vote in people's minds and talk about the future."

"You can do that after you win," she said.

"No time like the present." He looked past us all toward the doorway. "Dane, can you check and see if it's possible to hire more security to guard the TV studio?"

Dane was standing just off my left shoulder, flush against the wall and still as a statue. The perfect bodyguard. I pivoted to face him.

"I'll call around and ask," he said. "Shouldn't be all that hard to get a few extra hands."

Jackson waved his hands in a, *There, see?* gesture.

"It's more than just the kids, sir." I pressed. "Lang betrayed us. That's the second member of your security team who's been negligent or betrayed you. Whoever is orchestrating all of this clearly has an in."

"We're less than forty-eight hours from the election, and then this will all be over." He lowered his voice and muttered, "It all be over." Lines bracketed from his eyes, and there was a determined gleam to his eye that didn't seem right. Why push this interview if he was so certain he was going to win?

Hours later, we pulled up to the entrance for the parking garage, and Dane leaned over to scan the parking pass that had been mailed to the hotel. Nothing happened.

"That's weird." He swiped it again. He punched in the number, wiped the reader clean with the sleeve of his blazer, yet the partition remained in place.

"Let's see if we can get ahold of someone who can let us in." I used my phone to pull up the email with the contact information for Travis Gore's assistant.

"This is Stacy." A crisp woman's voice came over the line.

"My name is Serena Black, and I'm part of the security detail for Jackson. We're having issues with our parking pass. Is there anyone who can come lift the gate?"

"I'll send someone out to you."

I sat on hold. It took fifteen minutes to determine that there was something glitchy with the system and the gate wasn't going to lift. Crapola.

"Well, what do you suggest we do?" I asked the woman on the phone, voice calm, though irritation flushed through me.

"The only thing I can think is for you to drop everyone off at the main entrance and then park across the street."

I took my phone away from my ear and stared at it. She had to be kidding. "I'm sure you understand what a huge security risk that is."

"What other choice is there?"

She was right.

I looked at Dane. "She's telling me that we'll to park across the street."

He snorted. "Seriously?"

I shrugged. This was beyond ridiculous.

"Are we going to keep loitering out here, or is someone going to take us inside?" Jackson snipped.

With a heavy breath, Dane put the car in reverse and pulled back around to the main entrance.

"All right, everyone out." I said, unbuckling my seat. "You park, and I'll get them settled."

"Roger that." He waited until the family and I were through the doors before pulling away from the curb. We checked in at the front desk, and the Jackson-could-be was whisked away for hair and makeup while a slender young man with a headset escorted the rest of us into the bowels of the building and pushed open a door marked, "Private Viewing."

"You'll be able to watch the entire broadcast from here with no interruptions," he explained.

The room was fairly large and had several small seating areas clustered along the edges highlighted by simply patterned rugs. A refreshments station sat at the back of the room with decanters of water and coffee and platters of fruit and pastries lining the long table. But the main focal point was definitely the three massive TV's that hung on the wall opposite the couches. They all had to be at least eighty inches and showcased different angles of the main filming set. I watched Jackson stride to his spot at the far left side of the crescent and take a sip out of the glass of water next to the microphone that jutted up from the desk.

"In case you're not familiar with how the show works, let me explain." Our escort said, "Mr. Gore hosts two political figures, typically who represent the opposite ends of the spectrum, and asks them questions to help create a more balanced conversation for the viewers. It can sometimes get a bit dicey but no one's taken a swing so far." He chortled as if with a private joke.

"How long is the entire show?" I took a turn around the room, eyeing the giant potted peace lily as the most likely place someone would have smuggled a camera or recording device.

"Forty-five minutes in total," he replied. "Most people are out of here in an hour and a half."

Alyssa flopped onto the couch in front of the middle TV and Logan inspected the pastry tray on the food table. I walked to the window on the far side of the room and looked out. The downtown streets were lined with cars but the traffic otherwise was light. Across the street was additional parking and a group of people all waving signs and yelling toward the building. There were only ten of them yet they made enough noise that I could faintly hear them over the noise of the city. A neon green sign read, "Semi-Trucks Cause Pollution" and another read "Jackson Doesn't Care About Mother Earth". Just what we didn't need—some random environmental group trying to get the media's attention.

I pulled out my phone and shot Dane a text. *You aware of the protesters outside?* I went back over to the food table and leaned against the wall, settling in. My phone buzzed a few seconds later.

Yeah. There's less than a dozen which shouldn't be too much of a concern if the group doesn't grow. Walking in now.

K. I've got the kids covered if you want to secure Jackson.

Roger that.

I stuffed the phone into my back pocket and turned my attention to the TV to watch Jackson in action.

In short, it was a train wreck.

The commentator was fixated on Jackson's abrupt platform change, stating that moves like that often ended a campaign yet it only seemed to foster momentum for him. The show host proceeded to list a plethora of organizations of individuals that added their support since his announcement to back a proposition to increase regulations for semi-trucks at state borders. Jackson seemed a bit dazed and robotic, his answers coming across as stiff and dripping with arrogance.

Current Jackson Robert Andrino was the guest across the desk, a raging Democrat, and practically foamed at the mouth the entire time. If I had a quarter for the number of times that man used the words "confused" and "traitor", I'd be able to buy some rare, limited edition version of an original Bac concerto.

Jackson's response to his reasoning struck a particularly bad note with Andrino, and the man practically jumped out of his seat.

"He doesn't seem to be doing a very good job." Logan's toy plane stalled at his side as he stared at the television screen with eyebrows knitted in concern.

I smiled at him. "Adults don't like change, and your dad sprung a big one on them. Don't worry, he'll get them to see the facts and come over to his side." I glanced at the magazine's lying on the table. "You wanna make me an origami animal?"

"With what? I don't have any paper."

I pointed at the magazines.

"You sure I won't get in trouble?"

"If you do, I'll fight them for you, and we can escape out the back door."

"Deal!" He leapt over to the table to begin ripping pages out of US Weekly. The harsh sound of paper tearing filled the air as I turned back to the TV.

The other commentator leaned forward in his chair, nostrils flared and jabbing his finger at Jackson, who seemed unperturbed by the man's ire.

Dane's voice buzzed in my ear. "Get ready to move in three. We're gonna leave before the in-person meetings to see if we can't avoid the crowd."

"Copy that." I clapped twice. "All right, let's get packed up and ready to get out of here." I didn't blame Dane for wanting to clear the building as quickly as possible. I could hear the shouts of the crowd outside, and they were fired up after the heated debate. Politics always made people's hidden crazy come to light.

Logan closed the decimated magazines as primly as he could before shoving the origami turtle into his pocket. Alyssa flipped her curls and looked up from her phone.

Two quick raps sounded at the door before it swung open. Dane poked his head inside and waved his fingers at me. I met him there, and he kept his voice low when he spoke.

"I moved the car as close as I could, but the protesters are quickly turning into a mob. They wouldn't let me through, and the closest I could park was about a hundred feet away from the sidewalk."

That wasn't good. More time in an angry crowd only upped the chances of some brainwashed protester doing something that would make national news. "How many people do you think are out there?"

"At least a hundred."

I swore under my breath. If the parking garage had worked, this wouldn't even be an issue.

"Okay. All we can do is stay close and keep movin', right?"

"Yeah."

"Let's do this." I turned to Alyssa and Logan, whose eyes were wide as the noise of the mob had grown loud enough for them to hear.

I said, "We're going to the car, but I need you to stay in the order Dane and I tell you, okay?"

They both nodded, blue eyes the size of discs.

I pushed open the door and ushered them into the hall. We met Dane and Jackson at the back entrance, where the shouts of the crowd easily filtered in through the door.

"Here's the plan," Dane said, addressing the other man. "The car's positioned just off the sidewalk, but we're going to have to fight out way to it. I'm going to make a path and you'll follow behind and we'll keep the kids in the middle with Serena bringing up the rear. Whatever you do, don't stop moving. Got it?"

Four heads nodded.

Dane flung open the doors. Noise slammed into us like a wav and we stepped into the ocean of angry chants, bouncing signs, and flashing lights.

Movement caught my eye, and I swiveled just in time to see a young man in a black hoodie make a hand gesture before fading back into the crowd.

Someone reached over the tape and shoved my shoulders so I stumbled slightly just as Dane stepped slightly to one side to grab the hand of an over exuberant protester.

Jackson jerked suddenly, one harsh movement, and his head snapped back at such a harsh angle that it threw him off balance. He stumbled back.

I reached forward to break his fall, and the brunt of his weight slammed into me.

The crowd screamed as I stumbled back into several other people. A sinking feeling filled my stomach. I looked at the man in my arms to see a red bullet hole leaking a small spot of blood in the center of his forehead. Shit in a bucket.

Dane looked back just as I lowered the him to the pavement.

"Groundhog," I yelled.

Someone screamed.

Dane ran back, wrapped a thick arm around Alyssa's waist, hauled her into the air, and started using the baton to beat back people out of his way.

I grabbed Logan and tucked him under my arm and whipped out a long reach taser. It took us a few minutes to beat and electrocute our way through the now frantic, scrambling crowd.

"Hang on, kid." I said, giving Logan a squeeze.

He didn't answer, and I didn't expect him to. When we'd practiced this maneuver at home, he was always a ball of giggles. What preadolescent boy wouldn't delight in being carried around like a sack of potatoes? Now, he was silent and stiff as a board. Terror evident in the tenseness of his muscles.

Hang on.

Dane reached the car and smashed the baton into the face of someone who came too close. He flung Alyssa inside and I was right behind, shoving Logan ahead of me and clambering into the car after him. Dane punched the gas before I was fully inside and I was dragged by the car for a few feet before I hauled myself into the backseat and slammed the door shut.

"What's going on? Why are we leaving dad?" Alyssa's voice was muffled as she struggled to pull herself upright.

"Buckle up, Alyssa." I ordered. The last thing we needed was for to fly through the windshield with Dane's evasive driving. I started to climb over the console into the front passenger seat just as he swerved to avoid a cluster of protesters and I spilled forward into a heap against the door. Good grief.

"How is dad supposed to be safe if both of you guys are with us?" Alyssa pressed. "We need to turnaround and go get him."

"You buckled, Logan?" I asked.

"Yeah." His voice warbled with adrenaline and fear.

"Go back for dad!" Alyssa screamed.

I pivoted in my seat. "Sit down and strap in." I ordered sharply and ignored the frantic wildness in her eyes. "The best thing we can do for you dad is to get you and Logan away from this madness and to safety so he doesn't have to worry about it."

"But—"

"Buckle."

She paused, warring with whether to not to press the issue. I calmly met her eye until her shaky hands reached back to pull the seatbelt forward across her chest. It sucked being a jerk to her but her young mind was in survival mode and was scrambling for assurance or control.

Alyssa feel silent, but her eyes were wide and frightened in her ashen face.

Logan curled into as tight a ball he could in the seat and rocked back and forth.

I found Brendan's name and hit call But before the phone rang Dane reached over and pulled it from my ear.

"No police." He said, tossing the phone back into my lap.

"You think they don't already know? I'll bet half that crowd was filming the effing thing and dialed 9-1-1 before we drove away."

"Doesn't matter."

"Why?"

"You think those people were all there and the police didn't already know about it?" Dane asked. "Most cities require that crowds like that have a permit to gather as a way to prevent loitering for days or disrupting civic peace. You saw that crowd. There were well over two hundred people in that mob, more than enough for the city to require a police presence. And yet there wasn't a cop in sight. Why is that?"

He voiced the fear niggling in the back of my brain. The protester had gathered outside the studio long enough to draw the attention of local authorities. Sacramento police would have been well within their rights to insist the crowd disperse if they didn't have a permit. Yet there were no police men to be found. The only answer made Beastie growl.

"You're telling me that you think the local authorities knew this crowd was going to be here and turned a blind eye?"

He shrugged. "I'm not saying anything for certain. Just my thoughts."

It was a conjecture—and maybe a desperate one—but I

didn't argue. Something was off here and we'd been blindsided by the ugliness of this thing with two traumatized kids in tow.

"So what's the plan? Go to the hotel and wait for the feds to show up?"

He nodded. "Something like that."

Made sense. If there was a hint of foul play from the local authorities, the next best bet was to lay low and until federal agents flooded in like the invasive ants they were. Invasive yet harder to pay off without someone noticing.

"I was calling Brendan." I told him. "He needs a warning about the shit storm that's rolling his way and needs to find Mrs. Jackson and get her in a secure location ASAP." I didn't wait for his agreement, just pressed the green button and waited as the phone buzzed.

It rang for a full minute before his voice kicked in. I hung up and tried again an got the same response. Shit in a bucket. This thing had already blown in our faces and now we're preparing for the shrapnel to settle in. At least the hotel was a defensible position and it wouldn't take long for the feds to track us down. And I wasn't opposed to shooting protesters, or anyone else, from the windows if I had to.

Dane stomped on the accelerator, and the car jolted forward. I gripped the overhead handle and hung on.

We made it to the hotel in a little under eight minutes. Inches from the front door, Dane skidded to a stop so fast and so hot that the bellhops jumped back for safety. We ushered the kids through the lobby, and I hoped we moved them fast enough that they didn't have time to hear the live footage of the protest that played on the TV screens from the sports bar off the main lobby. I caught a glimpse of one of the screens as we hustled past—a male reporter interviewed a pair of young women with an EMSA truck flashing in the background. What a mess.

We strode past the reception desk, me all but carrying Logan, and the doors to a recently emptied elevator started to slide closed. Dane reached forward and caught the door with a massive hand and I hustled inside. I hit the elevator button for the twentieth floor.

"Were they talking about Dad?"

Logan's voice cut through the turmoil in my head, and I looked at him. His stiff body and pale features indicated shock. I needed to get him moving and focused on something else before he became completely unglued. Not that I'd blame him, but we needed to survive before we could grieve.

"She could have been talking about something else. Another event." His voice was soft, as if trying to convince himself this was a bad dream. I wished that were true.

"I clearly heard dad's name," Alyssa jerked against Dane's hold on her arm but would only end up yanking her shoulder out of socket before she budged the large man.

"Calm yourself," Dane snapped, giving her a bit of a shake.

She beat his arm with her small fist. "You tell me where my dad is!" she yelled but tears pooled in her eyes.

The elevator dinged and the doors slid open. A quick glance showed that the hallway was empty. I wasn't sure Logan was up to walking so I swung him into my arms like an infant. He didn't fight me. Alyssa was still screaming so ended up covering her mouth with his hand, her tears spilling over his thick fingers, and duck waddling them both down the hall with her in front of him.

I swiped the card and we poured into the hotel suite. I set Logan down and he swayed a moment before widening his feet and staying still. Better than Alyssa—the moment Dane released her, she sank to the floor with fat tears rolling down her face. Until she got herself together—*if* she got herself together —she'd be dead weight.

I looked at Logan. "Can you find a blanket for your sister?"

His eyes were watery, more with shock than anything else, but he gave me a slow nod. Brave boy.

"What about dad?" He asked with a shaking voice.

I touched his cheek. "I will tell you what I know as soon as we get Alyssa calmed down, okay?"

He nodded and moved like a zombie through quicksand, and I watched his slow, robotic steps until he disappeared into his room.

"Let's move her to the couch, get her out of the doorway." I told Dane. He picked up the crying girl and placed her on one of the couches in the main suite. I flipped on the TV and turned to a nature documentary hoping to distract her. She barely noticed.

"Well this is a cluster," Dane muttered.

That was the understatement of the decade. When was the last time a major U.S. political candidate was gunned down in the street? Like...never. This was like some movie plot from a communist director's screenplay.

Dane's phone pinged and he stepped away to read the text.

Maybe there was something on Jackson's laptop that would give us a clue to this whole situation. I walked to the other side of the suite and stepped into the dark room. The first thing I noticed were the pillows on the bed. The bed was pristine, save a slight crinkle in the top coverlet and depression in the pillows as if Jackson had tried to nap a bit before the gig tonight.

A siren sounded in the distance, and I moved to the window to see if I could see it from there. I peeked out the curtain and nearly jumped out of my skin when a window washer paused mid swiped waved back. He and a second man stood on a balanced platform connected to wire in the roof that allowed them to scale the windows without being at risk of shattering the glass. My hand eased off my gun and I let the curtains fall back in place. Who was washing windows at eight o clock at night? It might be too hot during the day but dang.

I shut the curtain without waving back. Did I need more attention? I think not.

Air shifted behind me, and something hit the base of my spine with enough force to slam me back into the windows. I gasped for breath. A hand grabbed and twisted the collar of my blazer and jerked. I flew backwards and slammed into the ground. Pain sizzled down my spine.

Dane loomed above me, a chilling expression on his face. Utter blankness.

I wheezed. "What the hell?"

He pulled a gun from inside his jacket. "It's nothing personal, Serena," he said, voice cold.

Pure survival instincts kicked in, and I rolled forward a hairs breadth before he pulled the trigger.

I felt the heat of the bullet whiz past my face.

My leg flashed out and caught him the back of his knee. His leg buckled, and he sank. I aimed a kick at his face, but he grabbed my leg in midair and, one handed, flung me into the windows hard enough for them to crack. He aimed a punch at my face but I threw up both hands to block it and head butted him in the jaw.

Blood spurted but a meaty hand clamped around my throat. He rose, me dangling in his grip, and slammed me back into the windows.

"Don't do this," I gurgled, beating at his wrist.

Dane turned his head and spat a mouthful of blood onto the carpet. "Lots of money at stake here. Apparently, there's a buyer who's been interested in these brats a long time, and he's willing to pay a lot of money to see them delivered to him unscathed."

"Traitor," I choked out.

He pulled me away and slammed me into the nearest wall. "Opportunist," he corrected. He reversed his hold so that the front of my body was pressed into the wall and used his arm at my throat and pressure at the back of my head to cut off my air supply.

Gray spots exploded in my vision. I clawed for his face but couldn't reach. I drove my elbow into his abdomen, but he only grunted as he took the blow and pressed harder against the base of my skull. At this angle, he could snap my neck. But he choose to draw it out.

His lips brushed my ear. "Just for the record, this isn't personal."

Neither was this. I slipped my hand inside his suit jacket and wrapped it around the butt of his nine millimeter. I jerked it from its holster, twisted my wrist at an awkward angle, and fired twice. Blood and stuff exploded around me, and Dane went limp against my so suddenly that I stumbled into the wall.

I wriggled my way out from under him, ignoring the sight of his face as his corpse slumped to the floor. For a moment, I stared completely confused.

What the hell was going on?

It took a moment before it occurred to me that there hadn't been a silencer on his weapon. Someone was bound to have heard the gunshot and come asking about the noise. Or call the police. A handful of swear words dropped out of my mouth before I could catch them. Freaking fantastic.

A light tap on the door made me jump. "Umm...Serena? Dane? Are you guys okay?" It was Logan. The doorknob started to turn and I sprang forward to slam it closed.

"We're all good here, bud," I told him.

"Oh." He paused. "I heard a noise..."

"Thanks for checking. I'll be out in..." I glanced around at the blood spattered walls and Dane's leaking corpse, "...A few minutes. Did you find you and Alyssa's backpacks?"

"I found mine. I'll go look for hers."

"Great idea." I waited until I heard his soft footsteps move away before I stepped back from the door. I stripped off my blazer which was coated in blood and thicker things and used the cleaner side to wipe my face and hair free of as much of Dane's DNA as possible. My mind warred with the possibility of calling the police and letting them sort out the nonsense. But instinct made me pause. Dane mentioned a third party —a buyer with the money and resources to invest in a long run kidnapping game. If such a person could get to the head of Jackson's security who knew what the scope of their reach really was? Or maybe Dane had been a plant all along?

The last thought made Beastie growl. The holes in my information made me want to hit something but I knew one thing for sure: I needed to get Alyssa and Logan to a secure facility and out of the immediate danger. From whoever killed their dad...and now this faceless kidnapper.

Someone knocked on the door hard enough to make it rattle. It came from the suite's main door.

"This is the Sacramento Police department. We were called about a disturbance that sounded like gunshots. Open the door." More pounding followed.

I frowned and checked my watch. I'd pulled the trigger less than five minutes ago and they were here? Unless they were already in the area, that seemed ridiculously fast.

I stepped out of the room, leaving just enough room to slide my body through without giving away a glimpse of the...mess in the other room. The TV in the main suite blared with footage from the latest news report and Logan stood in the door of his room, a black backpack dangling from his hand as he stared at me with wide, questioning eyes. But it was Alyssa moving toward the main door that grabbed my attention.

"Alyssa, don't!" I shouted.

She looked back at me with a desperate gleam in her eye, hand on the doorknob. "Daddy always said the cops will help us. They'll help us find him," she said and pulled it open.

The two uniformed men on the other side of the door didn't look a bit surprised to suddenly be staring into the tear streaked face of a twelve year old girl.

"We were called about a disturbance. Can we step inside?" The man stepped forward even as he spoke and forced Alyssa to shuffle backward to stay out of their way.

"Who called?" I asked and the front cop met my gaze with bright hazel eyes.

"Building management," he responded. "Apparently there is a VIP staying in this suite and the manager wanted to ensure everything was alright."

The second cop slowly prowled the room, his massive six foot plus frame filling the space with an energy that made

Beastie perk up.

Beastie growled at the men and I agreed. Something was off but I didn't want to risk pissing them off by implying that too quickly. Still, I forced a small, pleasant smile as I said, "There's a candidate for the US senate staying here but he's...at a meeting right now. We don't' expect him back until later. If we were being too loud, I apologize. We'll be quieter from now on."

Movement made me turn my head toward Logan's room. The second officer stood in the doorway pushing Logan in front of him with a massive hand covering his mouth. "Found the boy."

Music rose in the depths of my mind and I followed the instinct when something flashed in the corner of my left eye. I stepped back and to the side in time to the dramatic violin sequence as the first cop's energy sharply shifted toward me. His baton sailed past my face and I grabbed it and yanked. He fell toward me and I crouched and did a partial turn that allowed me to drive my elbow into his ribs twice.

The beefier cop flung Logan aside and lunged for me, hand going to his waist. I felt my fingers creeping toward my own gun but I reverted and snatched the baton out of Hazel Eyes' hand and flung it at Beefy Boy. It nailed him right between the eyes. Shooting a cop was a great way to end up on the crap of almost every agency with some cute alphabet mishmash name and I didn't need any more corpses to be responsible for.

I flipped Hazel Eyes over my shoulder and he hit the floor with a thud. He swung his legs around as if to trip me and I jumped to avoid it just as Beefy Boy closed in and shoved me mid-air. I flew backwards and Alyssa screamed. It slammed into one of the couches and flipped over the edge of it.

I pulled myself up and glanced at Alyssa who was cowering near the suite door. "Alyssa, get your brother and go hide in your closet." I needed to get them out of the way before they got hurt.

The larger man rounded the couch and exaggerated symbols and horns flared in my head when I caught sight of the massive blade glinting in his hand. It had to be the length of his forearm and twice the width. Definitely not a standard issue weapon.

He lunged with long swipes like a windmill and I scrambled back to avoid them. I counted the timing of his swipes—it was a staccato three-fourths beat—and on the pause I used both hands to grab his wrist and twist sharply into an arm bar. The bone snapped and he roared in pain. I canted his arm at an angle and tried to shove the blade into his chest but he fought the motion and the knife buried itself into his shoulder.

He screamed again and drove his fist into the meat of my thigh. My leg buckled and I went to one knee and he tackled me. It was like being hit point blank from a pissed off King Kong. I instinctively titled my hips and rolled us, my hand scrambling along the floor. Me on my back with a man this size on top of me was bad news. My fingers closed on the baton. I did a monkey scramble around so I was on his back, slipped the baton around his throat like a bridle, and pulled back. His back arched at an unnatural angle and he reached back, grabbing at my clothes as I cut off his air supply. He tried to grab my braids but I swept them out of his reach.

The other cop leapt off the back of the couch with a battle cry. I wrenched the baton back and twisted sharply. A crack like someone stepping on a thick branch and the man beneath me went limp. I dropped the baton and used both forearms to block a vicious kick to the face that sent me back. I rolled with the momentum and leapt onto my toes in a crouch. Hazel Eyes landed a flurry of punches and kicks and I blocked them, studying the rhythm of his moves. He paused a fraction too long between strikes and my fist lashed out and buried itself in his throat. Twice. His hand flew to his throat yet he still kicked out, choking against the rapidly swelling flesh of his esophagus.

He went for his gun and I stopped him as the weapon barely cleared the holster. We grappled for it. Of the two of us, he was stronger but his face reddened and eyes started to bulge as body went critical with the need for air. I jerked and twisted the gun at an angle, trying to pull free of him but his hand clenched hard trying to fight me.

The gun fired and he jerked as if I'd punched him. He collapsed to the floor and the clarity slowly faded from his eyes as blood leaked from the bullet hole between his ribs.

My chest heaved as I sucked in breaths and stared at the corpses as my mind raced. This was a cluster from start to finish.

"Can we come out?" Alyssa's voice was muffled through the wall.

"In a minute," I said, crouching next to one of the bodies. "I'll tell you when." I quickly rustled through his pants pockets and pulled out a basic brown wallet. One glance made my stomach drop. In the very front laminated pocket was his police ID badge—a quick check of the other body and I found the same thing. There wasn't a cuss word emotional enough to sum up the emotion coursing through me...so I said several.

It didn't matter that they'd clearly were intent on stealing the kids and attacked first.

Didn't matter that Dane had tried to kill me not fifteen minutes before.

From the outside looking in, I'd just executed a rogue killing spree and slaughtered two police officers and a member of a now murdered Senate candidate's staff...and I was about to flee the scene.

Because Alyssa and Logan were in danger from an enemy I couldn't identify. Because this enemy had somehow infiltrated the local police and sent assassins to finish the job. Because, now, I didn't know who to trust.

In for a penny, in for an effing pound.

CHAPTER 15

"**K**ids! Time to move."

They popped out of their rooms at the same time, both wearing black skinny jeans but Alyssa rocked a dark red, almost black hoodie while Logan wore his trademark dark green jacket. Alyssa's hoodie would stand out, but I'd deal with that later.

I ran to my room and snatched up the black backpack on the closet floor just as police sirens screamed in the distance. Adrenaline surged in my veins. We were out of time. I walked over to the large main windows and murmured a quick prayer that the window-washing contraption was still there. This room was situated on the north side of the building, which faced away from the street and overlooked an alleyway. Away from the busy street and prying eyes. Perfect. The only thing that marred the view was a window washer's platform that dangled at an even height with the windowsill. Perfect.

I pulled my Smith & Wesson from my waist holster and stepped back as I attached a silencer. I shot the corners of the window, the gun jerking with soft pops. The glass broke and shattered toward the ground like glittering rain.

I turned back to the kids. I said nothing, I reached out and grabbed one of the cables of the window washing platform and swung it towards me.

"This is our way out of here." I told them. "Step down." I reached out a hand.

Alyssa looked at me like I'd lost my mind.

Logan looked concerned but reached forward and grabbed

my hand. Brave boy.

I smiled. "Take a big step and use a wide stance to stay balanced. Grab the rail with both hands."

He did. The platform creaked with his weight. "Your turn, Alyssa."

"Isn't there another way?"

"If there were, we'd be using it." I said, "Get on."

She slowly stepped forward.

"Step into the opposite corner as Logan," I told her, bracing the platform against the windowsill. It was situated just below the ledge, so it was a step down into the cradle. Alyssa stepped down but wobbled, making the platform rock.

"Easy," I said. "Now grab the rail with both hands and widen your feet, it will help

distribute the weight." She shifted.

Good. Now my turn.

I stepped down onto the platform and stepped into the far corner from the kids, hoping to balance our weight. I grabbed the lift lever. "Now crouch down but still keep hold of

the rail."

They did.

Going slower would be safe but we couldn't risk someone seeing us on a lower floor. So I pushed down on the lever and notched it at the second highest speed. We dropped like a tower of terror at an amusement park. The kids screamed but we were going too fast and the wind caught and carried away the noise. We careened toward the street. I counted floors and when we hit the sixth floor, I applied the break.

It squealed in protest and the lift only slowed a little bit. The ground rose quickly into view. I jerked it back and pressed the brake again. This time it slowed. We wanted to slow down gradually or risk the cables snapping from the stress.

We came to a stop just inches from the gray pavement

The entire fall took less than a minute.

"Everyone off."

It took several seconds for them to register what I said. Both clung to the rail with a death grip.

Alyssa shook so hard I thought she'd fall over. I reached over and grabbed an arm and forced them to stand. We could be scared and shaky later.

The lift deposited us at the back of the building, and I jogged to the corner and peered out over the street. No black cars littered the street...yet. The sirens, however, were growing closer. Most likely police backup, and I knew our window of time was quickly closing.

I scanned the street and focused on a black sedan that was only fifty feet in front of us. Our ride out of there. "Stay here." I told them over my shoulder and then casually walked to the car. I stood in front of it as if I owned it and pulled a small device from my utility belt. I inserted it into the lock and twisted. The sirens grew louder. Come on, I muttered under my breath. A few seconds later, the doors beeped unlocked. I waved to the kids, and they ran to the car. We piled in and I reached under the dashboard, fiddled with a few wires, and the car purred to life. Just in time too.

Three police cars skidded past us and screeched to a halt in front of the hotel, six officers jumping from the cars and running into the building. I put the car in reverse and slowly backed into the alley we just left and waited for the street to clear before I shifted the car into drive and drove away. I kept to the speed limit though my heart was pounding. I checked the rearview mirror several times to make sure no one was following us. After a mile or so, I relaxed.

"Alyssa, do you have your phone on you?" I asked.

"Why?" Her voice had a tremor in it that told me she was still high on adrenaline.

"I need you to find me the nearest car rental agency. We need to offload this car before the owner realizes it's been stolen."

She pulled her glittery purple encased phone out of her hoodie pocket and tapped on the screen. Several minutes later, she said. "There's a rental place a mile up the road."

"Right or left side of the street?" I asked

"Left."

I hit the turn signal and got over into that lane. I held my hand out toward her. "Can I see the directions?"

She placed her phone in the palm of my hand.

I rolled down the window and threw her phone out. The grey minivan in the other lane honked and swerved to avoid running over it.

"Hey!" she screeched.

I ignored her. "Logan, where's your phone?" I glanced in the rearview mirror to look at him.

He silently pulled out his brand new smartphone, a present from his mom, and handed it to me. I gave a brief nod in the mirror and flung his outside as well.

"You're insane," Alyssa muttered.

"Phones are the first thing that they'll track and they'd find us before sundown." I said, "You know that."

"Maybe we should just go the police. Then we won't have to run from anyone." She said, desperation flashing in her eyes.

"Like the cops back at the hotel?" I shot back.

She didn't reply, just slouched in her seat and stared out the window. Twenty minutes later, we swapped the stolen sedan for a black Nissan pathfinder. The lady was skeptical when I asked for an older car model, trying to upsell me on all the sweet packages that came with newer cars. I wasn't interested. An older car meant it was less likely to have excessive electrical parts and devices that could be hacked to find our position. The sales lady became straight up suspicious when I paid cash for the whole thing. At first, she didn't want to accept that much money, saying they don't have a safe on hand.

I pressed.

She argued.

Still, I won.

For the next five hours we drove in silence. I was tempted to turn on the radio so I could stay updated on what the media was saying, but the kids had been traumatized enough without reporters and politicians justifying or explaining his death in a cold hearted manner. Alyssa and Logan were already having a hard time processing all that they'd seen in the past six hours and I wasn't interested in adding to the trauma.

I tried calling Brendan, thinking I could persuade him to set up a safe house for Alyssa and Logan. Even if I were under fire, the kids didn't deserve to be pursued like criminals simply because I toted them around everywhere. I ended up leaving a voicemail and setting the phone aside. He'd call back.

We hit the Nevada border in the wee hours of the morning and I decided that was enough for the night. I searched the highway for a small yet reputable looking hotel and saw one directly off exit 186. The desk clerk barely looked up from his computer screen as he put me in a king bedroom on the third story and I was booked less than ten minutes later. I handed him cash and noticed the small streak of red on the back of my hand. I used a few pumps of the hand sanitizer on the desk to get rid of it. Hopefully, he hadn't noticed.

The kids waited in the car while I grabbed the key, and I made them pull their hoodies as far over their faces as possible before they got out of the car. I'd played with the idea of having them dye their hair, but their café au lait skin and golden curly hair was so distinctive I'm not sure it would have helped much. Better to just hide it all together and pray no one looked too closely.

We piled into the room.

It was simple with a clean looking king-sized bed and bathroom. It smelled faintly of bleach, which was definitely better than any of the alternatives. The only thing I wasn't thrilled about was the balcony, which posed the greatest security risk.

"Go to bed," I told them. "We'll take showers and start fresh tomorrow."

Both kids nodded, their faces a combination of weariness, confusion, and lingering fear.

As they settled in the bed, I grabbed the chair at the desk and dragged it across the carpet to shove it in the corner behind the door. This position allowed me to watch the windows and catch any intruders by surprise who might decide to burst through the doors.

I drew my gun and settled into the seat, draping the gun across my lap. Logan shifted on the bed but he was the only thing that moved. Beastie stalked the corridors in my head, ready for action and I hummed a few bars of my favorite Schubert symphony to calm her. I was as ready as I could be for any trouble. Hopefully, there would be none. Hopefully, we were just far enough from the shit storm that we could avoid getting hit.

Hopefully.

I waited a few extra moments to make sure they were asleep before pulling out my phone and dialing Brendan. There wasn't a doubt in my mind that this had already erupted across political America and that the news stations were already eating it up. If I knew him, he was pacing the floor like an anxious wet nurse. Again I got a voicemail. I angrily closed the call. Where was he and did he have any idea what the hell was happening here?

My phone pinged and it was a notification from one of the few news stations I subscribed to since most of them were sensationalized trash. I opened it, expecting to see a headline reminiscent of "Senate Candidate Murdered" or "Nanny Gone Rogue" but, when I clicked the link, a familiar face stared back at me from the clipping of a newspaper article.

WAR HERO AND BELOVED POLICE CHIEF FINALLY PASSES AFTER A HARROWING BATTLE WITH CANCER.

It was a picture of my dad in his military uniform—Joseph Black. The photo captured the warmth of his eyes. The way they sparkled mischievously as if he harbored an unspoken joke.

Pain, visceral and crippling, seared through my chest, and I struggled to breathe past it. The wave of emotion was just as confusing as it was paralyzing. This couldn't be right...and yet the picture: dad healthy and smiling in his police chief uniform. Long before the days of chemotherapy and targeted radiation; of long nights vomiting any food that touched his stomach and reduced him to the skeletal figure I'd said good-bye to four days ago.

He'd been doing better. His doctors had been so impressed with his progress that they considered cutting back on the frequency of his hospice visits. What went wrong?

A muted video thumbnail ran in the lower left corner and I read every caption that looped across the screen, each one a shard flung at the glass veneer of my soul.

A Yale graduate and decorated war hero.

Saved the Secretary of State during his third tour.

Served as Police Chief for Oklahoma County for thirteen years.

Dearly loved father of two children.

My vision blurred at the last. A multitude of questions flooded my mind—how long ago had this happened? Why hadn't my family called me? Their numbers were programmed to automatically bypass my phone's security settings so they could reach me at all times, anywhere in the globe

But it never rang.

Was I such a horrible person that I didn't even deserve to know when my father died? It's not like they knew that you really cared, a small voice said. That voice made me flinch and pain shoot through my chest.

Tears slipped down my cheeks as that thought rattled in my head. It wasn't like I could call Julien and demand answers; the encryption code that would secure my phone wouldn't finish loading for a few hours. So I was stuck with the yawning silence of no information and Beastie's growing anger.

I needed a distraction, anything to avoid the searing emotions that threatened to erode the control I had left. I gave into my sick curiosity and typed Jackson's name into the search bar. Right now, we were flying blind and how no idea if there were any suspects for the Jacksons assassination or if there was a massive man hunt for whoever left a body in a four star hotel.

I clicked on the first local video that popped on to my screen, and my stomach sank. Jerky footage from smartphones and ground level snapshots of the riot outside Travis Gore studios flooded the feed. People screamed and ran, signs littering the ground as they hurried to get away. One news station created a dramatic montage of the moment the Jackson went down—captured on someone's smartphone—and the chaos that ensued.

One headline caught my attention. It was uploaded less than an hour from Sacramento so I pressed play.

"This just in," a female reporter chimed. "As the details of the horrible assassination of Oklahoma senate hopeful, Davis Jackson, unfold, it appears that authorities have identified a suspect. The details are still unfolding but following the brutal murder of a trusted staff official, at the moment, she is our prime suspect."

A picture popped on screen beside her. My stomach dropped.

It was me.

CHAPTER 16

I closed my phone and fought the urge to launch it across the room. Beastie snarled. What did I think would happen? Especially leaving Dane's headless body in the hotel room for the maid to stumble upon. That didn't leave much to the conversation except that I'd lost my chili and decided to shoot up the place as my sanity, cool points, and professionalism ran for the door. What other story was there to believe?

Closing my eyes, I leaned my head back against the wall and let thoughts filter through my brain. It was safe to assume that a handful of local and federal agencies now had my face flashing across their desks to try and bring me in. We'd be a high priority catch and we now had people from both sides of the law coming at us from every angle. Freaking perfect.

My main goal was to get the kids into protective custody. I could do nothing about clearing my name until they were out of harm's way.

I felt eyes on my skin. It woke me from a mild doze. I didn't move my head, which was leaned against the wall, and let my gaze rove around the darkened room. A single lamp in the far corner gave off enough light for me to see but wasn't bright enough to catch outside attention if anyone was watching through the windows.

I looked around, trying to figure out what disturbed me. Nothing stood out but Beastie paced in her cage, my senses tingling. Slowly, I sat upright. A glance towards the bed and scanned the children. Fine there. Neither had moved since the last time I'd seen them—Logan starfished over the bed, and

Alyssa huddled into a ball in the corner.

My eyes went to the balcony. I'd drawn the curtains and weighed them down with a few of the books on the table to create a seal that made sure no one could look in or move the curtain without me noticing. But it was easily our weakest point of defense and it didn't take a genius to see that.

I rose and quietly crossed the room, careful to avoid the creaky spots in the floor. Gun raised, I approached the double doors. Once I reached the curtain, I paused, held my breath, and listened.

Nothing.

Didn't mean there wasn't something lingering out there. I put my back flush against the wall and, with the tip of my gun, moved the curtain to one side so I could peek out.

A man was leaning against the balcony rail, arms and ankles crossed as if he were casually waiting for a friend instead of lingering outside the room of one of the nation's newly minted most wanted persons. Who was on a hair trigger to boot. He didn't move. I kept my gun raised but the braid flung over his right shoulder gave him away.

Freaking Talon.

Relief rushed over me in a strong wave. I told myself it had everything to do with not having another enemy to fight—and completely ignored how the surge of panic calmed inside me when he shot me a lopsided grin. It was just a side effect of stress. I was new to the whole, "forced to clear my name" lifestyle and it left me a bit tense.

That didn't mean he'd get away with being stupid.

I moved the curtains and slid open the balcony door. "I should shoot you on principle, Orsoto." I snapped, keeping my voice low so I wouldn't wake the kids.

His grin was white and unrepentant as he stepped across the threshold into the room. "That wouldn't be very nice," he whispered, matching my tone, "Especially considering all of the trouble I took to find you."

"No one asked you to." Infuriating high-handed man...If I

wasn't beating back the urge to hug him, I'd probably be more contrite.

He shrugged. "Saw your face come across the police desk as a wanted criminal. I packed my bags and came to find you."

Just like that. He knew I was in trouble and dropped everything to swoop in and help. Emotion surged through me, and I had to look away a moment to hold back the moisture that misted in my eyes. I cleared my throat. "I've got everything under control." I gritted out.

"So I can tell from the twenty seven newscasts blaming you for the assassination of a soon to be U.S. Jackson."

"How did you find me?"

He smirked. "I'm a marine. I've got my ways."

"I've got zero patience for bullshit, Orsoto. Spill it."

He gave me a look. "It didn't take a genius to know that you'd move the kids away from the center of drama. I simply cross referenced your last known location and checked hotels for late night check ins within a hundred mile radius. I also knew that you wouldn't play to the norm and would avoid the sleazier motels since that's where people would look first." His assessment was straightforward and on point...and the likelihood of someone else arriving at those same conclusions were high. We needed to get gone.

Talon was on the same page because he stepped, filling my space. "Let's get on the road." He said. "You tell me where you're headed and I'll drive so you can get some sleep."

"Talon—"

"Woman, don't argue with me." He said. "We don't have time. Tell me—what's the plan?"

The air was tense with my silence. Everything in me screamed not to say a word. The last time I trusted a man like this, I got burned and ended up a prisoner in a shit hole in Syria. Staring into his eyes, something else warred deep within me.

"There's no place I can trust." I finally said. "My best option for them is a safe house."

"Makes sense. You got one arranged?"

"My contact's not responding." I shook my head. "Truly, I was just going to drive there and demand sanctuary, at least for the kids."

He nodded, taking the whole jacked up situation in stride. "Let's get them up and moving and we can figure this out on the road. It wasn't easy tracking you, I knew what signs to look for, but I wouldn't put it past more motivated players to not be far behind. It's too dangerous to stay here too long."

Motivated players? Like bounty hunters, contract assassins, government bloodhounds...a whole list of highly trained hobbyists and professionals fueled by the thought of fame or fortune flicked through my head. All of them scenting blood in the water. Effing perfect.

I woke Alyssa first, knowing she'd be a good stabilizer for her brother.

"Wake up, hon." I murmured, gently shaking her shoulder. "Wake up." She jerked beneath my hand and her eyes popped open, hazy with sleep. They cleared a bit as she focused on me. "I need you to get you and your brother up and ready to go. We leave in five minutes."

"But we haven't been here—" Her eyes shot to Talon and her lips shut.

"Don't be afraid. This is my friend, Talon, and he's going to help me get you and Logan to a safe place. You can trust him."

Skeptical hazel eyes flicked back to me. "We haven't had much luck with "help" the past few days."

Guilt welled in me. The past forty-eight hours had been a nightmare, a disaster neither she nor Logan should have experienced. She was right to be suspicious. "Do you trust me?"

She blinked and then nodded.

"Good." I shoved the cascade of emotion that her affirmation caused in me toward Beastie who pounced on it willingly. "I trust him and so can you. Now wake up Logan and let's get out of here."

With Talon hustling the kids and me wiping down every

surface in the room, it took us less than ten minutes to be dressed, packed, and out the door just as the first rays of coral morning sun peaked over the horizon. We piled into Talon's car, and the engine roared to life. We pulled out of the parking lot, my eyes alert and scanning for any movement or glint.

"Call Thorne." Talon said.

I turned my head from the window and stared at him. As in the same Luke Thorne who he'd almost gotten into a brawl with at the hospital? That one? I obviously need to get my ears checked. "Excuse me?"

"Call Detective Thorne."

I stared at him like he had two heads. "Why?"

"Has your other contact gotten in touch with you yet?"

I was silent. That was all the answer he needed.

"Do you or these kids have time to wait on him?"

He was right and I knew it.

"How do you think Luke will be able to help?"

"He works in a special unit. No one will look twice about him requesting one."

The more I thought about it, the more it made sense. "I don't have his number saved."

Talon reached across me, popped open his glove box, and pulled out a cell phone. He pressed a few buttons and handed it out to me.

"You have Luke Thorne's number saved in your phone?" I couldn't quite keep the incredulity out of my voice.

"I don't like the man," Talon said. "That doesn't mean he's not useful."

That mercenary logic totally fit Talon.

I dialed. It rang several times, long enough that I thought he wouldn't pick up. I couldn't blame him for that. Why would he?

Please, I breathed. Please, let him answer. My head bowed, struggling under the weight of what I would do if he didn't.

"If it wasn't for the fact that we have a mutual acquaintance who's currently in the middle of an epic crapfest, I'd have just let it ring." Luke's smooth voice said over the phone.

"Luke." Relief made my voice breathy, which I hated.

I could almost feel his attention snapping forward. The energy on the phone changed drastically. "Is this a secure line?"

"No."

"Give me three minutes. I'll call you back." He hung up with a click.

I set the phone on my lap.

"That was fast." Talon said.

"He says he'll call me back."

"But you didn't give him the number."

"I know."

"That phone has a device that scrambles the number code so it'll take more than whatever rookie move Thorne has up his sle—"

The phone buzzed in my hand, cutting Talon off. He looked a bit petulant around the edges as I put the phone to my ear. Macho men didn't like to be wrong. For the first time in nearly three days, I wanted to smile.

I hit the green button. "Hello?"

"I've transferred you to a more secure line." Luke said. "That will keep our connection from dropping."

"That's fine with me." I could hear noise in the background. "Are you at your office?"

"Unfortunately, leaving is not an option at the moment." he replied, the vague formality of his words enough. He was at the office and didn't want our conversation to catch attention. Got it. "You have become a person of interest for a variety of agencies, my friend." he said. "There are regional and national entities looking into the...incident."

"Oh believe me, I'm intimately aware of that" I said. "What are they saying?"

"Nothing good." he hedged.

Non-answers were almost worse than the truth. "Tell me."

"Word on the street is that you are part of the crew who assassinated Jackson and that this hit has been in the works for months." He said. "One source said that you were hired on illegally, under the table, which made it easy to pass out information."

"That's what I've gotten from the news."

"It gets worse," he said.

Dread filled my gut. "What is it?"

"Several entities have placed a reward bounty for your arrest."

Crap. That meant lone ranger yahoos and weirdos trying to taze and bag me at every turn. I was quiet as I processed how that would affect what I was trying to do.

"Are you safe?" he asked.

"Besides some scrapes and bruises, we're fine."

"We?"

"I have Jackson's kids in custody."

He swore. "That complicates matters. A lot."

"Leaving them to the fate of whoever is after them was not an option."

"What are you talking about?"

I debated for a moment but decided to lay it all out for him. If he was going to risk his neck, he needed to know the full extent of the hell that had been unleashed and was traipsing unhindered up the main street of my life. So I told him about the late night car chase that forced us to leave town and the kidnapping attempt at the museum.

"Is there anything you need from me?"

"Yes." I took in a breath. "I need you to organize witness protection for the kids. 24/7 security. A safe house, a shack, anything. The more off the grid, the better."

He made a strangled sound and fell silent. I stared at the road and watched the yellow lines fly by as the silence ticked on. I wouldn't pressure him. If he helped, it had to be of his own volition. I needed him to be all in and I wouldn't beg or subterfuge to make that happen.

After a long minute, he huffed a breath. "I can't make any promises." He admitted. "This will be damn near impossible to explain to the Captain but I might be able to do something.

"Anything you can do I'll appreciate."

"Give me a couple of hours and I'll call you." he said. "Where are you?"

"On the move." My answer was vague on purpose. Just because he trusted his secure line didn't mean I did.

"Right. I'll text you when I know something."

Got it. Hope surged but I fought it back down. "Thank you."

"Stay sharp, beautiful. I'll call you soon." With that, he hung up.

I stared at the phone. Something warm blossomed in my chest at his calling me beautiful. I hit the off button and handed the phone back to Talon.

"What did he say?"

I updated him, swallowing past a surge of discomfort. Was it really that? the voice on my shoulder asked. Or do you just not like having to ask for help? Perhaps both.

My phone vibrated and I looked down to see a text from Brendan. Text? Seriously? I opened it and read the message.

Saw the news. What the hell happened. Jackson and two cops injured. Dane dead. Authorities here are saying you've gone rogue and are out of control...

A pang reverberated in my stomach. Crap. The last thing I needed was a manhunt on my plate, with persona non-grata being yours truly.

Answer your phone and you might already know the answer. Jackson killed. entire thing a set up. Dane and the cops were dirty.

A minute or two ticked by before he responded.

It's a madhouse here. Phones ringing off the hook, news crews picketing the house, FBI sniffing through every room and computer looking for clues. It's full on lockdown. Things aren't looking good on this end.

I gritted my teeth and Beastie paced restlessly. Yeah, the article last night had summed that up for me.

I'm trying to figure that out. Any information you can pass along will be helpful.

It took so long to respond, I didn't think he would.

It's too risky. FBI is monitoring everything.

I understood. This was so far outside his purview and the feds probably danged the real possibility of jail time for his negligence. Not that he could really be blamed, but government agencies always loved a good scapegoat.

I can find who assassinated the Jackson. Anything you send, I'd be grateful for.

A brief silence. *I'll see what I can do.* Another pause. This one longer. *Sorry about you dad.*

Sorrow crashed through me like a wave and it crushed my windpipe making it hard to breathe. Beastie growled at the surge of emotion and it was a faint noise in the back of my mind compared to the wail rising in my chest.

My phone vibrated again.

I've got something you might could use. When can you meet?

That statement pulled me out of the sinking pit of despair that I quickly fell into.

Whatever works. I'll use it. ASAP.

A pause. Then. *Meet me at the funeral.*

Emotion rose and, for a moment, I was blind with all the things I couldn't process right now. There was no doubt in my mind that I wouldn't be welcome. All of this probably confirmed to Julien that I was an unstable and unhealthy variant who shouldn't be allowed near the family and didn't want me tainting the day. Add that to the fact that it would unquestionably be the one place that the authorities would monitor and it should have been an easy no.

Should have been.

Going to the funeral was a bad idea. Yet, when Dad's laughing face flickered in my head, everything that was whole and good in me was tempted to respond that I'd be there. I forced my fingers to open and let the phone slip into my lap until the urge went away.

"Serena," Talon's voice was a welcome distraction until I saw the expression on his face. I knew him long enough to know that look. He was about to say something that he thought would hurt me and he didn't want to but felt obligated to do it. pulled made me look at him. The hesitation in his eyes made my breath catch. "There's something I think you need to know. Your dad—"

I couldn't do this. Couldn't hear this. I could barely breathe around it. I didn't want his sympathy or compassion. I wanted to find a deep dark hole and bury myself in it. "I know." I cut in sharply.

He was silent a few beats. "How did you know?'

"Saw it on the news back in Sacramento. The ambulance explosion made national headlines."

Silence stretched.

"How you doing?"

"Peachy."

"Babe." It was a gentle chastisement and an invitation to talk all in one.

I said nothing. This was the last conversation I wanted to have, with anyone.

"There will never be anyone like your dad, Serena. He was a one of a kind. Generous, loyal, compassionate." His rumbly voice was deep, quiet...almost reverent and that weird pain surged in my chest again. "I'll miss him, too. More than I think he knew."

I didn't acknowledge him, simply stared out of the window and tried not to let the vortex inside me swallow me whole. Talon picked up my left hand and I watched through the window reflection as he brought it to his lips before settling our linked hands on his knee.

He held my hand like that for a long time.

CHAPTER 17

We drove east for another six hours before Talon's phone buzzed with GPS coordinates. Luke. For the next dozen hours, we switched off driving in shifts until we reached our location—a sprawling neighborhood just outside of Chandler, Oklahoma. With condominium-like duplexes all smushed together in endless rows like books at the library. A place to hide in plain sight in the midst of chaos. Perfect.

The first splatters of sunlight barely crested the horizon on Saturday morning as we pulled into the driveway of a white painted duplex—one of three dozen on that street—the kids only stared.

"Everyone out." I said spurring them on. "Bring your go-bag."

"Where are we? Is mom here?" Logan asked hopefully.

Guilt twinged my gut. But if the kid knew, he'd freak out. And I needed him calm and lucid until then. "This is a house that will keep you safe from the bad guys trying to get you. Your mom's still in Brazil with the humanitarian council, remember?" His face was so crestfallen that I added, "But once we think the safe is clear, we'll take you to her. Okay?" Lies, but necessary ones to keep him from a full out meltdown.

Alyssa looked at me, her suspicious glance an attempt to hide the fear in her eyes. Logan stared up at me like I held the sun in a perilous grip and nodded his head.

I turned and saw Luke standing in the front door of the house, waiting for us. He gave a short wave.

"Any bags I can help with?" He asked as we got closer.

I shook my head.

Alyssa was staring at him with an awestruck look. His smile ratcheted up about a hundred kilowatts. "Hey, pretty lady. It's good to see you again, even under these conditions. How you doing?"

Alyssa's cheeks went pink. "I'm fine, Detective Thorne," she replied, her voice small but eyes wide.

"That's good to hear." He winked at her.

The color on her face flamed to red.

It might have been hilarious if I wasn't so busy trying to keep them from seeing my fractured soul. "Stop flirting with a twelve-year-old, Luke," I chided. "Kids, inside."

Luke stepped back, and we trudged inside, Talon bringing up the rear.

"Thorne," Talon grunted.

"Orsoto."

I rolled my eyes. Men and their primitive greetings.

"We appreciate you housing us last minute," Talon said.

"I'm not doing it for you." He turned to look at Alyssa and Logan who stood in the living room with lost expressions on their faces. "Okay, quick tour of the house. Both bedrooms are on one side of the house. Serena, I thought you might appreciate your own room. Alyssa and Logan, you share the last one."

I forced a smile but the chaos inside me was too much. Luke's voice was drowned out of a punctured reservoir of emotions.

I made turkey and American cheese sandwiches for the kids from the fridge stocked with basic supplies, made sure they were settled and doing as okay as could be expected, gave Luke and Talon an abbreviated summary of events since the kidnapping attempt at the museum, and secured my own telephone lines. The walk to my room was done with rigid, forced steps. When the door clicked shut, I began to shake.

I didn't stop moving until I was in the bathroom and turned the knobs on the shower. My skin itched, and an obsessive desire to get clean ping ponged in my mind. I needed to wash away the last twenty-four hours. Get my head on straight.

I stared at myself in the mirror until steam fogged up my reflection. My face warbled, slowly disappearing as steam crept up the glass until my entire reflection was hidden from my gaze. Overlooked and overwhelmed once again. Rage welled and spilled over. I turned toward the steaming shower and slid back the door. I stepped in, fully clothed. Blistering hot water immediately soaked me but I found solace in the pain. I sank against the tile wall until my knees hit my chest. Jackson, dead. Dad, dead. Alyssa and Logan wanted by an organization I'd yet to identify. Me on the run from half a dozen or more government and private agencies.

Such a shit storm. I'd done nothing to predict or stop it.

It was too much.

My mind felt like it was melting and exploding all at the same time. Beastie pounced and prowled back and forth. All but smothering the emotion laden insecurities in my life.

I wrapped my arms around my knees and found solace in the blistering hot water that pounded into my skin.

I had to pull this together. There was no other choice. But the how and working it out was overwhelming. I had connections but none that would help me with the news labeling an accomplice political assassination. My options for supplies were limited. Dane's laptop was the only thing I had to go off of for information on who put out the hit on the Jackson's kids... then hopefully I'd be able to trace that back to the people who hired him in the first place.

It felt like I was grasping at straws.

I rested my head on my knees and sucked in a breath full of steam.

Something rattled the shower door, but I ignored it. When the it slid open, my head slowly drifted up to stare at the tall man now framed by steam. Prussian blue eyes met mine, the expression carefully blank.

Luke studied me for a moment. He didn't say a word, just stepped into the steaming tub and sat down beside me. I was afraid he was going to chat, garble his condolences and give me a "these things happen" speech. But he did none of that; simply sat and let his body heat soaking through my side.

"It's not your fault." He deep voice echoed off the shower tiles. It was nowhere near as deep as Talon's, but it was still nice.

Maybe so, but it was hard to believe that when the weight of correcting it rested solely on my shoulders

"I'll do whatever you need me to do, Serena. Help you in any way I can. Just tell me how."

I looked into his eyes and saw the seriousness of his words. He knew the risks—I didn't have to outline them point by point. Losing his job was the least of his worries. Jail time and no pension was a very real possibility. And yet he'd risk that... for me.

I didn't know what to do with that.

I glanced at his chest. It looked strong. I leaned over and put my head on his chest. I don't know when the tears started. But once I noticed them they came in a torrent, silent and copious.

The water turned cold before the tears ran dry, casting chills over my slick skin. My clothes itched...and never once did he move.

CHAPTER 18

The hard tub floor and the chilly water expedited my pity party. When I could no longer feel my fingers, I knew it was time to get up and at least pretend to find solutions instead of wallowing in the grief that threatened to strangle me with every breath.

Luke stepped out of the shower before me and held out a fluffy white bath towel for me to step into. I let him wrap me up, knowing I should say something, anything, but only watched with hollow eyes as he grabbed a hand towel from one of the cabinets.

"My grandpa used to tell me that sometimes you have to let out all of those violent emotions before you can see clearly enough to do the next right thing," he said, voice low and soothing as he dabbed droplets from my face with a hand towel. "Even if the next right thing is only being brave enough to face to the next problem."

Wise words. But that philosophy only worked if you had hope that the problem could be solved...and deep down I knew the truth. Failure was inevitable. The question was, how much damage could I mitigate before it all came crashing down?

I shrugged and struggled to find my words. "A person can only take so much tragedy."

"True." He threw the damp towel into the sink before grabbing a bigger one. "But *you* are stronger than the average Jane...and there are good people willing to help you traverse the rough road ahead." I wasn't prepared for him to step close, wrap his arms around me, and begin squeezing water from my braids. He kept maximum distance between us, the only point of contact light brushes of his skin against mine, and he avoided making eye contact, giving me space as he focused on my hair.

I should have stepped away, created more room but it felt like my heels were drilled into the floor.

I slowly shook my head. "I can't drag you guys into my failure. This situation is a crapshoot and it's only going to get worse if I can't produce hard evidence that I had nothing to do with Jackson's murder. Evidence that's as elusive as the reason someone would want to take him out to begin with."

"We've got time."

"No, Luke, we really don't." I watched our reflection in the mirror and the dress shirt he wore was plastered the muscles of his back and shoulders. Muscles that rippled when he gave my braids another gentle squeeze. "How long will it take for your office to figure out there's a house being unofficially occupied? Two days? The wise thing would be for me to cut ties with the group but I don't trust the system enough to just give Alyssa and Logan over to it—I've seen this kind of political manipulation before and it never ends well for kids."

Luke met my gaze then and I instantly drowned in the stormy indigo depths. "For some of us," he murmured. "Letting you leave is not a viable option."

I knew what he meant. He was a good man and I'd caught him up in a situation that could potentially end his career yet the blaze in his eyes told me I couldn't dislodge him if I tried. What had a done to create that kind of loyalty in a man I barely knew? It was half gratitude, half apology that made me hitch onto my toes, lean forward, and kiss his cheek.

I didn't expect him to slide an arm around my waist and bring me flush against him. Didn't expect him to brush my cheek with his free hand before softly placing his lips on mine.

For a moment, I let myself enjoy it. The warm strength of his body. The rasp of his skin as he brushed his mouth back and forth against mine. I sank into it for a split second, letting the chaos of thoughts quiet under the gentle insistence of his kiss.

But reality was never far away. Beastie yowled in protest at the invasion of our space. I was a federal fugitive and if I hadn't made it to Interpol's top ten list, it was only a matter of hours before that happened. The amount of space I had for an emotional entanglement was negative a thousand and I couldn't be selfish enough to drag Luke down with me.

Or Talon, for that matter. Who was prowling the house somewhere.

Crap. I should be mitigating the drama, not adding to it.

I shoved his chest and took two giant steps back. "That was...inappropriate. I shouldn't have done that. I'm apologize." My words were blunt, tone colder than a Siberian iceberg but delivery was the last thing on my mind.

Luke's mouth quirked in a quizzical smile but nodded. "No, that's my fault. I'm usually better at picking my moments but I'm not myself around you." He shot me a small smile as he pulled open the bathroom door. "You've got a lot on your plate and there isn't time for that."

But the gleam in his eye implied that, at some point, he'd make time. I didn't get a chance to shoot that down before he turned and strode into the bedroom and through the door. I stared at it frozen to the floor as a myriad of emotion swirling through me. Panic that I was repeating history. Fear that, when he realized just how much I was holding my shit together with duct tape and determination, he'd be disgusted. A warm glow that secretly enjoyed his soft kiss. I didn't want to string him along but it seems like it was all I seemed to do.

And then there was Talon. God, I was such a mess. That thought alone made we want to find some cheap whiskey and pound it.

That was out of the question so I did the next best thing: hunted.

I swapped my waterlogged clothes for black leather jeggings, a turtleneck, and a cropped jacket. Then, I pulled open my go-bag and grabbed Dane's phone and black box the size of tablet that was a state of the art decoder that could decipher gate codes, unlock electric cars, and disarm security systems in less the sixty seconds. I plugged the iPhone into it and waited. But Dane, apparently, was no rookie. There was an encryption code lock on the phone that rewrote itself every time I tried forcing it open. I tried several different hacking techniques but nothing seemed to penetrate. After an hour of trying, I conceded defeat.

I flung the phone to the bed and fought back a scream. This only left one option and it wasn't a good one—a clandestine meeting with Brendan...at my dad's funeral. Beastie huffed at the thought. The list of ways this could spiral out of control was two miles long, starting with how neither Luke nor Talon would ever agree to letting me walk into a public event that was sure to have more cops and federal agents than a FBI convention. Brendan's motivation was also suspect. Why risk his position helping a federal criminal? His motive didn't pan out but I couldn't do anything about that.

All I could focus on was the next right thing: which was getting myself to that funeral.

Pulling a small laptop out of my bag, I did a quick search of my father's name. Five hundred results popped up immediately and, for a second, I was tempted to let the pictures, videos, and news stories drag me back under the ocean of grief inside me. My nose stung as I forced myself to skim the page and it didn't take me long to find a local news article stating the location of dad's burial service: the Arlington Memorial Gardens in Spencer, Oklahoma. A popular resting place for highly decorated cops and military...and the funeral was tomorrow morning at ten a.m.

Ten minutes later, a map of the area surrounding the funeral home and its surroundings was burned into my brain and a plan crystallized. There was no way I'd be able to enter the funeral crowd from the parking lot—I'm sure local authorities would set up some kind of screening system to try and catch me if I tried to slip in that way. The church funeral would be the most heavily attended but also the most watched. That was a no go. The burial site might be an option. I glanced at the screen again to confirm the location—Arlington Funeral Home & Memory Gardens in Spencer, Oklahoma. Remote, dense woods flanked the southern and western edges of the property, and there seemed to be a small building in the center of the property. A quick search later and I saw that it was a funeral facility house within the gardens.

Bingo, baby.

I could sneak into the facility and hide there until people showed up for the burial. At some point, the building would be busy with people taking bathroom breaks...and then I'd slip into a group of commiserates and walk until I found Brendan and make him tell me his news.

Anything to clear my name.

Anything to remove this crushing weight of failure that I felt every time I glanced at my dad's picture. I'd make this right...so that my father wouldn't be buried thinking his daughter was as horrible and unstable as the criminals he'd spent a lifetime fighting.

That thought lurched me into action. I picked up my phone and shot a quick text to Brendan.

I'll be there.

Once the little green send bar swooped across the screen, grabbed my backpack, and dumped the contents onto the bed. I did a quick inventory, checking to see what I was low on and what I could persuade one of the boys to loan me. I glanced through the contents of a makeup kit that would make the artist for the last Star Trek movie jealous and made sure I had enough facial putty to pull off the plan in my head. If I was going to walk through a crowd of dad's friends, people I'd known since I could walk, then I'd need to alter my appearance enough that there was no way they, or the plain clothes cops that would no doubt be in the crowd, would recognize me.

I was shoving things back into the bag when the door swung open and I glanced up just as Talon strode inside. He shut the door, hard, and it made me really look at him; the tension vibrating off him made me frown. The Native American war lord was pissed and I had no idea why.

His eyes flicked to the mess on the bed. "Ever get any leads from Dane's phone?"

"Unfortunately, no. It's embedded with a self-encrypting security system that changes the password every time I try and force my way through the server." I rolled a thin sweater that was lined with thermal heat tech and placed it in the backpack.

"Fancy." He rumbled.

I know right. I was dying to know what information was so important that he'd go to such lengths, expensive lengths, to keep it concealed. Hopefully, Brendan could give a few insights.

"You goin' somewhere?"

There was a dangerous timbre to voice, one I hadn't heard before. But I had zero time or inclination to deal with how big a gasket Talon would blow a gasket if he got the slightest hint that I was going to try to attend my dad's funeral. I already knew it was going to be teeming with law enforcement agents from at least three agencies trying to snare me. Was it wise? No. Was I going to be talked out of it. Absolutely not. So I did what any self-preserving, minimal drama, totally stressed out woman on the edge would do.

I lied.

"Just repacking," I told him in a smooth voice as I threw in a few extra magazine clips. "Trying to take inventory and see what refills I can ask Luke for."

Talon's scoff was a harsh rumble. "Of course you'd ask Thorne. I can only guess at how helpful you think he's already been in this whole situation."

That made me pause and straighten to look at him. "Now what's that supposed to mean, Orsoto?" His tension affected my Zen and I could feel Beastie stirring in the back of my mind but I was a bit puzzled by this hostility. "Luke has done nothing but put his career on the line to help me and without his help we'd still be driving up on and down Route 66 hoping someone would answer our calls. I didn't ask for his help and I certainly didn't ask for yours—"

"What was he doing in here with you this afternoon?"

My mind blanked. Surely he wasn't talking about...but the blaze of jealousy made his jaw clench and muscle tense. I scrambled for something to say. "He was...checking on me. He knew was upset because of dad and wanted to make sure I was okay."

"I'll bet there's lot of things you can make okay in the shower." Lightning gleamed in Talon's eyes and there was a wild emotion I couldn't quite name but his implication spiked my own anger.

"Don't be a jerk," I spat. "You could just ask instead of implying that I'm a whore seeking emotional comfort but even then I don't owe you an explanation for anything that happens between Luke and I."

Talon silently drilled holes into my skull with those flashing eyes and silence descended. Then just as suddenly, he cracked his neck and pushed off the door and began slowly walking toward me.

"I recognize." He started, voice deep and so, so grumbly. "That the last forty-eight hours have been traumatic for you and you've been forced to make a lot of hard decisions in a short amount of time."

The look on his face triggered danger bells in my mind and I inched away from him, matching his forward steps with my own backward ones.

"Normally, I'd wait," he muttered, edging closer. "Give you time to grieve your dad, clear your name…. but you've forced my hand."

What on earth was he talking about? With no warning, he lunged for me, hands outstretched, but I ducked under his arm and spun back to face him. "Cryptic isn't your usual style." I said, backing away even as he whirled and stalked toward me. The room really wasn't that big and I hit the wall sooner than I expected. Talon used that to his advantage and yanked me into his chest before I could retaliate.

"What the hell is your prob—"

"If you think"—he shook me a little bit— "that I will stand aside and watch you fall in love with another man, you're out of your mind." His arms wrapped tightly around my back and held me flush against him.

"Love? What are you talking about?" There wasn't much room to maneuver so I rammed my knee into this inside of his thigh, causing his knee to twist at a painful angle. His leg buckled and I used that bit of space to ram four fingers straight into his solar plexus. He gasped and I spun out of his loosened grip and lunged for the door.

I yanked it open an inch but Talon put a big palm against it and shoved it closed once again and pressed into my back.

"I'm talking about Luke," he growled into my hair.

"Let go, Talon."

"Not until you tell me that I must have been dreaming when I walked past your window and saw Thorne kissing you."

I flung an elbow back into his ribcage but he only grunted like it was a fly swat. "That's none of your business."

"I'm painfully aware that *you* really believe that."

My eyes narrowed and I twisted around until the door was at my back and I could stare into his silver eyes. "Sarcasm isn't appreciated. There is literally nothing to say about this." Okay, maybe close eye contact with an emotional Native American war lord wasn't such a great idea.

"Luke seems to think otherwise—"

"I don't care." I snapped.

"You're determined to bury your head in your armpit and pretend this thing between us doesn't exist."

"It doesn't!" I cried. "It can't. Julien hates me enough without thinking that I weaseled my way into a relationship with his best friend. Luke's out of the picture and so are you."

"Now Julien's the reason you can't *see* me?" He shot back, frustrated. "See what's been in front of your face for years? Do you expect me to wait until you and Julien bury whatever crap it is that you've put between him so I can go to him and tell him I'm in love with his baby sister? Considering the mature way you two have handled yourselves the past week, that's not likely to happen anytime in the near future."

"You of all people know exactly how unstable I am. You shouldn't *want* this."

"Stop lying to yourself. You've been pushing people out of your life for years. It's all you seem to know how to do."

Anger flushed through me. Could he blame me? Look at what happened when people came into my life—either they hurt me or I failed them. And the common denominator was always me.

I didn't know how to make him see that. "What do you want from me?"

"This."

He wrapped my braids around a fist and gently titled my head back, his free brushing against my cheek in a delicate career. His mouth, however, was a different matter altogether. Hungry. Plundering. He kissed me like a man starved of light and trying to soak all of it up at one time. The dichotomy of his touch, sweeping caresses against my skin but his lips aggressively plundering mine made something snap inside me. If he thought I'd shrivel under the force of his passion, he was dead wrong. I lifted onto my toes, buried a hand at the base of his brain and kissing him like I was drowning. And maybe I was. Drowning in the conflicting emotions of liking two men. In Beastie's plaintive roar and the music sweeping through mental corridors. In the crushing failure of Jackson's assassination and the burden of protecting his children.

For a moment, with Talon's lips on mine, the noise in my head quieted and all I could focus on was the feel of his mouth and clutch of his hands.

By the time he lifted his head, I was a hot mess trying to rebuild the bricks of my mental fortress that he'd just blown crater sized holes in.

"I have no intention of letting you slip away from me."

"You don't get to make that decision." My voice hitched as I tried to catch my breath.

He let me go and strode for the door. "The funeral is going to be the first place they look for you." He had his back to me, hand on the door, braid mused from where I'd clutched him to me. "Local PD...FBI...free agents trying to collect a buck and a trophy...there's going to be a cocktail of players there, all with eyes out for you."

I knew this. I'd gone over the dozens of ways someone could snatch me in a situation like a crowded funeral. But it wasn't going to stop me. I needed whatever information Brendan had to help shed light on Jackson's murder and clear my name. The way I saw it, I had no choice—and it was personal both ways.

So I said nothing.

And Talon knew me well enough to recognize that I'd already made up my mind.

"You think your brother will just stand by and watch you be dragged away, your family's name run through the mud?"

If local PD was doing the dragging, Julien probably would likely hogtie me himself Any other agency? Absolutely not. He'd draw weapons before letting that happen, if only to save face.

"Someone could get hurt. Your stepmom, Julien, your dad's co-workers, family. You. Don't go, CeCe. Wait it out—it's safer for everyone that way."

He wasn't wrong and I knew it. It just didn't matter. Something inside me was pulling me to the funeral and I couldn't fight it.

When I didn't say anything, Talon pulled open the door and stepped outside. But his disappointment lingered in the air.

CHAPTER 19

T he bathroom tiles of the Arlington Memorial Gardens women's restroom gleamed, and the lack of debris in the corners told me that an obsessive compulsive janitor must work there. I would be intimately acquainted with the habits of the cleaning staff—I'd spent the last six hours in the corner stall in the women's restroom waiting for dad's burial ceremony to begin.

It was too much of a risk to take Talon's car. I'm sure the moment the authorities clocked him back in town he'd have a tail, plus I didn't need another lecture from him. Luke was an option but I needed another alpha male jumping down my throat at how dangerous this was like I needed a nail in my foot. So, he was out of the picture also. In the end, I was reduced to the ultimate desperate scenario: calling Uber. This was the safest way to keep anyone from tracing me back to Alyssa and Logan. From what I gathered on the news, there still wasn't a clear motive or suspect for the murder of Jackson Davis...except me, of course.

So, I snuck out of the condo and had the Uber driver pick me up in a neighborhood half a mile from the safe house and then drop me at a sketchy gas station in Spencer, Oklahoma that was half a mile away from the funeral home. After weaving through a dense grove of trees at two am in the morning, disarming the antiquated alarm system took less than two minutes and I slipped through the funeral home parlor in the wee hours of the night.

Now I waited for people to begin filtering through the

building so I could slip into the crowd. I checked my watch. It read six fifteen am. Still hours to go. I set the alarm on my phone before allowing myself to doze but my dreams were restless and violent. Filled with flashes of exploding cars and the distinctive sound of water dripping on stone. Beastie growled, the tension and low dose adrenaline was making her edgy. Her and me both. I rose earlier than planned and stood before the large mirror with my makeup bag open. An hour later, I took a moment to examine my work.

I'd applied facial putty to my nose, elongating it, and snapped false dentures into place to alter the look of my teeth. Small changes that subtly shifted the length of my jaw and cheekbones. I sharpened my cheeks with a variety of facial powders and even added an indent in my chin using black eyeliner and tactful smudging. Lake blue eye contacts completed the look. The final effect made me look like one of those emaciated models with sunken cheek bones and a pinched mouth.

It was half past nine when heels clacking on the tile alerted me that people had finally arrived. Several women walked into the bathroom and I waited until I heard a stall door close before I stood, flushed the toilet, and walked out. There was a small line inside the doors four women deep and the next woman moved into my vacated stall. I washed my hands and checked my reflection. My braids were stuffed down the back of a black trench coat fastened in place by a large silver buckle and I tugged on a slouchy beret to cover the rest of my hair and part of my face.

I dried my hands and followed two women out the door and through the building. Just before I stepped outside, I snagged the oversized black sunglasses dangling on the collar of my black turtleneck and slid them over my face. A wave of people lingered just outside the building and broke off in small groups to walk to the gravesite. I slouched my shoulders, making myself as small as possible and followed.

It had rained the night before and thick water droplets clung to shoes and soaked socks as people made their way across the burial site. The early morning sun created a golden haze over the field, just enough warmth to cause steam to puff in the air. I sucked in a lungful of pine scented crisp air.

Hazy, mellow, frosty morning...dad's favorite time of day.

The crowd moved all around me. People lingered, the sadness hovering over the gravesite like a veil that we were hesitant, weren't ready to tear.

They mingled, hushed voices consoling and remembering at a respectful distance. My brain picked up bits of pieces of conversation, things like "he pulled me out a burning tank in '91" or "we shot our way through a band of gangbangers" and "one day a check showed up in our mailbox and we knew it was him"; it all filtered around me like trickling water as I watched my family. The line of people wanting to speak with my stepmother was at least twenty people deep, all waiting to console and encourage and remember with her. Three men in dark grey coats and sunglasses stood on the far side of the casket, their presence unobtrusive yet there was a watchful energy around them that drew the eye.

Federal agents assigned to trail my family. I'm sure they indicated it was for their protection and a courtesy to dad; only a fool would believe that. If it were just a handful of officers, that would make sense. But on my first sweep of the area, I clocked more than a dozen agents scattered across the graveyard. This wasn't a show of support for a fallen comrade—this was a thinly veiled manhunt with me at the center target. I cinched my trench coat a little tighter.

A few boldly let their weapons show but I knew they wouldn't really risk firing shots into the crowd; innocent civilians hurt was bad for reports...and promotions. Their only really option was to arrest me but I couldn't let that happen. I wouldn't clear my name cooling my heels in someone's jail cell, letting the bureaucrats take over the investigation. With Alyssa and Logan safely installed in a safe house, I could focus on what needed to happen.

My cousin Marcus never left my stepmom's side, arm

wrapped around her shoulders and hand holding hers as soldiers, civilians, and friends came to speak with her. Yvonne looked flawless as usual—she'd paired a black tea dress with a black velvet blazer and a wide brim church hat—but there was weight in her shoulders that hunched her back, made her lean heavily into my cousin as she'd fall at any moment. As if he was the only thing keep her from being a puddle on the damp, cold earth. I'd never seen her so…shaken.

Out of nowhere, music fluttered in my head, half startling me. I checked on Beastie but she only sat in her cage with eyes roaming for trouble. She wasn't unstable enough to trigger the music generally used to calm her and it left me puzzled. But the song didn't wane and I started to hum a cello accompaniment under my breath. It took nearly ten bars for me to recognize the son—Amazing Grace, dad's favorite.

Hot tears splashed on my cheeks. They felt conspicuous to me and burned as memories flashed before my eyes. Dad's booming laugh that always managed to pull a smile out of me. My arms wrapped around him as he let me ride the motorcycle for the first time. His arms on my shoulders as he corrected my gun stance. The pride on his face when I told him I'd been offered a job at Homeland Security.

I had to remind myself that no one would look twice at a woman crying at a funeral. In fact, the opposite was more likely to draw attention.

A large black man strode to the head of the gravesite and ushered people to draw closer. When the crowd closed ranks, there were close to a hundred people present, and the man opened his Bible and began the final eulogy as dad's casket was slowly lowered into the earth.

I stayed on the fringe of the crowd and distracted myself by searching the seas of faces for the one I'd come to meet with. The law enforcement and military contingent immediately caught my gaze; the high and tight haircuts, straight posture, and uniforms were a dead giveaway. There was a hard set to their faces, a glint in their eye that testified to the violence they'd seen and wouldn't hesitate to unleash it on you given the right circumstances. I didn't linger on those faces. The best of us could sense when they were being watched and the last thing I needed was trigger a cop's third eye by staring too long.

After my sweep of the crowd, worry curdled my gut. Brendan hadn't responded to my last text but I didn't think anything about it since I'm sure his life was a barrage of reporters and police all wanting an inside story. At first, I thought he might come in disguise but there was no need for that—staying to help his uncle meant that he had a clear alibi for the cops and he wouldn't be a high priority person to watch. Which meant we'd have an opportunity to really talk...if I could find him.

My eyes drifted over the crowd and paused once again on the man who stood head and shoulders above everyone else, leather wrapped braid swaying in the November breeze. Talon. I'd known he'd be here...that the same love and compulsion that drove me would woo him to this gravesite as well. Dad had been...well, father to both of us. Watching Talon clench his fists and a sheen in his eye, I knew that he felt the loss as deeply as I did. Maybe deeper. This was the second father figure he'd buried in his life.

When the funeral diggers began tossing dirt back onto the grave, the ceremony was over and people began breaking away, some going off to their cars, others lingering to reminisce. Talon made his way over to where my family stood and the moment Julien caught sight of him, he broke away and drew him into a fierce, back pounding hug. As he pulled away, Talon said something that made Julien jerk and look at him with surprise that he quickly hid. When Talon moved to greet my mother, Julien swept his eyes over the crowd with a frown on his face. Oh crap. Suspicion flared. Had Talon told him I was here? Beastie rumbled, ready to be angry but I forced myself to ignore the cold stirring in my core. He wouldn't do that, he knew it was too risky and...

"Talon!" Yvonne screamed when she saw him and fell into

his arms in a dramatic heap as if the strings holding her up had snapped. "I didn't think you'd make it," she sobbed, loudly. "When we couldn't get ahold of you, we thought you might have gone after Serena to talk some sense into that girl's head. What's wrong with her?" She dissolved into tears but saying my name was like hitting the magic button on a game show. They were suddenly surrounded by men who created a perimeter or black sunglasses and grey trench coats around them. No doubt ready to jump down Talon's throat...once he got rid of the dramatic armful that was my stepmother.

Her reaction made me frown. She hated theatrics—thought anything other than a calm voice and relaxed demeanor was tacky and ghetto. I remember when I cried after breaking my toe walking down the stage after a cello recital and she punished me for being too loud. Perhaps the funeral threw her over the edge but I never imagined...this. I thought she'd be more resigned...

"You shouldn't be here," a voice from my left grumbled.

I froze. It was Julien. Just like that, I was sweating in my turtleneck.

His tone was casual but there was a tightness around his eyes that told me he was holding his emotion in check. Beastie grumbled. We knew how quickly that emotion could turn volatile.

"I'm not staying." I meant it as a reassurance. "I couldn't miss it, though. He wouldn't have wanted me to." And the information carrot that Brendan dangled before me was to alluring not to take. If I could find him.

"He would have understood your present circumstances," Julien berated. "You being here is a danger—"

Yvonne wailed, louder this time, and Talon patted her back soothingly and he swept his eyes over the crowd as if searching for help. I realized that the whole production was a distraction. Create a big enough scene with someone who potentially had information and all of the sudden everyone was looking at my mother and her obnoxious scene and no one noticed Julien slip away. To find me.

I turned to face him, knowing that we'd draw more attention standing right next to another and talking out of the sides of our mouths. "I didn't do it."

"There's four dead bodies that say otherwise. Four. That's strong evidence."

"It was a cluster long before I entered the picture. There are other players in shadows—and I have no idea who they are or what they want."

"Plus Jackson's missing kids. Word is that you're going to ransom them back to their mom."

"And what do you think?"

"I have no interest in conjecturing about your guilt," His voice was sharp and I flinched. "What would *he* say about this mess that you're in?"

My throat tightened. Dad would be furious...and disappointed. But I also knew he wouldn't leave me to dangle in the wind. "He'd help me I could," I countered under my breath.

"I know what he'd say. He'd say you're capable of getting yourself out of it, that you always had a plan and boldness to see it through," Julien scoffed. "For a long time, I thought he was making up that crap. For a long time, I thought that the reason he invested so much in you was because he was unimpressed with me. I wasn't enough so he had to make do with you as well."

"Dad never—"

"He'd always say things like you were strong and bold and had a moral compass that would always point true North. That you'd never leave a comrade in danger. That you'd claw your way out of any hellhole because you were brave. Honestly? I thought he was making it up to make you feel better about yourself. And I thought all you did was ride the wind of greatness with zero of the responsibility to carry on his legacy. That's what I thought...until I read your Homeland file."

My gaze snapped to his and Beastie growled. Read my file? That wasn't possible. My missions were often highly classified and only the upper echelon of the government could access it. Hell, it had probably been redacted so much that it looked like the resume of a Walmart employee.

"I know what you're thinking," he said. "With everything that's gone down the last couple of days, there's been some psychological evals done on you to determine the likelihood that you'd go off the rails this far. I convinced a buddy to let me...glance."

He'd know, then. About Syria, the diplomat's death and the gruesome death of his daughter. All my fault. All due to my bad judgement call—an unforgivable crime in my profession. "Julien, I can explain."

"Explain what? You're saying that you didn't' do those things?"

"I'm saying that it's more complicated than that."

"Really?" He sounded dubious. "It can't get more complicated than raiding a Nigerian slave camp to extract the daughter of a murdered diplomat who was forced to be a child soldier."

My mind blanked.

"Report stated that you rigged a bus with a bad transmission and ended up saving twenty-one kids that night."

I had nothing.

"I read enough that you don't owe me or anyone else an explanation." He cut in. "Dad didn't know of the things you've done. But I do...and I know he'd be proud, prouder than he already was."

Tears burned in my eyes. "I need to go."

"Yes, you do." It was matter-of-fact but had no heat, no vehemence. "But don't stay gone, Serena. Dad wouldn't have wanted that. Neither do I."

I couldn't meet his eye, couldn't handle this new openness, and didn't quite know what to make of it. I looked over his shoulder into the tree line to give myself a minute to pull it together enough to say something. Anything. But glint of light made me focus in harder at the grove of trees. I scanned the area but nothing jumped out at me. If a gunman was hiding there, it'd be impossible to tell. Lead hit my stomach. I needed to leave before some money crazed yahoo got it into their thick skull to do something stupid like open fire in a crowd in hopes of nabbing me wounded. Beastie roared in agreement.

"I've stayed too long." I told Julien. "Tell Yvonne—"

Julien's body jerked a millisecond before something white hot slammed into my right shoulder, the force strong enough to spin us both around and knock us off our feet. I knew I was shot before I hit the ground. Pain flared bright and I gasped as fire ran the length of my arm. My body wanted to curl in on itself, to protect itself, but I fought that instinct and forced myself to be still, making myself as small a target as possible and not give whoever was shooting a reason to keep firing. Beside me Julien moaned and my heart jerked.

I sucked in a breath and ignored the scream of pain as I flung my legs over my head in a backwards roll until I knelt over him. "You with me?" I asked. Blood oozed from a small hole in his shoulder. Crap. I pressed my left hand to the wound to staunch the flow.

His hand squeezed mine and I stared into his clear hazel eyes. "You need to go."

He was right but I didn't want to leave him. "Only if you—"

Another bullet hit the ground next to my hip and I rolled several feet away from him to squat behind a large tree. Someone screamed and people began running through the gravesite.

"I'll lay down cover for you." Julien still lay on the ground but he craned his neck to stare at me. "Run like hell."

"Got it."

"One." His good hand drifted to his hip and rested on the butt of his gun.

"Two!" I pulled my own weapon and glanced behind me.

A family secret: we never counted the three.

We both sprang into motion at the same time. Julien rolled to a crouch beside the tree and fired several shots into the tree line. I jumped to my feet and started to run for the line of cars on the other side of the cemetery but a stream of bullets in front of me forced me to dive to one side. I landed on my bleeding arm and screamed but kept rolling. Once shots broke out, chaos erupted. Some people ran for their cars, others, the cops, pulled out weapons and started shooting into the woods.

A glint to my left caught my attention and I whipped my head to look just a man I didn't know pulled a small gun from inside his black bomber jacket and pointed it at me. I lunged for him just as he squeezed the trigger and the soft pop of a silencer sounded with bullets hitting the tree behind me. I slammed both hands into the shoulder holding the gun arm and pulled him close enough to knee him several times in the torso. He grabbed my braids but I pulled back enough to shoot him point blank in the heart.

He started to fall but a caught him just enough to adjust my aim and shoot through his chest at woman who pulled a gun from her purse and pointed it at me. Blood bloomed at her throat and she collapsed.

More bullets sprayed the ground around me.

Rolling to the right, I slammed into a large gravestone, which rattled, but forced myself upright enough to fire three more shots a trio of suits charging toward me.

I had to get out of here. I glanced toward the line of cars that snaked down the street but it was too far to sprint to with bullets flying thickly through the air. The snick of a gun cocking made my blood cold. I flung myself left as a stream of bullets peppered the gravestone above me, bits of rock raining over me. My back slammed into something hard and uneven, winding me and causing fresh pain to sear down my arm. I came up into a crouch and realized that I'd been backed into the infamous tank monument that the cemetery was known for.

And it put me that much further from my escape route.

An arm wrapped around my throat from above and squeezed. It startled me and I screamed but it came out as a muted gurgle. I tried to stand but the concrete beneath was slick and my feet kept slipping. My right hand scrambled to grab my dagger but it came up empty. Crap. I'd already buried in it another assassin's throat. I tugged on the arm with my left hand, trying to give a bit of space so I could lower my chin and breathe but it was weak and did little more than hold on to the crook of the elbow. I re-routed and pulled my Glock and pointed it above me at a vicious angle and pulled the trigger.

All I got was a click.

It was empty.

Hell.

The black spots grew and I wheezed. My mind raced. *Think, Serena.* With a shaking hand, I took the gun apart and the pieces fell on the ground around me. My hands scrambled to grab the part I wanted: the slide. I turned it over in my hand and stabbed the sharp metal into the arm around my throat. A deep cry, a man's voice, in my ear and he jerked. His arm loosened suddenly and a body fell from above and hit the ground in front of me with a thick thud—A tactical tomahawk buried deep in his forehead.

Sky blues stared back from the corpses as I sucked back huge lungfuls of air.

Strong hands grabbed my right arm and yanked me to my feet. Talon shot a man approaching with a mini Uzi before turning stormy gray eyes to me. Lightning sparked in their depths. Oh yeah. It was safe to say he was pissed, but I wanted to throw my arms around his neck and hug him. I lost badass points for that but I didn't care.

"I've got a car on the east side of the cemetery." he said. "I'll lay down cover fire and you run like hell."

I grabbed the handgun from his thigh holster, cocked it, and nodded.

He started to lead me around the statue but a fresh wave of gunfire from the woods made us both jerk back. It was like the shooters doubled and were doing their dead level best to keep us trapped there.

Faintly, I heard the roar of a car engine underneath the clamor of gunfire but I had no chance to think more of it because a chunk of statue crashed to the ground, inches from my foot. Crap! I huddled closer to Talon.

The screech of car tires jerked my gaze from his and I lifted my gun prepared to shoot. A Range Rover with blacked out windows zoomed past us, dirt and grass flying, and did a screeching one-eighty turn that put the front of the car facing Talon and me. Bullets peppered uselessly off the armored glass and metal. The car impatiently honked several times. I squinted at the windshield, trying to see who was driving, and my mouth dropped open in shock. Surely it couldn't be...

The driver's side window began to lower and I truly thought whoever was inside must have a suicide wish. A small but distinct gun barrel peeked out from the top of the glass and the semi-automatic opened fired with the noise of a sawed off shot gun. Talon and I both covered our ears, so close to the powerful weapon that it was deafening. But it was the distraction we needed.

I rose in a crouch and bumped Talon's knee as I did. He looked, a question in his eyes. I pointed at the car and, before he could stop me, dashed for the Rover. I barely made it four steps when I felt Talon's strong arms around me, propelling me forward even as he shielded me from errant bullets.

We both made it to the car. I ripped open the side door and Talon all but shoved me inside.

The gunfire ceased as soon as the door opened.

"About effing time," the familiar female voice groused. She tossed the subcompact machine pistol into the passenger seat, released the park brake, and stomped her foot on the gas. "Were you guys waiting for an invitation?"

The car fishtailed in the slick grass and I slid across the leather seats into the door. Talon's large body slammed into me and I gasped, stars dancing in my vision as pain shot down my arm. Talon immediately pushed himself off me.

"Bad things tend to happen to people when they get into strange cars, Leah." My voice shook a bit from a heady mixture of pain and adrenaline.

Deep brown eyes, so dark they looked black, shot me an irritated gaze through the rearview mirror.

"I'm saving your ass yet again."

I grinned. "So it seems."

"You got any mags in here?" Talon rumbled. "I'm out."

Leah smirked and I must say it wasn't an altogether comforting expression. "I'm not." She kept one hand on the wheel as she reached back and pressed the pad of her forefinger into a small indent in the back passenger seat. A loud beep sounded before the seat popped open. I stared. It was hollow and filled to the brim with handguns, ammo, and small grenades. Part of me wasn't surprised. Leah was the most crazy, prepared assassin I'd ever met.

I gave the address to the safe house and she plugged it into her navigation system. I sat back against and pretended stars weren't dancing before my eyes with each breath.

"Why is no one following us?" I asked through gritted teeth. "We've got to be the hottest item in town?"

"They might be dealing with a few...unexpected vehicular malfunctions. I've heard that Oklahoma weather can be difficult on standard issued cars." Leah held up a hand to showoff dark smears of oil and black gunk.

"You disabled the cars?" Talon asked.

The smile she shot us was a bit manic. "Cops really should make those things harder to break than simply pulling a few wires."

Right. "How did you know where I was?"

She shot me a look in the rearview mirror. "Hon, anyone that knew you for five minutes knew that your dad was the main man in your life. You'd amputate your arm before missing his funeral."

"That doesn't explain why *you're* here."

"Have you seen your face in the news lately? Political assassinations? Kidnappings? You're swimming in crap so deep you can't see the shore." She shrugged. "Plus, I'm between gigs and was bored. Why not help my bestie?"

Talon raised quirked an eyebrow and mouthed, "Bestie?"

Oh shut up. I yelped as Talon pressed a wad of gauze over the oozing wound in my shoulder.

"Don't bleed on my seats," Leah warned.

"Screw you." I groaned.

"Too late for that." Talon muttered. He held the gauze in place with one hand and reached for a bandage roll. As he began wrapping, the pain seared and I shifted a bit, trying to get away from the pain.

"Why didn't you tell me that you were going to the funeral to meet Michaels?" His breath brushed against my skin as he spoke.

I looked out the window and focused on staying still.

"Serena—"

"I knew the atmosphere was going to be unpredictable," I said.

"That was a given."

"I didn't see the point in dragging you there with me, especially if there was a real possibility we'd both walk out of there in handcuffs."

"That's not your call to make," he shot back. "You know you could have asked me to back you up. Why didn't you?"

Leah hit a pothole in the road and pain made everything go fuzzy around the edges. I yelped.

Talon growled.

"I'm trying." I looked at him and wished I hadn't. Lightning still sparked in his eyes.

We finished the drive in silence; Talon vibrating anger like a taunt cello string, me gritting my teeth against the growing pain and desperately wishing for an aspirin, and Leah brooding over God knows what. She's one of my closest friends but she's intense, crazy, and scary AF.

Not that I'd ever admit that to her.

The drive was short, thanks to the fact that Leah drove like a raccoon on bath salts. If my shoulder wasn't throbbing in time with my heartbeat, I'd probably be nauseous from all of the sharp turns. I scanned the street and my eyes zeroed in on the front door—it was pulled mostly shut but dangled from a single hinge. Dread hit my gut and Beastie growled.

I snatched a Beretta 45 from the conceal cover, shoved open my door and was out of the car before it was fully in park.

"Serena wait."

I heard Talon's voice as if in a tunnel. I lifted the gun,

ignoring wrenching pain in shoulder, and cautiously entered the house. The door didn't make a sound as I shoved it open with my foot and stepped inside. Mid-morning light streamed through cracks in the blackout curtains, giving the whole house a dim, hazy feel. Haunted. Abandoned.

I moved through the living room into the hallway where the kids' room dead ended. Blood on the wall made my stomach clench. Shit. Please don't let it be theirs...please don't let it be theirs, I chanted over and over in my head as I neared their room. I moved closer I noticed the door look as if it had been kicked open viciously, splintered jutting out at all angles.

I felt a presence come up behind me on my left and I knew it was Talon.

"Laundry room's clear. But we've got a body in the garage." He whispered.

I nodded, throat to tight to speak.

Talon laid a hand on my arm, stopping me. I looked back and he made a signal to let him go first. The beast growled, saying we could handle it. Pain throbbed in my shoulder and, for once, I ignored her. I nodded at Talon and he swept past me. He bumped a shoulder into the door and pressed into the room, me close behind.

The scent of blood was thick in the air but I made myself check for flickering shadows or any persons leaping from the closet or underneath the bed before I gave it my full attention. When I finally looked, my stomach heaved.

Luke lay face down in the middle of the room, a puddle of blood pooling around his head.

Seeing his prone form made the realization of what happened crash over me. My scar twitched and the beast roared inside my head. There was only one conclusion that made sense: somehow, an unknown party had discovered the location of this safe house and infiltrated.

The kids had been taken.

And it was all my fault.

CHAPTER 20

I 'll admit, I lost it.

My shit, all of my cool points, leaked away like Luke's blood soaking the carpet. Beastie raged in my mind, hurling accusations and every single one of them was on point. I'd failed them, and we had no idea where to begin searching for them. Anger at myself boiled inside. I picked up tableside lamp and flung it at the wall.

"That's not helpful, Serena," Leah snapped, crouching beside Luke. "Go find me a first aid kit."

My mind latched onto the task, anything to drown out the self-disgust ricocheting through me. I turned on my heel and walked out the door toward the master bathroom, brushing past Talon, who was dragging a body out of the second bedroom. A man lay dead across the bathtub, strewn across the blood streaked surface. Normally the sight wouldn't phase but right now my stomach churned. He wore head to toe black but an oversized hoodie stood out from the professional tactical clothing of the other men I'd seen. Three so far.

Against my better judgement, I stepped closer and examined him. Young face but clearly marked with spots from drug use. Dark bruising around his neck told me Luke had been forced to snap it. The hoodie covered most of his upper body but his fingers were riddled with tattoos. One tattoo in particular looked familiar. A circle with a three thick lines cutting through the center. Something about it registered as familiar.

"Serena, hurry!" Leah's voice snapped me into action.

I rummaged through a few cabinets before I found a massive first aid kit underneath the sink. Without another look at the corpse, I ran back across the house and knelt beside Leah. She'd managed to turn Luke onto his side and we could see a deep gash on his left temple. A few minutes later we had his head bandaged. Talon helped us lift Luke and put him on the couch in the living room. His eyes were flickering and the occasional moan tore from his lips. Pain was the best remedy to jolt someone from unconsciousness.

The whole time I helped Leah with Luke, I racked my brain to remember where I'd seen the tattoo before. When Luke was settled, I pulled out my laptop and a quick search later, I found several mugshots of petty criminals within the last few months and all of them had the same tattoo, in various places. I didn't know how all the men were affiliated but I knew that marking led back to a single source—Nicholas "Slade" Stone.

When I saw his name, my stomach clenched.

But if he was our only lead, I'd make deals with Lucifer himself to bring Alyssa and Logan home safely.

I stepped into the backyard, phone in hand. Leah followed me outside. "I don't like the look on your face."

I stared down at my phone. She'd definitely take issue with the vague plan forming in my head. Perhaps it was blood loss or exhaustion that made this seem like a good idea but I was out of good ideas.

"Who's that? Who are you calling?"

The words tumbled out of my mouth before I could hold them back. "You remember that brand of whiskey I had you look up a few days ago?"

"Yeah."

"Turns out a powerful person sent it to me as...a gift." More like a bribe. "And his number in case I felt the need to reach out."

Her eyebrows cinched. "I'm getting the feeling you're not telling me the whole story."

"You ever heard the name Slade?"

Those eyebrows shot into her hairline. "As in Slade the

man who runs the largest drug operation in the Midwest...that Slade?"

I shrugged.

"And you're going to call him? Why?"

"Those markings on the men? I've seen it before...on one of Slade's guys. Luke just checked and there's several cross reference to that tattoo and his organization. Maybe he's got information and he can help."

The look she shot me said it all. "This is not a plan, Serena. This is a desperate patchwork of really bad ideas."

I didn't respond. Mainly because I was thinking the same thing. Reaching out to Slade was risky...but so was wasting time chasing hazy leads that might not produce anything but frustration. We'd debated all logical options but nothing was concrete enough to move on. I had a direct connection—relationship was too strong a word—with Nicholas and, at this point, he seemed to be the only one who could point us down the right path.

And let's be honest here, this wasn't the first time I'd made a deal with the devil. Right or wrong, legal or illegal, I was willing to do a lot to ensure those kids came home safe and as unscarred as possible. Alyssa and Logan didn't have time for me to balk at moral semantics.

I let out a breath and punched in the number.

Leah shook her head at me. "You and I both know that making deals with men like Slade put you in a vulnerable position that they are all too happy to exploit. He'll make you walk a mile of sin before he's satisfied."

I held her gaze and let it ring.

"You sure Talon won't dip out once he knows who you're making your bed with?"

Talon was rock solid—he'd traverse up an erupting volcano for me and insist on going down first, despite being so pissed at me he hadn't looked at me since Luke came to.

Pick up, I breathed. Please, please pick up the phone. More because I didn't want to hear any more of Leah's excuses, I told myself. It had nothing to do with the cold that yawned in my middle and grew steadily colder and larger with each passing hour those kids remain missing.

"And even if he stays, you'll have your hands full corralling to PMSing pissy macho men and conducting a rescue miss—"

"Few people have access to my personal phone," a slightly accented voice drawled across the line. "Even fewer whose numbers I don't immediately recognize when they call. You have my attention."

"Mr. Stone. This is Serena Black. We've never actually met in person but—"

"Ah, yes." His voice was low, so painfully low and masculine that is sounded like he was growling. "I know who you are, filly. I wondered how long it would take for you to call me. "I couldn't tell if the accent caused the drawl or the drawl caused the accent but whatever and why ever it worked to create a cultured cowboy tone that trailed across my skin and left goosebumps in its wake. There had to be laws against using that kind of voice against an unsuspecting female public.

"Trust me, it's not my habit to consort with renowned drug lords." I snapped then cursed myself for my lack of reserve.

"We're consorting now?" He seemed amused. "That's a big step up from you sending back my gifts. Were they not an adequate apology?"

"My blue blood automatically makes accepting bribes from men like you a conflict of interest. And if even if *I* could justify it, my brother would find it harder to understand."

A warm chuckle filtered through the phone. "Semantics, darlin'," he drawled. "Tell me something, filly, am I in trouble?"

The question threw me. I was torn between telling him to shove this "filly" nonsense into the nearest orifice or being charmed by it. The beast rumbled warningly but I ignored her. "Not from me." We've got to play nice-nice...for now.

"Then call me Slade."

"Very well." It was an easy enough request. "And this is a business deal, Slade, we just haven't gotten to that yet."

Silence yawned over the line and his surprise shifted the energy across the line. "I see." The drawl was heavier but there was a sharpness to the calm words. "Did someone instigate a conversation that I was not aware of?" Interest sharpened.

"I think your men know you well enough to understand that would be a bad idea."

He grunted. "Touché. You've got my attention."

I paused, gathered my thoughts, and then plunged forward. "I need information."

"Oh?"

"I'm tracking two children who've recently disappeared and the trail has gone cold and—."

"Something's led you to believe that I have information you need to locate them."

"Yes."

A pause. "Information's a valuable commodity in my world. Not something to be sold cheaply."

"I realize that."

"It's also risky." He went on. "Especially considering who you're affiliated with. Why should I put my operation at to disclose such information to the daughter of a blood enemy? Well, a dead blood enemy."

Beastie snarled at him. It was a low blow, a blow designed to discombobulate me and turn me into a mass of rash emotion. All men thought they could manipulate me and he was no different. Time to reeducate him.

"Is Lily out of school for Thanksgiving yet? I know the Deer Creek school district has a special calendar when it comes to national holidays." I asked casually.

Silence. Dangerous silence. But sharp interest turned into anger that crackled across the line.

"I'd hate for her school to keep her late and for her to miss out on Thanksgiving preparations. Nothing creates better memories than being elbow deep in raw turkey or making popcorn chains."

"Are you threatening my niece, Miss Black?" The question

was laced with absolute venom and I knew I needed to proceed carefully to avoid making an accidental enemy.

"Absolutely not." I said firmly, let him hear the conviction in my voice. "I'm simply asking about the health and wellbeing of a child that you love. And it is well known that you love your niece, Slade, would do anything for her."

Silence.

"You'd tear heaven and hell apart to keep her from danger."

More silence.

"You'd sign a contract with Lucifer himself if it meant keeping her safe."

"These children you're looking for mean so much to you?"

My throat tightened and I forced my words past. "Yes."

"Why?"

"Doesn't matter." I hedged. "What matters is what I'm willing to exchange to get the information I need."

"I see." Another pause. "You've piqued my interest. Meet me at Surge. Today, 2pm. Don't be late." With that, the line went dead.

I let out a rough breath. I lowered the phone and hoped the slight tremors in my hand did show.

"So? What did he say? Did he agree to meet with you?" Leah asked.

I blew out a breath. "Yep."

Leah shook her head. "You've got balls of brass, sister." Her sardonic tone didn't quite hide her jealously and it made me smile. Leah saw it as her personal life mission to find the wildest person in the room and one up them by a thousand. If she had any clue about the fear beating at the back of my mind, she'd save her jealousy for someone less chicken shit.

"You know the boys are never going to for this." She nagged matter-of-factly.

I nodded. My mind was already turning over possibilities and arguments to help them see reason.

"You got a plan to convince them this isn't sheer insanity"

I walked back to the back door and slid it open. "That's why

I've got you. You're the craziest person I know and an expert on how to convince people to do stupid shit."

She cackled and glowed at the compliment.

Even if I had to tranq-dart them both, nothing would stop me from taking the meet with Slade today. Nothing. Not Satan or demons or God himself. Though, if God wanted to help things a bit, I wouldn't argue.

CHAPTER 21

To say Luke had a shit hemorrhage when I told him I'd arranged a meet with the infamous drug lord was a serious understatement. He ranted. He railed. He used every drop of cop logic and moral high ground that he could come up with to dissuade me from doing it. He got so worked up that I was afraid he'd pass out from over exertion and rage, the bandage wrapped around his head a glaring reminder of how he barely cheated death. Emphasis on barely. Still, I let him yell, knowing he needed to get it out of his system before he was ready to listen to me…or help.

"You're a fool if you think Slade intends to just *give* this information away." Luke scathed.

"Don't insult me." I warned. "I'm fully aware of the kind of man I'm dealing with."

"I hope you are. Because Slade will run you through the shredder for his own sick entertainment if you step into this world with him."

"That's what I told her." Leah chimed in.

I shot her an acid glare. Don't help me. Then I met Luke's burning gaze calmly. I wouldn't defend myself twice. Slade could name is his price—no cost was too high.

"If this is the way you want to handle things, I can't be involved." He said it like the words were torn out of him. What he didn't say spoke louder. It killed him to admit it.

"I know. I've compromised your job enough."

"If—"

"You don't need to make excuses, Luke. I've put you in a

perilous position already. You've risked so much already and I can't keep asking you to do that."

He met my eyes then and truth shone in his midnight eyes. He'd give me everything if I let him. My chest constricted.

"Serena—" he took a step towards me but Talon stepped in before he could finish his thought.

"Our options are limited and so is our time." He rumbled. "We'll miss our window to help the kids trying to go through more traditional methods."

Luke wasn't satisfied. "We have no idea what this guy's angle is." He argued.

"True. But we don't have time to waste on wishful thinking or plans that put us at risk of being arrested before we can retrieve Alyssa and Logan. That tattoo is our only link to the kidnappers and it points straight to Slade. He's our only and best lead." Talon glanced at me. "I'm in."

Air whooshed from my lungs. Something squeezing in my middle loosened just enough for me to breathe. It was silly to admit but I knew that if Talon was with me I'd storm the bastille with no trouble. Even with the anger still lingering in his eyes.

Luke was pissed and didn't try to hide it. Still, when we all strapped up and exited the house, he followed.

We piled into Leah's Range Rover since it was the least likely car to be traced by the feds and took off for the club. Silence filled the car as we drove through downtown OKC, each person in their own world of thought. Anger shimmered off Talon and he sat in the front seat clearly pouting.

We pulled into Surge's parking lot with ten minutes to spare. The moment we turned off the car, the pair of burly security guards eyed us suspiciously, both wearing dark jeans and not attempting to hide the shoulder holsters peeking from their jackets.

"Isn't it a little early for full on security?" Leah asked she pushed open her door. "Unless I'd totally missed the announcement that morning ragers are the new trend."

A glance at the clock read a quarter to noon. Definitely too early for the pre-gamers who frequented this place. Either they were updating club policy or the establishment was on high alert. Interesting.

I filed that bit of information away and flung open my car door. They were expecting us and quickly did a weapons check. Clearly someone warned them that we'd come armed and they did the cursory check but let us keep our guns. That surprised me and I silently breathed a prayer that this meeting wouldn't end in a blood bath.

The guards, one tall with inkjet hair and the other shorter but stacked with muscle, led us through the still empty club. A bartender stood at the bar wiping down glasses and a pair of women dressed in skimpy corsets and sheer robes practiced what looked like a burlesque routine on stage. We wove through the tables and walked down an emerald lit hallway with VIP rooms. Just past the bathrooms, we can to a stop at a locked door. One of the men scanned their badges and the door unlocked and they push it open. We stepped inside a lush room decorated in golds and browns with a hint of red, plush couches and ivory marble tables scattered throughout the room.

"I'll let Slade know that you are here," The dark haired guard's accent hinted at Caribbean heritage.

Luke settled in the scarlet and plum patterned couch in the far corner, brooding, Talon leaned casually against a wall, and Leah perched on the arm of the couch facing me, her back to the door, letting one leg swing like a lazy pendulum. I sat in the left corner of the taupe couch that faced the door. Giving the door my back wasn't an option. Tense silence descended.

Leah shifted and I looked up. Her dark eyes met mine and then flickered at something over my head, slightly to the right. I recrossed my legs, and used the movement to toss a nonchalant glance over my shoulder.

A camera. Effing fantastic.

I settled and jerked my head at her to let her know I saw

it. Honestly, I wasn't surprised; I'd be shocked if a man like Nicholas Stone wasn't prepared to cover all his bases at any given moment, even going so far as to store blackmail material. And in a room like this, I'm sure the footage would go one for weeks. The entire club was no doubt littered with cameras and wired for sound recording. Still, once I knew it was there, I could almost feel the eyes watching us. It didn't matter though. We weren't here to make a nefarious deal…simply ask our questions and be on our way.

The dark haired guard returned not five minutes after he left. "Slade is ready for you." We all stood and made our way to the door but the guard never moved.

"Just you," he ordered, looking at me. "Everyone else has to wait here."

Talon turned to face me. He said nothing, but the look in his eyes wanted to know if I'd be all right.

I nodded at him. This wasn't my first time to deal with men like this and I wasn't afraid or intimidated.

Talon stepped aside and as I followed the man out of the room I felt his eyes on my skin like the warmth of the sun.

The security guard led me down a dark hallway that dead ended at a door. I walked up to it and knocked, three solid taps.

"Come in." a familiar voice washed over me and I paused. I'd been steeling myself against his voice but it still washed over me in a wave of warm molasses.

I twisted the knob and pushed open the door.

A man sat at a mahogany desk on the opposite end of the room, reclined so far back in a matching leather chair that I thought he might tip over. He spoke into a cell phone but waved me over with a flick of his wrist, not even turning in my direction. I strode through the lush, masculine room—decorated chocolate brown leather couches and dim yellowish light casting out of vintage fixtures and swirls of black in the lamps, fur rug, and couch pillows. It was modern and masculine, with a hint of welcome that surprised me.

The lair of the drug lord. Music boomed in my head as a dramatic crescendo.

Let's be honest. This wasn't my first trek into the bowels of the crime underworld and the subtle hints of goth intimidation like the lacquered black skull imprints in the wall made me want to roll my eyes. It was classy intimidation at its finest —too bad I was hard to impress. Be it the slums of India, sheik tents of Kazakhstan, or the Victorian homes of London, classy intimidation was always a theme and this was the Midwest version done to a tee.

Too bad the effect was lost on me. I'd stood before some of the slimiest people in the world—one power hungry drug lord in Oklahoma wasn't going to phase me. The man was more important than the room, though some let the atmosphere intimidate them before the main event ever opened their lips. I focused in on the man at the far end of the room. What did an Oklahoma drug lord look like?

Nicholas Stone was not at all what I was expecting. He was tall, not quite as tall as Talon but that played well with the thick muscles roping under his designer shirt. A sand colored shirt strained against his massive chest and biceps, the color contrasting nicely with his dark pewter slacks and vest. His dark brown hair was swept back but long on the ends and stubble shadowed his cheeks. It was as if someone had carved a bear from stone—a grumpy, suspicious bear if the look in his eyes had anything to say about it.

He leaned back against the desk, slowly scrolling through a black tablet that looked like a child's cell phone in his hands. He didn't look up until I stopped a dozen feet from the desk and the eyes, he leveled on me were as cold and blank as an icy night.

Pushing off the desk, he strode around it, hand outstretched. "Miss Black, it's so nice to finally meet you."

"Slade," I slid my hand into his paw and gave it a firm shake. "I appreciate you taking the time to meet with me." The words came easily but they burned the back of my throat. I'm sure he had more entertaining things to do than meet with me but, as my momma always said, "Politeness never hurt nobody." I'd learned to lead with courtesy when dealing with the elite scum balls of the world. Especially since I was the one coming to ask a favor. Still, Beastie batted at her cage in disagreement. I took in a slow breath and let the opening bars of a Bach piano solo drift through my head to calm her.

"Can I get you a drink?" He gestured at the crystal decanter and handful of glasses resting on a bronze platter on his desk. "It's bourbon."

It was a subtle reminder that he knew my preferences, a hint of what else he might know. Beastie's growl drowned out the music in my head.

I gave a tight smile. "I better not. I wouldn't want my reflexes hindered."

The corner of his mouth twitched. "With how popular you've been the last few days, I'll bet those "reflexes" have gotten quite a workout." as he reached over and filled a crystal tumbled a third of the way full. He cradled the drink in his right hand and leaned back against the desk. "In my experience, avoiding cops can be highly exhausting...or pure entertainment. Especially when you know what you're doing as you clearly do." He took a sip of whiskey, watching me with eyes the same color as the expensive liquor in his glass.

"We all have special skills."

"Indeed, we do. But yours, Miss Black, are quite impressive. I recently viewed a video with interesting footage of you showcasing your...abilities against several of my associates. I'll have to see that my men are better trained from here on out."

"If you're referring to the...incident at your club a few ago. As ridiculous as this is to admit, it was pure accident that I ended up there. It's not my usual scene."

"It certainly isn't," his eyes glinted. "You're more used to dodging the bullets of terrorists and paid assassins while you evacuate the brats of corrupt diplomats and foreign politicians to safety.

My stomach dipped and Beastie's growl gurgled in my ears. I shouldn't be surprised that he had somehow accessed private servers and found this out about me; I'd bet a kidney that he had some strung out tech lackey in a basement somewhere awaiting orders. But hearing the words never made it easier—nothing would. The only thing I could do was try to atone for my failure and move on. And all of that hinged on retrieving Alyssa and Logan.

So I swallowed the cold rage surging up my throat. "I save children from twisted the manipulations of the power hungry. You traffic them right back into their arms. Same coin, different sides."

His eyes glinted over the rim of his glass. "What makes you think that I'm into trafficking?" The question was casual but it belied the tension strumming across his wide shoulders.

"I hear it's one of the more lucrative arenas."

"You spend a lot of time researching these things?" The sardonic humor in his voice was completely at odds with the blankness in his eyes.

"I've spent my entire professional career dabbling in all the dark industries that rely on the exploitation of innocent people. Protecting my clients from it. There's nothing on your resume of sins that I haven't seen replicated in a dozen different ways on three continents."

"I'll consider that a challenge." He rumbled.

"My sources are confident that you run a trafficking in the city. Maybe not directly, but you're the brain behind the operation."

"And you trust these sources?" His voice was smooth like the whiskey he swirled in hsi glass. Calm, disinterested even.

"I trust corpses," I snapped. "And Danny Verangaz's bullet ridden corpse lying outside the OKC police department hints at your involvement."

He scoffed, an amused sound, and shook his head. "I'll be the first to admit that Danny was a pawn whose head had swollen with his own self-importance. Arrogance and ego will get you killed in this world—especially when you forget where you land in the pecking order" He rolled his shoulder. "If I wanted him dead, I wouldn't put on a production of shooting him in front of the police station. That's old school shit you see in Westerns...not something you'd see from someone who's trying not to disturb the waters."

Damn it. Everything he said made sense and echoed my initial thoughts when I learned of Danny's death. But like the kraken, death tended to follow him along.

"That's not the corpse I was referring to."

He quirked an eyebrow at me, the only sign that he was even listening, but the energy in the room spiked. I had his full attention.

"Several men raided a police sanctioned safe house that was protecting the two kids of the recently murdered Davis Jackson." I watched his eyes, waiting to see if there was a hint of surprise or discomposure. "One of the corpses found had an interesting tattoo. A mark that linked him back to a gang that's rumored to run jobs for you from time to time."

"Aren't these the same kids that you're reported to have kidnaped after you plotted with an unknown terrorist organization to kill the Jackson?"

He was baiting me. I didn't give him the satisfaction of reacting though cold swirled in my gut.

"What is it exactly that you hope to accomplish here?" He set the glass on the desk behind him and leaned forward. "You hope that I will give up the name of a trafficking ring that may or may not exist so that you can storm the Bastille and save the day? Seems a bit naive for a woman of your experience."

Anger surged strong only to cover up my fear. His eyes were cold, completely unaffected at the thought of innocent children being auctioned off for a life of sexual abuse and misery.

Slade's relentless gaze never let up. "Tell me: what hold do these children have over you that would make the daughter of the most respected police chief in the city beg to meet with me?"

"It was my job to protect them and I failed. I have to make that right."

"Are you ready to visit hell to see them saved?"

I shrugged. "Hell and I are old friends."

He wasn't amused. "The question isn't "Can I survive this". The real question to ask yourself is how many times can a soul sustain trauma before it's beyond repair?"

A frown tugged at my lips. Those same thoughts continually swirled through my mind...the difference is that I served my country and gained back psychological instability. It made me curious about his story, about what made him who he was. I shook off the thought. Curiosity was bad when you're talking about mob bosses.

"I'll give you the names of the men who've been running flesh behind your back." I told him.

The smile he gave me was all condescension. "If you believe that I killed Verangaz for his involvement in trafficking, what's to say that I don't already have a list of his accomplices?"

He had no intention of giving me any helpful information. He was toying with me and I wouldn't be an amusement any longer.

"I'm wasting my time with you," My voice shook from the anger I was trying to suppress. I turned on my heel and headed for the door.

"Just a moment, Miss Black."

My feet paused but I didn't turn around.

"Information is not what I want from you," he admitted. "But you do have something that is of value to me and it's what I will barter with you for."

Hope rushed through me but was tempered with suspicion. I pivoted on my heel to face him. I cocked an eyebrow at him.

"You're a woman of extraordinary talents and immense composure under pressure," he pushed off the desk and took two long steps until he towered over me. "I'm going to be in a position soon where I will need someone with your skills to be on my staff to protect...certain assets that are extremely valuable to me."

I looked at him like he'd sprouted fangs and a third eye. "I mean no offense when I say that making a deal with a drug dealer is the last thing on my mind."

"But you will," he said, utterly confident. "Or your hope of finding Alyssa and Logan before they're sold off to the highest bidder dies with you."

Beastie snarled at him—because he was right and we both knew it. My mind whirled with possibilities. The only thing that made sense was that he must have someone he wanted to protect but no one he trusted enough to do the job. No one, except me.

"There's no way I could be on your staff in any official capacity." I told him.

"Of course. This will be a clandestine arrangement shrouded with the utmost discretion."

"What's the duration of the job?"

"At the moment, that's hard to say. Six weeks at the least but it could be longer."

"And who—?"

"When the time's appropriate, I'll give you all of the necessary details." He cut in. "I realize that you'll need more than a few days' notice to adequately prepare and I give my word that I won't spring the job on you. That wouldn't benefit you or my asset."

Vague

Working for a criminal lord? That was a sin Julien wouldn't forgive and I wasn't sure I'd be able to blame him. But I didn't have a choice and the longer I hedged, the more vileness Alyssa and Logan had to endure.

I looked him dead in the eye. "I'll do it."

Surprisingly, he didn't crow or smirk in victory. Simply stuck out his hand and we shook on it. "Then I will give you a name. Rashawn Perkins."

I etched that name in my memory.

"He's the gatekeeper for a collection of individuals with specific sexual preferences and he works with specialized vendors to organize and setup events that cater to their tastes."

Read: he organizes sex auctions for groups that solicit children.

"Know where he can be found?"

A slick smile tugged at the corners of his mouth. "That would be step too far. I'm sure your "sources" can help you track him down."

Smug bastard.

CHAPTER 22

Frustration tightened my chest as I lowered the phone from my ear. Damn. Another dead lead. We'd been at it for nearly an hour, making calls, scouring confidential government sites, Leah even managed to convince a reprobate cousin of hers—who I hoped was legal— to hack into the city webcams and pull live feed through city cameras. Still, nothing. Ole Rashawn either didn't exist or was an expert at being smoke on a radar.

After the meeting with Slade, Leah drove to the Ferris wheel just outside of downtown and parked in front of the quaint recreation area. Luke had insisted on traipsing to the police department to search the system for hits on Rashawn Perkins but he was in no condition to drive so Talon ended up playing taxi driver. Not before he shot me a warning look of, "Don't do anything stupid". Honestly, I was in too much pain to consider stupid right now. That and we had no time to be chasing our tails.

Every second wasted diminished the possibility of rescuing those kids. I couldn't articulate why I believed that; from the moment they disappeared this ominous clock loomed in the back of my head, each passing second punctuated by the boom of a drum. It didn't simply mark the passage of time...it was a countdown. I knew that, when it reached zero, Alyssa and Logan would be far beyond my reach.

My hand spasmed and I launched my phone across the room as it spilled over. I buried my head in my hands as it hit the wall with a dull thud, ignoring the sharp twinge of protest that zinged through my shoulder. The aspirin I'd taken had worn off a few hours back and I wasn't about to take something stronger that would cloud my judgement or fuzz my clarity. I let out a deep breath, hoping it would take the fear and pain and anxiety with hit but all three stayed, weighing down the middle of my back as if an anvil dropped between my shoulders. Fear yawned and swirled in my mind. I wasn't going to be able to find them...I'd fail them too. I hunched over further, hands pulling at my braids. If I failed them, I would never be able to look at myself in the mirror again...wasn't sure I could live with myself.

Help me find them. The words slipped past my lips, no breath behind the words just a desperate silent plea. I instantly scoffed. What right did I have to ask God for anything? I wasn't sure He was even checked in? How desperate was I that I would cry out to the very God who let my dad die the slowest, most painful death imaginable? I'm so pathetic.

"I take it that conversation didn't go well."

I sighed and let my hands fall into my lap as I looked up at Leah. Yeah, the conversation was a big fat dead end. I shrugged.

"Maybe you need to take a breather. Clear your head and come back to it." She suggested in a blasé tone but concern shone in her eyes that reminded me of polished obsidian crystal.

Anger flared. I didn't need sympathy. I needed answers and, clearly, they wouldn't fall out of the sky by divine arrangement.

"Pull up the file Luke sent one more time. Maybe we missed something the first time." It had been less than an hour and we already had several files, alternative names, and photos to search through. We scoured the information several times already but maybe fatigue, or overzealousness made us overlook something simple.

Leah gave me a look but propped her legs on the steering wheel and let her fingers fly over the keyboard. I tried reading over her shoulder the words blurred, fatigue catching up with my tired burning eyes.

"Skip to the photos." They'd be easier on my eyes and often revealed more information than anything else.

Her hands stalled over the keys. "I guess you think you're too badass to say please."

I rolled my eyes.

"A little common courtesy never hurt anyone."

"Leah."

"I'm just saying."

I huffed out a breath. "One, I don't think I'm badass, I know it. and two...please?"

She nodded, a satisfied smile twitching her lips and she double clicked the mouse.

I rolled my eyes again. Sheesh—managing women was so much more trouble than it was worth. But a smile played at the corners of my mouth and I had a sneaking suspicion that was what she was going for.

A slideshow popped up on the screen and Leah blew it up so it filled the screen. Leah clicked through them slowly and my eyes flickered over every single one.

Rashawn Perkins didn't fit the bill of the average sex trafficking slimeball. From the pictures, he looked like a businessman—crisply pressed pants, blazers in an array of colors, ties. Thug was hard to hide though. It was there in the glossy coldness of his eyes...the tattoos swirling down his body.

There were pictures of him entering and exiting clubs. He didn't have any social media accounts, which should be standard protocol, but you'd be surprised at how stupid people can be in that regards.

"Zoom in there."

Leah manipulated the mouse and zoomed into the picture. It was a picture of Rashawn and a group of women. His arms were slung over the necks of the women closest to him and grazing the shoulder, and boob, of the ladies on the ends. Yet, it wasn't a party photo or picture at the end of a night rave. They were all dressed in professional clothing with the women wearing pantsuits and skirts and Rashawn rocked a blazer and tie and there seemed to be a caption at the top of the picture.

"Is this cropped from a Facebook post?" I asked.

"Probably," she moved the mouse to view the picture from different angles before double clicking. The photo expanded back to its original orientation.

"Focus in on the windows of the building their standing in front of." Sometimes the reflection of a street name or identifying marker might be captured in the windows just enough to give us more of a clue. Leah zoomed in and inched the picture across the screen, bit by bit, as we both searched for anything that stood out.

Something red was reflected in the background and I had her zoom in. Elation zinged through me. It was the name of a hotdog restaurant. One quick search later and the only eatery in the city with that name was located on the NW side of town. Leah quickly panned the picture so we could see what every side of the street looked like…and on the south end of the street, stood a gleaming office building with black outed, super reflective windows that matched the picture.

Bingo, baby.

Twenty minutes later, Leah parked Luke's car in front of the building in the photo. She shoved the lever into park, etched muscles rippling through her arms, but left the engine running.

"You good?" she asked

I frowned at her. "You asking me that because you really want to know? Or cause you're worried?"

"Just checking?" she shot back, flicking her dark hair away from her face. "Cause we're probably going to have to convince him that we're serious and it's going to take more than banging around like apes to do it. You okay with what you will have to do to get the information you want?"

I almost laughed. Was I worried? Ha. The only word that came to mind at my current psychological state was fragile and I didn't want to admit that.

"We do what we gotta do to make sure Alyssa and Logan get to come home." I said.

She nodded and threw open the car door. "Be back in five." She hopped out of the car and sauntered into the building—cause that's the only way to describe the confident, swaying, seductive yet dangerous way Leah moved. It was both an invitation and a warning. Paired with the painted on black skinny jeans, cropped turtleneck sweater, and bolero hat, if Rashawn was half the ladies' man he seemed to be, he wouldn't be able to resist.

I clenched my jaw and shifted over to the driver's seat, ignoring the way my stitches pulled at the movement. Rashawn officed out of a ten story building directly off Northwest Expressway in the heart of the city. Despite the sign that boasted brand new renovations, the dingy white paint and cracked sidewalk made me think it was an older building that was given a facelift. And in the very first row, a mustard yellow Lamborghini was double parked, half covering a handicap parking spot. Something only a complete jerk would do. What would have been ideal was to park directly behind it but Leah parked two rows over that angled us with enough room to maneuver. I could make it work.

I twisted the rearview mirror until the main entrance was in line of sight.

I was so beyond worried. At this point, I was trying to keep Beastie in check as she screamed warnings and bombarded me with violent images, trying to keep my shoulder from falling off, and trying to keep everyone from seeing how close I was to failing. Oh, and not going to prison would be nice.

The door to the building glinted, drawing my attention as a black man in a navy suit and mini dreads flopping on his head burst through and ran down the sidewalk toward the Lamborghini. Leah was behind him, her face twisted with concern and a hand covering her mouth as if she were afraid of his reaction.

Time to move.

I yanked the gear stick to reverse, looked over my shoulder, aimed, and stomped on the gas. The man whirled back to Leah, yelling in irritation—likely that his precious car was unmarked—when I wrenched the wheel and backed straight into the Lambo's passenger door. Metal crunched and I think I heard the man scream, almost in pain.

He stared, horrified, with his hands clutching the sides of his head, and, for a moment, I thought I might have seen a tear slide down his cheek. But rage contorted his face and he stormed to my window, spewing curse words.

"Look what you just, you stupid bitch. You tore up my car. Are you blind as well as ugly? Can you not see a yellow sports car." He yelled as he beat on the glass with an open palm.

I rolled down my window. "I'd consider my looks average." I snorted and pointed my gun straight into his face. Surprise paralyzed him and whatever insult he was going to hurl next died with a choked noise. "What do you think, Leah?"

"*I'd* give you a solid eight and a half." She said from behind him.

Gee thanks.

"Get in." I ordered calmly.

"I wouldn't think of going anywhere." Leah casually suggested. From the severely arched angle of his back, I knew she must be pressing her gun into his spine. "If you tried to run, we'd shoot you and leave you to die on the street like a dog."

"What do you want?" he wheezed out.

I beeped the locks and Leah reached forward to pull open the door and spur Rashawn into the back seat. His body stiffened, as if to resist her. Leah rolled her eyes at me over his shoulder and slammed the butt of her gun into the small bundle of nerves at his back. He spasmed and Leah shoved him inside and climbed in after him.

She threw a black cloth sack at him. "Put that on."

"If it's money you're after, I can cut you a blank check today." He offered.

She lifted her gun until the barrel of it brushed his nose. "Put it on." she warned.

"Or cash. I can give you cash—any amount you want."

Leah pulled back the hammer and it snapped back into place with a loud snick.

Rashawn jumped. He swore a blue streak as he shoved the mask over his head.

I drove to a storage facility in Luther and through the maze of white garages to the last one in the final row. I jumped out of the car and banged on the door twice—three quick reps, two slow. A second later, the door was raised and Talon stood in front of me.

"You got him?" he asked, eyes on me.

I could hear the other car door opening and Rashawn stepping out with protest. "First try."

"Still think this is a good idea?" He assessed me with serious eyes and it rankled Beastie's fur. No one was forcing him to stay. If things got too deep for him, the door was just as open for him as it was for the rest of them.

To conceal all of this, I shrugged and kept my face neutral. "It's the only one we have."

"Maybe not," Luke conceded.

"What do you mean?" I frowned.

"I had a team do a sweep of the safehouse after Alyssa and Logan were taken," he explained. "If a house is breached or compromised, there's a process to analyze how it happened, scrub it clean, and put it on the market to sell cause we can't use it again. In doing so, I asked them to check for prints to make sure we didn't miss anyone who might have recently been there."

Talon voiced my question, "I'm guessing you found something?"

"Possibly. We print checked all of the kids' personal items and guess who's prints showed up on the broken doll Alyssa had in her backpack? Brendan Michael's."

I quirked an eyebrow. "How is that possible? She's had her doll with the past week and Brendan stayed back in OKC because his uncle broke his hip or something."

"I thought it seemed strange as well," Luke agreed. "But I checked the record from the team who did the sweep of Jackson's home after he was murdered and Brendan's prints showed up on Alyssa's dolls. Like all of them."

Talon frowned. "So he's either a sick bastard with a doll obsession or—"

"It might be more than an obsession and he might be some twisted pedophile." I finished.

"Only one way to find out."

"Make way," Leah called, shoving a stumbling Rashawn. "Don't let his filth get on you."

We stepped aside so she could force Rashawn into one of the air conditioned storage units. It was the size of a large shed and was lightly filled with a random assortment of furniture that lined the wall. Luke leaned against a dresser stacked with cardboard boxes and stared at us with blank, bright eyes—a look every cop had in their own way. In the middle of the room was a waist high, square red oak table—probably used as an end or entryway table—with a fold out chair pushed against it. Leah forced the taller man to sit in it but left the hood on.

I gave Luke a chin lift. "How's your head?"

"Fine. How's your shoulder?" The stark lines around his mouth and grayish complexion told me the truth.

"Fine." I spotted a dining room chair with a low seat, walked over and grabbed it, and plopped it in front of the table.

Rashawn jumped and cast frantic glances at each of our faces but remained silent.

I sat and stared at the man across from me. I glanced at Talon who leaned against the only free sliver of wall a dozen feet from Rashawn's chair. At my head nod, he took a long step forward and snatched the hood off.

The other man sucked in a breath and coughed. He had deep umber skin with a subtle golden glow and round eyes and wide, full lips. I bet his smile was his favorite tool to use to lure women to him.

He coughed to clear his lungs. "I don't know who you are

or what your goal is, but I'll tell you this right now: you're all dead." He shook his head as if to clear it.

I leaned back into the seat, keeping my body relaxed though Beastie shifted with anticipation in my head. "Look at me." The order was sharp and his eyes snapped to me. I let him study my face and it took about ten seconds for recognition to dawn.

"I know you," he spat. "You're the woman who's accused of murdering that US Jackson."

"That's right."

"Pretty ballsy walking around as if there wasn't a price on your head."

"And you'd know all about ballsy, wouldn't you?" I said. "I've been wondering why someone would take a job like yours and I think, deep down, you're an adrenaline junkie. An addict. And acting as the gatekeeper for the largest sex auction ring in the region gives you just the hit you need."

He an eyebrow but didn't rise to the bait. In fact, the straight set of his shoulders meant that he was calm, unaffected. I needed to inspire the correct amount of respect before I could get him talking.

"I'll cut the crap," I told him. "Our intel suggests that you are intrinsically involved in a sex auction ring, the largest in the region. This same intel tells me that the children of Jackson are likely to be at the next event. You're going to tell me where that is."

"You lost two children?" he mocked, laughter in his voice.

"I didn't lose them. They were kidnapped fifteen hours ago."

"Don't know how you think I can help."

"That mark on your left forearm? I found a similar one on one of the corpses at a safehouse after the Jackson's children were taken. It links to a local gang that's known for pedaling flesh and your name is at the top of our informants list."

"I have no idea what you're talking about. I'm a businessman, work in product sales for a startup company. I pay taxes and vote and this is a violation of my rights"

His smooth, cultured zone pissed me off. "You're going to

tell us who you work for and give us the details of the next auction."

"I can't give you information I don't have."

I looked at Leah and nodded for her to close in. She came and stood directly next to me, absently flipping a wood handled hammer over and around her palm. "This is my friend," my voice was conversational as if discussing my favorite restaurant. "She has many skills. She can read braille, tap dance, cross stitch...my favorite thing she can do? She has the concerning ability to beat information out of weaselly creep like you."

Leah sat at the table and dumped a small lid filled with tiny nails on the table.

"Just to be clear," I said as Leah chose a nail. "You are going to tell me where the sex auction is going to be, how to get in, and who's in charge. Otherwise, Leah" I nodded at her. "Will nail your fingers to the table."

Rashawn squirmed in his seat.

Talon reached around him from behind and braced Rashawn's shaking arm.

"Hey! Get off me, man."

"Lots of tiny nerves in the fingers." I informed him calmly "It's the reason our touch is able to pick up extremely delicate things. It's also the reason why small injuries hurt like a bitch."

"You have no idea who you're messing with." Rashawn squirmed but Talon didn't budge and panic began to slide over his face.

"Give me a location." I demanded.

"Suck my—"

Leah drove the nail into the flesh of his finger just below the first knuckle.

He screamed. His whole hand starfished with the trauma, fingers splayed. He looked at Leah with wild eyes as the pain seeped in. "You crazy bitch."

"What do your people want with the Culwell Jackson's children?" I asked.

He shook his head as if to clear it, dreads flopping on his head.

Leah looked at me and I nodded.

She drove another nail straight through the knuckle in the middle of his finger. Bone crunched. Blood spurted in a thick stream and splashed on some of the boxes as Rashawn screamed.

"Hey!" Luke shouted. The blood had arced his direction and he was forced to move as it splattered the place he'd just been.

I shrugged at him. Hazards of the job.

Rashawn was hunched over, sweat dotting his forehead. Talon no longer needed to hold him down.

"Do I have your attention?" My voice was droll as if asking what his favorite flavor of ice cream.

He shook his head, as if that would clear the pain. "You have no idea what you're messing with." he heaved. "This is so above your head you have no idea that sharks swimming in this—"

Leah slammed a third nail home, driving it through his nail bed. He choked on his scream making it a pathetic mewling sound.

I frowned at her. Really?

She shrugged.

"They're payback." he gasped as if he'd just sprinted a 5K. "Jackson's kids were taken to fill a debt."

I kept my face blank but my mind whirled. That could have a dozen different connotations. "What do you mean?"

His chest heaved as blood and sweat mingled dotted his face. "I don't have details. I never do. All I know is that Jackson owed a debt that he couldn't pay and his kids being on the market is someone collecting their payment."

"*Someone* being the leader of the sex ring, right?"

He shook his head, lips pursed as if battling against telling us more.

Leah slammed the hammer into the wood of the table. He jumped sharply, tugging at the nails in his finger and making him cry out.

"Look," he wheezed. "All I know is that this specific auction is retribution payments. Someone doesn't or can't hold up their end of the bargain and these kids mean something to them and so we kidnap them and sell them."

I looked over his head at Talon and let the frown play on my face. This confirmed what I'd suspected after the car chase that led us to leave for California: Jackson had been over his head in something and trying to escape the consequences. But I still had no idea what that was or who he could have made a bargain with that would have resulted in his death.

But the auction was a starting place. To clear my name and recover Alyssa and Logan.

"And the next auction is...?" Leah asked.

He clenched his jaw but I knew that look in his eye. It was fear.

I leaned in. "You think there's any coming back from this? That the people who run this auction won't know it was you who told us how to get in?" I cocked my head. "How do you think they'll respond? I can guess. If they don't kill you outright, they'll turn you into a eunuch as a warning to the next poor schmuck who takes your job. Then they'll sell your daughter to the same sick bastards you've been working for. It's a bitch when the system works against you."

He licked his lips, breathing hard. "I'll need some assurances..."

"If you help us," Luke chimed in, "And if your intel is good then I can promise protective custody for you and your family until your court hearing. What happens after that is out of my hands."

"That's not good enough," he snapped, voice ragged.

Luke shrugged. "That's all I have to give."

I leaned back in my chair and we waited. Silence was the interrogator's greatest weapon—sometimes letting the mind run rampant with all of the twisted possibilities did a better job than threats ever could.

Rashawn swore harshly and I knew we had him.

"The next gathering's tonight. Eleven pm near the fair-grounds."

I glanced at my watch and saw that it was just seven o'clock. We had four hours to craft and activate a plan. Beastie flicked her tail, lazy eagerness in her movements. I could do this, save Alyssa and Logan and, maybe, step a little further out of the shadow of Syria's failed mission. I ignored the hint of desperation that trickled through my thoughts.

Time to go hunt down a sex auction.

CHAPTER 23

Several hours later Talon, Leah, and I walked across a beat up parking lot towards an even more dilapidated building. Rashawn's directions took us to a decrepit shopping strip just off I-40, in that strange part of OKC that was close enough to downtown for the eerie light of the Devon Tower to cast a dim blue glow over the cramped, rundown buildings. Sporadically placed streetlights offered little in the way of visibility and seemed to accentuate the darkness of the early a.m. "Sketchy" defined everything about this situation.

Two cars sat on either ends of the small parking lot: a black Mercedes sedan and black Escalade. Both gleamed with the sheen of money.

A normal person wouldn't even notice. But cop intelligence told me differently. An expensive car idling outside a rundown building in a part of town where that the car payment alone was more than any resident in that zip code saw in year was worth taking note of.

That, more than the sketchy location, told us we were in the right place.

To my right, my weak side, Talon vibrated with tension, pure hostility radiating off him and, whether intentional or not, solidifying the bodyguard vibe we were going for. A small part of my brain noted how scrumptious he looked in black leather pants and a partially unbuttoned sheer black shirt. A large silver pendant of a bird in flight rested in the middle of his chest. When I'd asked him what kind of bird it was, he'd grunted, "Harpy eagle," and turned away. Angry much? Even in the dark, his eyes flashed warning. It only to his overall look—foreign, expensive, and lethal. Mmm. My favorite kind.

Leah matched his badass vibe. A fitted blazer with slits from elbow to wrist and hip to hem cinched in at the waist with thick braided leather along the seams. Thick braids cascaded over each of her shoulders, sharpening her features. She'd gone for a thick metal and leather choker at her throat and a matching cuff on her left wrist.

Side-by-side, they looked like a pair of pissed off Native American warriors sent to earth to enact justice. Which was disturbingly on point.

We made it to the building and Talon pulled the door open for us. I started forward but Leah grasped my arm holding me back, her glance silently reprimanding. The dim light caught the series of black dots that starbursted out from the corner of her eyes and down her chin. War paint she called it. I got the message. I was the rich client, they were the bodyguards. Despite its shoddy appearance, I wouldn't be surprised if this entire place was strung with cameras and we didn't want to make whoever was watching suspicious. Any slipups and we'd get dead before we got lucky.

Following Rashawn's instructions, we turned left and walked down the long corridor, lit only by the street light shining through the cracked windows. It smelled like old pipes and mildew and my nose tickled. The only sounds were our footsteps echoing in the big, empty space and the occasional wind gust whistling through every sliver and crack. Based on the exterior, I expected the concrete floor to be littered with broken glass and trash but, on the contrary, it was swept clean. My four inch heels had no trouble at all. I guess it would be bad for business if buyers broke their crooked necks on a dirty floor. Tragic really.

The hall turned sharply right and up ahead it dead ended. A vast wall loomed and the only way through it was the locked metal door. We came to a halt in front of it. A small keypad situated below the door handle caught my attention. There was a small keypad below the door handle. I sucked in a breath and let it out. Here goes nothing. Please let this be right, I breathed, and pressed in the code Rashawn had given us.

9-4-7-7-1. Pause. 7-4-9-7-1.

Click.

The light shone green and the entire door vibrated with a loud boom as if someone hit it from the other side. It whirred several times before the door handle jerked with a small clicking sound. Access. I let out a breath of relief as Talon stepped forward, pushing down the handle and shoving the door open. It smoothly swung open and intense white light flooded through the opening, blinding me. It took a few seconds for my eyes to adjust. I blinked several times and waited for them to clear before following Talon down a spiral metal staircase. Leah brought up the rear. The angle of the staircase was steep and I walked slow to avoid rolling my ankle or worse. I huffed out a breath. Right, make the women dress up and then have them navigate this steel trap of death. Even in four inch platform sandals, it still was a broken ankle waiting to happen. Not that I needed another thing on me screwed up.

The staircase sharply curved several times and on the last curve I could finally see the landing area.

Four men stood at a large metal door. Three of them were tall, muscled, and wore shiny black shirts tucked into black slacks. All of them alert with frosty gazes radiating hostility and readiness. Over paid strip club bouncers? Not likely. Bodyguards for a horde of pedophiles and creeps waiting to buy children for perverse entertainment? Bingo, gentlemen.

The fourth man leaned casually against the wall, seeming not to care about the wrinkles he causing in his obviously expensive cobalt blue suit. When he saw us, his eyes lit with anticipation and he pushed off from the wall.

Showtime.

I lifted my chin with a haughty tilt and let my gaze flit between the men as if sale at the mall was more impressive than they were. Talon lifted a hand and I grasped his palm for extra balance as I stepped off the last stair but dropped it as soon as I was steady without a thank you or backward glance. I strode up to the door, letting the hips and hair sway with every step. Confident, superior, and in charge.

I came to a stop in front of the men, leaving half a dozen feet between us, and prattled the codeword, "Aardvark.".

"Good evening, madam. You're card, if you please." The man in the cobalt suit said. With a smooth olive face and dark hair flipped back in a modern hairstyle, I guessed him to be in his early twenties. It seemed the induction into a world of crime and debauchery started younger every time I looked up.

I opened my satin clutch and pulled a blank white card from an interior pocket, courtesy of Rashawn. Flashing it up so he could see what it was, I held it out to him.

Cobalt Suit took the card. "Thank you," His voice was smooth as olive oil and cultured with accent that tickled my ears as faintly Mediterranean. He pulled a palm sized black tablet from inside his blazer and held the card long ways in front it. A faint blue light shone out. I held my breath. Lettering briefly appeared on the card but instantly disappeared once the light left the surface. Hmm…black light wording. The tablet beeped once and he looked back at me with curious eyes but held out the card.

"I've not seen you in this circuit before."

"You wouldn't."

"Why is that?"

"I'm not from around here."

He stared hard. "Didn't realize we were hosting any out of town guests tonight."

"I'm a last minute replacement." I shrugged.

"I wasn't informed of any exchanges." He drawled confidence. "And I'm in charge of the list so either this alteration happened within the last few hours or you're lying."

The energy in the room went electric. Talon practically vibrated violence and the muscled men at the door looked ready to jump us at any moment, one even pulled back the flap of his blazer to reveal a holstered gun at his hip.

Most people would be sweating into their eyeballs, tension making them slip up and give themselves away. Not me. This wasn't my first delve into the world of the illicit and illegal. My nerves of steel could handle anything this pup threw at me.

"He must not know who I am," I tossed over my shoulder to Leah. "If he did, he'd know that I cut out the tongue of the last man who called me a liar."

One of the guards inched forward as if to put himself between me and Mr. Cobalt Suit but the young man threw out his hand and shook his head.

"Is that a threat?"

"Just information." I babbled. "For your knowledge and your benefit." The underlying threat was unmistakable. "Let me help you out," I drawled lazily, smirk firmly in place. "My friend is Rashawn Perkins who could not make it tonight. I am Diamond and, please, feel free to check my sources. I'm sure Rashawn will appreciate the thoroughness of any investigation."

Read, he'd lose his chili at the implication that he'd send a mole straight into the heart of your operation.

His eyes narrowed but I could see uncertainty weaving its way in. He sighed and looked down at the tablet's screen. "What's your last name."

"Mine."

The tapping paused. "Diamond Mine?" The scoff in his voice was unmistakable but he was too well trained to actually give into it. "We require real names here, as collateral."

"Who says that isn't my real name?" I asked and cocked my head to the side. He didn't miss the hostility.

Indecision hovered in the air. His eyes flickered past me. "Both of them cannot be here." He eyed Talon and Leah behind me, tall pillars of hostile Native American energy.

I rolled my eyes. "I always take two guards with me."

"With respect, I could care less about what you "always do"," his accent made him put slightly too much emphasis on the final word. "Every guest is allowed one personal guard onsite, no exceptions. One of them will have to wait outside."

Frustration blitzed through me but I smiled instead pounding his head into the wall. Crap. There was no way I'd be able to convince Talon to wait outside the building without making a scene and if I sent Leah, I didn't entirely trust that she'd actually make it to the car. She's the kind of person to "accidentally" stumble into a camera room or set off the security system just to laugh at the chaos.

I could work around this. "Fine. Leah can stay here and keep you boys' company," I flicked my hand at her. "Talon, you'll come with—"

"I'm afraid you misunderstand me." Cobalt Suit interrupted. "One of them must wait outside the building or in your vehicle. We cannot have any outstanding shows of force that might make our other guests...uncomfortable." Finality echoed in his tone and the muscle heads beside him straightened at his tone, tense and ready for any sign of trouble.

I flashed him a machete smile. If he thought I'd be intimidated, I'd quickly give him a much needed education.

"That's totally understandable," my voice smooth as cocoa butter. "However, where exactly do you suggest my people wait? Directly outside the building doors? That's sure to get the wrong kind of attention this late at night in this part of town. Especially when said parking lot is filled with hundred thousand dollar cars in a part of town that doesn't see that much revenue in a year. Not to mention the fact that half of those vehicles probably have unregistered license plates—a juicy bust of a cop with sharp eyes. And all of that..." I waved my hand in the air, searching for the right word, "Drama would be your fault. It's pretty hard to regain client trust once you have a reputation as a police crashing the party, don't you think?" I cocked my head at him and let the question linger in the air.

Uncertainty shimmered in his eyes.

"I won't be long. I have...particular tastes and I'll know fairly quickly whether or not you serve what I'm looking for.

One quick look and I'll be out of your hair."

His lips flattened out in a thin line. After a beat of silence, he rolled his shoulders, looked back at his screen and finished typing. He snapped his fingers in the direction of the other men and one of them stepped forward, pulling a marker out of his pants pocket.

"This is our official seal." Cobalt Suit clarified. "If you to step outside for any reason—a phone call, medical emergency—this allows you access back into the auction, one time." He held up a finger. "If you exit and try to reenter again, you will be forcibly removed from the premises."

The meathead grabbed my left hand and roughly pressed the marker hard enough for the indention to bit into my skin. Thank God he hadn't grabbed the other side—if he'd treated my right arm that roughly, I'd be passed out on the floor.

"Any questions?"

I smirked at him. "Not for you."

His jaw clenched but he flicked his hand at the other men. The one closest to the door grabbed the handle and pulled it open for us. Voices immediately hit us, all low but distinct and, for some reasons, loud in my ears.

"Enjoy your night." He said, the picture of elegant politeness.

I smirked. "Oh, we will." I strode into that room like I'd been there a hundred times before.

The lighting was the first thing I noticed— a subtle reddish glow that created a perversely relaxed atmosphere across the cavernous room. An open space tastefully sprinkled with expensive couches and armchairs clustered together to accommodate mingling and gossamer white curtains floating down from ceiling high cement pillars. It reminded me more of a modern, luxurious coffee shop or smoking lounge than the site of a sex auction. Men and women meandered around the room, most chatting amiably in groups of twos or threes and some sitting off to the side, eyes aimed on the empty stage. Clearly waiting. Most were dressed in varying degrees of business casual, with slacks and casual yet stunning dresses being the most common with the occasional jeans and cowboy boot throw in.

What caught and held my attention were the young people scattered around the room—girls dressed in loose white night-gowns walked the room serving drinks from crystal platters. Boys—in that awkward, unfinished state between puberty and manhood—stood still as statues across the room, some jumping at the nearest sharp command from a guest. All with skin ranging from pure obsidian to smooth café-au-lait. All with kinky wavy hair in various shades of brown and black, from honey gold curls to ebony black coils.

My stomach churned. It was a nightmare zone for mixed kids.

"Would you like a pamphlet, ma'am?" A soft voice at my elbow startled me. I looked left and a young girl with creamy brown skin and thick black ringlets that cascaded down her back stood beside me, a white booklet extended from her small hands. Sky blue eyes stared up at me.

My throat tightened but I forced myself to nod and take a book from her. "What's this?" I asked.

"A guide of all of all the merchandise for sale tonight." Her voice was adorable—high and sweet and melodic—the kind of talking voice a child radio station would love.

And it was completely robotic.

I stared into her eyes and saw nothing. No curiosity...no joy...no life. She couldn't be more than ten years old and these monsters had leeched everything that made a child special from her very soul.

My jaw clenched. If I tried to speak, I'd scream. All I could do was nod. The girl walked past me, swinging wide to avoid Talon, and moved to the next adult, a grossly overweight man with cigar in his mouth and a lecherous gaze. My eyes were hot as I watched her walk away but frost swept through my gut. The rage that beat at my mind was hot as lava but the cold place in my soul, the place where killing was simplest and justified, was frigid. For a moment, I truly let myself consider pulling the blade strapped to my thigh and stabbing every person in the room over the age of eighteen. The beast roared her assent and it echoed in my ears.

Control, Serena. Control. I sucked in a breath and held it, waited for the desire to leave the room bloody and vindicated to pass.

Something moved behind me and heat trickled up my spine as Talon stepped close. His hand brushed the small of my back, a subtle touch that anchored me. This was a game of the right moment and flying off the handle would only expose our hand and put these kids at even more risk. I wouldn't help anyone losing my cool.

"Steady." He rumbled in my ear.

Right.

I let out the breath and glanced at him over my shoulder. His face was petrous, totally void of emotion, fully in character of the good little bodyguard. He glanced down at me and, for a moment, I saw lighting in his eyes. A deadly storm gathered inside him and there'd be hell to pay when he finally unleashed it. His anger helped me pull back from the frosty ridges of my mind and pull myself together.

"Perhaps we should take a seat." He suggested.

I nodded. Excellent idea.

I spotted an open seat on the far side of the room, slightly away from the heart of the action but with full visibility of the stage and made my way towards it. I sat and casually glanced around the room. Just in time. A man appeared out of a side door on the far side of the stage.

Tall, lean but not in an off putting way, and dressed to the nines in a black ensemble. He moved with grace and authority. I without a doubt, I was looking at one of the masterminds behind this sick gathering.

His dark gaze cut to me. I felt Talon stiffen as the man made his way towards us.

"You don't feel like mingling?" the stranger asked when he was within ear shot, voice thickly accented.

I shook my head. "Not tonight. I'm jet lagged beyond belief."

"I can understand that. I heard your flight was less than ideal."

"Planes aren't my thing. Especially when I'm to get off that death contraption only to be interrogated when I arrive."

"You refer to Dmitri." He said. "Our humblest apologies. He is...eager and very capable to do the job but he's still in training and, at times, it shows. The organizer of this event heard of the issue and sent me to smooth things over with you. We'd hate to lose your goodwill."

"And the goodwill of the Albuquerque system." I reminded.

He gave a small smile. "Of course."

I took a deep breath and let it out with a dramatic huff. "It's not the first time I've been carded at the door. But never by someone so young." I leaned forward.

"That can be surprising."

"It sure is." I held out my hand. "Diamond Mine."

The man took my hand and brought it to his lips, eyes never leaving mine. "Charmed." He murmured against my skin. "I am Javier, assistant to the organizer."

I smiled, dazzling and sultry at the same time. "Ooooo, a foreign man. They're my favorite kind."

"What makes you think I'm a foreigner." There was smile on his lips but something dangerous lurked in his eyes.

"The whole package." I waved my hand at him. "The olive skin. The curly hair. Cultured voice. All deliciously exotic... Unless you're a really good actor with a spray tan, which is possible."

The sinister emotion slowly leeched out of his eyes and he smiled once more, a slight quirk of his lips. "Caught." He admitted. "I'm originally from Miami."

"I knew it!"

"So is that you're looking for?" he asked. "Dangerously exotic?"

"Something like that."

"I'm not quite sure if what we're offering tonight will suit those tastes."

"That's what I'm here to find out."

"Indeed." He murmured. "Please don't hesitate to let me know if there's anything we can acquire that will be more...satisfying for you."

Bile churned in my stomach. But I forced a smile. "I appreciate the offer. I'll keep you updated."

He nodded and held out his hand. I slipped mine into his and he raised my hand to his mouth and kissed the back of it. I shivered. More from the inscrutable look in his eyes than the feeling of his lips on my skin. He released me and turned to thread his way back through the room, stopping to talk and laugh with guests. Something about his presence left a greasy film on my skin.

"I'd like a drink." I told Talon abruptly.

He stared at me, eyes blank of emotion but an eyebrow kicked up at my tone.

"From the bar." I explained.

His eyes flicked that direction, where Javier chatted with a slender, pale woman in a short tangerine gown; despite their agreeable faces the tension between the two was obvious and I wanted to know they were talking about. The bar was close enough to hear but far away enough that it wouldn't be obvious.

Talon looked back at me. "Whiskey? No ice?"

I grinned up at him. The man knew me too well.

He nodded and headed for the bar, walking the length of the room instead of cutting straight through the middle. His pace was measured but intent—slow enough that he'd be able to pick up on bits of conversation but no one would be suspicious of his lingering.

I sat back in the cushioned chair and let out a breath. My shoulder throbbed and all I wanted to do was massage until the ache faded or rip it off and beat the nearest lech with it. My gaze drifted across the room, taking in every face and accent. I'd remember all of these degenerates—down to the last leggy botoxed blonde or balding pedophile. Be it prison or a coffin, their days of freedom were numbered.

The thought made me smile.

Movement to my right flashed in the corner of my eye and I tensed. I'd deliberately chosen this seat to avoid anyone standing behind me. If someone lurked near me, I definitely wanted to know who and why. I threw a bored glance over my shoulder as if casually scoping the area.

A young girl standing in the far corner of the room caught my attention. She carried a crystal tray with tumblers filled with a clear liquid. Like the other sad children here, she was easily ten pounds under weight, bones showing clearly despite the sheer gown draped over her. Such thinness made it difficult to determine her age. But something familiar pinged in my mind.

When she shifted, I noticed the cuff around her ankle. It was connected to a thin, almost elegant chain that was bolted into the pillar she stood beside; she couldn't have more than twenty feet of length before the chain caught. Even from this distance, I could see the skin around her ankle was darkly bruised and scabbed over.

A man snapped an order at her. When her head whipped in his direction, I got a clear view of her face. It hit me like a ton of bricks.

Oh my God.

Memories flooded my mind, that face unlocking a vault of nightmares I intentionally ignored and pretended didn't exist.

The convoy car exploding.

Flesh burning as I tried to pull bodies from the flames.

A young girl screaming as masked men dragged us apart.

The gunshot

Blank onyx eyes.

I would know that face anywhere. Hers was the face that had haunted my sleep for two years and was secretly the reason I was belly deep in a sex auction trying to save two kids I barely knew.

Sakira.

I stood, and my feet moved of their own accord. I crossed the room as if sludging through icy water. I had to get closer, had to be sure I wasn't hallucinating in broad daylight. She'd gone to attend to the man who'd summoned her. When she arrived, he grabbed her arms and yanked her forward, ignoring the fear quivering off her and the wide eyes watching him like a trapped animal. Those eyes sealed the deal—large almond eyes the color of gleaming obsidian stone. This was without a doubt the Syrian diplomat's daughter, the one I'd failed so many years before.

The man pulled her behind the pillar and then jerked her into him so roughly that the chain caught and her leg jerked with the motion. He pulled up by the arms. The look on his face was calm, as if he were having a conversation about the weather, but his eyes glinted with feral anticipation. He held her suspended with one hand along her waist and rocked, the way you'd rock a baby, but the look on his face and the way his free hand stroked her thigh made it anything but harmless.

The beast roared and my mind blanked. I walked faster. I tried to breathe around the stifling rage, tried to remember the plan and all that was at stake even as the beast bodily threw herself against the bars of the cage.

"Serena, what are you doing?" Talon's voice sounded in my ear but it was muffled.

What was I doing? My steps slowed as I tried to get control of myself. "Talon." I breathed his name on a whisper, but it was a cry for help.

"Talk to me. What's happening? What's going on?"

"Southwest corner," was all I could gasp out.

He was silent a moment. "Is that—?"

I nodded as if he could see me.

"I need you to keep it together, Serena." His voice was equal parts soothing and firm. "We can't act until we know exactly what we're dealing with."

He was right but Beastie still screamed with rage. I focused on sucking in slow deep breaths. I could do this. I was fine. I could handle this.

I really was—until they led her on stage.

One of the armed guards unchained her from the wall and walked her to the far side of the stage. The man never touched her but her fear vibrated off her in palpable waves. By the time she stepped up the stairs, the beasts had had enough.

Protect her. Save her. The tigress yowled in my mind as she threw herself bodily against the cracking cage bars. *Make it right.*

Pain shot through my skull as I struggled for self-control. Give it time, I told myself. We can't rush the moment or we'd risk everything. I pressed my feet into the floor and leaned against the seat, trembling with the control to stay put when everything in me screamed to throw myself onto the stage and save her.

"Easy." Talon murmured in my ear. "Our time will come."

I turned my face towards him. "I can't watch this. I can't fail her again."

A pause. "What are you talking about?"

"The Syrian diplomat's daughter."

The energy behind me changed and I knew he understood. He of all people should understand. He was the who found me, surrounded by bodies, in the musty hellhole in Syria and pulled me back to the world, into the light, literally. He'd seen her body just like I had, knew what her death had broken me.

But now, redemption stood before me on the stage.

Talon placed a heavy hand on my good shoulder and spoke into my ear. "She's not our target, Serena."

"I can't leave her here."

"I know." He murmured. "But if we move now we risk losing any information and leads to Alyssa and Logan. If we bide our time, we can save them all—Sakira included."

I let the wisdom of his words wash through me and relaxed into the chair. We had to bide our time. If I flew off the handle, the kids would disappear on an impossible trail to follow and the likelihood of recovering them diminished to almost nothing. I had to be calm. I could see this through.

For a moment, the thought was enough.

Until the "emcee" of this horrible event walked behind Sakira, grabbed the neckline of her gown, and ripped it down the front, exposing her to the room.

My mind blanked and everything went silent except for the beast's enraged roar echoing in my ears. I failed once. I would not fail again.

I leapt from my seat, ripping away from Talon's hand, and rushed the guard standing closest to us. I pulled the blade from my thigh and buried it in his neck before he could even jerk in surprise at the attack. Blood burbled from his mouth. I ripped the gun from his hip, pointed at the stage, and fired several shots, aiming high to avoid hitting Sakira.

By the time the room registered what had happened, the emcee was dead.

A guard swiped at me and I ducked beneath his arm, firing twice into his armpit and ripping his gun off with my free hand. I shoved his toppling body into another man who leapt from around a pillar.

"Plan Zulu." Talon yelled into the mouthpiece.

Bullets peppered the area in front of my feet and I leapt left behind a pillar as the ground was sprayed in front of me. Flashing movement to my right. A large man came up on me and tried to conk me on the head with the butt of his AK-47. I ducked, spun behind him and shot him in the back of the head. As he collapsed, I grabbed his gun and, with an enraged yell, I ran for the stage, sending clients and guards ducking for cover.

I leapt onto the stage and knelt next to her prostrate form. Blood stained her gown. Had I hit her accidentally? I ripped the corpse off her and knelt beside her still form, trusting Talon to cover me.

"Come on!"

Her body jolted violently and her head slowly lifted to look me in the eye.

"Can you run?" I asked. "I'm going to get you out of here."

Bullets pinged off the stage. Time to go. I wrapped my left arm around her waist and hauled us both off stage. Talon stood at the base, AK's looped around each arm and he sprayed the room.

"Let's move!" I yelled.

I looked to the door just in time to see Leah fling something towards the back of the room and the pin flew through the air. Shit.

"Grenade." I shouted and ducked behind a pillar, just as the bomb exploded. I covered Sakira's face as cement, glass, and smoke exploded through the room.

"Moving." Talon yelled and I followed him as he blazed a trail, stepping over hunched bodies and shooting anyone who stepped in his way.

We sprinted through the store and up those spiraling stairs. Someone must have alerted Luke—that or the gunshots gave him a clue that the plan was going to shit—because he was right there with the car when we burst through the doors.

Five seconds later we were all safely shoved inside.

Talon cast a backward glance at the building and so did I. Smoke wafted out of broken windows like smoke from a dragon's nostrils.

Subtle, real subtle.

Sakira trembled in my arms.

CHAPTER 24

"Someone want to tell me what the hell went wrong back there?" Leah asked as Luke merged onto the highway at breakneck speed.

There was no excuse I could give, wanted to give. What could I say? That I'd flown off the handle because of the raging beast that still flung herself against the bars of my mind, still urging me to fight and claw my way out of the uncomfortable situation. I was a hot mess and had almost gotten everyone killed for it.

So I said nothing, stared out the window at the passing city.

Talon's anger filled the space and it felt as if the pressure dropped like a tornado was close by. The moment the car stopped in front of the safehouse, I flung open the car door and rushed inside. Unfortunately, Talon was hot on my heels.

"Serena—" He snapped, voice tight with suppressed fury.

Beastie snarled at him. He had no right to judge us.

"I'm guessing things didn't go so well." Luke stated, limping out from the small kitchen, eyes on me.

I ignored him too.

I walked through the living room toward the hall with the bedrooms. I had to get away from Talon's aggressive energy. Strong hands gripped my upper arm and forced me to stop. I looked over my shoulder at him and begged him with my eyes to let me go.

"Talk to me." he demanded. "Tell me what the hell that was and how opening fire into a room filled with professional criminals and—"

"I couldn't leave her."

"You think I don't know that?" He shook me enough to jar. "Me," he hit his chest. "I know what she means to you. I know what losing her did to you. Do you think I'd callously walk away from an opportunity for you to finally silence those damn demons you are so determined to let dictate your life? You know me better than that."

"You were telling me to wait. She would have been molested on that stage right in front of us and I could not—"

"Nothing worse than she's already experienced and you know that."

"She's a child."

"We had a plan." Talon roared.

"You need to take your hands off her and calm down." Luke appeared on the other side of Talon, close and in his space.

The look Talon shot him was filled with venom and if Luke had any common sense left in his brain, he'd step back.

"Luke, you should sit down before you fall down," I said, trying to get him to back away from the other man.

Luke never took his eyes off Talon. "I might. After he takes his hands off you." Men really aren't that smart. Even with a bandage on his head with a red spot the size of a small orange seeping through, he stepped closer to the taller man.

Talon stalked out of the room. What was his problem.

"That was fun." Leah drawled as she pulled an avocado from the fridge, voice both managing to sound bland and disappointed.

Trouble maker. "Where's Sakira?" I snipped.

She sent me a glare back. "I got her started in the shower while Talon was chewing you out."

I shot her a glare.

She pursed her lips in a I'm-not-scared-of-you look and pointed towards the hallway Talon had stomped down. The message was clear: go after him. Beastie yowled in protest but I shoved it down. She'd done enough damage for tonight. But I knew Leah was right and I didn't want to leave

Didn't mean I wanted to do it either.

So I let the humiliation at being called out in front of everyone and failing to control Beastie, yet again, and putting everyone in danger fuel my anger and I stomped to the room that he and Luke shared. I knocked twice before shoving open the door.

"What the hell was that, Orsoto?" I asked, trying to keep my tone normal but my voice shook from the effort.

He stood by the window, but didn't turn around at my outburst, only shot an irritated look over his shoulder before turning back to stare out into the night.

I shut the door, hard. "You're going to ignore me? Real mature?"

"Why should I respond when it seems you have it all figured out." Talon sat on the bed and began unlacing his boots.

"As much as you've been busting my butt about "being a team player" and "trusting the team" you did a real good job of demoralizing everyone."

"You don't want my opinion." He bent forward to reach the lower laces and his braid swooped over his shoulder, pooling on the floor. "Just some kind of confirmation that you're doing the right thing."

"I *am* doing the right thing."

"No," his sharp voice whipped across the space. "You did what you *wanted* to do. Screw your team, screw the plan…you acted on your first impulse and that's all that mattered to you."

"I still have nightmares about her death, Talon. When I saw her, I couldn't leave her. How could I when I had the chance to make right what I did wrong so long ago?"

A sigh lifted his shoulders and poured out from his chest. "At what cost?"

"I couldn't control it."

"You know what, Serena? That line doesn't hold up when your actions start getting people killed."

I stared at him. Did he think I was a nuclear weapon of unstable emotion for shits and giggles? "How dare you." My voice was low and tight with anger. "You have no idea what›s like to live with something inside your head that you can't control."

"You think I don't have my own voices inside my head? Forget the military, I've had voices whispering, prodding, spurring me to unspeakable since my dad killed himself. Voices prodding me to drunkenness, telling me I'm nothing and will never be able to remove the stain that my father's drunk abuse and suicide painted on my family. Voices telling me to end it. And at some point, I had to decide that I couldn't listen to them anymore. Had to tune them out in order to survive. You haven't made that choice because you think that voice protects you, safeguards you from hurt or harm…when all it's really doing is eroding the relationships in your, poisoning your view of people and yourself and making you unable to accept help."

"People aren't the problem." I snapped. "It's *me*—and every jacked up thing going on inside my head. Me and this crushing failure that I cannot seem to outrun and I can't let it win."

"Who said you're a failure?" he challenged. "How many purple hearts *do* you have? How many times has Homeland Security given you some kind of award for bravery, courage, and determination to do your duty? A dozen? Those don't speak to someone who doesn't measure up."

I scoffed. "Every time someone looks at me, they expect me to fail. No one looks at the black woman and assumes I'll succeed, that I'll surpass status quo and thrive. They expect me to cater to victim mentality and give excuses about why I can't meet the standard."

"Isn't that what you're doing already?"

His words slapped me in the face and I stumbled back against the door. I couldn't expect him to understand…but something what he said slid deep inside me like a knife of acid.

He was silent a moment, eyes piercing mine and I found myself frozen beneath the weight of his lightning gaze. Silence I could handle. What he said next, I could not.

"Do you know what I found when I pulled you out of that hellhole in Syria?"

The tone in his voice made something lurch inside me and I frowned. I barely wanted to think of the feral, broken creature he'd pulled out of that cave compound, much less talk about her.

Unfortunately, Talon had no such qualms.

"I found you." His voice rumbled, "Standing amidst a pile of bodies and fighting off a Syrian warrior with a knife you'd stolen off a corpse. You took down six men with a fractured collarbone, busted ribs, and over seventy-two hours of torture. And those ten seconds I saw you fight, you fought like a hellcat, desperate and determined not to be recaptured. You were going to save yourself, no matter the cost—the exact opposite of this victim mentality you've spouted ever since."

My chest heaved as emotions stormed through me. A kaleidoscope of memory flickered in my head of those horrible days chained to a cave wall.

"But when you heard my voice, you collapsed. Fell to the ground as if someone had cut your strings. And when I scooped you up from the carnage, the first thing you said to me was, 'I knew you'd come.' Over and over and over until we fought our way out of the darkness and back into the light."

Humiliation burned in my chest. I remembered, all too well; it still washed over me in an ocean of sound and all I could think was one thing: I was so pathetic.

"Something inside of you told you I was coming, knew I wouldn't leave you to suffer like that."

I looked away. He refused to see it, the weakness that made me such a failure. That was the reason that Alyssa and Logan had been taken in the first place and why we all put our professional careers on the line to save them.

"And I knew that, knew you trusted me to find you, and it's what burned in my chest, made me blaze through the impossible until I discovered you in that cave." He stood and took a step toward me. "Trust, Serena. Trust is what makes this whole thing go 'round. You'd know that by now if you didn't run or scoff or retreat into your shell of fear every time every time someone asks you to put your faith in them."

"At least that shell is a safe place." I snapped.

"That shell is killing you!" he yelled. He took a breath to calm himself. "It's killing you, CeCe." His voice wavered with emotion and the look in his eyes—disappointment, pity even —made something crack inside. His words struck a chord deep in me, directed at the fragile truth that I'd clung to this whole time. That people couldn't be trusted—at some point they'd manipulate or betray or leave me. But Talon stood before me, eyes flashing and chest heaving with anger and something else I couldn't identify.

Talon was trying to burst my protective bubble.

A truth that now seemed shrouded with lies and inconsistency.

I looked up at him as wet pooled in my eyes and slid down my face. "I don't know how to move past this."

"Do you want to? Really, genuinely want to?"

"I don't know."

His lips kicked up in a small smile. "That's the most honest you've been in a long time."

My throat was too tight for words. It felt like I was in a tornado of emotion, things swept up inside me and flung out into the world for all to see. Fear rose up at the thought and swirled with the ice in my gut. I stood paralyzed, looking at him with wide eyes that glimmered with tears and fear. Yes fear.

He reached up and swept an errant braid from across my forehead, fingers skimming across my skin. "You know I'm here for you. Always."

The muscles in my throat squeezed until it was hard to breathe.

"But," he rumbled leaning closer until his strong face is all that vision and I was caught in the storm in his eyes. "If you have any doubt, any hesitation at all..." he brushed his lips across my forehead, down my cheek, kissed the corner of my mouth and I nestled into that embrace.

My chest tightened and breathing choked. I couldn't help it.

His tone, his smell, his strength beside me, all familiar in a way that turned my resolve and my stomach to slush.

The arm around my waist squeezed me tight, pressing me into him as his lips brushed my forehead. My breath caught. The tenderness threatening to unravel me. I simply focused on breathing and dissolving into a puddle of goo on the floor.

Talon pulled me closer, still careful of my arm, and I felt his lips sweep down across my nose heading toward my lips.

"I can't." My breathing hitched.

He paused, lips hovering over mine a hairsbreadth. "If you're afraid of what Julien will think, I'll talk to him."

For a moment, I sagged against him. There was no judgement or anger in his voice, just respect. I wanted that kiss, wanted it so badly it thrummed in my body and made my chest ache.

Something loud crashed against the wall and I jerked back against his arms. The sound came from the bathroom.

I touched Talon's chest to get his attention as he stepped forward to go investigate. "I'll go."

His arms loosened and I stepped into the hall just as Leah rounded the corner. Beastie yowled in protest but I ignored her as I stepped inside the steamy bathroom and shut the door

Sakira.

CHAPTER 25

The girl was huddled in the middle of the tub, knees clutched to her chest and black hair obscuring her face as steaming water cascading around her. For a moment, I had a disorienting sense of falling, as if I tripped on a memory and awoke staring into the same face that had haunted me for so many years. My stomach revolted and I swallowed down bile that threatened to surge up my esophagus.

I took a cautious step forward. "Sakira?"

She jerked when I said her name, as if I'd slapped her, but didn't look up.

I moved to the tub and sat on the edge, as far from the water spray but flecks of water still peppered my skin. I was careful not to touch her—she'd experienced enough unsanctioned touch in the last couple of years. But the urge was strong. Part of me still couldn't believe she was alive and not a rotting corpse in a Syrian mountain cave.

She looked at me with those endless onyx eyes. "I—I know where they're going to take them." Her accent was thick but no less lyrical for it. Her English had been passable before her kidnapping but now it was clear and easy to understand.

I lifted an eyebrow. What was she talking about?

"The other kids at the auction." she explained. "They won't keep them here long; they never do after an…an event and especially not the ones who received low bids. They'll pack them up and ship them out like express goats to the next location. The highways here make it easy to move us from city to city without being noticed."

"Wait…are you saying you've been here before?"

She nodded. "The organizers of this circuit ship merchandise—"

"People, Sakira." I gently corrected. "You are not and have never been "merchandise". No one is."

She swallowed. "Right. Oklahoma City is a big trade route and people are circulated through here all the time. I've been on this circuit for five months and have been through here a few times. There's a truck repair yard off the highway with the big water park and it's their favorite spot for emergency exports."

"Were you exported often? Did no one ever…want you?" There was no sensitive way to ask the question but I needed to be sure that her information was halfway accurate.

"They told me I was one of the special ones," Her lips twisted in a bitter smile. "I was only allowed to be presented in auctions with other special kids like me."

"Special? You mean, kidnapped like you?"

She shook her head.

I thought back to the auction. "Mixed race?"

Another head shake. She was hesitant to tell me and my stomach churned. I didn't want to think of the myriad of sick ways that a sex ring would label a child as "special" and the thought of what might have happened to her made my skin crawl.

"You can tell me, even if it's painful or embarrassing."

"Kids whose parents are important, like in politics or world affairs" she explained finally. "We're not allowed to talk to each other but we always manage a few words, especially when there's only one or two guards watching us. Did you see a boy with dark skin and really blue eyes?" I nodded. "Yesterday, he told me that his father is the king of Sudan but his mother wasn't married to him so she sent him away to protect him. That's when the men caught him."

My mind whirled with the information. "So, you're telling me that the men who kidnapped you in Syria specialize in taking children of important people and..."

"Moving us within sex groups as blackmail?" she finished for me. "Yes."

My mind whirled with the implications. Part of me wanted to question the reliability of the information coming from her. The six months, she'd experienced enough trauma to break the psychological stability of grown men. I shoved that thought aside. I wouldn't dishonor her struggle by disregarding what she had to say.

Her information was the best lead we had on recovering Alyssa and Logan and figuring out who was behind Jackson's death. And it was far more convoluted than I would have guessed. But before I went chasing down truck stops through the city, I needed to be sure I was on the right track to finding Jackson's kids.

"I need you to try and remember if you've seen these kids before," I told her as I pulled my phone from my back pocket and scrolled through my downloaded pics. The one I wanted was halfway up the page, the Jackson family at a rally somewhere in Oklahoma and their faces on fully display. I twisted my wrist so she could see the screen. "Have you seen either of these children? They would have been added to the group in the last few days."

She studied the pictures. After a moment, she nodded. "She was in the room with me before tonight's auction," Sakira pointed at Alyssa's face. "I don't know why she didn't go out with the rest of us but she was still chained to the wall when we walked out."

It felt like water rushed through my ears. Alyssa had been there tonight...and I left her. Emotion flood me and I fought not to drown in the deluge. Focus, Serena.

"He was there too."

Sakira's finger didn't rest on Logan or even Jackson's face. She had zoomed in on a familiar face toward the back of the stage and could barely be seen behind Jackson's body. But that mange red hair was too distinct to go unnoticed.

I blew up the photo as much as I could and pointed. "You saw this man? At the auction?"

She nodded.

"What...?" I was too stunned to form a question.

"He didn't stay," she explained. "He met with some men and then left with a gray briefcase."

A payout? What the hell was Brendan Michaels doing accepting money from sex slavers? I struggled to put the pieces together. "Let's rewind a second. You think the men who took you will ship everyone out of place near a large water park in the city."

"That's right. A repair shop for the large trucks with the big wheels."

"Semi-trucks?"

"I think so."

My mind reeled as I processed her words. "Are you sure?" I didn't want her to think that I didn't trust her information but I'd be a fool for not checking. "There are dozens of larger cities with outlying towns that look like OKC."

"I'm sure," her voice was firm but she didn't meet my eyes. "If I was...good...they'd let me walk around sometimes, afterward. I'd pay attention to street signs and highway names in case I ever had a chance to escape."

A flood of emotions surged in me at her words but I focused on pride. Despite what they tried to make her, she wasn't a victim.

But she wasn't done.

"There's a small window in the room that the guards usually keep us in. It's high off the ground and looks kind of small but I could slide through if I needed too."

Her words caused the surge of thoughts to come to a screeching halt in my head. "What? No. I'm going to call the police and get you in protective custody and we'll focus on tracking down whatever family you have left. You're not going in there."

"You need to know if the two people you're searching for

272

are even down there," she reminded me, voice soft but strong. "Why risk you and your team's life for people who aren't even there?"

What she said made sense and it angered me. Didn't I just rescue her from hell? I wasn't about to send her straight back into fire. "I appreciate your offer, but the answer is no. We'll figure out."

The determined glint in her eyes told me differently.

CHAPTER 26

M otels rank on my top five list of "Sketchiest Places on Earth." It didn't matter that I'd slunk through some of the world's dirtiest slums and dangerous ghettos, one thing always remained the same—motels were breeding grounds for skanks, criminals, druggies, and unidentifiable diseases.

And this one was no different.

"What are your three primary strike points?" I tossed the question over my shoulder as I finished setting up the small hi-tech laptop on the nightstand dresser Talon had moved to the window for me.

"Anywhere on the neck, the heart, and the groin." Sakira's soft, accented voice responded.

"Good. And how long should you hold before letting up?" Leah asked, eyes focused on the girl as she wiped down a long pistol with a cloth.

"Three long seconds—one potato, two potato, three potato. Five to be sure they stay down."

I turned to face the teenage girl. "Good. Now, say the attacker grabs your hair..." I reached up and gently rested my good hand on the top of the thick crown of jet black hair. We'd been at this for an hour, and I was trying to be subtle, watching for any signs that my movements triggered flashbacks or she was getting ready to freak out.

Sakira was made of stronger stuff.

"I tase him here." She touched the inactive stun gun to the inside of my elbow. "And, when I get an opening, here." She reached out and placed the cold tongs on my neck.

"And what if he gets you on the floor? Tries to get between your legs?"

I felt eyes on me as I asked the question but I didn't care. Sakira had already experienced the worst the world could do to a woman, had her innocence ripped away in the most horrendous way, and I was giving her a tool to take back a small measure of control. Anyone who attacked wouldn't be easy on her ,and neither would I.

She didn't even flinch. "Let him hold onto whatever he likes and tase his ass until he pees himself." Her eyes glinted with determination.

Her grit should have settled me, given me a bit more reassurance that I was doing the right thing. But all I could see was the bullet hole dripping blood in her forehead from years ago.

"Remember," I said, trying to shake off the image. "If have to defend yourself, tell us what's happening in the coms and someone will get to you. Your job is not to defeat your attacker. Your job is to stay alive until Talon or Leah can get to you. That's it."

She nodded. "I'm ready."

I stepped close to her and placed my good hand on her neck. "Whatever happens, they will not retake you." Conviction made my voice waver, and I swallowed past the tightness.

"I'm not afraid." She looked down at the stun gun a long moment before meeting my eyes again. "If I...can help someone not be what I was forced to be...it's worth the risk."

Her bravery made my throat clench tight. The smile I gave her felt brittle, but it was all I could do. I had no words. Inside I knew that a few hours of self-defense training wouldn't be enough to keep her safe. It's why I should be going with her, to make sure no foul person lays a fingernail on her again. But I wasn't. My stomach dipped. So I didn't say anything, just nodded in reassurance. Silently impressed by her courage and equally terrified that we were inviting a repeat of two years ago.

"Leah had something she wanted to show me as well."

I gave her the space to step around me and cross the room to where Leah sat on top of the dresser that held the motel TV, carelessly swinging a leg like a lazy cat as she cleaned her gun. Sakira purposely skirted the bed, giving it a wide berth. I didn't blame her. The military drove out the majority of prissy sensibilities I might have inherited from my mother, but a clean mattress was not one of them. If the bed looked remotely unclean, I refused to have anything to do with. And the king sized bed in the room we checked into was a particularly concerning specimen. It told the story of its visitors without emitting a single squeak—mysterious stains, the stale scent of cigarette smoke, and the potential for flesh eating critters.

We didn't have a choice though. This motel was just over three-quarters of a mile from the semi-truck repair yard owned by Brendan's uncle, and Luke flagged it as the best place to set up base. Between the large expanse of overgrown grass that stretched between the two buildings and the shoddy trailer park on the west side of the motel, it seemed the perfect place to avoid suspicious eyes and still control the mission from a central location.

The perfect place for me to stay behind and let others pick up my slack.

A presence came up behind me and I didn't have to look to know it was Talon. "You gonna make it?"

I shot him a dirty glance over my shoulder and turned to the long range rifle we'd set up at the only window in the room. He knew better than to ask stupid questions. If I didn't think too hard about the fact that I wasn't going to be active in the field, I could almost pretend things were normal. Ignore the fact that the bullet wound in my shoulder and Beastie eagerly prowling inside my head made me a liability to the team. Ignore the fact that I told Talon to run point on the mission in a wild attempt to activate on the concept of trusting the people around me.

He made it harder by refusing.

I needed some form of leadership, he told me. Control. Like I was some unstable, argumentative ninny who couldn't take orders from someone other than myself.

How well he knew me.

As mission leader, I tried to slip myself into the action just a little bit, saying I'd be in charge of onsite reconnaissance to make sure no unexpected players messed up our plan. Talon was having none of it. When Luke threw in his lot with Talon, saying that if he was going to play a more passive role because of his head injury—he agreed to scout his resources for the OKCPD and see if he could convince anyone to bring backup—then it made no sense to send me into the field with a bum shoulder. I ranted and railed but eventually agreed that I'd stay behind at the motel and manage the coms and reconnaissance from an eagle eye view in the room. Leah wisely, stayed out of it but when I finally relented she shrugged her shoulders with a wry smile as if to say, "Oh darn, two attractive men putting themselves on the line to keep you protected. What a hard life you live." Traitor.

Now, we were less than half an hour away from activating our play, and Beastie was a pacing, snarling mess inside my mind. It felt like between one breath and the next my cool points would disappear and I'd disintegrate like a bullet hitting water. I knew I wouldn't be able to hide this from Talon so I ignored him, fiddling with the sights on the rifle while he watched me with stormy eyes.

I felt him move and glanced his way as he leaned against the wall next to the window. Whatever. He could study me all he wanted but it didn't mean I had to talk to him.

"Serena—"

"She shouldn't be going and we both know that," I hissed under my breath. I set the sight down with a bit more force than I intended and it clattered on the dresser.

"We don't have much choice. She's the best option." Leah said.

"I want to go, Serena." Sakira chimed in, her accent making

my name as soft as the wind rustling through trees.

Talon stepped close. "I told that I'll keep her safe and I mean that."

He couldn't be sure of that. Once you stepped into a storm with people like these, all certainties and control went out the window. Anything could happen…and Sakira would be right in the middle of the chaos.

"Do you trust me?"

I looked at him. "It has nothing to do with that."

"Then what?"

I stared into his lightning silver eyes, swirling with kindness and concern and understanding, not judgement because my hot mess was showing.

"I can't lose her again." The words came out tight and whispered and quivering with the emotion I couldn't suppress. "I can't lose any of them. I wouldn't survive that." There, the raw truth out and open in the world.

Talon stepped forward, gently wrapped me in his arms, and laid his forehead against mine. "I give you my word that Sakira will make it out of the building unscathed." He squeezed me. "We all will."

Wetness pooled in my eyes.

"Trust me."

Beastie roared in opposition, clawing at the bars of the cage to be set free and take over. For the first time in years, I did something new—I closed my eyes and focused on shutting her in a cage made of steel bars of determination and will power.

A high pitched beeping sounded through the room, and Talon pulled his cell phone from his pocket and turned off the alarm. That was the sign that it was time to get this show on the road.

"All right kids, it's party time!" Leah chirped, snapping her Kevlar vest in place, one of the rare times she actually wore one. Tonight, she was on keeping Sakira on track and eliminating any threats that came her way and she was armed to the teeth to do it.

I walked over and handed Sakira an earbud. "Here, put this in and make sure it's secure."

She did and turned her head to let me inspect.

"Looks good. Just remember that one tap means no and two taps means yes." I adjusted the Kevlar vest beneath the long sleeved black shirt she wore. "If you can't see Leah, that doesn't mean she isn't watching out for you. She'll have you covered one hundred percent of the time, okay?"

Sakira gave me solemn eyes and said, "The only reason I agreed to do this is because I knew you'd take care of me. I'm not worried...and neither should you be." With that, she turned and walked to the door where Leah waited, leaving me speechless.

Her faith in me was overwhelming. She had suffered years of rape and abuse because of me yet was willing to go back into the lion's den because she believed I'd pull her out again. My throat tightened and Beastie yowled once again that we shouldn't let her go. I opened my mouth to voice a final protest but a strong arm looped around my waist and Talon yanking me into him. I was about to tell him where he could shove the macho ape bull crap, but his head descended and lips slid along mine before I got out so much as a growl. I put my hands on his chest and shoved but that only made him cinch me in tighter until I was flush against him and we moved against each other with the bite of weapons biting into our skin.

Something inside me cracked and I found myself slipping my good arm around his neck and kissing him back like he was water in the desert. Talon growled against my lips, the vibration ruffling through me down to my toes.

When he finally let me pull away, my legs were shaky.

"You've got to stop doing that." I snapped but my breathy voice made it a weak complaint.

"What? You'll let the warrior go off to battle without giving him something sweet to think of?" He grinned down at me.

Normally I'd have responded with some remark about how I fight my own battles, but tonight proved me that wasn't the case. "That's too sexist to even deserve a response," I told him.

He grinned at me and swiped his bag off the stained coverlet and joined Leah at the door while I shook myself out of my Talon fog. I took a moment and studied the group. Dressed in black, hair slicked back into braids that swung around their waists, and armed to the teeth, both Talon and Leah looked every inch the Native American assassins that they were. Even Sakira didn't stand out of place, with her high cheekbones and exotic onyx eyes making her seem like part of the team.

"See you on the other side," I called to their backs as they strode for the back exit.

The door clicked shut and the volatile emotion swirling in my gut surged into my throat. I should be with them. It was a coward's move staying behind—or the weakest link. I couldn't stand to be either.

But the look in Talon's eyes pierced through my swirling fear and resentment. Protecting Sakira, bringing Alyssa and Logan home safe and sound was just as important to him as it was to me. It was more than that though. Something in his eyes asked me to trust him, to trust him to bridge the gap for what I couldn't do. He needed it just as much as I needed him to succeed. I inhaled a deep breath and held it—held it until my chest ached and lungs burned and a slightly tremor in muscles and the look in Talon's eyes made that swirling panic recede at last.

Even when I failed, Talon pulled through. If there was anyone who could bring back Alyssa and Logan, it was him. And the team needed me to do my part.

I turned and walked back to the room's only window. A Blaser R93 Tactical bolt action rifle sat on a three prong stand directly in front of it, ominous even in the dingy yellow light. When Talon pulled this thing from the trunk of his car, even Leah looked impressed.

I snagged the chair and sat at eye level behind the gun. A state of the art laptop the size of a book sat on the dresser to my right and I reached over to tap the green button that activated the small buds in our ears.

"HQ comms are up." I said into the air, settling to peer through the gun's scope. "Everyone check in"

"This is Eagle Eyes, all is good." Talon's voice rumbled over the line.

Leah chimed in. "Pocahontas can hear you loud and clear."

"What about you, Butterfly?" I asked, clicking through the frequencies.

A pause. "Umm...this is butterfly checking in." Sakira's voice was shy but strong.

My throat clenched hearing her voice. I shoved it down. Talon and Leah would protect her with their lives—there wasn't anyone else I'd trust her with. "Okay, hon, just keep your earbud in your ear and follow any instructions we give you."

Two quick buzzes came through the line. Smart girl.

Desperate people did desperate things and our plan was as straightforward as it was insane. Leah would escort Sakira back into the warehouse where the children were kept, and she'd tell us if Alyssa and Logan were there. We'd all agreed that we wouldn't leave the children in that warehouse behind even in the kids were nowhere to be found. In the meantime, Talon would act as the buyer from the Syndicate and try to force whoever oversaw the money exchange into giving him the children. Based on what we knew from Rashawn, the Syndicate rarely sent the same person twice to close out a deal so there was a real shot we could get all the kids loaded into a semi-truck and drive into the horizon before anyone was the wiser.

So many variables. So many things had the potential to go wrong. I didn't focus on those. If it didn't help my nerves, keep me calm and steady, I pushed it aside.

I peered into the scope and focused on the building. It took a few seconds to zoom in on the entrance. It had no windows so all I could do was scan the outside and surrounding area to make sure no ugly surprises headed their way. All I had was the info on the comms and my belief in them.

Through the rifle scope, I tracked the black SUV Talon drove up to the building door. He sidled the car and honked the horn three times—twice fast, three times slow in sets of four. He did this over and over for at least four minutes. By the time the fifth minute, I was ready to lose it. This entire scheme would go awry if we couldn't even get the guy to open the door.

On the sixth round, the double bay doors finally slid open.

"Headed inside." Talon rumbled over the line.

"Copy that." I told him. I watched the doors close but they were just slow enough for me to see Talon step out of the car, black trench coat swirling around his ankles. Then the doors shut, blocking my view, and leaving me only with the sounds the comms could pick up.

My gut clenched. This wasn't the first time he'd been in hot water. He'd be fine. I muttered this under my breath and mentally slapped myself. Talon was a former Marine—this he could handle.

I muted his line and switched over to the other frequency. "What's the ETA on arrival on site?"

A moment of dead air.

Then Leah's voice crackled over the line. "Butterfly is inside the warehouse. Boosted her through a window."

Air whooshed from my lungs.

"I'm going to do quick reconnaissance, see how many men are on site. Stand by." Leah whispered.

"Copy that." She'd be fine. She volunteered for this, I chanted to myself. She'll be okay. Sakira had survived two years of hell—she could handle this.

Beastie growled a protest in my head but Talon's words swirled in my mind. I could choose to do it on my own or I could trust the people around me. My fingers clenched around the rifle's handle. The look on Talon's face after I blew the sex auction infiltration flickered through my head like a snapshot —disappointment, sadness, but the most jarring, pity. I never wanted to cause that look again.

The laptop beeped, drawing my attention from my thoughts, and I focused on the screen. A weather app popped up on the blacked out screen, showing heavy thunder clouds moving into the area. I reached over and clicked on the message, skimming through the information. Heavy rain. Extreme lightning. Severe winds.

Crap. I'd checked the forecast yesterday, and it mentioned nothing of a thunderstorm at the time. Just when I needed bipolar Oklahoma to be on her weather mediation. Lightning would interfere with our comms, which was dangerous for a mission built on verbal cues.

I needed to tell the others and stat.

I clicked opened Talon and Leah's frequencies and opened my mouth to speak but a harsh voice coming through the com made me pause.

"You're not the regular guy." A man's voice crackled faintly.

I focused on Talon's comms and turned up the volume.

"After last night's debacle, we've been forced to switch things up in order to keep the trail clear," Talon's voice rumbled over the line. "It would be in everyone's best interest to avoid a repeat of last night." The threat was subtle.

"I had nothing to do with that. And from the way it sounds, neither did Baxter." Lightning flashed and the man's voice wavered. I turned up the volume to Talon's mic.

"Happened on your turf. That's reason enough to make us… concerned."

The man swore. "This is crap."

Talon didn't respond.

"Listen man, I'm not doing jack shit until I confirm that you really work for The Syndicate."

"Feel free to call. My boss highly enjoys conversations with hired muscle."

A pause. "Look, I just do what I'm told, and no one told me to expect a new courier."

"You think they inform you of all their plans? I'm the money man and they shuffle me around from job to job minimal information and hope I don't get shot in the face for asking the wrong questions."

The man gruffly laughed. "I can relate."

"I'm sure you can. Now, let me inspect the merchandise and I'll be on my way."

"Why would I do that?" Back to suspicious.

"So I can make sure it's all there."

"You don't trust my work? That I do what I say I'm gonna do." Whoever this guy way, he's a hothead.

"I'm about to hand over ten million dollars...In my work, I don't trust anyone."

Headlights flared in the western distance and drew my attention. A frown tugged at my lips and I swung the rifle so I could zoom in on the activity. This late at night, traffic was light and consistent mainly of semi-trucks blazing down I-40. I leaned forward and peered through the scope, scanning until I found the lights. Everything was tinted green with night vision but it didn't distract.

Please let them keep driving, please let them keep going, I muttered under my breath as I watched the three cars approach the exit. My scar twitched. How likely was it that three black SUV's driving in an unbroken line would be unaffiliated with one another and only coincidentally headed toward a sex trafficking drop-off point? About as likely as a meteor striking the same place twice.

Dread surged through me when I watched through the scope as all three SUV's exited the highway. Shit. The Syndicate convoy was early

I glanced at the clock and it read 12:15 am.

Lightning streaked suddenly across the sky, flashing through scope and making white spots burst through my eyes. I jerked away from the scope and blinked several times, clearing my vision. I reached for the comms and turned on an open frequency. I had to warn them.

"Heads up. We have activity coming from true west—three black SUV's following one another." I said into static.

There a pause and then, "Copy that. How far out?" Leah' voice broke halfway through as another streak lit the sky. Crap.

"Be advised. Five to six miles from the rendezvous point." I tracked the progression. "All three vehicles are exiting the highway now." I zoomed into the first car, the powerful lens covering that distance easily.

"Butterfly, what's your status?" I asked.

Static filled the line.

"Pocahontas, can you get a visual on Butterfly?"

Nothing.

Lightning pierced the sky in a brilliant flash.

Dread filled my gut.

"Eagle Eyes, buzz your comm if you can hear me."

Nothing.

Shit.

The storm was interfering with our comms. I had no idea if they could hear me and it wasn't allowing them to respond. There was no way for me to know if they knew the Syndicate was literally two miles from them.

Beastie roared in my head. Can't leave Sakira. Must go save her.

I breathed around that voice and squashed it. Talon had this. I had to trust him. I tried the comms again.

"Syndicate convoy is t-minus three minutes from location. Does anyone copy?"

No one responded.

Two gunshots ripped through the comms, loud enough to make me wince. I froze. The noise had sounded from Talon's line.

I switched over to just his line, hoping it would be more stable. "Eagle Eyes, I heard gunshots. Talk to me? Are you good?"

Thunder boomed outside in the silence, mimicking my heart in my chest. Come on, come on...

His comms clicked twice.

Relief coursed through me. He was alive. For now. "Do you

need back up? I can be there in four minutes."

Silence.

I leaned forward and swung the rifle around until I caught sight of the SUVs. They pulled in through the parking lot and started down the long road through a forest of semi-trucks.

I adjusted the controls and tried his line again, but still found static. Shit, shit, shit. I checked the scope. The SUV's were closing fast, a mile and a half, two miles out tops. They were almost to the winding road that would lead them through the lot to the main building. Then it would be too late.

Maybe if I closed the distance, it would stabilize the connection. Talon was flying blind until he knew that Sakira had eyes on Alyssa and Logan and God knows where Leah was. I could either wait here and pray that coms came back online. Waiting put everyone in jeopardy, and I couldn't let that happen. Everything inside me vibrated for me leap into action.

But I'd promised Talon.

Promises can be overridden in a crisis, Beastie hissed.

I sat back in the chair. No. I told him I wouldn't step in unless he asked me to. I tried him again. Nothing.

I got up and paced the length of the room twice hoping that would get rid of the energy building inside me. It didn't help.

But I'd wait. I peered through the scope once more and swore. They were almost to the gate. We couldn't risk such a devastating surprise. Cars like that could hold up to fifteen men—way too many for our coalition to deal with. Not to mention the number of BU's men who were already inside. Surrounded by the enemy on both sides.

I had to move. For my team…For those kids.

I jumped up and walked over to the dresser where a sole black military style bag sat on the dresser. Unzipping it, I pulled a subcompact machine pistol, two retractable Sai blades, and a variety of clips and quickly shoved them in holsters at my back, waist, and ankles. I pulled out a preloaded morphine syringe and stabbed it into my shoulder. Once the pain in my shoulder dimmed from fire to just a smoldering burn, I jogged to the door. I know I promised Talon I'd stay out of the fight...but all my people were about to be surprised in a dangerous way, and I had no way to warn them. I could be a stabilizing force, a force to turn the tables.

I went back to the laptop and tried again. "Eagle Eyes, I am here to provide backup. Please respond."

I grabbed the butt of the rifle and swung it back toward the barn. The black SUV's had pulled in front of the warehouse and close to a dozen or so men piled out. I swept the scope over the other men, memorizing faces and the way they moved and filing it in my brain. Something glinted through the scope... glasses? I zoomed on that person, and Brendan's face filled the screen. A frown pulled at my lips. He was supposed to be in Nevada investigating Jackson's assassination. Had he been reassigned? Suspicion blitzed through me and I watched him walk into the building with the other men. What was his association with the Syndicate? Was he undercover?

I scanned the car Brendan had exited, checking to make sure no one else was there. Something swayed in the very back of the car, technically the trunk, but tinted windows covered the space. The windows were tinted so darkly it was hard to tell and I zoomed in more, hoping to increase visibility. A dark shadow moved through the space. Definitely man shaped. What was Brendan doing? Several reasons a man might be hanging out in the back of car flickered through my head but none of them made sense.

I twisted the dial on the scope and upped the magnification to the highest level. The shadow swayed and was still dark and shapeless but something bright was wrapped around their head like a fluorescent head wrap. My breath shuttered to a stop in my chest. I should recognize that head wrap...I'd done one just like it a few hours earlier.

Luke.

I scanned the car but all I could tell he was immobile in the backseat, barely moving. A thousand thoughts raced through my head but I knew this for sure—he wasn't there by choice.

He was their trump card and I had no idea when they planned to show it or how they intended to use it. Whatever it was certainly wouldn't be in our favor.

Just then, the doors to the warehouse opened once more and I watched Brendan stride angrily for the car. Crap. Time's up.

I couldn't begin to guess why they had him but instinct told me that they were keeping him a surprise for a reason—one that could only be deadly for Talon.

My whole body vibrated with the need to leap up and charge in to the rescue. Talon knew there were more players. He knew the situation was evolving and not in our favor. He knew I was there waiting for him to put me in play. I sucked in a breath and let it out slowly. He knew what he was doing.

He'll get everyone killed, Beastie roared, bodily throwing herself against the bars of her cage and my body shook with the vibration.

No. Talon knew what he was doing. He must have a plan. But I could feel control fading away; could feel myself slipping into the same violent headspace that caused me to lose it during my reassessment mission and blow the entire operation. So much at risk…but I couldn't control myself.

I stumbled back from the rifle and caught one of my legs on the edge of the bed that sent me sprawling. I landed hard on my knees, head in my hands, and screamed. I was going to fail to control Beastie and let her takeover. Again. Blow the entire mission and watch everyone who mattered to me get slaughtered before my eyes. Again. It felt like I was fracturing at the seams. There was no way I'd be able to live through something like that a second time.

"God, help me!' The words were torn from the depths of my soul and I screamed them.

Beastie roared in protest and flung herself against the cage. I swayed with the force of the chaos in my head, knew that if I reached for that gun, I wouldn't be able to control my actions.

I suddenly remembered a card Miss Soto had sent me during my first few weeks at Homeland. It had arrived out of the blue and I only kept it because she was the one who gave it to me. Etched on the card was a prayer that I mumbled even now, "God, my soul is like a turbulent sea. Grant me peace of mind and calm my troubled heart".

A sensation poured over me like being doused with warm water and with it came a calm so foreign, yet so welcome, that it slid around me like a blanket. Beastie's terrified motions stilled and she even lay down in the corridors of my mind, tranquil for the first time since my devastating days in Syria. I froze, waiting for her to rebel against the calm and torment me yet again.

But she was quiet. At peace, almost.

I wanted to be baffled but my spirit knew the truth. God had come through.

The laptop on the dresser beeped loudly, drawing me from my reverie. I jerked my head up in time to see a green vibration rend across the screen and the earpiece in my ear buzzed.

It was Talon signaling for help.

Finally.

I was up and out the door before the final vibration faded from the screen. As I jogged down the stairs, I didn't spare a thought for the room full of weapons lying around, several that could be traced back to one or two government agencies. Hopefully we'd be back before housekeeping in the morning.

Hopefully.

I exited a door that opened to the motel's east facing back door. I was instantly hit with the smell of ozone, acrid and sharp, as lightning ripped across the sky, for a moment illuminating the field that stood between me and the warehouse. My eyes tracked a path, and I took off and didn't stop until I was flying at a dead run across the slick, muddy grass. I was bent nearly in half, and waist high grass slapped at my face; I could feel my braids dragging along in the mud.

Urgency a staccato beat in my heart.

CHAPTER 27

It was cold enough that my breath puffed out in harsh clouds as I ran.

It took four minutes to sprint the length of the field and the entire time my brain whirled with the myriad of ways the situation could devolve. We needed a diversion. Something that would startle everyone and allow Talon enough time to make a move that would help him escape or gain the upper hand.

Luckily, I had one in mind.

Several rows of semi-truck tractors—a.k.a., the front part —were arranged across the gravel road and all narrowing the eye to the main office building and warehouse. I stopped at the first line of trucks I came to, the back row, and crouched low. I pulled on the door handle of the semi cab I leaned against. Locked...not for long it wasn't. I scanned the ground around me and quickly found a rock large enough to do the job.

Lightning streaked, thunder bellowed loud enough to make the metal quiver, and I flung the rock into the driver side window. The sound of shattering glass was absorbed by the chaotic weather. Rain pelted me harder as I stepped on to the low rim of the semi and snaked my good arm between the teeth-like shards of glass at the opening. I fumbled for the door handle and pulled. The door clicked open and I just as carefully removed my arm before hopping to the ground and pulling it open all the way.

Scattered, staticky words came through the earbud, disjointed and hard to understand, as I slid into the driver's seat and searched the obvious places for a hidden key. But threats always had a way of standing out.

"Your face is familiar but it's not because I've seen you on this circuit" a new voice crackled, whiny yet distinctive and it made dread surge through me. Brendan.

Time was running out. I ripped open the dash and fumbled with the mess of dangling wires.

"If he's not with you and he's not with us, then…" Another new voice, this one thick with a Mediterranean accent. A gunshot rang out and my fingers slipped from the wires. I glanced up but was just far enough away that I couldn't see through the windows.

I touched my earpiece and spoke just above a stage whisper. "Buzz twice if you're alive."

More noise scrambled through the lines, men shouting at each other but Brendan's voice came through most clearly.

"This is not your operation. You have no control here and I won't be usurped by a European bastard! You don't move product without my say so and you sure as hell don't shoot anyone without my say so."

"You are a vessel, a means for temporarily storing our products before our guys ship them out," Mr. Accent snapped back. "We chose to work with you because your uncle's business gave us the most legitimate cover story but don't think for a moment that we won't replace you for someone more amenable to our expectations."

Brendan's scoff sounded like a choked snort. "With the amount of "product" you move? There isn't another type of business that would be a legit cover for what you do. The feds would be down your throat in a minute. Trucking is your best, and only, option."

"We'd work a way around that. We always do. In short, you are irrelevant and would have remained so without our money and resources."

This was bad. Piss on conversations like this usually had one outcome: bullets flying until the deadliest group remained standing. And Talon, Leah, and the kids would be right in the middle of that mess. I twisted the two wires around each other and hoped I wouldn't electrocute myself into next week.

"Red is dead. Green is clean." I muttered under my breath as I stripped the wire casings with hands that shook from cold and adrenaline. The engine jumped and roared to life. Hell yes! The headlights came on and I quickly flipped them off. Darkness was my cover. I put the semi into reverse and backed it out. I yanked the gear shaft to first gear and it slowly shuffled down the loose gravel road toward the buildings.

"Talon, buzz me if you're alive. I'm comin' in hot." I yelled over the noise of the truck as lightning split the sky. The rumble and creaking could easily be mistaken for thunder and buildings groaning beneath the force of the wind.

I was still half a mile away from the main building and I'd need every meter of that to get this bad boy going fast enough for what I needed to do. The cab lurched and growled toward the building and I was hoping that without a heavy load, the engine would shift more quickly. I noticed the scope lying on the passenger floorboard and I leaned over and snatched it up. A quick adjustment and I could see through the panels of glass into the room and my gut clenched. Both groups of men —Brendan's backwoods truckers in flannel and boots and the suave mystery men in blazers and trench coats—were scattered throughout the room with guns pointed at each other. At least thirty men all ready to unleash on each other at the drop of a pin. I scanned for Talon but my gaze froze on the scene in the middle of the chaos: Brendan standing behind Luke and pointing a gun to his head.

Even through the scope, I could see the blood running down the sides of his faces from his head wound and he swayed on his knees, as if staying upright was all he could do. I tapped my earpiece several times until sound flooded back through.

"He'll tell us," Brendan screamed. "He'll tell us how they figured out where we were or I'll shoot his friend in the head."

Swear words flashed in my brain. My heart pounded as I shifted the lever into third gear and watched the speedometer creep past fifteen miles per hour. Come on, come on.

"Leah," I yelled. "If you can hear me, you need to force everyone away from the southwest corner. I'm comin' in with a bang." I wrenched the lever into fourth gear. There was no way that windows like those could support the weight of the roof of a building like that. A more stabilizing structure had to be in place and that's what I was betting on.

I stepped on the gas and slid into the next gear. Yes! With one hand keeping the steering wheel steady, I fastened my seatbelt. Then I picked up the semi-automatic and pressed the button to let the driver's side window down.

Technically, I was coming at the building from the back half and its windows were less prominent than the impressive display at the main entrance. But that only meant I was not the focal point and no one, yet, had noticed the semi-tractor rolling towards them at thirty-five miles an hour. I twisted the wheel to adjust the angle so I'd hit the south east wall from the back and slide into the main area where the drama was.

"I'm coming in hot," I yelled, hoping the comms worked long enough for my team to brace.

The building loomed less than one hundred feet ahead. It was now or never. I used the butt of the gun to slam down the headlights lever and bright lights exploded from the front of the truck. I threw up a hand to protect my face and eyes from any debris that would fly upward and braced. One moment momentum...the next...impact.

Even hitting a wall that was seventy percent windows, the brick and mortar provided enough resistance that it felt like being flung face first into the ground. The truck lurched and slowed a bit but I jerked the wheel enough to guide me into the main area.

"Get some!" I screamed and pulled the trigger. The gun lurched in my hand as a spray of bullets blitzed across the section of the room that was opposite of where I'd last seen Talon and Luke. Men screamed and leapt out of the way. I dropped the gun in my lap and grabbed the steering wheel with both hands and tugged sharply, making the truck do a one eighty spin so that the back portion of the truck smashed into the main windows at the front of the building. It rocked to a halt with the cab facing the interior and the back wheels sticking outside.

Dust flooded my lungs and I coughed as aggravated bumps and bruises let me know they didn't appreciate the rough treatment. Bullets peppered the front of the cab and I ducked behind the dash. I gripped my gun tightly and shoved open the door with my left shoulder. I peeked the gun around the door and sprayed bullets toward whoever was firing. I glanced around, looking for a better cover spot but it was essentially a large open room with all of us shooting at each other. Behind the truck door had the best protection at the moment.

Beastie growled a warning and I swung around and nearly shot Talon in the chest.

"Because sneaking up on me is a great idea," I yelled at him.

He fired two shots behind "Next time I'll knock," he said. "You got a lock on the kids?"

A man in plaid tried to jump over the back of the truck but I shot him midleap. "They're still in the backroom."

"I'll find Thorne. You get the kids."

Sounded like a plan to me.

Talon crouched behind the semi's bumper and blitzed the mob with heavy fire and I used the opening to combat roll across the debris sprinkled floor into the narrow hallway that led into the bowels of the building. Music flared in my head and out of the corner of my eye I glimpsed a fist swinging toward. I swept left to avoid the strike and caught the man's arm caught his arm with the barrel of my gun before whipping it away from his body and shooting him twice in the chest. The way now clear, I sprinted down the hall and mentally followed the map Sakira had created for us. I turned into the first doorway on my right which was a storage area that yawned with rows and rows of electrical plugs, hand held equipment, and a variety of spare parts for large trucking equipment. At the back of the room, in the southwest corner, was a door metal just as

Sakira described. I put my back to the door so I could keep an eye out for any movement behind me and knocked hard on the door—five quick knocks, two slow—to signal it was me

I waited a few seconds and then did it again. Nothing.

My mind whirled. Maybe Leah hadn't made it inside. If so, that meant Brendan's men were still guarding the children inside and were definitely on high alert with all of the gunshots. There wasn't a chance they'd open the door with calm threats. Crap. I'll have to find another way ins—

Something thudded on the other side of the door so hard that it made the metal sound like a gong. I swung around, ready for anything to spring out. A few seconds later, the door jerked open and Leah stood there out of breath with mud streaked face and sweat and blood trickling down her neck.

"Thought you decided to take on the whole village of crazies by yourself." She quipped.

"I'm not quite up for that much excitement." I gently rotated my shoulder, hoping to lessen the tightness that was causing pain to shoot into my neck. Gunshots that sounded close made us both flinch. I stepped inside and almost tripped on the body of a man slumped just inside the room, his chest a mass of bullet holes.

I gave her a look. "Looks like you already took care of the problem."

"What?" She bolted the door behind her. "Not up for trying to stampede a group of malnourished, terrified kids through a gunfight?"

That made me survey the room. A single light bulb was the only source of light in the small room, only slightly larger than a small shed, but it was enough to see the dozen or so children huddled in a corner, all of them staring at me with wide eyes. A small bundle rose from the pile of humans huddled in the corner and raced toward me. I opened my arms, and Logan flung himself at me.

"I knew you'd come." Wet hit my neck as he wrapped his arms tightly around me. "I knew you'd come."

Mist gathered in my eyes as I let myself absorb his weight. He was alive. Another body removed itself from the pile and rushed over to glue itself to my side. I rested my head against Alyssa's curly hair and squeezed her tight.

"Are you guys alright? Are you hurt?" I asked.

They both shook their heads. I set Logan on the ground and knelt to look at them more closely. Their blue eyes were wide and bright with adrenaline and fear but that would help keep them alert and alive until help came.

"Where's Sakira?" I glanced up and saw her standing with the group of other children. I reached out my hand and she tentatively came forward and grasped it hard. "How you doin'?"

She nodded but I could see that fear was quickly clouding the courage in her eyes. Being back in this nightmare room would only heighten that fear, accentuate the horrible memories she'd rather forget. I needed to get her out of here. I needed to get them all out of here.

Leah bustled around us and I didn't ask what she was up to.

"We're going to find a new way to escape but we're not leaving anyone behind." My eyes went toward the window that Sakira had to slip through in order to get back inside. Maybe we could squeeze everyone out that way. It would take time...and that was quickly running out.

"Working on that." Leah's voice drew my attention to where she was crouched in front of the far wall and hurriedly attached something to the wall. I stepped closer and my eyebrows shot upward. "Tell me that isn't C-4."

She shrugged, still messing with it. "Okay. I won't."

"You just happened to have a stick of C-4 on you?"

She looked over her shoulder at me. "Some people carry extra chap stick. I carry spare explosives." Her grin was a bit maniacal. "If I remember correctly, this wall leads to the main yard and we can sprint into the field for cover."

Trust the team, I chanted to myself. I took a breath and forced myself to ignore Beastie's roar of warning. "Sounds good to me." I turned my attention to the kids in front of me. ""I'm proud of all of you guys. But we're not out of the fire yet. We're going to blow a hole in the wall and use it to escape the building." I looked across the room at the half dozen other terrified kids staring at us with wide, hopeful eyes. "Sakira, I'm putting you in charge of getting everyone back to the hotel and hiding them inside or in the trailer park."

She frowned and started to shake her head but caught herself mid-motion and let out a breath. "I think I can do that." She said, eyes glistening and it was hard to tell if it was from tears or determination.

"I know you can, sweetheart." I smiled at her. "Leah and I will shoot anyone who tries to stop you guys. Okay?"

She nodded.

Gunshots pinging off the door made us all jump. Time was up.

"Let's do this." Leah shouted.

I ushered everyone over to the group of kids still huddled in the far corner. There were about nine or so of them, all with hunger sharpened cheekbones and clothes two sizes too big. I hunched in front of them and their eyes were riveted on me. "Alright guys, I know it's been a rocky night but I'm a friend of Sakira's and I'm going to help you go home. But to get home, you'll have to run as fast and as far as you can and follow every direction Sakira gives you. Think you can do that?"

"Home?" A small, cracked voice asked.

"Home. I promise."

Leah jogged over to us. "Ten seconds."

"I need everyone to curl up as small as you can and cover your head with your arms, like this." I pulled my body in tight like a roly-poly to show them. "Hurry!"

The urgency in my tone seemed to snap them out of their suspicious or incredulous stupor and they all hunched into tight balls. Logan flopped down next to me and curled tightly into my side. I wrapped arms around him as Leah counted softly under breath.

Three. Two. One.

The explosion wasn't really that bad. It was like a giant had kicked in the side of the building, sending bits of wall and wire spewing into the room. Some of the kids tried to stand immediately but I pressed them back to the floor, waiting for the final bits of brick to stop pelting us. The moment the dust settled, Leah and I leapt to our feet.

"Let's go, let's go, let's go," I yelled, gently tugging kids to their feet and hustling them to the makeshift doorway as Leah dashed through the hole to make sure nothing hostile waited on the other side. Logan wrapped his arms around my waist and didn't want to let go. "Run into the field, kids." I told them, clapping at the running ones to make them go faster. "Go fast as fast as you can, stay low to the ground and don't stop until you hit the motel."

Sakira ran past me, pushing a boy with short kinky hair and brilliant blue eyes in front of her. Alyssa ran to but paused looking for her brother.

I peeled Logan's arms away from me and met his frightened stare. "Trust me?"

He nodded, golden brown hair flopping into his face.

"Follow your sister and don't stop until you hit the hotel." I jogged us both to the hole the size of a large doorway and tucked his hand inside Alyssa's shaking one. I pulled her in tight for a hug. "Help the others get away." I murmured into Alyssa's hair. "I'm trusting you guys."

Bullets peppered the wall over our heads and I looked over my shoulder to the barrel of a gun pointing through the diagonal opening from the door hanging on its hinge. I raised my gun and let loose a spray as I spun all three of us out of the way and through the hole. We stumbled over chunks of wall and ran into the chilly downpour outside. I instantly focused on the sounds of close gunfire and men yelling—the fight had moved outside. Fear tried to douse the adrenaline pumping. Any of the kids could catch a stray bullet in this environment but there wasn't any help for it.

The only way through was through.

Leah waved from her position at the corner of the building, her back to the wall and gun raised. The rest of the children were in a single line behind her, like tattered mice following a bloodthirsty Peter Piper.

"Fighting's hot," she yelled over the boom of thunder. "But if we can get them into the field, they'll be as safe as we can make them."

I nodded. I switched out ammunition clips and ignored the twinge in my shoulder. Let's do this. "Lead the way for your friends, Sakira. Leah and I will make sure no one follows you."

Sakira's black hair was plastered around her body like a soaked curtain and she nodded. Without further encouragement, she sprinted into open darkness and the kids followed her in a flood. Leah and I moved with them, weapons high. We were way too close to the fighting and I didn't want anyone stumbling across a runaway creep lurking in the tall grass. Nonstop lightning streaked across the sky and lit our way through the rain-slick grass.

A shape loomed out of the darkness and something hit my hand hard, trying to knock my gun away. Music roared in my head and I ducked as a large arm swung over my head. I blocked a punch at my face, waited for lightning to flare long enough to illuminate the plaid shirt and sneer on his face, and kicked out, aiming for the ribs. A man's grunt rang in the air. He swung at me again and I swooped low to grab my gun, and shot him in the chest as he raised his fists to strike me again.

Heart pounding, mind crystal clear, senses heightened…it was crisp and adrenalized and I felt alive.

A few feet ahead, Leah shot a man who leapt out from behind one of the parked SUV's. Thunder boomed and it shook the ground. A few of the kids screamed but kept running. I counted to make sure the last kid cleared the final line of cars and rushed into the tall grass that waved over most of their heads. Leah followed them into the field and I was about to follow, casting one final look around to make sure we weren't being tailed and that's when I saw it. Talon fired into the building from behind an SUV with two men sneaking up on his left, using the partially exposed semi-truck to conceal their approach.

I raised my gun and fired but it clicked empty. Crap. It was barely a thought in my mind before I was flying down the slick gravel at a dead run. My feet crunching on the gravel drew the men's attention and I ripped the strap over my head and used my good arm to fling the gun at the man closest to me. It hit him in the chest but was the distraction I needed. I ducked beneath his wild punch and aimed a vicious kick at his left knee. The joint crumpled inward and he screamed, pitching forward straight into my spinning hook kick that caught him in the jaw. This caught the second man's attention and he swung his gun toward. I swayed to one side, letting the barrel brush past then, then grabbed his wrist and drove my elbow into his ribs three times. Wrenching his wrist, I yanked the gun from his grip and shot him point blank in the chest.

A third man leapt on top of the fifth wheel with a battle cry and trench coat flapping in the wind and a long, wicked blade flashing in the light. I stumbled back, raised the gun to shoot but he was too close and his blade sliced through the barrel. Now useless, I flung the gun at him but he swiped it away in midair. No matter. I needed my hands free anyway. I pulled the long metal rods from my belt and pressed a small button on the handles to release the studded batons. I twirled them like samurai swords, ready to deflect an attack.

The man lunged at me but I dodged, feet moving in time to the clash of violins and cellos in my head. It was a deadly dance. He backed me back against the grill of the semi but I still fought. As rain poured down over us and lightning painted the sky.

I dodged a deep lunge and brought the baton down hard on the outside of his elbow, snapping the joint with brute force. He roared with fury and elbowed my jaw hard to jerk my head back and make me see stars. I struck out again even as I stumbled back into the grill avoiding his blow. Strange energy prickled the air and made the hair on my arms stand straight up and stomach gurgle. What the hell was that? I blocked another blow as Beastie growled a warning but it was too late. Silver, hot energy exploded around us, making the truck hum like a gong and knocking me backward.

I flew through the hole in the wall and smashed into the grill of an SUV outside. Rain slicked down my face as black spots bubbled behind my eye and pain thrummed everywhere...my back...my shoulders...it all felt like I'd been someone had sideswiped me with a thousand pound boulder. A bright ringing echoed in my ears and I struggled to orient myself. I tried to stand but flopped back down as my legs felt like noodles.

Get up, Serena. I told myself. You need to move.

All I could do was twitch on the ground.

I reached up and grabbed the nearest hard surface and pulled. My muscles quivered like Jell-O on an unstable table and I felt about as stable as a slinky. I wrapped my elbow around the thing stabilizing—a car headlight—and got to my knees. Everything quivered. I'd just been struck by lightning. The air smelled like ozone and even a bit like burned flesh. I didn't spare a thought for whether it was mine or not.

A random bullet pelted the ground next to me but I ignored the melee going on around me. After a tense few seconds, I got my feet under me and used the car's hood to pull me upright but pain surged and doubled me over. I collapsed against the hood of the car. It was cool, blessedly cool, beneath my cheek and I took a moment to rest and take stock of my injuries.

Right shoulder, on fire. The numbing medicine had worn off about the same time I smashed into the building. Searing pain across my right ribs. My left ankle moved wrong. My hands trembled and motor functions felt...glitchy at best. Guess only comic book superheroes got supercharged from a lightning strike.

I was surrounded by enemies and knew I couldn't linger...I also knew I probably couldn't walk worth a damn right now. If it hadn't been raining I'm sure I'd be sweating.

I was so focused on staying on my feet that I didn't hear the gravel crunch nearby. Out of nowhere, something hard smashed into my stomach and doubled me over with the impact, breath ripped from my lungs. Gasping, I looked up at the figure haloed by the car headlights.

Brendan.

His mangy red hair was plastered to his head and glasses slipped further down his nose due to the rain. But there was a light in his eyes that I hadn't seen before—arrogance, cruelty. He stood differently. A thick black briefcase dangled from his left hand and I realize that what he must have hit me with.

He gave a low whistle, glancing over his shoulder at the still steaming semi-truck. "That looked like it hurt." He said.

I tried to push away from him.

He swung the suitcase again and I barely raised both my arms in time to block it as it smashed into me, sending me staggering to the left, using the car to keep myself upright. My left foot caved beneath my weight and my vision tiled and I ended up on my hands and knees in the gravel.

"Poor, Serena." His voice was a sarcastic shout over the wind. "Poor, talented, favorite Serena." He kicked my ribs viciously on the last word, hard enough to flip me onto my back.

He stood over me, a sadistic smile on his face. "Money is power and in *this* world it's the only thing that matters. It's not a popularity contest. No one overlooks me. As long as I have this stuff," he hefted a case to show me. "I'm in control."

I could hear sirens in the distance. Hopefully, police sirens. They would rescue the kids and my team.

Lightning flashed again and something glinted out of the corner of my eye. One of my batons. I used a last surge of strength to swing out my right leg and slam it into the flesh of his lower calf. He stumbled and I rolled myself backward and snagged the weapon in my left hand.

Brendan roared and struck at me with the briefcase. I let it brush past my nose, then lunged forward, holding the baton like a dagger and smashed the end of it into Brendan's throat. Twice. His gurgled and stumbled back.

His eyes bulged but not with defeat—with revenge. He warbled a word that sound like, "Bitch" and reached for something behind his back. Chances it was a gun.

I tried to stand but my body spasmed—a late neural reaction to the lightning strike—and I writhed on the ground. Helpless. Vulnerable. All I could do was stare into the lightning lit sky.

A gun fired. I kept my eyes open, rain falling into my face. My body relaxed as the spasm passed. I'd meet death fully conscious.

But the searing pain never came.

A body thumped to the ground beside me and I whipped my head to look. It was Brendan—a bullet hole leaking red in the middle of his forehead. I slowly moved my head to look over in the direction of the shot.

A man in a police uniform stood a dozen or so yards away, gun raised. Lightning illuminated his face. My heart wrenched. It was Julien. More uniformed police flooded around him, into the field and quickly subdued the chaos. The fighting was over, at least for tonight.

Nearly an hour later, blue and red flashing lights lit up the sky and I stared out of the back of an ambulance over the gravel lot filled with police cars, cops and federal agents, and a handful of men sitting in puddles on the ground. When the EMT's tried to strap me into the gurney, I straight up refused and they ended up shooting me up with some sort of sedative that made the gray at the edge of my vision slowly creep in and forced me to lay down. I made the EMT in charge, a tall brunette woman with more muscle than most of the men, promise that she would wait to load me up last after her team checked everyone else. An ambulance had already loaded up most of the children from the auction and carted them off to the hospital to be examined and a squad car had followed in order to provide security. Based on Sakira's information, it wasn't a far stretch to think that there were some very important people who'd be extremely interested, some desperate, to know those kids were alive and the OKCPD was going to ensure their protection to the fullest extent.

My gaze swept over the field and settled on Talon. He stood next to Captain Dawson and several other officers as a man in a black suit spoke to them. He must have felt my gaze because his head lifted and our eyes met. I gave him a small smile and he jerked his head at me in a macho man chin lift and lifted his hand in a "five minutes" gesture to let me know he'd be over to chat with me once his conversation was over. It wouldn't matter. I wasn't sure I'd be conscious in five minutes.

Gravel crunched nearby and I slowly turned my head to watch Julien come to a stop near my gurney.

"You look like you single handedly fought a war." He said with a hesitant smile.

"Apparently, this is the better-looking side of being struck by lightning." My voice was scratchy as if I hadn't spoken aloud in weeks. "Could be that guy." I tried to raise my hand but the best I could do was flick my fingers in the direction of the black body bags that were lined up in a single row inside the building.

"No kidding." He frowned in that direction. "I just wanted to let you know that I just received a call that Brendan's uncle is in custody and on the way to the station to be questioned. He's claiming that he had no idea what his nephew was up to but a quick look at their accounting for the past two year suggests otherwise."

"I'm surprised you found him in town."

"Considering he was in a wheelchair, I can't imagine how far he could have gotten." At my quizzical look, he kept going. "Apparently he managed to break both his knees falling off his roof. Sounds plausible but the bruising on his face suggests that he was beaten at some point as well. Not sure if those are related so I asked for the report from the hospital as well."

A punched in face and two broken knees? Sound like

old school mafia tactics to me. He was either dangerously clumsy...or someone decided to personally deliver a message and make sure he understood.

"I'd make sure he has police protection," I rasped. "Just in case whoever it was did that to him—" I snapped my mouth shut. Julien was a grown man and a well-trained officer, he didn't need any lecturing from me. "Sorry."

He did something that completely shocked me. He leaned down and brushed a soft kiss on my forehead. I froze and stared up at him, both trying to keep my expression clear so he wouldn't see the pure confusion but also wanting to give him something so he didn't think I was an unfeeling gnome.

"I missed your nagging," he quipped as he straightened. "You know...before you got mean."

The smile on his lips was the only way I knew he was kidding and it choked a surprised laugh out of me.

The EMT captain walked over, bag in hand. "You're the last one to go and we're ready to load you up," she said, tossing her bag into the truck.

Another man grasped the other side of the gurney and when the pushed it back to give them room to actually shove me into the van, gray dots exploded in my vision. A single word popped into my head: ow. As they pushed me into the truck, I glanced a final time over the yard and landed on Talon. He waved a hand in my direction, a soft smile playing at his mouth.

His flashing silver eyes were the last thing I saw before they closed the ambulance doors.

EPILOGUE

S now was a fickle sight in Oklahoma, even in December.
Today though, the slate gray clouds were low, and the air was brisk with a subtle scent of charcoal—if I had to guess, we'd see flurries by dinnertime. Which gave me just enough time to finish this visit.

Frost deadened grass and packed down leaves crunched underfoot as I wove between the headstones toward the iconic tank statue in the center of Arlington Memorial Gardens. I still wasn't moving at a hundred percent—getting your butt toasted by lightning was the electrical surge of a lifetime and tended to overload and reprogram the wiring. It had been a month since the sex auction bust and I still had moments where my limbs would twitch randomly in a charley horse or communication between my brain and legs would blink on and off I'd stumble like a drunkard. It wasn't all bad, though. The most unexpected blessing? Beastie—that ever prowling tigress in my head—had been reduced to something the size of a kitten locked in the cage of my mind.

A feral kitten. With sharp claws.

But I no longer battled overwhelming urges that were impossible to control. I definitely could see why electrocution therapy would never quite appeal to the main market but, hey, a reset from the heaven's and this was the most emotional and psychological stability I'd experienced in the past six months. Maybe even my whole life. I wasn't about to question why God chose that particular method. It hurt like hell though.

My thoughts strayed as I came to a stop at a headstone

that gleamed with a newness that struck at my heart: Joseph Clemens Black. Shriveled flowers and blown out candles were strewn three rows deep all around it and the sight made my eyes sting.

"Hey dad," I murmured. I knelt and rearranged the flowers on the skinny side of the headstone, clearing space for me to spread out a blanket and lean back against the cool stone. I breathed the frigid air and finally felt the urgency in my chest release as I looked around the cemetery. A woman with auburn hair and a slight hunch in her upper back dusted the slabs free from dirt and leaves, going stone by stone up and down the rows despite the rapidly descending temperature. There was only three weeks until Christmas and she looked like the kind of person who had a abundance of last minute shopping to do; yet she didn't rush her pace and took time honoring the dead with her excellence.

Once Julien told me that I was officially no longer a suspect in the murder of Davis Jackson nor responsible for the kidnapping of his kids, this was the first place I wanted to come. I wanted to say goodbye in the right way—no FBI or epic shoot-outs or sympathetic onlookers. Just me and dad's spirit hovering over this place.

It was the most peaceful I'd been in a long time.

Beastie, in kitten form now, looked up from playing with her tail when footsteps and the rhythmic crunching of leaves signaled someone's approach. It was probably the old woman leaving. When a large presence settled on the other side of the gravestone from me, she growled low in her throat. I opened my eyes but the pine and leather cologne gave him away.

"I'm sure it's purely coincidental that we both decided to visit on the same day," I said, trying for irritated but I couldn't quite keep the smile out of my voice.

"Could be," Talon rumbled. "Or I could have asked your brother where you'd be and detoured to see you."

I let my head rest against the concrete slab and relaxed. The sound of something unscrewing was followed by a stout, sugary smell. Out of the corner of my eye, I saw Talon hold out a steaming thermo liquid and I didn't hesitate to reach over a take it. One sip and thick, sweet chocolate slid over my tongue. Now *this* was how hot cocoa was supposed to be—none of that pre-packaged, powdered nonsense.

"You're the first stalker who's ever brought me a bribe." I joked, taking another sip.

"Your dad taught me that recipe," he said. "Apparently melted chocolate bark is the way they used to drink it in regency England and that little trivia tidbit appealed to his more refined self. Seemed fitting that we'd celebrate your first visit as a non-criminal with an ode to him."

"Non-criminal?" I huffed. "I was always innocent."

"And now the FBI agrees with you."

I picked up a handful of leaves and chucked them over my shoulder at him. All he did was laugh.

"Auntie told me that you were looking at establishing your own security firm."

I shrugged and took another sip from the lid. "Yeah. Seems to be an unmet market here for personal protection and none of the competition really has the credentials I bring to the table."

"Why not go work for one of them?"

Yeah, no. "I'm determined never to say "Yes, sir" to anyone ever again." That was only about sixty percent true. "Besides, I'd much rather have total control over my operation: I can decide how to vet potential clients and create process that make sense to me. I'd hate to join someone else's' team only to have to ignore the kinks that they're not interested in working out."

"Makes sense."

"It won't be anything large. I don't want to bite off more than I can chew." I'd managed a few tactical teams with Homeland but nothing this permanent. "It might grow, might now but I've got a few women I plan to ask to join the team."

"You planning on asking that hellion Leah?"

The concern in his voice made me chuckle. "She is a bit

wild," I conceded. "But makes a great wing woman and cares about the job, regardless of whatever nonsense is coming out of her mouth."

"She doesn't strike me as the kind who'll want to settle down long to accept a single location gig."

"True. But I can be pretty convincing."

"That you are," the smile in his voice was obvious. "Got business name in mind?"

I smiled over the rim of the thermos. "Lethal Nannies Inc... or something like that."

Talon snorted before outright laughing in short bursts. "A bit on the nose, but seems to fit."

"Logan thought so."

"You spoke to Jackson kids recently?"

I shook my head and remembered he couldn't see me. "No. I figure we'll all need time to detox from things before they're ready for me to check in with them. It's just a nod of the hat to what he called me when we first met."

He slid something across the leaves and I twisted my head to get a better look. It was an envelope, crisp and white against the decaying leaves, and from the top of it peaked two slips of paper. Tickets. For the OKC Philharmonic holiday concert. Tonight.

"Aunt Elana will love those." I said, "She mentioned the other day on our walk how she'd like to go. It'll be a great Christmas gift for her." I pushed the envelope back toward him.

He was silent.

I took another sip.

"Those aren't for Auntie," he rumbled and my stomach clenched at the tone his voice got to me. Something moved in the corner of my eye and Talon shuffled back until our shoulders touched and he could look me in the eye. His silver eyes sparkled. "I got those tickets for you and me."

"What like a date?" I quirked an eyebrow at him but a smile pulled at my lips.

"Yes."

I shrugged. "I'm not sure I'm really a "dating" kinda girl."

A slow smile spread over his face and his silver eyes sparkled. Those eyes should be illegal. He wrapped a hand around the back of my neck and leaned in. "I'll convince you," he murmured, his breath warm and smelling of chocolate.

Pillowy snowflakes started to drift down from the heavens as his lips sealed over mine. Cleansing snow that signified new beginnings. With Talon.

My lips quirked. That sounded good to my soul.

ABOUT THE AUTHOR

Kat Lewis

Kat Lewis is an up-and-coming thriller author and recently launched her career with her electrifying debut novel, Rogue Defender. She is a passionate advocate for those escaping the horrors of human trafficking and uses her writing an avenue to spread awareness. She has served as the President and Vice President for the Oklahoma Christian Fiction Writers (OCFW) and is an active volunteer with WriterCon. When not writing the next installment of her Lethal Nannies series, she can be found browsing for cute shoes, eating chips and queso, practicing Krav Maga, or searching for her pet rock. Connect with Kat on her website at katlewisauthor.com.

Made in the USA
Coppell, TX
22 April 2022

76936837R00175